NAPOLEON

MAX GALLO

NAPOLEON

The Song of Departure

Translated from the French by William Hobson

MACMILLAN

First published 2004 by Macmillan
an imprint of Pan Macmillan Ltd
Pan Macmillan, 20 New Wharf Road, London N1 9RR
Basingstoke and Oxford
Associated companies throughout the world
www.panmacmillan.com

ISBN 0 333 90797 3

1 3 5 7 9 8 6 4 2

A CIP catalogue record for this book is available from
the British Library.

Typeset by SetSystems Ltd, Saffron Walden, Essex
Printed and bound in Great Britain by
Mackays of Chatham plc, Chatham, Kent

To Stendhal and André Malraux,

and for my son

Where might I be attacked that a historian may not defend me?

Napoleon on Saint Helena

Very well, he left France smaller than he had found it.
But that is not the definition of a nation. For France he had
to exist . . . Let us not set too little store by greatness.

De Gaulle, quoted by André Malraux, *Fallen Oaks*

PRELUDE

❧

*This plain would make
a fine battlefield*

4 APRIL 1805, a little before dawn

THE EMPEROR OF FRANCE, Napoleon Bonaparte, stood in his stirrups, pulling on the reins of his Arab as it pawed the ground.

Caulaincourt, grand equerry and aide-de-camp, and the rest of the Imperial suite kept a respectful distance. Their horses stamped and jostled, and every now and then, the officers' sabres clattered.

The Emperor was in front of them alone.

He looked at the ruins looming out of the fog. He recognized an avenue of lime trees and, at the end of it, the monastery of the Order of Minims. This was all that remained of the Military School of Brienne, which he had attended for five years, from when he was a little boy of not yet ten, who was teased by the other pupils because he had a bizarre, foreign name: Napoleone Buonaparte. *Napoleone* – they thought it sounded ridiculous, like '*Paille au nez*' Straw on the Nose, and they used to chant 'Napoleone Buonaparte, Paille-au-Nez' to try to provoke him.

Only twenty years later, on 2 December 1804, in Notre Dame, he had taken the Emperor's crown from Pope Pius VII's hands and crowned himself.

He was Napoleon Bonaparte, Emperor of France. He was only thirty-six years old.

HE HAD COME FROM Paris the day before because he wanted to see this part of the country and this school again, not knowing that it was now no more than a heap of rubble that bore witness to the tumult of those intervening twenty years. Shut down in 1793 and sold as national property, converted into a caisson factory and then, after the workshops had been moved, sold again for a pittance, the school had finally been demolished in 1799 and used for raw materials.

He had spent five years there, the hardest years of his life, alone in a country where, to all intents and purposes, he was a foreigner.

But he had become Napoleon Bonaparte, Emperor of France, and in the meantime, only twenty years had passed.

IN PARIS on 30 March 1805, Pope Pius VII had come to pay his respects before returning to Italy. Napoleon had told him that he would shortly be leaving for Milan, where, in the cathedral, Cardinal Caprara was going to crown him King of Italy. Once again, Pius VII had bowed his head before the Emperor and, as he was now soon to become, King.

Napoleon had set out from Paris on 31 March in the direction of Troyes.

As if he were making a pilgrimage to the places of his lonely childhood and those years at the military school, he had agreed to spend a night in the Château of Brienne which dominated the village.

Cheering crowds had lined the road from Paris to Brienne. He had leant out of the door of his coach. At the entrance to the towns and villages, he had mounted his Arab and, straight-backed, set it prancing on its hind legs, as he acknowledged the people's adulation. When he had entered Brienne towards noon on 3 April 1805, he had had to rein in his horse because country folk from miles around had jammed the streets.

He had recognized the ramp which led up to the esplanade on which, set in vast gardens, the château stood. Madame de Brienne had been waiting for him outside, on the steps. She had greeted him deferentially and shown him to his rooms where, she murmured, the Duke of Orleans had once stayed. Napoleon had gone in, opened the window and looked out at the Champagne countryside, that landscape that had seemed so different and alien and hostile when, as a ten-year-old, he had found himself stranded and alone in its midst.

In his five years at the Military School of Brienne, he had heard hundreds of times about the marvellous parties the de Briennes threw, with hunting in the forests and dancing in the château. Often the sound of orchestras or horses in full cry would carry to the schoolyard.

Bonaparte and his classmates had only once been invited to visit the château. It was Saint Louis's Day, 25 August 1783. Madame de Brienne had noticed the thin, olive-complexioned pupil with the curious name, Napoleone Buonaparte, but her attention had only been caught for a moment. He had merged back into the hundred or so pupils of the school, that anonymous throng of boys in blue woollen uniforms, with coats with white lining, red cuffs, lapels and collars, and white buttons emblazoned with the school's arms.

In the château's gardens, Bonaparte had joined the crowds of people wandering the avenues; the whole district had been invited by the castellan and his wife to celebrate the King's feast day. There were stages for travelling acrobats, singers and players; ropes had been strung between trees for tightrope walkers, and coconut and gingerbread sellers threaded through the crush, hawking their delicacies.

Bonaparte had walked along in silence, his hands clasped behind his back.

That had been twenty-two years ago.

Now he was Emperor of France, and Madame de Brienne was inviting him to come and have dinner and join her afterwards in the drawing room.

THE OTHER GUESTS were introduced to the Emperor.

A local curé, dressed in a brown frock coat, approached and, with a bow, said that he had been one of Bonaparte's teachers at the military school, which had been run by Minim friars.

'Who are you?' the Emperor asked, as if he hadn't heard.

The curé repeated his name.

'The purpose of cassocks,' Napoleon said flatly, 'is to enable priests to be recognized at all times and under all circumstances. I do not recognize a curé in a frock coat. Go and dress yourself.'

The curé disappeared, then returned, embarrassed and humble.

'Now I recognize you,' said Napoleon, 'and I am very glad to see you.'

He was the Emperor of France.

He grew impatient over dinner. The guests fell silent. Intimidated, the majordomo knocked over a sauceboat in front of the Emperor. Napoleon burst out laughing and the atmosphere instantly relaxed. Everyone got up from the table in a hubbub of conversation, and then the Emperor withdrew.

He slept little, and before dawn he had gone down to the

courtyard, mounted his Arab and set off from the château to revisit the military school, which, as the fog thinned, he saw was a ruin. He couldn't envisage it being rebuilt. It would cost millions.

The past would not rise again.

Suddenly, with two sharp jabs, he spurred his horse into a gallop, crossed the Brienne and set off down the Bar-sur-Aube road alone. In a few minutes he had disappeared. Usually kept on a tight rein, his charger raced along at breakneck speed, leaping ditches, plunging into woods, its hooves drumming the stony paths. Whenever the Emperor changed course, he recognized a landscape here, a village there. Alone, perfectly alone, the Emperor galloped through the countryside on the trail of his memories, and imagined Caulaincourt and his staff panicking and trying to catch him up.

A shot rent the fog-bound silence.

Caulaincourt was calling: they had to set off again. The Emperor rode back, his eyes fixed on the towers of the Château of Brienne. He had been galloping for more than three hours and, as he told his astonished officers, he had no idea where he'd been. His horse was exhausted and dripping with sweat, and blood trickled from its nostrils.

On that day, 4 April 1805, the Emperor left Brienne for Milan, where the Italian crown awaited him.

While the château was still in sight, he leant out of the window of his coach and ordered it to stop. The sun lit up the towers, and glinted off the sheaths of his escort's sabres and the facings of their uniforms.

'This plain,' said Napoleon, 'would make a fine battlefield.'

PART ONE

❧

Granite heated by a volcano

15 August 1769 to October 1785

I

BORN IN AJACCIO to Charles Marie Buonaparte and Letizia Ramolino on 15 August 1769, the child who enters the parlour of the Royal Military School of Brienne on 15 May 1779 has not yet celebrated his tenth birthday.

He stands very straight and still with his hands behind his back; thin face, protruding chin, delicate frame in a tightly buttoned, dark blue coat, chestnut hair cut very short, grey eyes. He does not respond to, or even seem to notice, the large, cold room in which he is asked to wait until he can be seen by the principal, Father Lelue, who, like all the staff, is a member of the Order of Minims. The child knows that he is going to be at this school for several years without being able to leave it once, even for a day, and will be alone in a country, the rudiments of whose language he has only just begun to learn.

HE TRAVELLED to Autun in France on 1 January 1779 with his father Charles, a tall, handsome man, with an aristocratic air, regular features, and immaculate, sometimes elaborate clothes.

Corsica, Ajaccio's alleys, the smell of the sea, the scent of pines, lentiscs, cane-apples and myrtles – his whole world as a child has had to be cast aside, like a guilty secret. He had to grit his teeth and bite his cheek when his father set off again, leaving his two sons at Autun College: Joseph, the eldest, who was born on 7 January 1768 and Napoleone; the former destined for the Church, the latter for the army.

He has three months at Autun, from 1 January to 21 April, to learn French, that foreign language shouted by the invading armies in the streets of Ajaccio. His father speaks it, his mother does not. Italian is all the Buonaparte sons have been taught.

Learn, learn: the child of nine clenches his fists and buries his sadness, nostalgia and what feels almost like fear: the feeling that he has been abandoned in this country of rain, cold, snow and slate, where the earth only smells of leaves and mud and never of the succulent plants he is used to. He wants to master this new language, since it is the language of the country that has conquered his people and occupied his island.

He strains every nerve, reciting the words out loud, repeating them over and over until they submit. He needs this language to be able, one day or another, to fight back against these arrogant French boys who make fun of his name; he does not want to have any dealings with them at all.

He is always alone in the courtyard at Autun, a pensive, sombre figure. While his brother Joseph is gracious, gentle and shy, Napoleone irritates his schoolmates with his haughtiness, which is that of a humiliated child, and his bitterness, which is that of one whose country has been defeated. So the boys tease him, provoke him. He keeps quiet at first, but when they say that Corsicans are cowards because they have let themselves be enslaved, he gesticulates furiously and bursts out, 'If the French had outnumbered the Corsicans by four to one, they would never have been successful, but they did so by ten to one.'

They make comments about Pascal Paoli, the head of the Corsican resistance, who was defeated on 9 May 1769 at the battle of Ponte Nuovo.

Again he controls himself, but the memories come back.

His father and his mother started off as protégés of Pascal Paoli. Youngsters of barely eighteen and fourteen respectively, they were part of Paoli's circle in Corte in the brief years of Corsican independence between Genoese rule and French intervention in 1767. In 1764, it was Pascal Paoli who put pressure on Letizia Ramolino's family to allow their young daughter to marry Charles Marie Buonaparte. The word of *Il Babbo* – the father, as Pascal Paoli is known – counts; the marriage took place. Two children were born and died instantly. Then, when Letizia had only just given birth to Joseph, she became pregnant again, just as Louis XV's forces defeated the Corsican patriots. They had to flee along paths in the maquis, ford rivers on foot.

At the College at Autun, the nine-year-old child cannot tell any of this to the Abbé de Chardon who asks him well-meaning but mildly ironic questions in the breaks between French lessons. 'Why were you defeated?' the Abbé wants to know. 'You had Paoli and Paoli is a good general, so they say.'

The child can't contain himself.

'Yes he is sir, and I want to be like him.'

Napoleone is Corsican. He hates this country, this climate, these French. He mutters, 'I'll do the French all the harm I can.'

He is a sort of voluntary prisoner, the son of a defeated leader. He has nobody to confide in, he cannot cry.

HE REMEMBERS evenings at his father's house in rue St Charles, the fragrances that filled the night air, the gentle lilt of voices.

His mother was severe — if they misbehaved, she would slap or whip them — but she was beautiful, loving. He remembers her sitting in the midst of her children, pregnant once more, calm and resolute. She would tell stories about the war and their flight after the defeat at Ponte Nuovo.

Everyone would listen — Charles' mother, Maria Saveria Buonaparte; Letizia's half-brother from her mother's second marriage, Joseph Fesch; her aunt Gertrude Paravicini; Camilla Ilari, Napoleone's wet-nurse and Saveria the maid, the family's only servant. Napoleone's devout grandmother, who went to nine masses a day, would cross herself a great deal.

Napoleone remembers every detail of the description of the Laimone in spate. Letizia Buonaparte had tried to ford the river but her horse had lost its footing, buffeted by the current. Charles had thrown himself into the water to save his pregnant wife and Joseph, but Letizia had managed to bring her mount under control and steer it towards the other bank.

How could Frenchmen such as the Abbé de Chardon or the boys at Autun understand Corsicans and their island, when they knew nothing of the murmur of the sea on its shores, of the narrow little alleys leading down to Ajaccio's port and the ochre fortress that commanded its bay?

Napoleone thinks of his races and his fights with the other children, Southerners like him, who spoke the same warm, expressive language and would sometimes make fun of him and his dishevelled clothes, singing,

Napoleone di mezza calzetta
Fa l'amore a Giacominetta

Napoleone whose stockings won't stay up
Makes love to Jacquelinette

He would throw himself on them and then drag the little girl, his classmate, off with him to the school run by the Beguine sisters where he learnt Italian.

Later, when he was eight, they would roam the quays of the port together, but they were already growing apart. He had started studying arithmetic. He would shut himself away in a wooden shed that had been built for him at the back of the house and do sums alone there all day long. Then in the evening he would come out, ragged, oblivious, and full of dreams.

DON'T TELL *anyone about any of that. Keep it to myself. Learn French.*

The victorious King's soldiers used to march past, parading through the streets of Ajaccio, that city that still reverberated with recent clashes and clan rivalries: splits between those who had remained loyal to Pascal Paoli after he had gone into exile in England and those who had thrown in their lot with the French.

The child knew that his father, Charles Buonaparte, was one of the latter.

The Governor of Corsica, Monsieur de Marboeuf, was a frequent guest at their house in rue St Charles. He was an inveterate lady's man, and Letizia's beauty perhaps was part of the attraction, but he had become friends with Charles, the son of four generations of nobility as attested by genealogists in Tuscany, where the Buonaparte family originated from. The governor was looking for support among aristocrats prepared to ally themselves with France.

Charles had played that card, as he had to, to get a position, an income, grants.

On 8 June 1777 he had been elected deputy of the nobility and had attended Corsica's States General at Versailles. He had returned dazzled by the might of the French kingdom, its cities, its palaces, its organization and its new, easy-tempered sovereign,

Louis XVI. At court he had petitioned the ministers, soliciting scholarships for his two sons: Joseph, who is intended for the cloth and Napoleone, for soldiering.

THE EIGHT-YEAR-OLD child listens to everything that is said in the house in Ajaccio.

He runs alongside the troops as they parade through the streets, fascinated by these self-assured officers in their blue and white uniforms. He does drawings of them and sets out his toys in battle order. He plays war games. He is a southern child who runs through the streets, climbs up to the citadel, rolls in the mud, has his own gang of scamps and stays out in the rain because everyone knows that if you are going to be a soldier, you have to be tough. He swaps his white bread for the brown bread of a private because he has to accustom himself to soldiers' fare.

When he finds out that his father has obtained scholarships for him and Joseph to study at Autun College, and that, as soon as he can speak French, he will go on to the Royal Military School, he trembles with excitement. He is heartbroken at the thought of leaving his mother, his family, his house, his city, but he has no choice. Other children have been born into the family: Lucien in 1775, Marianna Elisa in 1777 and Louis in 1778. Pauline will follow in 1780, Marie Annonciado Caroline, in 1782 and Jerome in 1784.

Admittedly the Buonapartes and the Ramolinos are not poor. They own three houses, vineyards, a property at Milelli, plantations, a mill, estates at Ucciani, Bocognago and Bastelica. They have influence. Their families are a veritable clan. However, they must think about their children's careers and how to maintain their status amongst the nobility of the kingdom to which Corsica now belongs.

So Joseph is to be a priest, and Napoleone a soldier.

Monsieur de Marboeuf promises to obtain one of the 'ecclesiastical benefices' distributed by his nephew Yves Alexandre de Marboeuf, Bishop of Autun, for Joseph. As for Napoleone being awarded a scholarship so he can go to military school, he gives his word he will arrange that too.

ON 15 DECEMBER 1778, the child of nine and a half kissed his mother and family goodbye. He stood between his proud, elegant father, who was going back to Versailles to represent the interests of Corsica's nobility, and his brother Joseph. Also making the journey were Joseph Fesch, who was going to study at Aix seminary, and Napoleone's cousin Aurèle Varèse, who had been appointed sub-deacon to the Bishop of Marboeuf.

There were no tears from the child.

He embarked and, as the vessel set off for Marseilles, he watched Corsica fade from sight. Long after it had disappeared he continued to inhale the scents of his country, his homeland. Once, when he was thinking about that moment during a French lesson in the prep room at Autun College, his mouth hanging open, his eyes staring into space. When the Abbé de Chardon told him off for not paying attention, he started and replied imperiously, in a thick Corsican accent, 'Sir, I know this lesson already.'

It was true, this solitary child had learnt quickly at the college, although there were still times when he would reminisce with his brother about the games they used to play on the island. Did Joseph remember their battles? How his pugnacious, quick-tempered younger brother sometimes knocked him down? Did he remember the Abbé de Recco who had taught the two brothers arithmetic? Napoleone excelled at that subject even then; he was passionate about sums.

Did he remember the day when the Abbé de Recco had divided the class into Carthaginians and Romans and, because he was older, Joseph was one of the Romans, and Napoleone was one of the Carthaginians, that is, one of the conquered? Napoleone had been in a fury until he had persuaded Joseph to swap so that he could be in the victors' camp.

Did he remember the May the fifth celebrations in 1777, less than two years ago, when the Buonapartes' tenant farmer had come to Ajaccio with two spirited young horses – and how, when the farmer had gone, Napoleone had leapt on one of the mounts and galloped off? He was only eight then. He had ridden all the way to the farm and astonished the farmer who had found him calculating how much corn the mill should grind in a day.

HE IS STRONG-MINDED then, this child, with a good brain and a fierce will. After his brief stay at the College at Autun, he has mastered the principles of French, the language of Monsieur de Marboeuf, the King's army, and Pascal Paoli's vanquishers.

'I have only had him for three months,' Abbé de Chardon reports. 'In those three months, he has learnt sufficient French to converse freely and even to manage a little composition and translation exercises.'

His father having managed to have the family's quarterings of nobility corroborated, Napoleone is now able to leave for the Royal Military School of Brienne. In the register of the College at Autun, the principal writes, 'M. Neapoleone de Bounaparte, for three months, twenty days, 111 livres, 12 sous, 8 deniers, 111*l.*, 12*s.*, 8*d.*'

This is how they spell his name! This is what they call him, the foreign child!

He clenches his fists and arches his back, so as not to collapse or give way to his grief, as the carriage stands waiting in the courtyard of the College of Autun.

Joseph, who is to continue his classical education at the college, breaks down and hugs Napoleone to him.

The younger brother knows that his last family tie is being cut, but he remains unbending.

'I was in floods of tears,' Joseph related afterwards. 'He shed only one, which he tried vainly to hide. After Napoleone had left, Abbé Simon, the sub-principal who witnessed our farewells, told me, "He has shed only one tear, but that shows his sadness at leaving you as much as all yours."'

THE CHILD is put in the charge of Monsieur de Champeaux, who first takes him to his country house at Thoisy-le-Désert.

There Napoleone discovers another universe, that of a French aristocrat's family. He knows nothing of their ways, but he holds his tongue, observes, and grows stronger. He goes on long walks through the countryside, amazed at its gentle, rolling hills, and thinks of the harsh, sunlit landscapes of Corsica, the fig trees he used to climb to gorge on the red, pulpy fruit, and of how his mother would come running to box his ears, if she caught him breaking her rule against picking the figs. Happy days of a mother's scolding, the fruits' white sap that stuck to his fingers!

He must not let anything show. He must listen, pick up new expressions, guess at the meaning of these words he has never heard before.

After three weeks, the Abbé Hemey d'Auberive, vicar-general of the bishopric of Marboeuf, whom Monsieur de Champeaux has sent for because he is too ill to travel, comes to collect Napoleone from Thoisy-le-Désert and accompany him to Brienne.

So this is where Napoleone Buonaparte finds himself on 15 May 1779.

II

THE CHILD IS ALONE.

He has had to force himself not to look round when the Abbé Hemey d'Auberive drove off, leaving him standing in front of the principal of the Royal Military School of Brienne.

Father Lelue struggles to pronounce this strange name, 'Napoleone de Buonaparte, is that it?'

The child says nothing. He feels himself being scrutinized. He knows he is small and broad-shouldered. He compresses his lips until they disappear and his face, whose large forehead and keen eyes are what people notice first, shows no expression, but he knows his olive complexion is a source of amazement in this grey country, this France where he's been left.

At Autun College, they used to make fun of his sallow skin. He never understood the meaning of their questions exactly, but he guessed the irony, the sarcasm. What had he been fed on as a child to grow up so yellow? Goat's milk and oil? In this land of cream and butter, what do they know of the inky taste of olives, or cheeses that are dried on rocks in the sun? He used to clench his fists.

Now he is following the principal down long, icy corridors lined with rows of narrow doors. As they are walking, Father Lelue explains that the child has been chosen because of his family's nobility, verified by Monsieur d'Hozier de Sérigny, France's court genealogist, to whose inquiries Monsieur Charles de Buonaparte, 'your father', replied diligently and meticulously. In response to Monsieur d'Hozier's question, 'What is the French for your son's Christian name, Napoleone in Italian?' Charles de Buonaparte explained that 'Napoleone is an Italian name.' It does not translate.

Father Lelue turns. The child does not lower his eyes. Then Father Lelue lists the school regulations, 'to mould character and stifle pride'. In the six years the boy will spend at the school, he will have no holidays. Every pupil has to 'dress himself, keep his effects in order and forgo any form of domestic service. Up to the age of twelve, hair is to be cut short. After that, it may be grown and worn in a pigtail, not *en forme de bourse*, tied up in a black silk bag, and powdered only on Sundays and holidays.'

But the child is not yet ten. Short hair, then.

Father Lelue opens one of the doors, steps aside and bids the child enter the room. Napoleone takes a couple of steps forwards.

He thinks of the vast room his mother had emptied of furniture so that the children could play in it. He thinks of the wooden shed built for him so he could devote himself to his sums. He thinks of the streets which opened onto the unbounded horizon of the sea. The cell where he will sleep is less than two metres square. Its entire furniture consists of a strap bed, a water jug and a wash basin. Father Lelue, who has remained in the doorway, explains that, according to regulations, 'Even at the harshest time of year pupils will only be entitled to one blanket unless they are of a delicate constitution.'

Napoleone looks the principal in the eye.

Father Lelue points to the hand bell next to the bed. The cells are locked by a bolt on the outside. In case of need the pupil should call a servant who is on duty in the corridor.

The child listens, stifling a longing to scream and run away. At home, he was called *Rabulione*, the one who touches everything, who gets involved in everything. Here, he is shackled by rules and discipline. Every pupil must leave their cell as soon as they wake up and only go back when it's time to go to sleep. They will spend the day in the prep room or taking physical exercise. 'Pupils must play games, especially those suited to developing strength and agility.'

In the corridor the child hears footsteps. Other pupils are arriving. He catches sight of them and guesses their families are wealthy by the look of their clothes. He hears their voices. French, all of them, from patrician families.

He feels even more alone.

'Pupils are to change underwear twice a week,' the principal adds. The child follows him along the corridor again, and enters the refectory after him. An austere, vaulted hall, this is where the school's hundred or so pupils gather to eat at huge tables, supervised by the masters. Bread, water and fruit for lunch and supper. Meat at both meals.

The child sits down in the middle of the other boys. They look at him and start whispering. Where does he come from? What is his name? *Napoleone?* Someone titters, and then bursts out laughing, 'Paille au nez'.

That is what it sounded like to them.

I hate them.

HE IS THE FOREIGNER. Don't his geography teachers say that, despite its having been conquered by France, Corsica is a dependency of Italy and hence a foreign country?

Napoleone accepts this, actively claiming a foreigner's role; he disdainfully cuts himself off from the other boys. When someone manages to pierce his armour, or catch him off guard, he retaliates.

Traps are laid for him. When a new pupil arrives in June 1782, he is pushed Napoleone's way. Egged on by the others, Balathier de Bragelonne, son of the commandant of Bastia, introduces himself to *Paille au Nez* as Genoese. Napoleone immediately challenges him in Italian, '*Sei di questa maledetta nazione?*' 'Are you from that cursed country?' The other nods. Napoleone rushes forward, seizes Balathier by the hair and the two have to be separated.

Napoleone retreats back into his isolation, a twelve-year-old Corsican patriot whose French spelling is so erratic that he writes in an illegible scribble to hide his mistakes, even though his style is growing more authoritative and his writing more incisive as his thinking develops in force and range. For the lonely child wants to gain the upper hand, remove all trace of his status as one of the defeated.

A foreigner? Perhaps. A subject, never.

He confides in Bourrienne, one of the few pupils he talks to, 'I hope one day to restore Corsica's liberty! Who knows? The destiny of an empire often turns on one man.'

Books stir him. He reads Plutarch again and again. History is one of his favorite subjects, along with mathematics at which, according to his teacher, Father Patrault, he excels. Listening to him solving algebra, trigonometry, geometry and conic section problems at will, the priest murmurs, 'That child will only be fit for geometry.'

The child does not demur. He likes the abstract puzzles that take him away from the humiliating, restrictive reality of his life, but he also likes the illustrated *Plutarch's Lives*, which allows him to escape into another reality, and one that is not an imaginary one, since it has existed. It is history and so it can return.

In him.

He identifies with the heroes whose fortunes he reads about. He is 'the Spartan'. He is Cato, Brutus, Leonidas.

He walks in the courtyard, his Plutarch in hand. No one even shouts at him any more. As the months go by, and he realizes that what he had sensed in a reflex of pride is true – that he is superior to most, maybe all, of them – he replies when he is spoken to. His manner is sour, cutting. He gives orders rather than defer to others. He judges his fellow pupils, and passes sentence.

Sometimes, in the corridors, he hears the rustle of feet slipping between the cells. These are the 'nymphs', pupils of ambivalent looks and virtue who are seeking a companion for a part of the night. Napoleone is revolted, and yet they court him. He has the delicate features and that insolence they consider attractive. He rejects his seducers furiously, lashes out with his fists and gets into fights, or chases them off, hurling insults. He suspects certain masters of indulging in 'the vices and licence of monasteries', and wages war against them, leading a revolt against the 'regents', who are assistants to the new principal, Father Berton. He is seized and thrashed, but he clenches his teeth and doesn't cry. He openly defies the master reprimanding him, who finally asks indignantly, 'Who are you, sir, to answer me in such a fashion?'

'A man,' Napoleone retorts in a loud voice.

He is an intransigent child, whose feelings are so sensitive under the carapace of his will that sometimes they erupt like a volcano, sweeping aside everything in their path.

One evening a dormitory master who has caught him reading gives him his punishment. He is to eat his dinner kneeling in the doorway of the refectory and, to compound the ignominy, he has to wear a pair of old, coarse breeches and outsize lace-up boots.

The part of him that wants to be a grown-up calmly obeys

until suddenly the child he still is begins writhing and screaming and rolling about on the floor, bringing up everything he has eaten. The mathematics teacher, Father Patrault, rushes up, disgusted that his best pupil should be treated like this. The principal concedes that the punishment was excessive and revokes it.

The man-child gets to his feet fiercer, prouder and more determined than ever not to submit. Someone who stands apart from the others, who is insular: that is what he is and what he wants to be.

ONE DAY the principal calls the boys together and announces that he is going to divide up a large expanse of ground near the school amongst them. These plots will be theirs to plough and cultivate and do with as they please, especially in September when the rhythm of the school slows to allow pupils not entitled holidays a little more free time.

Buonaparte listens to the principal, his face strained, his eyes fixed.

As soon as Father Berton has left, he accosts his classmates and opens negotiations. For days on end this boy who is usually so aloof lays siege to them one by one. Then, one day he stops. He has got what he wanted; two of them have given him their piece of land.

After that, as the weeks pass, whenever he has an opportunity, he is to be seen working on his plot, transforming it into a fortress. He drives in stakes, erects a palisade, plants small trees and constructs an enclosure, his 'island', which soon grows into a veritable hermitage, as it is called by the other boys. Withdrawing there every break, he spends his time alone, reading and thinking.

There in the summer in the shade of his arbour, he can give himself up to nostalgia. Even at this time of year, Champagne is sad and monotonous and the sky is dull without a hint of the intense, spotless blue of southern skies. He remembers the wooden shed behind the family house.

'To be deprived of the room one was born in, the garden one played in as a child, one's father's house – that is what it is not to have a country,' he revealed one day – a momentary weakness. Those pupils who approach his 'island', his place of retreat, are met with punches and kicks, no matter how many of them gang up on him. Buonaparte's rage and determination are such that they retreat, accepting that he has carved out his own separate 'kingdom'.

'My comrades feel little affection for me,' he says.

At times they even hate him, because he is proud, cantankerous, haughty, solitary and different.

They make him pay.

The principal has organized the pupils into a battalion consisting of several companies. They drill, dress, march past. Each company's captain is chosen according to the results of their schoolwork, and Napoleone is nominated to be one of them, until the pupils' staff council summons him. He appears, full of scorn, before this court martial formed of thirteen-year-old boys. He listens to its sentence, which is delivered in due form. 'Napoleone Buonaparte,' they declare, 'is unfit for command since he keeps himself aloof and refuses to strike up friendships with his comrades.' He is to be removed from his command, stripped of badges and reduced to the lowest rank in the battalion.

He listens, makes no response to the affront, as if it is powerless to affect him, and takes his place in the ranks. All eyes follow him; the boys whisper amongst themselves, admiring such steadfastness.

In the days that follow, he is shown signs of regard. He stood up for himself; his courage was evident to all. He accepts these marks of respect and joins in a few games, even organizing some, such as when they build a whole fort in the schoolyard that winter of 1783 and he takes command of it for a snowball fight.

He remains inaccessible, however, a reef that nothing can breach, and the more the years pass the more different he feels, unable to share in the joys of these French. Even if, like all the other pupils, he dutifully attends mass, taking communion and reciting the prayers, he still refuses to 'convert' to these people in whose midst he has now lived for several years.

Command them, perhaps. But be one of them? Never.

IN 1782, HE IS thirteen, a thin fellow with hair so stiff and unruly that, against school regulations, a wigmaker has to dress it. The sub-inspector general of military schools, Brigadier Chevalier de

Keralio, comes to Brienne on his tour of inspection in September that year. Each of the pupils is seen in turn; he consults their files, studies their results and questions these children who report themselves to him like veterans.

Monsieur de Keralio is satisfied with Buonaparte's interview. The young man has merit, excels at mathematics, is 'of good constitution, excellent health, four feet, ten inches, ten lines tall', but weak in social accomplishments and Latin.

Monsieur de Keralio recommends that Napoleone Buonaparte be admitted as soon as possible to the Military School of Paris, whose cadets include the best scholarship boys from all the military schools. After which he can return to Toulon.

Buonaparte is elated, despite his face showing not a flicker of emotion as he listens to the royal inspector. He only has a few months more to spend at Brienne. He hurries back to his hermitage, where he grows calm: the future seems wide open, like the sea. Buonaparte dreams of the sea and ships. Other Corsican aristocrats have served in His Majesty's navy. Why not him? He could see the Mediterranean sky again, cross from Provence to Corsica.

However, it is only a matter of months before all his hopes are shattered, and the adolescent once again turns in on himself. Keralio is replaced in June 1783 by another inspector, Reynaud des Monts, who considers Buonaparte too young for the Military School of Paris, refuses his choice of the navy and steers him towards the artillery, the arm traditionally intended for pupils who excel in mathematics. In any case, according to the new inspector, it is too soon to think of leaving Brienne: this Napoleone Buonaparte has only spent four years and four months in the school. Patience!

Angry and bitter once more, Buonaparte withdraws to his hermitage. Brienne has nothing more to teach him. Anyway, mathematics are the only classes he still attends. He has lost interest in Latin; he knows all the other subjects. He reads and chafes at the bit, refusing to join in school life.

On Saint Louis's Day, 25 August 1784, when the pupils are extolling 'Louis XVI, Our Father', he does not join in the processions. There's singing in the corridors and, a school tradition, the boys let off firecrackers. Suddenly there is a more violent explosion; sparks from a firework let off by one of the school's neighbours have set fire to a powder-chest. Panic sweeps the pupils, who take to their heels and as they stampede, knock down the palisade of Buonaparte's enclosure, snap the trees and destroy his hermitage.

Armed with a pick, he throws himself in their path, trying to stop them and defend his territory, indifferent to their fear or any danger they may be facing. They hurl abuse. He threatens them with his pick. They accuse him of selfishness, callousness. They shout that perhaps the celebrations in honour of the French King have exasperated *Paille au Nez*, the foreigner and, who knows, the republican, since that had been the dream of an independent Corsica.

Napoleone does not deign to respond, even though fury wells up in him at the thought of having to stay – heaven knows how much longer – at this school. If he is to escape, he must have greater self-control: he is fifteen now a man in charge of his family's destiny.

Besides, by August 1784 he is no longer alone at Brienne. His brother Lucien has been at the school with him since June.

What a wonderful month that was!

On the 21st, Napoleone Buonaparte is told he is wanted in the parlour, and there, waiting in that big room, he finds his father and one of his brothers, Lucien, the youngest Buonaparte. Napoleone doesn't rush over to them. He backs away instead, so as not to shatter under the weight of emotion. It is more than five years since he has seen any member of his family.

He looks fixedly at his father. There he is, this same tall, wiry figure, with a horseshoe wig in a black silk bag with two black silk ribbons falling to his ruffle. It is as if he never left. He is as elegant as ever, in a frogged silk coat trimmed with braid, and he wears a sword. However, his features are drawn, his complexion yellow. Charles Buonaparte, who has just taken his daughter, Marianna Elisa, and two of her cousins to St Cyr, complains about his health. He tells his son that he cannot keep down anything he eats and that his stomach pains are becoming more and more acute.

Buonaparte listens, watched by his brother Lucien who is amazed by his brother's apparent lack of tenderness or emotion, but when Buonaparte learns that Joseph has decided to leave the college at Autun to pursue soldiering like him, he argues with all the confidence and authority of a head of family, as if his father's illness immediately pushes him to assume this role.

The visit is a brief one. Lucien stays at Brienne, where Buonaparte will look after him and guide him, and Charles sets off for Paris, saying that he will return to Brienne on his way back to Corsica.

Napoleone accompanies him to his coach.

When the horses move off, he turns brusquely towards Lucien and speaks to him like a schoolmaster.

NAPOLEONE IS FIFTEEN. Already his role has changed. On 25 June, he takes up his quill. His writing slopes, and he makes plenty of spelling mistakes, but he expresses himself clearly and forcefully. It is the voice of a fifteen-year-old adult speaking in the letter to his uncle Fesch. He does not hesitate to judge one and all, from his brother Lucien – who is called the chevalier because he's the youngest – to his elder brother Joseph. Every sentence indicates a man who compels his feelings to bow to his reason, a man who can think for himself, who forms his opinions by himself. He has developed his own mind by opposing those who surround him. The child who has had to defend himself, turn in on himself so as not to dissolve into nostalgia and sadness or disappear into the crowd, has grown into an autonomous, independent soul, able to analyse problems, resolve them, and then draw the appropriate conclusions. Fifteen years old!

He writes:

My dear Uncle,
    I write to inform you of the passage of my dear father by Brienne. He left Luciano here, who is nine years of age and three feet eleven inches and six lines tall. He is in the sixth class for Latin and is intending to study all the different parts of the curriculum. He shows much disposition and goodwill; we must hope that he will turn out well. He is in good health, is fat, lively and mischievous, and as beginnings go, we are content with him. He knows French very well and has forgotten Italian entirely . . .

I am convinced that Joseph, my brother, has not written to you. How could you expect him to do so? He only writes two lines to my dear father, when he does write. In truth, he is no longer the same person . . . As to the profession he wishes to enter, the ecclesiastical was, as you know, the first he chose. He persisted in this resolution up to the present time, but now he wants to serve the king, in which he is wrong for several reasons . . . He has not sufficient courage to face the dangers of an action. His feeble health does not permit him to bear the fatigues of a campaign, and my brother only looks at the military life from the point of view of a garrison . . . He will always come off well in society, but in a fight?

Buonaparte, writing fast, proceeds with the indictment. Joseph, who knows no mathematics, will not make an officer either in the marine branch or the artillery. Infantry then? 'Good. I understand. He wishes to spend all day doing nothing, loafing about the streets . . . What is a tiny officer of infantry? A good-for-nothing three-quarters of the time and that is what neither my dear father, nor you nor my mother nor my dear uncle the archdeacon want, since he has already shown some signs of levity and prodigality . . .'

This is a younger sibling talking about his elder brother! An adolescent – already, to some degree, a man – who feels responsible for his whole family, as if he was its head.

A few days later, Buonaparte takes up his quill again. He has suffered a fresh disappointment. His father will not be returning to Brienne. He is going directly from Paris to Corsica.

My dear Father,
    Your letter, as you can imagine, did not give me much pleasure, but reason, the interests of your health and the family which are very dear to me made me praise your prompt return to Corsica and have altogether consoled me.
    Besides, being assured of the continuation of your goodness and of your attachment, and of your readiness to help me come out well here, how could I be anything but contented? For the rest, I am eager to ask of you an account of the effects which the waters have had upon your health and to assure you of my respectful attachment and of my eternal gratitude.

A loving son, a 'respectful' son attached to his family and a grateful son who salutes the efforts of his father to help him 'come out well' at Brienne, he none the less continues his letter with advice to his father concerning Joseph's choice of studies. He hopes that he will place his elder brother in Brienne rather than Metz 'because that will be a consolation for Joseph, Lucien and me'. He hopes that his father will send him books about Corsica. 'You have nothing to fear, I will take care of them and bring them back to Corsica when I come, even if it be six years from now.'

'Adieu, my dear father,' he concludes. 'The chevalier – Lucien – embraces you with all his heart. He works very well, and did very well at the public examination.' Then he addresses his respects to all the members of the family, and he signs it, 'Your very humble and very obedient son, de Buonaparte.'

IN THE LETTER to his father, an apparently anodyne passage – 'The Inspector will be here on the 15th or 16th of this month, at the latest, that's to say in three days. As soon as he has gone I will tell you what he has said' – marks Buonaparte's impatience. For he has another interview with Reynaud des Monts who has been briefed by the ministry to send up to the Military School of Paris 'all scholarship boys from the smaller schools who commend themselves not only by their talents, their knowledge and their conduct but also by their aptitude at mathematics'.

During his inspection of Brienne in September 1784, he chooses five of the Minims' pupils to become gentlemen cadets and go to Paris. The first name on the list is Montarby de Dampierre who has opted for the cavalry. The second, Castres de Vaux, has chosen the engineers. The three others are candidates for the artillery: Laugier de Bellecourt, de Cominges and Napoleone Buonaparte.

When he hears his name, the youth simply looks up, and his feelings can only be discerned by a brilliant glint in his eyes.

He knows what leaving means: escaping the routine of Brienne, first and foremost; these places he knows all too well, this grey, oppressive landscape. He will be abandoning Lucien here – that pains him – but he can become an officer in a year, and then his brother Joseph will have a scholarship and it will be his turn to go to Brienne to attend Father Patrault's mathematics lessons.

Buonaparte hides his joy, but he walks faster, pacing up and down the courtyard, hands clasped behind his back. An obstacle has been overcome. He is moving forward. Everything is possible.

HOWEVER HE HAS to wait. The days drag by impossibly slowly, and it is only on 22 October 1784 that Louis XVI, 'having awarded Napoleone de Buonaparte, born August 15, 1769, a gentleman cadet's place in the company of gentlemen cadets established in my military school', requests 'the Inspector General, Monsieur de Timbrune-Valence, to welcome him and make him known in the aforesaid place'.

On 30 October Napoleone Buonaparte leaves Brienne with his four schoolmates and a Minim who is going to supervise them.

First they take the coach to Nogent and there board the water bus for Paris. The sky is grey, and now and again there's rain, but how can a gentleman cadet of fifteen succumb to melancholy when he is making his way to the capital of the kingdom of France, where the King will welcome him as a scholar at his most prestigious military school?

This is what a foreigner, a citizen of a conquered land, a Corsican can seize hold of, when he knows what it is to want something.

'I want this,' murmurs Buonaparte.

III

BUONAPARTE WALKS through Paris. He is 'a short, dark-skinned young fellow in knee-breeches with red facings, sad, gloomy and severe in manner', but his hungry eyes devour the city.

He stops regularly to let the Minim escorting his four comrades from Brienne go on ahead. He wants to discover this spectacle on his own, experience all the heady thrill of it alone, for although his face is stiff, inside he is quivering like a bow.

He is only fifteen years and two months old, but he understands this city; he intuits it as a vast theatre, a wide open horizon. He crosses the Pont-Neuf, with its jam of carriages and carts. Barges are moored to the quays; street-porters force their way through a motley crowd of people in every manner of dress, from the studied elegance of a young aristocrat to the tatters of a young woman with ample breasts and bare arms.

People push by him without even a glance, but he sees everything. He sees those buildings at the corner of Place Dauphine that stand stiff as guards in red uniforms with white facings, and the rows of town houses over the bridge, with their lines of coaches waiting in front of them. He sees spires, domes, squares, the Champ de Mars and gold cupolas accentuating the grey slate roofs. He is exhilarated. He breathes this air with its mingled smells of excrement, horse dung and sweat. He listens to the sound of wheels on cobbles, the tramp of crowds hurrying through the narrow streets, the voices – French voices – which for the first time do not feel hostile or foreign.

He thinks of Corsica, its sea, its sky, its landscapes, the beauty of its creeks, its language, his family, but Paris, this vast, bountiful, teeming metropolis, is a sea as well. He is finished with dry Champagne and Brienne's narrow horizons. In this city where everything seems to be in motion, where royal magnificence displays itself at every turn in monumental buildings and statuary, the adolescent feels less a foreigner than in the confined universe of a provincial school. The wind blows here as it does on the shore and the uprooted young southerner rediscovers in the capital the sort of grandeur he had grown accustomed to, watching the sea and its immense skies.

When one of his schoolfellows, Laugier de Bellecourt, hangs back to nudge him in the ribs and share his delight at being here at last – in this city overflowing with life, where the liberty of morals is evident in every body, in every bold look – Buonaparte draws back.

Laugier de Bellecourt, his junior by more than a year, was close to him for a few months at Brienne, but Napoleone was quick to reject that ambiguous friendship: Laugier de Bellecourt with his gentle, girlish air was probably one of the school's nymphs. Buonaparte has not forgotten. He turns away. He wants to be left alone to enter this town, and catch his first sight of the Military School of Paris on the Grenelle plain, not far from the Hôtel des Invalides.

As he approaches it, he is secretly overawed by the beauty of this palace with its high quadrangular dome. He waits until last before going in to admire the eight Corinthian columns, the pediment, the statues atop it and the clock framed by garlands. He passes through one of the iron gates, and enters the recreation yard lit by twelve great street lamps.

The cadets' quarters are in the right wing. He walks through rooms where boys play backgammon, chess and draughts, when the rain drives them in from the yard. The parlour has none of the austerity or coldness of its counterpart at Brienne. It has a large portrait of Louis XV, white calico curtains and red Abbeville damask hangings. The banquettes and chairs are upholstered in tapestry with a motif of green and white roses. Buonaparte looks into the classrooms, which have papered walls with gold fleurs-de-lys and the King's monogram gleaming against a blue background. The doors are glazed and framed, like the casement windows, with hangings. The luxury, magnificence and abundance dazzle the adolescent.

He eats his first meal in the refectory, sitting at a table for ten. The helpings are generous, the meats followed by dessert and fruit, and the pupils are waited on with ceremony. Among the gentlemen cadets, alongside the scholars, he notes young members of the high nobility who pay two thousand livres a year to attend the school. If it wasn't for their haughtiness and their lack of academic success – they attend the lessons, but they don't study – there would be no telling them apart from the general run of 126 cadets. However, from the day he arrives Napoleone senses that a Duke de Fleury or a Laval-Montmorency, a Puységur or a Prince de Rohan Guéménée, cousin to the King, will give him a scornful look and then turn away, to show that they are of another breed and that a scholarship son of minor Corsican nobility is only French because his island has been conquered by the royal army.

At the start these looks taint Buonaparte's enthusiasm, but at the same time, what does that crowd think? He did not give in when he was a child of nine; do they imagine that he will lower his guard when this city, these halls, everything proves that he is a victor? This certainty makes him milder-tempered, even though he remains intransigent, unyielding. The beauty of the place, the attention shown to the gentlemen cadets, even the presence of these descendants of the most illustrious families in the kingdom reassure him that he is one of the select few who are called to command. His pride swells; his sensitivity is simultaneously soothed and heightened. 'They' have shown him recognition – all well and good – but let them not provoke him: he will only be all the more determined to defend his origins and his beliefs. However, if he is shown respect, he is friendly, since he is no longer the raw-nerved soul of before. This first success has bandaged some of his wounds.

At the school, everyone initially shares a room with an older boy who is chosen to be their infantry instructor. In Buonaparte's case, it is Alexandre Des Mazis, who proves to be attentive, amiable, and even considerate. Buonaparte responds to his overtures and accepts his companionship. The room is small and boasts an iron bedstead, chairs and a set of shelves in the window recess, on which three pairs of regulation shoes stand in a row. The room opens on to a larger one with wood panelled walls, which is lit by sconces and heated by earthenware stoves: this is the dormitory.

So, no expense is spared in the military school and by the time Buonaparte has seen the armoury and admired the sixty horses in the riding-school – the finest Spanish chargers, some of which cost between 800 and 1,000 livres – he is convinced that he is being treated as the son of a lord.

Yet once again he draws back. He must not let himself be corrupted by this luxury which he knows, with utter lucidity, is only transient. He knows his family's means. His scholarship has shown him a world that otherwise would have been wholly unattainable. Now he must lay claim to as much of it by work and talent as he can because all this luxury will disappear the moment he leaves the school.

Buonaparte understands this.

He distances himself from his former schoolfellows who fritter their time away in dissipation. 'Sir,' he says to Laugier de Bellecourt. 'You have intimacies I disapprove of. Your new friends will be the ruin of you. Choose between them and me. I am leaving you no middle course. You must be a man and decide. Take what I say as a first warning.'

However, Laugier de Bellecourt does not resist temptation; his behaviour confirms the suspicions Napoleone Buonaparte had at Brienne.

'Sir,' he says to him curtly. 'You have scorned my advice; that is the same as renouncing my friendship. Never speak to me again.'

NAPOLEONE WORKS with fierce determination. Some boys, especially the boarders from grand families, make fun of him. This dark-skinned little chap is 'argumentative and never stops talking'.

He won't tolerate such remarks. In the schoolyard, he rushes into the fray, fists clenched. He dishes out wallopings to these scions of the high and mighty. He may be, as he says, *'un petit noble'* yet still he emerges victorious from these confrontations.

Sometimes antipathy turns to hatred.

With every word, every look, Picard de Phélippeaux, a scion of Vendean nobility, goads Buonaparte. He is the elder by two years; he came to the school in 1781. Their rivalry is not academic. They hate each other instinctively, as if one sees the scholar as the incarnation of all the new men who will turn the stable, monarchist world upside down, while the other senses in the Vendean a sworn adversary of movement, the aristocrat bent on suppressing and prohibiting all change. They issue challenges; they fight. Their regimental sergeant-major, Picot de Peccaduc, puts himself between them at evening prep so that they won't come to blows, but they kick each other so hard under the table that he has bruised legs.

Often Buonaparte will be walking with his hands behind his back in the armoury school, between fencing lessons, when suddenly he will freeze. From a group, a voice is shouting a word, a phrase. They make fun of Corsica, they provoke him. He leaps forward, seizes his foil and charges the group, amidst hoots of laughter.

But he isn't laughing.

He becomes indignant when cadets claim that a small French force conquered the island. These are the same slanders as at Autun and Brienne and he has to refute them, 'You were not six hundred, as you claim,' he answers, 'but six thousand, against benighted peasants.'

Why should a great people have been compelled to make war on a little nation? It is a sign of 'inferiority'.

'Come,' he says finally to his friend Des Mazis, 'let us leave these cowards.'

He cannot keep his peace for long, as at any moment a detail, a comment may remind him of his origins. When he kneels to be confirmed by Monsignor de Juigné, the latter is surprised by his Christian name, Napoleone, which is not that of one of the saints of the calendar.

The adolescent looks up, stares at the clergyman, and then says brusquely that there are a host of saints and only 365 days in the year.

He will never be made to keep silent. Even in the confessional, he will reply sharply if he is attacked. When, in January 1785, he is listening to the priest to whom he has just confessed – as every cadet must do each month –he suddenly cannot stifle a roar. The priest is reprimanding him, talking to him about Corsica and the duty of obedience he owes to the King, whose scholar and grateful subject he is. In any case, the priest continues, Corsicans are often bandits who suffer from the sin of pride.

'I did not come here to talk about Corsica,' cries Buonaparte, 'and a priest has no business lecturing me on this matter.'

Then he punches the grille between him and his confessor, breaks it and the two men come to blows.

HIS DAUNTLESS defence of his country, the mania, almost, with which he vaunts the exploits of Pascal Paoli, show that he is not one of those prudent souls who calculate every action. This adolescent is first and foremost a force that responds to the promptings of emotion.

Domairon, his humanities teacher, is struck by his 'bizarre amplifications'. 'He is granite heated by a volcano,' he says. The history teacher, De Lesguille, adds that this young cadet is 'Corsican both in character and nationality' and 'that he will go far if circumstances favour him'.

But Monsieur Valfort, the principal, is worried. He is told that this cadet, a King's scholar, declaims verses he has written portraying his homeland rising up in a dream, handing him a dagger and prophesying, 'You will be my avenger.'

A caricature by his classmates circulates, showing him as a vigorous young cadet striding haughtily along while an old teacher tries vainly to restrain him by hanging on to his wig. The caption reads, 'Buonaparte, run, fly to Paoli's side to rescue him from his enemies' clutches.' It's a strange state of affairs. This gentleman cadet, a future officer in the King's army, sees himself as the 'avenger' of Paoli who has been defeated by the King's troops, and he neither hides his opinions, nor his determination.

Monsieur Valfort and the school authorities send for him. He is so young, this Corsican patriot! His unguarded enthusiasm is, in some sense, proof of the purity of his character and besides, patriotism is a virtue for these officers, but they consider that the love of Corsica should not outweigh the gratitude he owes his monarch's generosity. Buonaparte listens, standing stiffly to attention. He is wearing the blue uniform with the red collar and white lining and silver bands. He holds his silver-embroidered hat in his hand.

He senses no hostility amongst Valfort and the other officers. He feels understood.

'Sir,' they tell him. 'You are a pupil of the King. You must bear this mind and moderate your love for Corsica which is, after all, part of France.'

He accepts their reprimand, but there is no change in his behaviour. He is unwavering, sure of himself. This assurance does not stem from the school's luxury – he remarks, almost reproach-fully, 'We are fed and looked after magnificently, treated in every respect as officers who enjoy great prosperity, far greater than most of our families could muster and far more than most of us will ever experience in the future.' He is a rock because he knows what he wants and because he is convinced that he has the qualities necessary to achieve his goal.

In their room, he explains to Des Mazis that he wants to skip a stage and acquire the rank of officer after just one year and be made a second lieutenant in a regiment. For this, Buonaparte says, his face tense, his body leaning towards his friend, he will have to pass the examinations to enter artillery school and become an officer at the same time. Instead of spending time as a pupil at artillery school first, he has to be promoted directly from gentleman cadet to second lieutenant.

It is a long shot!

'I want this,' says Napoleone Buonaparte.

This supposes that he knows, in their entirety, the four volumes of Professor Bezout's *A Treatise on Mathematics* – which the cadets simply call the Bezout – and that he can reply to all the questions put by the examiner, Laplace, an eminent member of the Academy of Sciences.

Buonaparte straightens up. He is going to take up this challenge, start learning, learning furiously, learn his Bezout, and pass both as a pupil and an artillery officer. When Des Mazis is in the infirmary for a few days, Buonaparte shuts himself in their room and doesn't look up from his mathematics textbook. What do the other subjects matter – spelling, Latin, grammar, German?

Baur, the German teacher, forms his opinion of Buonaparte on his results in his classes. When he notices he is absent in September 1785, at exam time, he asks the rest of the class where he is. Buona-parte is applying for the rank of second lieutenant of artillery, he is told.

'He knows something, does he?' asks Baur.

'What?' the class replies. 'He is one of the strongest mathematicians in the school.'

'Oh well,' says the German. 'I have always thought idiots were the only ones fit to study mathematics.'

Buonaparte neglects his dance lessons as well. He has no interest in the tenets of good breeding and manners which are taught at the Military School of Paris to enhance the brilliance and prestige of the nobility. This impatient adolescent, turned in on himself and obsessed by the goal he has set, has no time to learn anything that is not immediately useful to him. Everything must be subordinated to passing the two examinations in one year.

What does it matter that he does not achieve any of the ranks open to pupils – sergeant-major, commander of a division, and head of a mess? Confident in his sense of efficiency and purpose, he makes fun of the three silver stripes proudly sported by some boys. He won't be awarded the cross of the order of Notre-Dame-du-Mont-Carmel either, like Picot de Peccaduc or Phélippeaux. He would have to spend three years at the Military School for that. Three years! He thinks he'll die just at the thought of it.

It takes him ten months to learn, equation by equation, theorem by theorem, diagram by diagram, Bezout's entire treatise. Dogged, relentless, he doesn't let himself be distracted by anything. Besides, the school regulations do not allow any leave, and make no provision for holidays. He only has one visitor in the school's echoing parlour, a cousin, Arrighi de Casanova.

Between lessons and revision, he often goes out onto the large, open expanse known as the Promenade which has eight oak benches and is bordered by deal fences. Two large sheds were built there at the beginning of 1785, followed by a sort of redoubt, to give cadets a clearer idea of a fortified city. Buonaparte walks rapidly up and down this promenade, a book in hand. He learns, recites out loud, and sometimes also composes poetry.

In January 1785, for instance, he copies out a clumsy poem on the flyleaf of his textbook:

> Great Bezout, run your course
> But first allow me to say
> Many a candidate you aid

> This cannot be gainsaid
> But I won't stop laughing
> When I've finished you
> At the latest in May
> Then I'll turn coach

That January he is certain that he will have finished studying *A Treatise on Mathematics* by May, in other words four months before the exam in September.

He organizes his work and revision time methodically, because the exams are hard and access to the artillery, like the engineers, is difficult, but a nobleman without a penny to his name, if he has talent, can rise through the ranks of this branch, since candidates are selected according to merit.

Twenty-five cadets have put themselves down for the artillery in 1785, but the school governor, Monsieur de Timbrune-Valence, only gives eighteen boys permission to sit the exam. Des Mazis, Buonaparte's friend who failed the exam in 1784, is top of the list, followed by Picot de Peccaduc. Buonaparte comes below his enemy, the Vendean Phélippeaux, and Laugier de Bellecourt is near the bottom, although given his dissolute ways, it is striking he has been selected at all.

When he sees the list, Buonaparte only indulges in a feeling of superiority for a moment: he is not afraid of his competitors – he knows he is one of the best mathematicians of the school – but there are the other candidates from the provincial schools to be reckoned with, especially Metz, the most prestigious artillery school, and he does not just want to settle for passing this first examination. He hasn't forgotten the officers' exam. So he redoubles his efforts, and tackles the third volume of Bezout's treatise in February 1785. Nothing must push him off course.

Then, at the end of that month, news comes that strikes Napoleone Buonaparte like a thunderbolt. He learns that his father died on 24 February 1785 in Montpellier. He was thirty-nine years old.

BITTER SORROW is etched on the adolescent's face. It grows gaunt, hollow-cheeked. He knew his father was sick, but now the abyss has opened up here, right in front of him, and he stands on the brink, about to fall in.

The principal breaks the news to him, and then, as is customary, suggests that Buonaparte go to the infirmary to cry and pray there and accept the suffering that destiny has imposed on him. Buonaparte remains silent for a moment, and then replies in a hollow voice that a man must know how to suffer. It is for women to cry. He asks to return to work as if nothing has happened. Sorrow is a personal matter. 'I have not lived to this day without having thought of death,' he says. 'I accustom my soul to it as I do to life.'

And yet his grief is extreme.

He learns how, over the past few months, his father had endured progressively crueller attacks of his illness – vomiting, unbearable stomach pains and an inability to eat.

Accompanied by Joseph, Charles Buonaparte had set off for Paris to be examined again by Doctor Lasonne, the Queen's doctor, but as soon as his ship had left Corsica in November 1784, it had met with a storm which drove it back to Calvi. There it had to put in, and they only reached Provence after another violent squall. At Aix, he found his brother-in-law, the seminarist Fesch, but his suffering was so acute that a doctor, Professor Turnatori, advised him to go on to Montpellier where renowned physicians such as La Mure, Sabatier and Barthez had their practices.

It was too late. In Montpellier, Charles Buonaparte's strength faded by the hour, although Joseph, Fesch, a Madame Pernom and her daughter Laure did everything they could for him.

Charles, the free thinker, the Jesuits' enemy, the Voltairean, called for a priest, confessed his sins, and prayed. He became hoarse, and then gradually his voice cleared, and in the hours preceding his death he called for Napoleone, the only son who could save him, snatch him from the dragon of death. In feverish outbursts, he cried that kings would tremble before Napoleone's sword, that his son would change the face of the world. If he were there, 'he would defend me from my enemies,' he screamed.

He tried to pull himself up, repeating, 'Napoleone, Napoleone', then fell back.

He died that same day.

The doctors performed an autopsy immediately after death and found, 'In the lower aperture of the stomach, a tumour of the length and volume of a large potato or a large prolate winter pear. The stomach lining towards the middle of its large curvature was very thick and of a hard, near cartilaginous consistency ... We can confirm that we found the liver engorged and the gall bladder extremely full of a very dark bile, having swollen to the size of a medium-sized pear in length ...'

Charles Buonaparte was buried in a vault in the Church of the Cordeliers.

IN THE DAYS after the announcement of his father's death, Buonaparte works even more unremittingly hard. He drowns his grief in study. When Alexandre Des Mazis tries to console him, he stops him, simply saying that now it is even more necessary that he succeeds. He has to be an officer by September. A pupil? That time has passed. Second lieutenant at the first try – that is what must happen.

He knows that from now on his mother will have to raise his four younger siblings in Ajaccio on an income of only 1,500 livres. The four eldest have been placed in schools and will be able to provide for themselves. So if he is an officer of a regiment and drawing pay by October 1785, then he will genuinely be the head of the family as he has been in spirit for several months already.

He writes two letters at the end of March: one is to his father's uncle, Lucien, the Archdeacon of Ajaccio, who, according to Buonaparte family lore, stashes all his money in a purse under his pillow; the other is to his mother.

As with all letters, he has to submit them to the masters who read all boys' correspondence and make any changes they see fit, so he masks as much of his feelings as he can. Nevertheless in the letter of 23 March, addressed to the archdeacon, the son's pain reverberates beneath the controlled style:

My dear Uncle,
    It would be useless to tell you how affected I have been by the tragedy that has befallen us. We have lost in him a father, and God knows what a father with his tenderness and love for

us! Alas! In everything he was the protector of our youth. You have lost in him an obedient and grateful nephew . . . Our country, I even dare to say, has lost an enlightened and disinterested citizen . . . And yet heaven lets him die, where? A hundred leagues from his native land, in a foreign country indifferent to his existence, far from all he held dear. A son, it is true, was present at that terrible moment; which must have been a great consolation to him, but certainly not to be compared with the triple joy he would have felt if he had ended his career in his own home, beside his wife and all his family. But the Supreme Being has not allowed it to be so. His will is immutable. He alone can console us. Alas! He has taken from us what we held most dear, but at least he has left us those who alone can replace him. Agree, then, to take the place of the father we have just lost. Our affection and our gratitude will be equal to so great a service.

I close by wishing that you enjoy health like my own.

Napoleone di Buonaparte

He re-reads the letter. The choice of guardian is a good one: the archdeacon is prosperous and influential. He will accept the role he is asked to play by this adolescent who is not yet sixteen, and yet has a gravely authoritative manner which marries sentiment and reason.

Five days later, Buonaparte writes the second letter, to his mother.

My dear Mother,

Now that time has somewhat calmed the first transports of my grief, I hasten to express to you the gratitude that your goodness towards us inspires in me.

Be consoled, dear Mother; circumstances require it. We will redouble our care and gratitude and be happy if by our obedience we can make good a little the inestimable loss of a dearly loved husband.

I close, my dear Mother, as my sorrow demands, by begging you to calm your own grief. My health is perfect, and every day I pray that heaven may favour you similarly.

Give my respects to *Zia* Gertrude, *Minana* Saveria, *Minana* Fesch, etc.

PS The queen of France gave birth to a prince, named Duke of Normandy, at seven in the evening on March 27.

Your very affectionate son,

Napoleone di Buonaparte.

Now, the ink barely dry, the wound still open, he must return to work. He does not hesitate. 'My sorrow demands.'

WHEN, AT THE START of September 1785, the academician Laplace enters the room in the Military School that has been prepared for the examination of gentlemen cadets applying for the artillery, Napoleone is ready.

He enters when his turn is called. Laplace is waiting, dressed in black, eyes half-hidden by a pince-nez. His appearance is severe, his manner grave, but his voice is gentle and his tone kind. He is extremely polite towards the candidates who are paralysed with fear, knowing their whole career will depend on their answers.

Napoleone does not lose his composure.

He looks at the platform on which two blackboards have been set up for diagrams and mathematical proofs. There are curtains of English linen at the windows and a row of tables for plans. Because the examination is public, there are tiers of benches covered in Abbeville damask for such artillery officers as happen to be in Paris, for the two representatives of the principal inspector of schools, Colonel d'Angenoust, and for his chief clerk, the war commissar Roland de Bellebrune.

Napoleone steps up.

He draws the diagrams with a vigorous flourish. His replies to the questions are terse and precise. He writes the equations on the blackboards. He knows the four volumes of Bezout's *A Treatise on Mathematics* in detail. He only makes minor mistakes.

ON 28 SEPTEMBER 1785, his name is forty-second in the list of fifty-eight youths admitted into the artillery as second lieutenants. There are four gentleman cadets from the Military School of Paris in all. Above him, Picot de Peccaduc is thirty-ninth and Phélippeaux, forty-first. Des Mazis, his friend, is only fifty-sixth.

He is ecstatic.

He strides up and down the recreation yard and the promenade.

He has attained his goal: in ten months' work, he has been promoted to officer grade without having first to become a pupil at an artillery school. All the other gentlemen cadets who have been made second lieutenants are older than him – Picot de Peccaduc and Phélippeaux by two years, Des Mazis by one.

His chest swells and he draws himself up to his full height. Perhaps this is what happiness is, he thinks, and then becomes sad for a moment, as his thoughts turn to his father – but his pride soon blots out his sadness. Those who came above him on the list had been preparing for the exam for years rather than months; he is the first Corsican ever to have passed out of the Military School; and in the entire artillery, there is only one other officer from the island, a M. de Massoni.

He is one of a kind.

His appointment to the rank of second lieutenant is backdated to 1 September 1785. He is sixteen years, fifteen days old.

He does not let himself be carried away with his success, but asks to be posted to the regiment of La Fère, which is stationed in Valence, where his friend Des Mazis, whose brother is the regiment's captain, should be going. The choice isn't prompted by friendship, but by the desire to be nearer to his family and Corsica. The regiment of La Fère provides the two companies of artillery that are garrisoned on the island; Buonaparte dreams of being posted to them. It is now more than six years since he saw Ajaccio.

DURING THOSE autumn days of 1785, Buonaparte is happy, perhaps for the first time since 15 December 1778, the day he left Corsica.

He fills his trunk with all the 'kit and caboodle' that the Military School supplies for second lieutenants – twelve shirts, twelve collars, twelve pairs of thick socks, twelve handkerchiefs, two cotton nightcaps, four pairs of stockings, a pair of shoe buckles and pair of garters – and for a long time he weighs in his hands his sword, his belt and the silver collar stud that is only given to gentleman cadets from the Military School of Paris. Then, accompanied by a 'gate captain', whose job is to supervise the young officers and pay their expenses, he leaves.

Paris, of which he has seen so little, offers itself to him that

28 October 1785, and he walks slowly through it, as if at the head of a triumphal procession, to pay a visit to the Bishop of Autun, Monsignor de Marboeuf, who lives on the ground floor of the abbatial palace of St-Germain-des-Prés; he is duly congratulated.

He is no longer 'the foreigner'. He has been accepted by this world into which he was brutally thrust as a child. He has not drowned. He has taken what was useful to him without abandoning what was important. He has donned its uniform without changing his skin or his soul. He has grown resilient, fighting his battles, never bowing before anyone, but remaining stiff-necked and holding his head high. He has learnt the language of Corsica's conquerors, but out of these new words he has created his own style. He has moulded the French sentence to the taut rhythms of his character.

He has seized what was necessary without letting himself be swallowed up.

ON 29 OCTOBER 1785 in the Military School's storehouse, the porter Lemoyne hands over 157 livres 16 sous to gentlemen cadets Buonaparte, Des Mazis and Delmas — who has been admitted as an artillery pupil — to cover their expenses on the journey to Valence.

The next day, in the company of his two classmates, Napoleone di Buonaparte steps into the coach that is to carry him South.

PART TWO

Always alone in the midst of men

IV

Buonaparte is impatient.

They only left Paris a few hours ago and already the stagecoach is stopping at Fontainebleau for dinner. It's been dawdling along. He walks about the yard of the coaching inn. They will sleep at Sens tonight; his friend Des Mazis assures him that the Lyon stage is famed throughout France for punctuality and the swiftness of its relays.

He walks out onto the road. When will he be able to gallop off alone, as he used to in Corsica as a child, go his own way and not be impeded by anything? The South still seems such a long way off, like a mirage that slips out of one's grasp. He has waited so long for this moment: to be nearer to Corsica and his family, to be able to see them again when his first furlough falls due, after a year's service.

At Sens the next morning, he is the first up. He circles around the coachmen, and is exasperated by the thought of the stages to come: Joigny, Auxerre, Vermanton, Saulieu, Autun.

Autun. He remembers 1 January 1779, when his father left him in the college there with Joseph. He feels calmer. This road he is taking leads to the sea.

At Chalon-sur-Saône, the travellers take the water bus and travel down the placid river to Lyon to join the Rhône. Buonaparte stands at the prow, his hair ruffled by a wind that carries new smells. The sky is different, brilliant, never-ending; the scenery is wild, with white stone gorges through which the river swirls. The bargees are a rugged lot. When he hears them talk, the accent reminds him of the peasants who used to come down from the backcountry to Ajaccio. Suddenly, looking around, he sees the same scrub vegetation and gnarled olive trees he knows from the family estate at Milelli. Then finally, Valence and its tiled roofs appear. This is not his 'country' yet, but Buonaparte is on the threshold and, after more than six years' absence, deeply moved to be thus reunited with the South.

THE THREE COMPANIONS make their way to the barracks of the
La Fère regiment, which is on the road from Lyon to Provence.

A wind is blowing. The shooting range lies on the other side
of the road, and soldiers are performing manoeuvres even though
rain is starting to fall.

The lieutenant-colonel introduces them to the regiment. All
the men, he says, have fibre, stamina, and cut a dash. The second
lieutenants will have to serve three months as soldiers and NCOs
to accustom themselves to the daily routines of those who will
be under their command. The La Fère artillery is hardworking
and tireless, he adds. They are early risers, with drill after firing
practice, apart from on market days, three times a week, when
they have theory classes so that the peasants and townsfolk are not
disturbed by the cannon.

'Good mathematician?' he asks, turning towards Buonaparte.

He reads the name of this short, beardless, pale, excessively
thin lieutenant again. He isn't much to look at, this cadet who has
been admitted as a second lieutenant first try. He is hollow-
cheeked, tight-lipped. None the less the lieutenant-colonel is
impressed. That face expresses firmness and obstinacy. He is
prickly and disagreeable, but he has backbone.

The lieutenant-colonel stumbles over his name, which is spelled
Napolionne de Buonaparte on the regimental list.

Buonaparte gives no indication he has noticed. Yet again, it is
as if his identity is fluid and uncertain to these Frenchmen who,
even so, have accepted him into their midst as a distinguished,
promoted figure.

He grows a little more sullen. He knows who he is: a Corsican
and an officer in the King of France's army who dreams of
returning to his country.

A few months later, in his lodgings in the Bou household, in
a big thirty-three-page notebook, Buonaparte writes with a quill
that catches, then flies over the paper, and then catches again
because his thoughts are too fast for his hand, 'The Corsicans
have been able, following all the laws of justice, to shake off the
Genoese yoke and they can do the same with that of France.
Amen!'

ON HIS FIRST evening in Valence, Buonaparte knocks on the door of the Bou household. It is opened by a woman of around fifty: Marie-Claude Bou, the daughter of 'father Bou'. She is lively, helpful. The room she shows him is of monastic simplicity but far larger than any he had at Autun, Brienne or Paris and it has a table. He puts down his books and his large notebook.

On the opposite side of the street, on the ground floor of the Maison des Têtes, Monsieur Aurel has a bookshop. Lieutenant Buonaparte can take out a subscription to the reading room there, explains Marie-Claude Bou. Here, she adds, he will have his washing and ironing done.

First night.

The wind rushes through the alleyways.

After the tension of those ten months at the Military School where everything was dominated by the challenge of the examination, a completely new way of life is beginning for the adolescent Buonaparte, who is not yet seventeen. Now he must assume responsibilities; he must command others rather than obey them. Even with the soldier's constants – guard duty, shooting range, officers' dinners – time here moves at a different rhythm. Every morning he goes to Father Couriol's on the corner of Vernoux and Briffard streets. He helps himself to two hot little patties from a steel shelf above the oven, drinks a glass of water and tosses the pastry chef a couple of sous. In the evenings, he dines at the Three Pigeons on rue Pérollerie with the other lieutenants of the regiment of La Fère. They discuss the day's exercises; Buonaparte speaks confidently.

HE COMPLETES his spell in the ranks in the middle of January 1786, and is made a regular second lieutenant. That first morning he puts on an officer's uniform: a pair of blue jersey breeches, a blue cloth waistcoat with open pockets and a royal blue coat with blue collar and lapels, red facings and pocket flaps with red borders. It has yellow buttons with the number 64, since he belongs to the 64th Regiment, and lastly epaulettes frosted with a bullion of gold and silk thread.

The emotion Buonaparte feels when he sees himself in the

apparel of his success, is so strong that he has to lower his eyes. Will he ever know a joy as great as this again? Will he ever wear a uniform as beautiful?

He heads towards the barracks and relieves the guard officer in the guard room on Place Clerc in the centre of town.

In the weeks that follow, he goes on manoeuvres with his company. He observes batteries being constructed. He attends classes in geometry, differential and integral calculus, and trigonometry which Professor Dupuy de Bordes gives the officers of the regiment. On certain days he learns how to draw up plans, outlines and maps. In the lecture hall, officers pass on their practical experience about how to aim and load the pieces of ordnance and ways to lay out batteries and mines.

He is attentive, hungry for knowledge, and reads the theoreticians of 'modern' warfare, Guibert and Gribeauval.

When he is questioned about these subjects, he answers with a precision that is astonishing for a second lieutenant of barely seventeen. His voice is deep and resonant; when he speaks he is terse and to the point and his passion is evident. He loves the profession of arms and studies with the same determination he applied to mastering Bezout's *A Treatise on Mathematics*. He feels at ease among these officers who are as passionate about their chosen branch of the service, the artillery, as he is. The demanding, specialized nature of it as a science fosters a mood of companionship which Napoleone Buonaparte warms to. Despite his Corsican patriotism, which remains unchanged, or even grows stronger, he feels comfortable with these comrades.

'The artillery,' he says, 'is the finest and best formed corps in Europe. The service is like a family, the officers are paternal in every way, the bravest and worthiest people in the world, as pure as gold, but too old because of the long peace. The younger officers laugh at them because sarcasm and irony are the fashion of the age, but they adore them and always do them justice.'

THE OTHER REASON Buonaparte's life is more harmonious than at any time since he arrived in France as a child is that Valence is part of the South, and the region is populated by hospitable Southerners.

'Corsican?' they ask him.

He is on his guard, replying with a wary nod, but people congratulate him on his origins; they find an accent like his, which is still Italian in its intonations, charming. He is introduced into the town's polite society.

He makes an effort to please, taking lessons in dancing and deportment, and, although he remains as clumsy and gauche as ever, he studies these French nobles whose elegance, nonchalance and brilliant manners and conversation seem innate. His own uniforms are often crumpled, as if creased by his abrupt movements. He wears wrinkled cravats, and his long straight hair falls to his shoulders, covering his temples. There is something rough and angular about him – no openness or grace, but a mixture of shyness, unsociability and brusqueness in the way he talks and carries himself.

Nevertheless he is invited to call by Jacques Tardivon, the former Prior of Platière and the Abbot of the order of St Ruf, on the recommendation of the Bishop of Autun, Monsignor de Marboeuf, who describes Buonaparte as a young officer with an impressive future, one of his protégés.

Monsieur de Tardivon welcomes him in the drawing room of the Hotel St Ruf, where Valence's nobility gather.

The uniformed Buonaparte makes an impression, despite his appearance. His silence is intriguing, the look in his eyes winning. Questioned by Monsieur de Tardivon's brother-in-law, Monsieur de Josselin, a regular guest at the Hotel St Ruf and former lieutenant-colonel of the Artois infantry regiment, Buonaparte answers briefly, but such succinctness commands attention.

He is singular, this young lieutenant.

He is recommended to the ladies of Valence, Madame Lauberie de Saint-Germain, Madame de Laurencin and Madame Grégoire du Colombier, who each have a salon, and Buonaparte visits these houses where the new ideas are afoot. He is at once shy, a charming quality, and daringly, almost provocatively plain-spoken. This touches these benevolent quinquagenarians. He is so young!

In this way he gradually grows accustomed to a social life, often going to Madame du Colombier's country house in Basseaux three leagues from Valence. He walks with a spring in his step through that Provencal countryside which reminds him of Corsica, the same smells and vegetation. His head is full of what he is reading. Just then it is Rousseau, who he reads again and again. He knows passages of *Reveries of a Solitary Walker*, *Confessions* and *The New Heloise* by heart. He feels a kinship with 'Jean-Jacques', as he calls him.

Madame du Colombier could be Madame de Warens, Rousseau's mentor. Not yet having experienced love, Buonaparte's pulse quickens in the company of this well-read, witty, distinguished woman who makes an effort to charm him. Sitting at her side, Buonaparte confides that he is thinking of writing a history of Corsica. She is enthusiastic. Has he read the works of Abbé Raynal? Monsieur de Tardivon knows this author who is now enjoying a considerable vogue. Whenever he travels from Paris to Marseilles, the Abbé always stays at the Hotel St Ruf. Madame du Colombier advises Buonaparte to write to the Abbé, and also recommends a bookseller in Geneva, Paul Borde.

Buonaparte writes to Borde immediately. He asks the bookseller for books that 'follow on from the *Confessions* of Jean-Jacques Rousseau. I also beg you,' he continues, 'to send me the two volumes of the *History of Corsica* by the Abbé Germanes. I shall be obliged if you will let me have a note of the works on the island of Corsica which you have or could obtain for me quickly. I await your reply to send you the money due.'

He subscribes, as Marie-Claude Bou has advised him, to the reading room of the Valence bookseller, Monsieur Aurel, and the books pile up on the little table in his room in the Bou house.

He reads constantly, and feels as if he is reading about his own life. Jean-Jacques is his double; he puts into words what this young man who is still undecided about the future, feels. Hasn't Buonaparte felt that he is different? Hasn't he been misunderstood and mocked like Rousseau? When Buonaparte goes to Basseaux, isn't he the solitary walker's brother? When he climbs the Roche-Colombe with a companion from the La Fère regiment and is elated by the beauty of nature in June 1786, isn't he just like Rousseau?

Buonaparte climbs, lost in thought and deeply moved. There is a vast, panoramic view from the top. He feels ennobled by the expanse he contemplates. His and Jean-Jacques's experiences correspond. 'I like to raise myself above the horizon,' he tells his fellow officer.

He comes back down at dusk, wondering. What will he be? A writer? A *philosophe*? A lawgiver as Rousseau wanted to be? An author who will define, like Rousseau, a social contract? Buonaparte swings from enthusiasm to dejection, from bold assurance to shyness. He is not yet seventeen. His life is only just beginning – what will become of him?

A few words of conversation with Mademoiselle de Lauberie de Saint-Germain are enough to move him deeply. He admires her beauty, her 'virtue'. He doesn't go beyond that.

He has never courted a woman, so when Madame du Colombier introduces her daughter Caroline to him, he instantly falls in love, but conceives of it only as a Platonic friendship. Caroline blushes. He pales. He confides to his comrade Des Mazis, who is passionately in love with a young girl from Valence, that for his part he wants to 'avoid those frequent visits that cause spiteful gossip and incur an alarmed mother's disapproval'. But the fact that one morning he pick cherries with Caroline in the garden at Basseaux is enough to leave him agitated for a long time. When he returns to his room that evening, he rereads the passage in the *Confessions* where Jean-Jacques describes how, in an orchard, he threw bunches of cherries to two young girls and they then threw back the stones, laughing.

He cannot sleep; he sees Rousseau's scene in his mind's eye and identifies with the writer. He is a young man bumping up against a part of life he knows nothing about, so he sits at his desk – reading and writing are ways to understand what he is, what he feels.

Over and over he reads the letters his brother Joseph sends him from Corsica. His nostalgia for his family and his island, for the scent of myrtles and orange trees, grows painfully acute. He dreams of the leave he is entitled to which, if it comes through, can start on 1 September 1786.

'I have been,' he writes on 3 May, 'absent from my country for six or seven years. What pleasure shall I not feel in four months when I see my compatriots and my relations once more! From the tender feelings that memories of my childhood pleasures evoke, can I not conclude that my happiness will be complete?'

Corsica is thus Buonaparte's *point fixe*, his certainty, and almost his obsession. It is the land that suffers the injustice of occupation, the island whose virtues Rousseau has sung, and the reef sheltering all the nostalgia he feels for his childhood and his family.

In June, when he learns that a compatriot, an artist by the name of Pontornini, is living at Toulon, four leagues from Valence, Buonaparte immediately sets off to talk of his absent homeland, and hear its tongue.

Pontornini gives him a warm welcome. Their conversation only stops when it gets dark and as they talk, Pontornini sketches a portrait of him, the first anyone has done.

Buonaparte looks at his even profile, the strong, slightly hooked nose, the delicate mouth, the long hair covering half his forehead and falling straight to his shoulders. His expression is that of a grave, serious young man with a thoughtful gaze.

At the bottom, in the right-hand corner, Pontornini writes, '*Mi caro amico Buonaparte, Pontornini, del 1785, Tournone.*'

THIS MEETING makes him long to return to his country even more and, as he waits impatiently for the day when he will set foot on his island again, he continues to write with the spontaneity of youth and the forcefulness of a mind inventing its own style. He is still taming French, and his use of this language is a mark of the deep, profitable effect his new country has had on him, almost in spite of himself, but he uses French to express the split that is making him suffer. He is a French officer and proud to have succeeded in becoming one – he feels, as he says, that 'being an ordinary second lieutenant in the artillery is an honour' – but, at the same time, he is also a Corsican patriot!

He dreams of returning to his country. In his room he pities and revolts against the lot which has been inflicted on the Corsicans. 'People of the mountains, who has disturbed your happiness?' he writes. 'Peaceable, virtuous men who spent days of contentment in the bosom of your land, what barbarian tyrant has destroyed your dwellings?'

Thus he denounces Genoa, but he worries too about the

aftermath of French victory. 'What spectacle awaits me in my country? My compatriots weighed down with chains, trembling and kissing the hand that oppresses them. These are no longer the brave Corsicans whom a hero inspired with his own virtues, the enemies of tyrants and luxury, but vile courtiers!'

How could he not think of his father, who was Pascal Paoli's comrade, but who, when France had won victory, solicited Monsieur de Marboeuf and sent his sons to French schools?

'How far removed men are from nature!' writes Buonaparte. 'How cowardly, bare and grovelling they are!'

His anger turns on those who have reduced his people to this state. 'Frenchmen, not content with having ravished everything we hold dear, you have even corrupted our morals,' he protests indignantly. 'The picture my country makes and my inability to change it is yet another reason to flee this land where duty forces me to praise men whom virtue bids me hate.'

He stands up and walks around the room. He repeats that phrase, 'duty forces me to praise men whom virtue bids me hate'. He hammers out each word, as if he wished to suffer still more from this split which he cannot control and which, with a seventeen-year-old's excessively romantic sensibility, drives him to despair.

He goes out, walks through the streets of Valence, enters the Three Pigeons, dines sombrely with his fellow officers, goes back to the Bou house, and takes up his quill again. 'Always alone in the midst of men,' he writes, 'I return to my quarters to dream and give myself up to the full force of my melancholy. What is its direction today? Death ... What madness makes me wish to destroy myself? What to do with my life, no doubt? Since I must die, would it not be better to kill oneself?'

A moment's weakness? A young man's indulgence? Buonaparte is torn, because he doesn't know how, nor is he yet able, to master the tensions he feels within himself. He thirsts for the absolute, for a cause that will sweep him up and compel him to take on fresh challenges. Until now, he has always had a goal before him: to become an officer. He has achieved it. Where should he go now, when he is on the threshold of his life?

To Corsica!

And make it his mission to restore his homeland's freedom, to be its avenger.

But deep down he already has doubts. He has spent as much of his life in France as on the island. It is here that he has left childhood, that he has developed his own way of thinking. It is here that he exercises this profession of soldiering he loves.

IN THE BARRACKS at Valence, the soldiers of the regiment of La Fère are falling in. Rioting has broken out in Lyon, amongst the silk workers. They must go and restore order.

The second battalion of La Fère, to which Buonaparte's company belongs, sets off and takes up quarters in the Lyonnais suburb of Vaise, near the workers' district of Bourgneuf. They disperse the rioters who are demanding a two sous rise in wages. They hang three of them.

Buonaparte gives a good account of himself in the affair, impatient to see order re-established, since it has been confirmed that he can set off on leave to Corsica on 1 September.

All goes well, without delays; the battalion returns to Valence on the expected date and he leaves from there.

Buonaparte travels down the Rhône valley. Every step he takes towards the sea, he is transported by his imagination. The Roman monuments and the landscape, resplendent in the autumn sun, enchant him.

'Mountains in the distant embrace of a black cloud crown the immense Tarascon plain where a hundred thousand Cimbrians lie buried,' he writes. 'The Rhône flows at its foot, swifter than an arrow, a road is on the left, the little town some way off, a flock in the meadow.'

And at the end there they are: the sea, the port and the ship that will take him to his childhood home.

V

THE FIRST THING Buonaparte recognizes, standing at the prow of the ship, are the smells of his island.

It is 15 September 1786. He is coming to the end of a journey that had begun two weeks before at Valence, but he has been dreaming of this for seven years and nine months, he realizes, as the violet peaks of the island's mountains stand out in the dawn and the walls of Ajaccio's fortress appear.

He is seventeen years and one month old.

He fills his lungs with the fragrant, almost warm air, heavy with the scent of myrtle and orange blossom which Joseph used to tell him about in his letters – and when the sailors drop anchor, the first man Buonaparte catches sight of, running towards the gangway, is his elder brother.

He must hold back his tears. He slowly disembarks, looking in turn at his mother, his grandmothers, *minana* Saveria and *minana* Francesca, his aunt *zia* Gertrude and his wet-nurse Camilla Ilari who is sobbing noisily.

They crowd round their *Rabulione*, then stand back to admire his blue uniform with red facings. Rabulione, an officer?

Letizia Buonaparte takes her son's arm, Joseph walks the other side. His younger brother and sisters, Louis, Pauline and Caroline, follow while the youngest, Jerome, who is only two, clings to his wet-nurse. Everyone has come. The big trunk, which is so heavy that two men can barely lift it, is loaded onto a cart. Joseph asks what's in it, and doesn't have to wait to be told – he guesses that it's crammed with books. They are the most precious possessions of this brother of his who suppresses his emotions and is already asking after the family's fortunes. How is Archdeacon Lucien, the rich great-uncle who agreed to take the clan's affairs in hand after Charles Buonaparte's death?

Bedridden and ill, is the sad reply; he has headaches and swollen arthritic knees and ankles which immobilize him; his appetite is healthy and he is as talkative, clear-minded and shrewd as ever but he is as good as crippled, suffering agonies the moment he tries to get out of bed.

Already Letizia is telling her son her worries about money, her concerns for the future of Lucien and her four youngest children. Lucien is still studying at Aix secondary school. She leans forward and lowers her voice – what will become of Joseph, her eldest? He intends to go to Pisa to study law so that, when he is a doctor of law, perhaps, he can take the same position his father held in Corsica's States.

From the first steps he takes on his island's soil, Buonaparte knows that he is the head of the family, the one who has a 'position' and is admired, but also the one who is asked for help, advice and protection.

He has barely been there five days before news reaches the Buonaparte household of the death in Bastia, on 20 September, of Monsieur de Marboeuf.

Letizia's eyes cloud with sadness. Who will help them now: support their petitions, obtain grants for the mulberry nursery, scholarships for the children?

Buonaparte reassures his mother, and tells her to give him time. He has six months leave. He will take charge of the house and the family's interests.

His mother hugs him. He is the son she trusts. She puts herself in his hands.

The young man of seventeen proudly holds up his head with the responsibility. He will take up this challenge too. It is his duty.

EVERY MORNING he sets off at dawn, on foot or on horseback.

He goes to the property at Milelli, where he played as a child, and where there isn't an inch of land that isn't charged with memory. He walks through the dense olive groves or goes into the cave with the roof held up by two enormous granite rocks. He reads under a tall green oak which was a landmark for him when he was a child, helping him find his way among the olives.

He takes the books from his trunk. One day he rereads Plutarch, another Cicero or Livy, Tacitus or Montaigne, Montesquieu or Abbé Raynal. Sometimes he and Joseph declaim passages from Corneille, Voltaire or Rousseau.

'Do you know,' Buonaparte tells his brother, 'that we are the inhabitants of an ideal world?'

No longer does he read to escape, as he did during those lonely years on the mainland. Far from failing to live up to expectations, Corsica fills Napoleone with joy. He follows its paths down to the sea. He waits for the sun to 'precipitate itself into the bosom of infinity'. The melancholy of twilight steals over him and Joseph finds him standing on top of a rock, leaning his elbows on a ledge, musing, his face grave, as the night darkens the sky. He starts when he notices Joseph and tells him that 'he is touched by the electricity of nature'. That evening, at the family table, he praises that 'island adorned with every gift'. It is Letizia who interrupts him. 'Nothing is decided here anymore, nothing,' she says.

He knows. What would he be if he hadn't studied at Brienne and Paris, she asks? He has become an officer of the French army. The kingdom is where careers are made.

Buonaparte listens respectfully. Then he goes up to his room and writes. He has not given up the idea of writing a history of Corsica, but in the few days he has been back, he has discovered to his surprise and consternation that entire swathes of the Corsican language have vanished from his memory. When peasants or shepherds address him, he doesn't understand them completely and he has trouble speaking to them.

What has he become, through no desire of his own? A Frenchman? French is the language of the books he reads with impassioned enthusiasm. French is what he writes in. Yet, when, deep in the Corsican mountains, a shepherd gives him a sheepskin to keep him warm at night and shares his cheese and ham with him, he is proud to belong to such an hospitable people. He observes these rugged, vigorous men, full of grit but generous, who welcome him trustingly without troubling to find out who he is first.

Their faces and their voices take him back to his childhood, and after a few days the language comes back. He even endeavours to recover the Italian he has lost. Sitting around the fire in a shepherd's hut, he asks his host to tell stories. He becomes intoxicated by their way of speaking with long silences, their stories that have the force of symbols.

When he goes back to his reading and sits 'sheltered by the tree of peace and the orange tree', he feels his resolve growing to carry through his plan and twin his destiny with that of this island, 'theatre of his first games'.

His mother approaches and he stands up. They go and sit side by side. She is straight-backed, a beautiful woman of barely thirty-seven, her body worn by her twelve pregnancies. Although lined by suffering, the loss of her stillborn children and her husband's death, her face is proud. Her expression and demeanour are wilful.

'You are the soul of this house,' she tells Napoleone.

He must take matters into his own hands. The archdeacon is not well and he is the one who usually takes decisions. What is being done about the nursery of mulberry trees?

In 1782, Charles Buonaparte had acquired a concession from the intendant of the realm to grow mulberries. He was to be paid 8,500 livres in advance, in return for which he would ship the mulberry trees five years later. But he only received 5,800 livres and in May 1786 the contract was annulled when the ministry abandoned the project. By then, however, Letizia Buonaparte had already put in the plantation.

Napoleone listens, calculates, his face grave. In all, the State owes his family 3,050 livres. He reassures his mother. He will fight to get their money, even if he has to to ask for a longer leave from his regiment in order to take up the matter with the authorities in Corsica.

Anyway, he also needs to think about the archdeacon's health and discuss the Milelli property with him. He can switch like this from melancholy reverie to meticulous organization, from thoughts of writing a history of Corsica to biting arguments with the archdeacon.

HE GOES TO VISIT his great-uncle a number of times and gauges his influence by the size of his entourage: an archdeacon in Corsica must be the equivalent of a bishop in France, he thinks.

The archdeacon is in bed, grumbling and complaining. He challenges Napoleone's plans, such as farming the Milelli estate, which he thinks will be a pointless waste of money, and the young man and the 68-year-old archdeacon argue about how the island's goats should be treated.

'We must get rid of them,' says Buonaparte. 'They destroy the trees.'

The archdeacon, who owns large flocks of the animals, is indignant, 'That's a very philosophical idea, to drive all the goats out of Corsica!' – but the conversation is interrupted. The archdeacon cries out in pain. He shows Buonaparte his knees and ankles.

On 1 April 1787, after one of their meetings, Buonaparte decides to write to Doctor Tissot, a celebrated doctor and 'member of the Royal Society of London, of the Medico-Physical Academy of Basle and the Economic Society of Berne'. He is particularly admired in Corsica for having declared that Pascal Paoli is the equal of Caesar and Mahomet.

> You have spent your days instructing humanity and your reputation has reached as far as the mountains of Corsica where doctors are not much turned to. It is true that the short but glorious eulogy you gave to their beloved general is reason enough for the deep gratitude, which I am delighted to find myself in a position to convey to you, in the name of all my compatriots . . .
>
> I dare to importune you to ask advice for one of my uncles who has the gout . . . My uncle has extremely small feet and hands and a large head . . . I think that having a tendency towards egotism he found himself in a comfortable situation which did not tend him to develop all his strength . . . His gout struck him at the age of thirty-two . . . cruel pains ensued in his knees and feet, his head is also afflicted . . . He eats well, digests well, reads, sleeps and passes his days, but without movement, without being able to enjoy the sweetness of the sun. He implores the aid of your science . . .
>
> I myself have been struck by a tertian ague, which makes me doubt whether you will be able to read this scrawl.

Buonaparte's writing is more cursive than usual, it is true, and shakier too.

A few days later, on 31 April, he sends a certificate of ill health signed by a doctor and surgeon of Ajaccio to his colonel with a request for five and a half months more leave to date from 16 May 1787. 'In view of my lack of means and the expense of the treatment,' he specifies, 'I ask that leave be granted me with pay.'

The response is favourable and his leave is extended to 1 November.

Buonaparte knows that if he wants to extract the 3,050 livres he believes his family is owed from the offices in Paris, he must go to the capital. His mother has been urging him to do so and is delighted when his leave comes through. Buonaparte, however, wavers over whether to leave for several weeks – weeks in which he speaks little, as if all his energy was devoted to answering the questions he asks himself and attempting to resolve the dilemma that pulls him in opposite directions. Is it to be France *or* Corsica, or France *and* Corsica. How can he pit one against the other when he depends on one and is attached to the other?

His mother quizzes him. She worries about his fever, but, whether it was a bout of malaria or something else, it has passed.

She asks him again if he is going to Paris.

He slips away, roams the maquis, spends nights with the shepherds, looks at the sky, gazing at it endlessly and musing in the silence, gripped by melancholy once again.

Then, at the start of September 1787, he announces to his mother that he is going to Paris, and embarks for Toulon on the sixteenth of that month.

There is a strong, bitter wind, that carries little of the island's fragrances.

He is eighteen years and one month old.

VI

BUONAPARTE LOOKS AT THE WOMEN. Since he arrived in Paris they are all he sees. They seem to brush against him in the rue du Four St Honoré, the little thoroughfare in Les Halles between the rue Coquillière and the rue du Faubourg St Honoré where he has taken up lodgings. He is staying in the Hôtel de Cherbourg.

He looks at the women so insistently that they turn away, but some stare provocatively back at him and several times he has been tempted to go and speak to them. He stops himself at the last moment, hurries away, goes back to his hotel, runs up the two flights of stairs, pushes open the bedroom door, leans his back against it to catch his breath, and then sits down at his desk.

He begins to write frenetically, almost furiously.

He draws up a detailed report for the controller general, going through the whole business of the nursery and setting out his arguments. He assures him that his father undertook the plantation in a spirit of patriotism and concern for the nation.

Then his thoughts stray; something is pulsing inside him which forces him to go back out again.

The city is there, offering itself up to his youth and freedom.

He walks the boulevards, prowls about the Palais-Royal where the women crowd in the half-light of the galleries, alluring and shameless, with their vulgar, provocative manner. He is eighteen. They call out to him. With his crumpled uniform, his straight hair, his youth and that hungry, timid look in his eyes, they can guess what he is looking for.

Is he coming?

He hesitates, walks away, and then addresses one of them coldly. Why has she chosen this trade, he wants to know. They send him packing. What does he want, this skinny youth, this little lieutenant? To talk? They laugh sneeringly. They are 'blockheads', he thinks. Stupid. He goes home, but his blood is boiling. It is the first time in his life that he is free, that he can allow himself to be led by his curiosity and desires.

He is not, as at Valence, the young officer constantly watched by mothers who, for one risqué gesture towards their daughters, would permanently bar him from their salons. Nor is he the dutiful son constrained by a mother, aunts, wet-nurse, grandmothers and every family in Corsican society to observe the customs and proprieties with scrupulous attention.

He is alone in a city where the women, all these women, seem there to be won, to be hired. Not having been initiated into the pleasure of sex, he is obsessed by their silhouettes displayed before him, but he struggles, as best he can, to resist, to curb his desires.

SOON AFTER he gets to Paris he takes one of the 'carriages of the Court' which, for a modest price, go to Versailles where the controller general has his offices. The coach is comfortable but slow. It takes more than five hours from Paris to reach the city of the Court and the ministers.

Buonaparte is kept waiting; when he is finally seen, he badgers the employees of the Office of Finances, has files opened, finds to his astonishment that there are no records concerning the plantation, but obstinately refuses to let that thwart him. Why have these documents disappeared? A family's fate is at stake.

By dint of persistence, letters and repeated visits to Versailles, he obtains an audience with the prime minister, Monsignor de Brienne, the Archbishop of Sens. He grows insistent, astonishing the minister with his firmness, which is palpable despite his unerringly respectful tone

On his return to Paris, he writes a letter to him, reiterating his arguments and revealing his indignation and wounded pride. After all, he says, 'this is merely a sum of money which will never make amends for the sort of degradation a man feels at being constantly reminded of his subjection'. He concludes that in awarding the appropriate compensation, Monsignor de Brienne will earn the Buonaparte family's gratitude and above all 'inner contentment, which is the paradise of the just man'.

HE WAITS FOR an answer. He wanders round Paris, goes to the theatre and becomes intoxicated with the light and smells of an easy-going city in which he feels anonymous, with no check but his morals, his sense of duty and the lofty considerations he turns to when he is alone in his room and takes up his quill and lets it run over the paper.

He composes a dissertation, a comparison between Sparta and Rome: the love of glory, on the one hand, which is the character-istic of monarchies, and the love of country, on the other, which is the virtue of republics. He pays homage to the English who have given a home not only to Pascal Paoli, but also to Baron Neuhof who had liberated Corsica from the Genoese in 1753. What emerges is not just dry and formulaic, but the ardent creations of a writer who gives free rein to his imagination, inventing, for instance, a letter from Baron Neuhof to the English statesman Horace Walpole.

Corsica, his destiny, makes his sentences ring.

'The venality of man's estate shall not sully my pen,' he writes at eleven o'clock at night in his room in the Hôtel de Cherbourg during that November of 1787. 'I only breathe the truth, I feel within me the strength to speak it. Dear compatriots, we have always been unfortunate. Today members of a powerful monarchy, we only feel the vices of its government's constitution and thus unfortunate; perhaps we shall only see relief to our ills in the course of the centuries.'

He stands up, his head swimming with the phrases he declaims. He paces up and down his room and, despite the advanced hour, is incapable of sleep.

He has requested a further leave of six months in order, as he puts it, to 'attend the deliberations of the States of Corsica, his country, to discuss rights essential to his modest fortune, for which he is obliged to sacrifice the costs of both legs of the journey, which he would not determine to do if it were not an absolute necessity'.

His leave is extended again, from 1 December 1787 to 1 June 1788. He must leave Paris, therefore, and return to Corsica and his family. It is his duty. His mother is alone with her younger children; her eldest, Joseph, is in Pisa where he is starting his law studies. Letizia needs Buonaparte, so he must try to conclude the process he has set in motion in Paris from there. He must abandon this city where he can watch the women, accost them. This is the desire he feels stirring in his eighteen-year-old's body.

He goes back out.

ON THURSDAY, 22 November, he goes to the Italian Theatre. The performance over, he walks at a good pace about the alleys of the Palais-Royal, and then, because there is a chill in the air, he goes into the arcades. The crowd in there is dense and slowly mills back and forth, men on their own searching for a woman, women on their own looking for a client.

Buonaparte stops by the gates. His eyes light on a woman with a pale face. He doesn't doubt that she is one of those girls he has already tried to talk to – ostensibly in order to understand 'the odiousness of their state' – but they have always been arrogant and rebuffed him.

This one is different. Her timidity encourages him and they exchange a few words.

'You must be cold,' he says. 'How can you stand going out in the alleys?'

'I must finish my evening, one must live,' she answers.

She is from Nantes.

He questions her with brutal directness, 'Would you mind, Mademoiselle, telling me how you lost your virginity.'

She answers softly, 'It was an officer who took it.' She hated him. She had to flee her family's anger. After him, there was a second, then a third man. Suddenly she takes Buonaparte's arm.

'Let us go to your rooms.'

'What shall we do there?'

'Well, we'll get warm and you will satisfy your desire.'

That is what he wants.

Later in the night, when he finds himself alone again, he paces up and down his room in the Hôtel de Cherbourg. Then, to calm himself, he begins to write, 'I left the Italian and began to walk at a good pace in the alleys of the Palais-Royal . . .'

He relates what he has just experienced.

'I had pestered her so she would not run away . . . by affecting a respectability which I wished to prove to her I did not possess . . .' a long-winded way of saying that he hadn't dared tell her he had never known a woman!

But he has got what he wanted.

He is a man now.

He can leave for Ajaccio.

VII

IT IS 1 JANUARY 1788, and Buonaparte is sitting facing his mother in the large room on the ground floor of the family house.

He landed at Ajaccio less than two hours ago, and his mother spoke gravely to him all the way from the port to their house, not self-pitying, but with anger and a sort of muffled indignation in her voice. Now, having sent away Napoleone's brothers and sisters, Louis, Pauline, Caroline, Jerome, whose ages range from ten to not even four, she resumes. She paints a picture of her life since his departure for Paris.

He listens, his face solemn, and without giving any sign of doing so, he thinks of the gulf between his first return to Corsica and this one. Even the crossing was different. Between Marseilles and Ajaccio, a strong, freezing wind threw up tall waves that struck the ship with so little interval between them that it sounded like rolling drums beating the alarm.

Napoleone stayed on the bridge, as usual, and, as soon as they entered harbour, he saw his mother, an upright, black figure.

When the gangway was lowered, there were no cries of joy. His brothers and sisters rushed towards their big brother who had returned, at last, but Letizia called them back. There were no enthusiastic exclamations at his officer's uniform, only anxious questions. My son, what did they promise you in the controller general's offices?

He explains the situation, saying he is hopeful that the affair of the mulberry nursery will be settled, but he has to admit that he hasn't received a response to his detailed report. He is going to pay a visit to the Intendant of Corsica, Monsieur de la Guillaumye, whose residence is at Bastia.

Continuing on from what she was saying on their way home, his mother describes her difficulties to him as they sit in the main room of the house. She has just written to Joseph in Pisa.

'We have no maidservant,' she says. She has asked Joseph to

find one and bring her back to Corsica so she can 'do our modest cooking. She must be able to sew and iron as well, and she must be dedicated.'

She lifts up her hand and shows it to Napoleone. 'Since I hurt my finger, I can't sew a stitch.'

He listens in silence. The disparity is always so great between how one would like things to be and how they are. Is this what life is?

He remembers the girl from Nantes whom he had possessed for a few minutes in an all too brief embrace in his room at the Hôtel de Cherbourg. She had left him frustrated, bitter, dissatisfied and ashamed of himself. He had always felt 'stained even by being looked at' by one of these women whose state he considers 'odious', and yet he held this girl to him, and discovered the pleasure of sex with her.

Pleasure? Love? Is that what they are? Always a world between one's dreams and what one achieves? And his family's situation, is it fated never to escape the plight his mother describes?

She is listing the family's expenses. The children are infants, Pauline is only eight, Caroline six. Lucien's fees at the secondary school at Aix have to be paid. She has to provide for Joseph, whose acommodation and studies at Pisa are expensive. The twenty-five louis Charles Buonaparte owed Lieutenant-General Rosel de Beaumanoir have not been repaid.

'Your journey to Paris . . .' she continues – but she stops and just adds, 'You know the family's situation.' She has told Joseph 'to spend as little as possible'.

Here it is, reality.

The city of Paris, that 'centre of pleasures', is a long way away. The expression has just occurred to Buonaparte and he mutters it to himself, like a dream or a reproach, as his mother tells him what he needs to acquire from Monsieur de la Guillaumye, the intendant. On Louis's behalf, he must petition for a royal scholarship to a military school, and he must request payment for the four thousand mulberry trees that Letizia has grown and delivered, as the intendant ordered. He must, he must . . .

Is this life?

Even if it is, one must never shirk.

NAPOLEONE writes to the Intendant of Corsica. He also goes to call on him several times at his residence at Bastia, and those journeys to the north of the island, those long rides, are the happiest parts of his stay.

Sometimes he puts his horse into a gallop when there is a suitable stretch of road, but most of the time he walks it along the mountainsides, discovering new panoramas, letting his mind roam, going back to Paris, to the galleries of the Palais-Royal, to that meeting with, as he wrote – and he often rereads that passage written in the moments after the girl had left – 'a person of the other sex'.

He stops.

He forces himself to drive away these thoughts that humiliate and embarrass him. Then he spurs his horse recklessly; it rears and refuses to budge.

If a shepherd or a peasant approaches, Napoleone dismounts and talks to them. He loves these encounters. He draws them out, puts questions, they trust him. He is taken to see one of Pascal Paoli's veterans who, when asked, tells him about the battles he fought. He writes the stories down when he gets back to Ajaccio. Often these men still have the memoirs they had printed secretly under the Genoese occupation. Buonaparte collects them, reads them and creates an archive. In this way he draws up the primary sources for his history of Corsica which he thinks about the whole time.

When he reaches Bastia, however, and cools his heels waiting to see Monsieur de la Guillaumye, reality strikes him again. Despite the intendant's attentiveness, honourability and amiability, Buonaparte feels subordinate – but he has to accept that this is what he is, a French officer whose family needs assistance, a young lieutenant who loves his profession and neither can nor wants to break with it.

On each of his trips to Bastia, he calls on the artillery officers garrisoned in the town. Traditionally, passing officers are invited to dine, and he does so a number of times.

They are older, but when, steered by him, the conversation turns to the question of 'governments, ancient and modern', he notes the ignorance of these lieutenants and captains. Some get to their feet, showing their boredom as he pursues the subject, unable to contain his passion. They murmur among themselves, loud enough for him to hear, that he is sententious, pompous, arrogant, pedantic and conceited.

Buonaparte lets himself get carried away defending the rights of nations. He is pressed on his views. What of Corsica, then? It is a nation, he replies. They are astonished. How can an officer speak in such a fashion?

'No one knows the Corsicans!' Buonaparte exclaims. He attacks the governor who he says is trying to prevent the Corsicans convene their Estates. The officers are stunned by the boldness of this Corsican patriotism.

'Would you use your sword against a representative of the King?' asks one of them.

Buonaparte is silent, pale.

HE RIDES BACK to Ajaccio that same evening, manhandling his horse, losing his way, edgy, almost infuriated. Is this living? Must he always subordinate his thoughts, his desires, his ambitions to mediocre reality? Must he gag himself to stop crying out what he feels? Must he hobble himself so as not to leave the path?

He touches his spurs to the flanks of his horse and puts it into a trot. It can't be helped if there is a dangerous drop.

He goes his way.

ON 1 JUNE 1788, after seeing Joseph who has come back from Pisa, Buonaparte, his furlough over, rejoins his regiment of La Fère which has been garrisoned at Auxonne since December 1787.

He is nearly nineteen years old.

VIII

WHAT NAPOLEONE SEES FIRST, when he arrives at Auxonne that 15 June 1788, is the mist hanging over the Saône.

The walled city rises up on the left bank of a vast meander of the river. In the distance to the north-east, above the haze, one can make out wooded heights which the coachman explains are the slopes of Mount Seurre. Stretching his arm further towards the east, he adds that, in good weather, one can see the Jura mountains beyond Dole and, in winter, even the Great Alps to the south. However, when the hot, rainy weather sets in, the Saône and the surrounding marshland sweat a dirty, humid vapour that sticks to your skin. 'There's a lot of fever round here,' says the driver, stopping the coach in front of the barracks of the regiment of La Fère.

Napoleone has barely paid attention to what he's been saying.

It is twenty-one months since he has seen his regiment, not that anyone will hold it against him. It is regular practice, in the royal artillery corps, to grant officers holiday *semestres*, irrespective of their individual leaves. He is impatient to renew friendships from Valence, and when he sees Alexandre Des Mazis, he rushes towards him.

Theirs is a warm reunion. The spirit of the regiment under the command of the marshal of the camp, Baron Jean-Pierre du Teil, who is also head of Auxonne's school of artillery, is excellent. Du Teil is honest, competent and passionate about this service to which generations of his family have been attached.

Des Mazis shows Napoleone the shooting range and the adjoining meadow where the gunners test their cannon and mortars, and then takes him to the Pavillon de la Ville by the barracks where the City of Auxonne provides the officers of the regiment of La Fère with free lodgings.

Buonaparte's room is number 16. Facing south, it is long and narrow, but it has an armchair, a table, six straw chairs and one wooden one.

Napoleone feels very cheerful. He goes to the single window and contemplates Auxonne's surroundings, those hills, those copses and the plain. It is hot and already humid. A few years ago, Des Mazis tells him, du Teil had to contend with an epidemic of fever which struck most of the pupils of the artillery school.

Napoleone opens his trunk and arranges his notebooks and books on the table. Des Mazis leafs through them and nods with recognition: The *Confessions* of Rousseau, *Philosophical History of Commerce in the Two Indies* by Raynal, the works of Corneille and Racine, *History of the Arabs* by Marigny, *Considerations on the History of France* by Mably, *The Republic* by Plato, Baron de Tott's memoirs concerning the Turks and Tartars, a *History of England*, a work on Frederick II, a study of the government of Venice.

Des Mazis shakes his head. There are not many like Buonaparte.

'What is the point of all this indigestible knowledge?' he asks. 'What do I have to do with what happened a thousand years ago? What do puerile discussions between men, reported in every last, minute detail, matter to me?'

He takes a few steps. He speaks of women, of love. 'Don't you feel, when you're in your study,' he continues, 'the emptiness in your heart?'

Napoleone shrugs his shoulders. 'Even when I have nothing to do,' he says, 'I feel I haven't any time to waste.' Then in a loud voice, hammering out each word, he recites some lines of Pope:

> The stronger a man's mind is, the more he needs to use it
> If he lets it fall asleep, there's a danger he will lose it.

'Nothing will change you, Napoleone Buonaparte,' concludes Des Mazis. But in the days that follow, he exerts a certain influence.

They're not twenty yet. Buonaparte joins in the pranks, games and jokes the young lieutenants get up to, sometimes with him as the butt. On the eve of a review on the firing range, he realizes that his cannon have been spiked. No anger: he just keeps his eyes peeled and doesn't let himself get caught by surprise again.

Sometimes, however, he does lose his temper. In a room on the floor above, one of his fellow officers, Bussy, plays the horn every evening which prevents him working. He takes music lessons himself, but those prolonged, repetitive, deafening blasts soon become intolerable.

He accosts the officer on the stairs.

'It must be tiring, playing your horn,' he says.

'No, not at all,' answers Lieutenant Bussy.

'Well it tires a great many other people. You would do better to go somewhere where you can play your horn at your leisure.'

'I am master in my own room.'

'You could have reason to doubt that.'

'I don't think anyone would have the temerity,' Bussy threatens.

'I would.'

He is ready to fight but the officers of the regiment prevent it going to a duel. Lieutenant Bussy agrees to play somewhere else.

BUONAPARTE knows how to make himself respected. He is known to be singular. He walks in the countryside alone, a book in hand; he stops to write something or sketch geometrical figures with the tip of his shoe or his scabbard. Every day he returns late to the Dumont *pension* where he takes his meals with the other officers.

They make fun of his unkempt appearance, but in a good-humoured way and he stands up for himself. He is not rich and, like many other lieutenants, bitterly resents the constant changes to their uniforms: black breeches instead of blue ones, an English frock coat instead of a overcoat. Who has to pay? The officers!

He would rather save his money to buy the books which pile up in his room. He continues to work like someone possessed, with astonishing determination, a sort of impatience, almost fervour, and a certainty that everything he does there will be of use to him – learning the profession of gunner, above all. He made a start at Valence, but now he realizes that he only knows the rudiments of this science of erecting batteries, firing cannon, siege warfare.

He goes to the theory lessons, and becomes one of the most assiduous pupils, a friend almost, of the mathematics teacher, Lombard, who has been teaching at Auxonne artillery school for over forty years. Lombard has translated from English *The Principles of Artillery* in 1783 and *The Range Tables* for cannon and howitzer in 1787, which are both by Robbins. Napoleone studies and summarizes them.

He wishes to acquire all the necessary knowledge, and his thirst to learn is such that Du Teil asks to see him and recommends he cultivate a hobby or take a rest because, in the final months of 1788, Napoleone is ill.

He suffers from a recurrent fever, no doubt brought on by the vapours that rise from the marshes and the ditches of stagnant water outside the city walls. He loses weight and grows pale. He eats little, and even puts himself on a dairy diet.

In January 1789, he is better and can finally write to his mother. 'This country is very unhealthy,' he says, 'because of the marshes surrounding it and the frequent flooding of the river which fills all the ditches with water that gives off an infected vapour. I have had a fever which lasted for days at a time, then left me for a brief period and then laid siege to me again . . . It weakened me, gave me delirium and subjected me to a long convalescence. Today, now the weather has improved . . . I am out and about again.'

Du Teil summons him and appoints him a member of a commission to study the firing of shells by siege guns, so Napoleone directs the manoeuvres, draws up reports and proposes new 'sustained, reasoned, methodical' tests.

Du Teil reads his reports, congratulating Buonaparte, and predicts that he will be one of the most brilliant officers in the royal artillery corps. That same evening in his room, Napoleone writes to his uncle Fesch, 'You must know, my dear uncle, that the general here has shown me great consideration, charging me to construct at the shooting-range several works that require great calculations and I have been thus occupied for ten days, morning and evening, at the head of two hundred men. This unheard-of mark of favour has set the captains against me a little . . . My comrades also show a little jealousy, but all of this will subside. What worries me most is that my health doesn't seem too good.'

SOMETIMES, amidst this austere regime, despite the satisfaction it gives him, another longing comes over him. He dreams of that 'centre of pleasures', Paris.

He dreams of going back to the capital. There are good grounds for it. He could go back to Versailles and put pressure on the controller general's clerks, since the affair of the mulberry nursery has not been settled in Ajaccio. Only he doesn't have the money for the journey. He appeals to his great uncle Lucien, the Archdeacon of Ajaccio. 'Send me a hundred francs,' he writes. 'This sum will be enough for me to go to Paris: there at least one can make one's way, form acquaintances, surmount obstacles. Everything tells me I will be successful. Would you see me prevented for lack of a hundred écus?'

The archdeacon turns a deaf ear.

Buonaparte then turns to his uncle Fesch, but he is elusive too. 'You are deceived in hoping that I should be able to find money to borrow here,' Napoleone replies to him. 'Auxonne is a very small town and besides I have been here too short a time to make proper acquaintances.' He expresses his regrets succinctly: 'I think about it no more and must abandon this idea of a trip to Paris.'

Farewell, dream of night-time walks in the galleries of the Palais-Royal! Those will come later; they will happen. For the moment, he reveals, 'I have no other resource here but work. I only dress myself once a week. I sleep so little since my illness, it is hardly believable; I go to bed at ten and get up at four. I take only one meal a day.'

IN HIS FEVERISH STATE, he projects himself into the future since the present, though agreeable enough, does not offer him the pleasure and intense exhilaration he expects. Only books and writing give him the heightened experience he needs, so he works as if he were preparing for a general officer's exam, or one in world history.

He repeatedly reads *General Essay on Tactics* by Guibert which he has studied already at Valence and he discovers *The Uses of the New Artillery* by Chevalier du Teil, the brother of Auxonne's commander. In so doing he steeps himself in the innovative ideas that French military theorists have been developing since the heavy defeat in the Seven Years War and, especially, at the battle of Rossbach in 1757.

Above all, with his quill in hand, Napoleone reads histories of the Arabs, of Venice, of England and France, and fills entire notebooks with notes.

Again Des Mazis is amazed. What's the use of it all?

Buonaparte doesn't answer him any more. Perhaps he thinks that if Pascal Paoli could become such a hero, when he was only a simple ensign in the Corsican guards under the King of Naples, then one day he too may be able to play a role in the service of Corsica. He knows that he is the only islander to have received an officer's training in the military schools of the French king, but he wants to go beyond the practice of war. He thinks that Corsica also needs a man who knows the workings of history, who can be a legislator and a politician.

One day, he is put under close arrest for twenty-four hours, and is shut in a dusty room which contains only an old bed, a chair and a cupboard. On top of the latter, Napoleone discovers an abandoned, yellowing work in folio. It is an edition of the *Institutes of Justinian* containing his codes and all the rulings of the Roman jurists.

Buonaparte sits down. He has neither pencil nor paper but he begins to read, learning those arid texts by heart and devouring the contents of that worm-eaten volume throughout the night by the light of a single candle.

He is startled when the guard appears in the morning. He hasn't noticed the hours passing. Now he knows Roman law.

Is it useful? He is convinced it will be, even if he doesn't know the exact circumstances or time when he will be able to put this knowledge to use.

THE OTHER lieutenants of the regiment of La Fère know his qualities, and when the time comes to draw up the regulations of their recently formed association, the Calotte, they turn to him. He immediately throws himself into the work with a boyish serious-ness, as if he was drafting the constitution of a state.

'There are,' he writes, 'fundamental laws from which it is not permissible to depart. They derive from the nature of the Primitive Pact.'

When Des Mazis attempts to moderate his passion, he replies that this association has specific goals – to assure equality between lieutenants, whatever their place in the nobility, to maintain a code of honour, to punish, if necessary, any who violate it and to defend lieutenants against possible injustices committed by senior officers. These goals conform to his principles; they are, in a word, republican.

He then adds, to Des Mazis's amazement and concern, that 'in all twelve kingdoms of Europe, the kings enjoy a usurped authority ... there have been very few kings who have not deserved to be dethroned.' Besides, why have kings at all?

Buonaparte picks up his exercise book and reads to Des Mazis from a dissertation he has begun. Men, he says, will soon feel that they are men. 'Proud tyrants of the earth, take good care that this sentiment never enters the hearts of your subjects. Prejudices, custom, religion – all feeble barriers! Your thrones will collapse if your people ever think when they look at one another, "We too are men."'

Des Mazis doesn't try to contradict him.

Napoleone holds out the complete set of regulations he has drawn up for the Calotte. The pages are fastened in the top corner by a red ribbon. Des Mazis leafs through them: the tone is grave; there is talk of laws, a grand master of ceremonies. Des Mazis is afraid the other lieutenants will make fun of its pomposity and lack of proportion.

He does not tell Napoleone next day that people laughed when he read out the document, because the lieutenants of the regiment of La Fère end up adopting Buonaparte's regulations.

BUONAPARTE confides his thoughts to Des Mazis, but he also remembers the argument he had with the officers in the garrison at Bastia, when he had imprudently revealed his feelings by eulogizing the Corsican nation. So, when he is a guest of the marshal of the camp, or the war commissary, or Lombard the mathematics teacher, he talks about *Cinna*, his favourite play by Corneille, rather than the audacious ideas taking shape in his head.

He is amazed himself when they spill out on the page of his exercise book, and sometimes he is alarmed by the path he has taken. He does not go to church any more. He still crosses himself mechanically, but he no longer believes. In his writings he aligns himself on the side of power, the State and Caesar, rather than on that of the Church.

He frequently reads Raynal, who speaks of the insurrection of the peoples as a 'salutary change', but he also instinctively despises anyone who submits. He declaims Raynal's exhortation, 'Cowardly peoples, stupid peoples, since the perpetuity of your oppression does not fire you with energy, since you confine yourselves to insults when you could roar, since you are millions and yet suffer a dozen children armed with little sticks to rule you as they please, obey! March without importuning us with your complaints, and if you cannot be free, then at least learn how to be unhappy.'

Napoleone walks alone through Auxonne with these words ringing in his ears. He will be one of those who roar. He will not let himself be ruled; he will not obey. He quickens his step. He feels immense stores of energy within him. He is like the muzzle of a cannon that one fills with powder. The charge is the books he reads, the notes he takes, the stories he writes, the reflections on the monarchy he composes in a fever. He does not know when the fuse will be lit, but every day, as if he hasn't much time, as if the battle is drawing near, he fills his head, the cannon's muzzle, with knowledge and ideas, in a prodigious effort of concentration.

He is sure that all this energy he is storing up will one day erupt.

One evening, rereading Guibert's *General Essay on Tactics*, he finds the passage that he read at Valence and has remembered, from time to time, ever since. 'A man will arise,' writes Guibert, 'perhaps from obscurity and the crowd, a man who will not have made a name for himself, either by his speeches or his writings, a man who will have meditated in silence ... This man will seize possession of opinion, circumstance, fortune ...'

Napoleone feels as agitated as when he went up to that girl who was standing by the gates of the Palais-Royal. This is the same desire, overriding any timidity, the same force that is urging him on – but how many evenings did he have to walk the streets before he came across that girl? How long will he have to wait for something to happen, like a spark, that will release his energy?

SUDDENLY, on 1 April 1789, the drum beats.

Napoleone Buonaparte runs towards the barracks, half-asleep after a night writing. The bombardiers of the regiment of La Fère have already fallen in, under arms, and the marshal of the camp, du Teil, strides furiously into the courtyard. He has received orders from the commandant in chief of the Duchy of Burgundy, the Marquis de Gouvernet, to send three companies at once to Seurre, several leagues from Auxonne in the mountains. The villagers of Seurre have killed two wheat merchants suspected of hoarding. 'And where, pray, are my captains and first lieutenants?' du Teil curses. 'On leave!'

So, he must entrust command to second and third lieutenants who aren't even twenty and have never experienced anything remotely comparable – but the marquis has insisted: three companies! Three companies it is, then. Buonaparte will take command of one of them.

IT IS BROAD daylight when they reach the village. Order seems to have been restored, although peasants are still gathered in groups at the corners of the lanes.

The men are billeted on the inhabitants, and Buonaparte lodges in rue Dulac. The leading citizens hurry round and show him and the other officers every consideration. The women are still in a state of great agitation: 'Wild beasts!' they exclaim, referring to the peasants. The salt-tax collector's wife is one of the most upset. She explains at length to Buonaparte how the salt store was besieged, and he is both attentive and sympathetic to her in her slightly overdone distress, which is not entirely unflirtatious. He deploys his men and sets up rounds of guard duty and patrols.

The situation is so tense that they decide to stay in Seurre for the foreseeable future.

Buonaparte brings out his notebooks and books, and time passes, week after week. Soon the detachment has been in Seurre for a month; Napoleone has been entertained by the local worthies, dancing at their balls, winning them over with his charm and joining in the general conversation.

All the talk is of the States General which the King is to convene at Versailles on 5 May. Some of Buonaparte's hosts are representatives of the Third Estate, and they speak about the kingdom's finances, the need to abolish the nobility's financial privileges.

Buonaparte listens, but volunteers little. He observes these conversations as one might a situation which only partly concerns one. It is as if he is leafing through the pages of a book, taking notes. He is not the author, since he does not feel that he is from this country. He is an officer here, but his homeland is elsewhere.

When he hears their arguments, and sees the passion these debates arouse among the nobles, he realizes the depth of his indifference. He is only a spectator. What matters to him is his destiny, which is bound to that of Corsica – but, it is true, what happens here, in this kingdom he serves, will affect his country's future.

AT THE END OF April, the villagers and the local peasants mass in Seurre's lanes again, brandishing pitchforks and yelling and shouting threats.

Buonaparte takes his place in front of his men. In a clear voice, he orders the soldiers to load their muskets, and then marches towards the hostile throng. 'People of Seurre!' he exclaims. 'Let the honest folk withdraw and go to their homes. I only have orders to fire on the mob!'

The crowd hesitates. Buonaparte, his sword raised, repeats, 'Let the honest folk go to their homes.'

His voice is steady. The demonstrators disperse. He sheathes his sword.

That evening, at one of the notables' houses where a ball is thrown in the officers' honour, the guests crowd round Buonaparte to congratulate him.

He did his duty, he says. He had no misgivings.

He feels nothing in common with that slovenly mob, those peasants, those paupers, common people.

He is Corsican: another breed, almost another race – a people of shepherds and mountain dwellers who speak another language; a people wholly dissimilar to that rabble which gathered in the lanes and slaughtered the wheat merchants.

He is Corsican, but he is also a member of the nobility. He has the pride that comes of descending from a line which for generations has set itself apart from, and exercised its authority over, the masses. He is an advocate of equality between members of the nobility – and even between all men, provided they show themselves worthy of it by their actions.

He is Corsican and a member of the nobility, but he is also an officer. Since childhood, he has understood the necessity of military order and a strict hierarchy. He is proud to be a member of that order, to wear an officer's uniform, even if it does belong to a foreign army.

No, he has nothing whatsoever in common with the rabble.

If he has been speculating about the role of kings, it is only because, as far as he can tell, hardly any of them have deserved to rule – but there has to be a hierarchy; discipline is essential, even if, at the heart of that order, there may be equality between those men who deserve it.

'I am an officer,' he repeats to those who applaud his determination and his courage.

BY JUNE he has returned to Auxonne with his three companies of bombardiers, but it is hard for him to stay shut up in his room reading and writing now.

He roams the countryside, and tells Des Mazis, who senses his nervous energy, that events are like natural phenomena. They arise from a combination of things and circumstances. People should know how to sense the tremors that shake societies to their core.

He often goes to Auxonne's bookseller, on the church square, to read the newspapers. The kingdom is stirring: the States General has met in Versailles; there has been pillaging on the streets of Paris; carts of grain have been stopped and emptied; soldiers have opened fire. Buonaparte knows something is starting.

He goes back to his room, where he has begun editing his history, *Letters on Corsica*.

He wanted to send it to Loménie de Brienne, but the Archbishop of Sens has been replaced by Necker, so he will send it to the new prime minister instead, but first he sends it to one of his old teachers at Brienne, Father Dupuy, for him to correct any mistakes and have a look at certain passages. He makes it clear to

Dupuy that the purpose of this is not to petition Necker; there's nothing he expects to gain from him. He merely wants to expound to the minister, who governs the kingdom with the authority vested in him by the King, the ideas of a Corsican patriot.

No, ALL THAT truly counts in Buonaparte's eyes is the opinion of Pascal Paoli. He senses that the ground is beginning to shake, that now is the time for swift action, and on 12 June 1789, he dashes off a letter to his hero at one sitting,

> General,
>   I was born when my country was dying. Thirty thousand Frenchmen spewed on our shores, drowning the throne of Liberty in a sea of blood — such was the odious spectacle that first struck my infant eyes.
>   My cradle was surrounded, from the day of my birth, by the cries of the dying, the groans of the oppressed, and the tears of despair.
>   You left our isle, and took with you every hope of happiness. To submit was to be enslaved. Our compatriots, weighed down by the triple chain of soldier, lawyer and tax-collector, live despised.

As he writes, the tone becomes more and more elevated. Little matter the reality of the facts: this is how Buonaparte, this young officer of twenty in the year of 1789, sees the history of his native land. He appeals to Paoli. He explains that he is writing his *Letters on Corsica* because he is 'obliged to serve'. He does not live in the capital, where he would doubtless have found other ways to act. He must therefore be contented with 'publicity'. He continues:

> If you condescend to encourage the efforts of a young man whose birth you witnessed, and whose parents have always been on the right side, I dare to predict a favourable issue . . . But whatever the success of my book, I am aware that it will raise up against me the whole battalion of French officials who govern our island and whom I am attacking. But what matter if it is in my country's cause?
>   Allow me, General, to offer you the respects of my family, and — why should I not say it — of my fellow citizens? They sigh

heavily in remembrance of a time when they had hopes of freedom.

My mother, Madame Letizia, asks me to recall to your memory the old days at Corte.

Buonaparte rereads his letter without changing a word. What he has written is what he has been carrying inside himself for years. He is like a jumper who, after placing his marker, finally makes his leap. In no uncertain terms, he both offers his services to Pascal Paoli and assumes the consequence of what he says about Corsica. 'I shall hear the thunder of ill-will,' he says. 'And if the bolt falls, I shall take refuge in my conscience, I will remember the legitimacy of my motives and from that moment I shall face it.'

When he receives a letter from Father Dupuy a few days later, sent from Laon on 15 July, in which his old teacher explains that he must temper the terms of his *Letters on Corsica* so as not to offend Minister Necker, Buonaparte rebels. His *Letters* are not a petition, but an act of war. He has written them so that no one will be in any doubt about what Corsican patriots think or who their standard-bearer is.

He does not hesitate for a moment. He is Corsican, with so violent a conviction that his hand shakes as he writes.

OFTEN HE HAS to stop, his impatience is so acute in this too, he is in tune with what is happening around him.

He opens the window and hears the call to arms. Shouting is coming from the river, the alarm sounds, and soon there are plumes of smoke rising into the air. Buonaparte goes into the centre of Auxonne.

It is 19 July 1789. A crowd of boatmen and street-porters has gathered and gone on the rampage, manhandling the syndic of the town, invading the apartments of the collector of taxes, burning his furniture and registers, and ransacking the tollhouses and the trade offices.

It is a riot.

Buonaparte returns to barracks where all the officers and soldiers are discussing the news: on 14 July, the King's fortified prison, the Bastille, was taken by rioters and its governor was beheaded. The guards sided with the crowd and turned their cannon on the Bastille. Buonaparte doesn't waste any time. He takes command of his company and sets off. Three bands of rioters are on the loose, but they disperse when they see the soldiers. Napoleone and his men patrol all night because everyone is afraid the *brigands*, as Auxonne's notables call them, are on their way.

By the morning of 20 July, these brigands, peasants from the surrounding countryside, have arrived. The tolls are burnt, the salt store is looted and the peasants only disperse when the soldiers are ordered to load their muskets. Calm is restored and the companies return to barracks. Buonaparte goes back to his room and, still steeped in the atmosphere of the clashes, immediately starts writing. He wants to tell Joseph what he has seen:

> In the midst of the sound of drums, arms, blood, I write you this letter. The rabble of this city, reinforced by a pack of foreign brigands who came here to pillage, began on Sunday evening to tear down the buildings where the farming clerks live, and they pillaged the customs and several houses. The general is seventy-six years old. He found himself fatigued. He called the head of the bourgeoisie and ordered him to take orders from me. After many manoeuvres we have arrested thirty-three of them and put them in jail. Two or three I think are going to be summarily hanged.

No interrogation. Order must prevail, even if, as Buonaparte adds, condemning the privileged, 'Throughout France blood has been spilled but almost everywhere it has been the impure blood of the enemies of liberty, of the nation, the blood of those who have been growing fat at the nation's expense for a long time.'

He may use the language of 'French patriots', but he reacts primarily as an officer who detests the 'rabble' and his thoughts, above all, are of Corsica. His own destiny depends on what becomes of it.

ON 9 AUGUST, he officially requests another period of leave to return to Corsica, but he is told he will have to wait for an answer, and he paces about his room and goes for walks as if he were under lock and key in that country.

Writing doesn't calm him, but it's the only activity which makes him feel he is doing anything.

He pens a letter to Monsieur Giubega, who is both chief registrar of the States of Corsica and his godfather. Privileges have just been abolished in a great wave of unanimity during the night of 4 August. 'This year begins in a very flattering way for good people,' writes Buonaparte. 'And after so many centuries of feudal barbarism and political slavery, one is always surprised to see the word Liberty enflaming hearts that luxury, nobility and the arts seemed to have disorganized.'

It is true, France amazes him. On that stormy August day, he thinks of Paris, that centre of pleasures which seems to have become a volcano, but, as far as he is concerned, this historic moment is only of value if Corsica can benefit from it.

He is so nervous at the thought that he might not return to the island that he goes to see du Teil, the marshal of the camp, who finally tells him that his leave is being approved, but that he must wait a little longer. He continues his letter to his godfather Giubega: 'While France is being reborn, what will become of us, we unfortunate Corsicans? Still lowly, will we continue to kiss the arrogant hand that oppresses us? Will we continue to see all the positions intended for us by natural law occupied by foreigners as contemptible in their morals and conduct as they are abject by birth?'

He is indeed of another race. At that moment, he despises the French people.

On 16 August, the regiment of La Fère openly mutinies. The soldiers march in close columns to the colonel's house and demand the contents of the regimental safe, the *masse noire* as it is called. Given their determination and numbers, their shouts and threats, the colonel acquiesces. The men share out the money, and then get drunk and force the officers to drink and sing and dance with them.

Buonaparte witnesses these scenes from a distance. He watches one of his comrades, Lieutenant Bourbers, be surrounded by frenzied soldiers who accuse him of having struck one of them. They want to slit his throat. Two senior quartermaster-sergeants rush forward and pull him away, but the lieutenant has to leave Auxonne that evening, dressed as a woman. They should have opened fire on the mutineers, Buonaparte tells Des Mazis, that abject mob flouting every principle of discipline.

This disorder disgusts him, even though the new politics seem to be 'a step towards the good', but all of this is secondary – Corsica is what Buonaparte thinks about obsessively. He wants his godfather Giubega to take action.

'Until now prudence has counselled silence,' he writes to him again. 'Truth has little appeal in a corrupt court: but now the scene is changed, so one's conduct must change as well. If we lose this opportunity, we are slaves forever . . .'

He wants to be back in Corsica and on 21 June, he finally receives official notification of his leave, which will last until 1 June, 1790.

THE FINAL DAYS at Auxonne seem interminable.

He goes back and forth between the barracks and his room. He stops in at the bookseller's. He hears the alarm being sounded several times a day. People run in panic through the streets; bands of brigands are said to be coming at any moment. But then gradually that great fear which has persisted for a month, like a recurrent fever, dies down.

When Buonaparte finally leaves Auxonne in the middle of September, order seems to have been restored.

ON HIS WAY to Marseilles, where he hopes to meet the Abbé Raynal before setting sail for Corsica, Napoleone Buonaparte stops at Valence.

He is given a warm welcome; everyone remembers this young second lieutenant. In Monsieur de Tardivon's drawing room, they are tensely discussing this revolution that is turning the country on its head; people are afraid of the brigands who have been burning down all the châteaux in the region.

Monsieur de Tardivon, Abbé of St Ruf, takes Buonaparte's arm and speaks slowly, in time with his shuffling steps. 'At the rate things are going,' he says, 'everyone can have their turn as king. If you happen to become king, Monsieur de Buonaparte, make your peace with the Christian religion; you will find it beneficial.'

THE NEXT DAY Buonaparte, standing at the prow of the boat taking him down the Rhône, fills his lungs with sea air.

PART THREE

*One's head full of great
public questions*

September 1789 to 11 June 1793

IX

ON 25 SEPTEMBER 1789, Napoleone is the first of the passengers to leave the ship and jump down onto the quay of Ajaccio's port.

It is hot, as if summer hasn't ended, and the city is drowsing in the early afternoon, disturbed only by the voices of the sailors and porters. Everything appears so calm, so peaceful, so different from what he has imagined, that he hesitates for a moment.

His mind is teeming with plans for Corsica. His memory is full of the din of rioting and images of violence. He remembers everything that has happened in Seurre and Auxonne and the conversations at Valence and on the boat going down the Rhône.

At one of the stages on the river, some patriots had tried to arrest a young woman, Madame De Saint-Estève, with whom Napoleone had struck up a friendship on the journey. They were amazed by the presence of an officer at her side, and thought the young woman was the Countess d'Artois, who was known to have left Paris to emigrate. Napoleone, luckily, managed to persuade the patriots of their mistake.

In Marseilles, the streets were thronged with patriots sporting the tricolour cockade. Speakers standing on bollards or carts were calling for vigilance, warning against the brigands. Before going aboard, Buonaparte met the Abbé Raynal, who encouraged him to continue with his history of Corsica. Then he spent the entire crossing pacing up and down the bridge, itching with impatience to attain his goal, and dreaming of the part he is going to play at Pascal Paoli's side – if *Il Babbo* comes back from England – or else in his place, if he cannot return to the island.

But now, look – here is Ajaccio sunk in a torpor, a slumbering city which seems to be outside history. For a moment Napoleone is seized by doubts. What if he has swapped the great stage of history for a backwater where nothing happens?

He sees Joseph coming to meet him.

WHAT IS happening in France? Joseph asks. What is this revolution? Joseph has received his brother's letters, of course, but French newspapers hardly ever arrive, and if they do, it is only a month after publication. None of the Corsican deputies to the States General, whether from the Third Estate – Saliceti, barrister on the Supreme Council ('I am now a barrister and member of the Supreme Council as well,' Joseph says proudly) and Count Colonna de Cesari Rocca, Paoli's nephew – or the nobility – Count de Buttafoco – or the clergy – Abbé Peretti – bring any news of the debates in the Constituent Assembly.

'Nothing has changed here,' Joseph adds. 'The governor, the Viscount de Barrin, does not publish any decrees voted by the Assembly. It is as if there had never been any States General, any storming of the Bastille. The island is still under military command.' Joseph suddenly points to some soldiers who are wearing the white cockade on their hats.

Napoleone is outraged. Doesn't anyone in Corsica know that a revolution has taken place? That privileges have been abolished? Is it possible that the great wind which has swept through the French kingdom, imposing the tricolour cockade on all, has not reached Corsica?

He is so disgusted that, on the way home, he changes the subject and questions his brother about the family.

Letizia is waiting for Napoleone, says Joseph. Her children are with her and they cannot wait to see their brother again. The only one missing is Marianna Elisa, who is finishing her studies at St Cyr. He hesitates, as if he's afraid of irritating Napoleone. Their future is uncertain, he says, like that of all Corsicans.

'I have only had one case,' explains Joseph, and then launches into a description of it for his brother. His client was found not guilty of murder, after he convinced the court that the man had been acting in legitimate self-defence.

'Lucien?' asks Napoleone.

He has returned from Aix, having left secondary school, and has not won a scholarship. Nor has Louis, who has been trying, without success, to solicit a bursary to go to military school, like Napoleone. Jerome is a little boy of five, Caroline will soon be eight and Pauline ten.

Buonaparte is silent for a long time. Then, as he enters rue St Charles and sees the family home, he announces severely that he's going to put everyone to work. There must be order, discipline, a strict daily routine. This house, he adds, ought to be a school for the children. There's going to be no shirking. The Buonapartes should be an example for Corsica.

NAPOLEONE barely has time to kiss his brothers and sisters, listen to Letizia complain about the difficulties of her life and lecture Lucien – 'more rigour, brother, less palaver' – before the house is full of relatives. They all ask the same thing: What is happening in France?

Napoleone answers enthusiastically, and is then reassured by what he is told about the state of public opinion in Corsica. People want change. Every day they wait for boats to arrive, because they want to know. The people are waiting for a sign from France to act.

In Ajaccio, on 15 August, the inhabitants demonstrated against Bishop Doria and forced him to hand over four thousand livres. They demanded the suppression of the admiralty's rights. The commander of the garrison, La Férandière, and his officers were powerless to stop them and they only dispersed when threatened with cannon. A committee of thirty-six citizens has been formed.

Similar outbreaks have occurred at Bastia, Corte, Sartène and all over the countryside. Exiles are beginning to return in the north and are forming into groups of thirty or so. Governor Barrin has given up trying to track them down, but he controls the towns. The people fear repression and punishment, but if they are appealed to, they will rise.

Napoleone listens and then delivers a rousing harangue. He condemns the 'cowards and effeminates who languish in a gilded slavery'. He is one of those who want to act. They listen. They talk endlessly.

It is the middle of the night before Napoleone finds himself alone again with Joseph, and he takes his brother out into the garden, despite the cool night air. The two of them, he says, can change Corsica and pave the way for Pascal Paoli's return, or else . . . Napoleone is silent for a few moments, then adds, 'or continue his work – be his successors.' He goes off alone, striding away vigorously.

IN THE DAYS that follow, Napoleone roams the streets of Ajaccio and the country lanes.

He assembles crowds, delivers speeches, and, quivering with emotion, proclaims all that he has written in the *Letters on Corsica*, all that he has carried with him for years.

Joseph goes out as well and in the evening the two brothers compare results.

At night, in his bedroom in rue St Charles, or else in his study in the country house at Milelli, Napoleone writes. He revises the introduction to the *Letters on Corsica*, praising Pascal Paoli's qualities even more emphatically.

In the morning, he gives what he has written to his brother Lucien for him to copy out. The Buonaparte house, people are starting to say in Ajaccio, is like a convent or a school.

Napoleone is not yet twenty-one, but with every passing day he gains more confidence in himself. He is alone much of the time, and goes for walks in the country. He loves the dense vegetation and the barren landscape further inland, where the salt marshes begin. Sometimes, when he comes back, he is trembling. The fever has struck again – they're not healthy, some of those places where he likes to walk – but he doesn't stop organizing rallies, or going on hikes, or writing almost every night.

For the first time in his life he discovers what it might be to have an influence over men. The more meetings he addresses, the more able and convincing he becomes. There are some people in Ajaccio who want to mount a coup, but Napoleone calms them. The governor has troops and cannon, he says. We must act prudently and rely on events in Paris to force the authorities of Corsica to concede.

ON 31 OCTOBER 1789, he calls on everyone who professes to be a patriot to assemble in the church of St Francis. People are astonished: this is the first act of a young man whose name is starting to be spoken of with respect. Napoleone walks up and down the aisles, with a book in his hand. It contains an address which he begins to read: 'When magistrates unlawfully usurp power, when, without authority, deputies take the people's name to speak against the people's wishes, individuals are permitted to unite.'

He demands that Corsica be delivered from 'an administration that devours, impoverishes and discredits us'. He appeals to the deputies of the Third Estate, Saliceti and Count Colonna de Cesari Rocca, but makes no mention of those of the nobility and the clergy, Buttafoco and Peretti.

'We are patriots,' Napoleone sums up.

A table has been brought into the church on his request. He puts the book on it, takes a quill, turns towards the assembled company and declares that this address must be signed and that he will be the first to do so. He bends down and writes, with a swift flourish, *Buonaparte, artillery officer*, then he straightens up again.

That night he doesn't sleep. He has just performed his first political act.

He gets out of bed and goes into the garden at Milelli where he is staying. This signature is the culmination of all his thinking up until now and, at the same time, it is a point of departure, the start of a road. He has no idea where it will lead or end, but he must follow.

One must act, act. That is the law he must obey.

THE NEXT DAY, he rides to Bastia. This is the capital, the seat of Governor Barrin; this is where everything is decided.

Napoleone finds lodgings. He organizes meetings of patriots, addresses them with authority. He is waiting, he says, for the delivery of two crates from Livorno.

When they arrive, he opens them himself and plunges his hands into the mound of tricolour cockades. Then he has them distributed to the people of Bastia and the soldiers of the garrison. After 3 November, the town is covered in red, white and blue, but the officers curb their men, imprisoning any who insist on wearing the new colours.

He must go further: act again, take another step, because action is a form of climbing.

Napoleone tells the people of Bastia to take out their arms and make a show of preparing them, sharpening their knives and cleaning their muskets. Then, on 5 November, they are to make their way peacefully to the church of St John where they will be officially enrolled into what will be a civic guard.

The tension is acute. Napoleone rides around the city.

Companies of grenadiers and chasseurs of the regiment of Maine are marching towards the church; the citadel's cannon have been trained on the city; officers are insulting the locals: 'Italian beggars, they want to thumb their noses at us, do they? They will have us to deal with!' Massoni, the only Corsican artillery officer other than Buonaparte, conspicuously decides to go to the citadel.

In the streets near St John, clashes suddenly break out between the soldiers and the people of Bastia. There's firing; two soldiers are killed, some Corsicans are wounded by bayonets.

Shortly after this, Barrin makes a concession. He distributes arms to the new civic guard. Meanwhile, the colonel in command of the troops now has no option but to leave Bastia. As his ship sets sail, the Corsicans send him on his way with shouting and hooting of their horns.

'Our brothers in Bastia have smashed their chains into a thousand pieces,' says Napoleone.

HE RETURNS TO Ajaccio. He knows these roads which he has ridden so many times before, but never, as at the start of November 1789, has he had the feeling of having caused events, made history. It intoxicates him in a way he has never felt before.

He is ecstatic when he learns a few weeks later that, on hearing of events in Bastia, deputy Saliceti requested that Corsica no longer be subjected to a military regime, like a conquered territory, but be integrated into the kingdom and governed by the same constitution as the rest of the country.

On 30 November, the National Assembly not only accepts this demand but also, on a motion tabled by Mirabeau, declares that all exiles who fought for the island's liberty may return to Corisca and exercise the rights of French citizens.

The news arrives at the end of December.

Napoleone immediately has a banner made and hung on the

façade of the house in the rue St Charles with the words, 'Long live the Nation, Long live Paoli, Long live Mirabeau'.

All over Ajaccio people dance and sing. A bonfire is lit in l'Olmo Square and the crowd shouts, '*Evviva la Francia! Evviva il rè!*'

Napoleone mingles with them. Te Deums are chanted in the churches.

Listening to the choirs and cheering, he feels the joy and pride that comes from causing all this. These dancing men and women, these jubilant people owe their happiness to him. Truly, he is one of those exceptional men, those 'heroes' as Plutarch calls them, who make history.

He is barely twenty years and five months old.

HE WRITES AND, perhaps for the first time since childhood, he feels whole, as if at last the two distinct parts of himself have been united. The Corsican patriot accepts the French officer.

France which had seemed frivolous to him, corrupted by loose women, depravity and idleness, has been reborn into a new, powerful, enlightened nation. It is radiant. It recognizes Corsica as a part of itself.

Napoleone is thrilled. 'France has clasped us to her bosom,' he says. 'From now on we have the same interests and the same concerns: it is only the sea that separates us!'

He gives up the idea of publishing the *Letters on Corsica*. What would be the use now?

'Of the many pecularities of the French Revolution,' he says, 'not the least is that those who put us to death as rebels yesterday, today are our protectors and inspired by the same sentiments as us.'

WHEN NAPOLEONE goes about the streets of Ajaccio, in those first months of 1790, on his own or with Joseph, he is hailed and enveloped in that affectionate, grateful curiosity which always accompanies those the people recognize as their leaders and representatives. People want to talk to him, however briefly, and they congratulate Joseph on his election to the Municipal Council.

A Buonaparte faction is gradually forming, and Napoleone

wants to show his supporters that, apart from being an instigator of events, he is also a humble patriot. He puts himself down on the register of the National Guard as a private, and takes his turn on sentry duty outside the door of Marius-Joseph Peraldi, who has been appointed colonel of the Guard.

Is anyone fooled?

From indiscreet comments, Napoleone learns that la Férandière, the commander of the garrison at Ajaccio, has written to the minister to denounce him. 'This young officer has been trained at the Military School,' writes La Férandière. 'His sister, at St Cyr, and his mother have been showered with the government's kindness. He would be much better off with his corps, since he foments constantly.'

Napoleone immediately takes the initiative and on 16 April writes to his colonel to request further leave, 'My shattered health,' he says, 'does not permit me to join the regiment before the second season of the waters at Orezza, that is to say, before 15 October.' He encloses a medical certificate with the letter, verifying his statement, and it is true that, from time to time, perhaps as a consequence of his walks in the salt marshes, he feels feverish.

On 29 May he is granted four months leave starting on 15 June 1790.

HE IS FREE. More and more nowadays, he has the feeling that his will and his desire can break down every door; that he just has to want something to be able to do it. When he has chosen a goal, he must set about methodically gathering the wherewithal to attain it; and then, if the will is still there, no obstacles will be able to withstand him.

He wants to stay in Corsica to continue 'fomenting' the island, and to galvanize Joseph to be part of the delegation going to meet Pascal Paoli on his way to Corsica.

He must be in Corsica for *Il Babbo*'s return. He cannot abandon the island just when its people are on the move and rallying to his hero, whom he has offered to serve.

On 24 June, Joseph sets sail for Marseilles. Pascal Paoli has left Paris after having been cheered at the National Assembly and received by Robespierre at the Jacobin Club. A Corsican delegation, which includes Joseph, is going to meet him at Lyon.

The following day, 25 June, Napoleone is at his desk when suddenly he hears shouting, the clamour of a crowd on the march.

For the previous few days, the municipality and people of Ajaccio have been at loggerheads with the French garrison. They are demanding arms and free access to the citadel, which La Férandière and Garrison Adjutant Lajaille have refused.

Napoleone seizes his musket and, without stopping to put on jacket, boots or hat, he goes down into the street.

The demonstrators recognize him and hail him as their leader. He hesitates, and then, because he is faced with what is already a riot, and because he knows to what extremes a crowd can go, he takes command of them and plays with their will, accepting that certain French should be arrested but protecting them from more serious acts of violence.

This is how Garrison Adjutant Lajaille comes to be arrested and imprisoned by the municipality, but by then Napoleone has stepped back, as he did in Bastia on 5 November 1789, and he only decides to resume a leading role when the municipality, having released Garrison Adjutant Lajaille, calls for a report to justify this 'day of 25 June'.

He accuses La Férandière of having fostered 'infamous plots against the law' and attempting 'an unpardonable rebellion'. He denounces those Corsicans who served the *ancien régime* French 'who live among us, having prospered in the midst of general degradation and now detest the constitution which restores our liberty!'

How, writing that, could he not be reminded of his father, Charles Buonaparte, who was one such Corsican?

ONE SUNDAY in July 1790, as Napoleone is walking in Place dell'Olmo with his brother Joseph, a group of Corsicans led by a certain Abbé Recco, the nephew of their former mathematics teacher in Ajaccio, rushes up. They accuse Napoleone of inciting the riots of 25 June and of persecuting the French and all Corsicans worthy of the name. Who is he? A Buonaparte, with a father who switched from supporting Paoli to being a courtier of Monsieur de Marboeuf, and a family that comes from Tuscany.

Friends of Napoleone step in and threaten to kill anyone who dares touch him, but he is unperturbed. 'Us, not French?' he exclaims. '*Orrenda bestemmia*, horrible blasphemy! I shall go to law against any scoundrels who utter it.'

They swap more insults, then both parties withdraw.

Napoleone returns with Joseph to rue St Charles. He is silent and thoughtful.

He has just understood the hatred that divides the people of Corsica into those who were followers of Paoli and stayed loyal to him, and those who, like Charles Buonaparte, agreed to cooperate with the French authorites. As for the future – there are those who have chosen to join the cause of revolutionary France and so feel citizens of that nation, there are those who have not renounced the white cockade and, finally, there are those who dream of independence.

IN SEPTEMBER 1790, Napoleone goes to meet Pascal Paoli, who has landed at Bastia. Since his arrival, *Il Babbo* has reigned supreme over the island, having his enemies, the French, arrested and going from village to village surrounded by a crowd of admirers and courtiers. Everywhere Paoli is greeted as the Saviour, the Dictator. Triumphal arches have been erected at the entrance to each village; the inhabitants cheer and let off their muskets.

Napoleone and his brother mingle with the young people who form a cohort around him; they ride in cavalcade and vie for the privilege of forming his guard of honour. He draws abreast of Paoli and looks around at this procession of which he is a member. He observes this old man who has lived in England for twenty years, drawing an English government pension of two thousand pounds sterling. He realizes that he is only one among many in Paoli's entourage. Perhaps his French officer's uniform and his father's stance render him suspect. And then there is the old rivalry between the people of Bastia and the people of Ajaccio, those *di quà* and those *di là*, this side and that of the mountains. Paoli mistrusts Ajaccio. The Buonapartes are from Ajaccio.

The convoy reaches Ponte Nuovo.

Paoli was defeated there by the French in 1769. He wheels his horse, dismounts, and complacently explains to Napoleone the arrangements of the two camps and the positions he had his men defend. Everyone listens respectfully to his account of the battle, until Napoleone curtly concludes, as an experienced officer, 'The result of these dispositions was as it should have been.'

Silence falls on the group. Pascal Paoli looks at Napoleone who does not seem aware of his insolence and is now congratulating the elder man on his heroic courage and loyalty to Corsica. The matter, however, seems closed and Joseph Buonaparte is elected to the Congress which Paoli convenes at Orezza, and re-elected President of the Directory of the District of Ajaccio.

Napoleone is satisfied.

His leave is expiring, 1790 is coming to an end. He both wants and needs to return to France – to receive his wages, but also because he now feels bound to this kingdom of which he is a citizen and officer. He also wants to take his brother Louis to the mainland to put him through military school and, if necessary, teach him himself and supervise his studies.

ALMOST EVERY DAY in that winter of 1790, Napoleone goes down to the port, but the winds are unfavourable. No ship is weighing for France.

He continues writing, as usual, and puts his brothers and sisters to work.

At the end of December, he is finally able to embark with Louis, but their ship is driven back to shore twice.

He must wait.

On 6 January 1791, in Ajaccio, he opens the city's first patriotic club, Il Globo Patriottico. He attends every meeting, passionately participating in the debates.

This man of twenty-one and a half knows how to influence men skilfully now. In France he learnt soldiering. In Corsica, as an instigator of events, immersed in the struggles between factions and clans and recognized as a proponent of change, he has learnt politics. He has played all sorts of roles and pushed his brother Joseph to enter the limelight of public office ahead of him, since he is still too young to take centre stage.

On 23 January 1791, in his study at Milelli, he writes a letter to Buttafoco, the deputy of the nobility, on behalf of the Patriotic Club of Ajaccio. The club decides to print it and he sends a copy to Paoli.

The piece is long and emphatic. As he attacks the deputy of the nobility, and lambasts a career that includes inciting Choiseul to conquer Corsica, Napoleone revisits each stage of the island's history. He denounces this Buttafoco 'all dripping with the blood of his brothers'. He invokes the deputies of the Constituent Assembly, 'O Lameth, O Robespierre, O Pétion, O Volney, O Mirabeau, O Barnave, O Bailly, O La Fayette, this is the man who has dared set himself at your side!'

Paoli's reply is brusque, however. He tells Napoleone 'he should say less and show less partiality'.

Napoleone grits his teeth. It has been a long time since anyone lectured him. In any case, has he ever allowed anyone to take him to task?

But he cannot stop reading the letter.

'Don't take the trouble to expose Buttafoco's impostures,' continues Paoli. 'Leave him to the contempt and the indifference of the public.'

Napoleone feels as if he has been slapped in the face, but he has chosen to be Pascal Paoli's man and so he endures the affront in silence.

Luckily, as January 1791 is ending, the winds turn.

Accompanied to the gangway by his mother, his brothers and sisters, as well as his friends from *Il Globo Patriottico*, Napoleone is at last able to set sail for France with his brother Louis.

As he stands at the stern, with a hand on his younger brother's shoulder, he feels doubts stirring within him.

His destiny is on the island – he wants it to be and he believes it will. Nevertheless, when the ship reaches the open sea and the peaks of Corsica disappear over the horizon, Napoleone, for the first time in his life, does not feel a wrench.

Something in him has changed.

X

IT IS THREE THIRTY in the afternoon of 8 February 1791, and Napoleone is walking briskly along the Lyon road. In the distance, under a low sky which threatens snow, he can see the spire of St Vallier du Rhône. Up ahead, just a few hundred metres off, are the first houses, or rather huts, of a little village. It is cold but, as often before a fall of snow, the air is damp, almost mild.

From time to time Napoleone looks round. His younger brother Louis has fallen behind on purpose. He is only thirteen and he would rather have stayed in Valence and waited for the stagecoach to leave.

'We will walk to the village of Serve,' Napoleone had said after talking to the coachman. 'The stage will pick us up there.'

And now here is Serve. Darkness falls abruptly. A peasant opens at his knock, greets the officer and young lad, and invites them in. They can wait there for the stagecoach that will pass through early in the evening, and then carry on to St Vallier du Rhône where it will stop.

Napoleone takes a seat and gives his host some money. He needs to put his thoughts into words. He talks with the peasant at length, while Louis drowses, and then a candle is brought for him. He takes what he needs to write out of his satchel and starts a letter to his uncle Fesch:

I am in a poor man's cabin where it is pleasant to write to you. It is four in the afternoon and the weather is chilly although milder. I have enjoyed myself taking a walk . . . Everywhere I find the peasants steadfast, especially in the Dauphiné. They are all ready to die for the Constitution.

At Valence I found the people resolute, the soldiers patriotic and the officers aristocratic . . . The women everywhere are royalists. It is not surprising. Liberty is a prettier woman who eclipses them all.

He breaks off. Louis has fallen asleep. He thinks of the situation in Corsica. The men he met in Valence seemed less competent than those in Ajaccio.

'We must not complain too much about our department,' he writes, but to draw attention to the island 'the Patriotic Society of Ajaccio should present Mirabeau with a complete Corsican costume: cap, coat, breeches, drawers, cartridge-pouch, dagger, pistol and musket. That would make a good impression . . .'

Napoleone stops writing. That noise of wheels and hooves growing louder is the stagecoach. He wakes Louis and dashes off a last sentence, 'I embrace you, my dear Fesch, the coach is coming. I must join it. We shall sleep at St Vallier.'

THEY FIND the travellers they had left behind at Valence in the coach, and pick up the thread of their conversation.

Napoleone defends the Constituent Assembly. He denounces the supporters of the *ancien régime* 'which will not return', he says, hammering out each word.

'What is called good society is three-quarters artistocratic,' he adds. 'That's to say, it hides itself behind a mask of being supporters of the English constitution.'

For himself, he admits, he is no supporter of moderatism.

In the inn at St Vallier, the conversation turns to the state of the nation. Napoleone repeats the word. Others speak of the *kingdom*, but since the capture of the Bastille and the formation of the Assembly, he argues, *nation* is the correct term for France.

Later in their room, while Louis sleeps, Napoleone starts writing again. Political preoccupations have receded into the background. He stands up, opens the window and goes back to the table. 'The ivy embraces the first tree it meets,' he writes. 'That, in a few words, is the story of love.'

It is snowing. He wants the cold to quash these feelings and desires that are troubling him. He will soon be twenty-two.

'What, then, is love?' he continues. 'Observe a young man of thirteen years of age: he loves his friend as he will his lover when he is twenty. Egotism comes later. At forty, a man loves his fortune, at sixty, only himself. What, then, is love?'

Napoleone takes a few more paces and closes the window again. Snow covers the silent town and countryside.

He writes a final sentence.

'If you have any feelings, you will feel the earth open up.'

TWO DAYS LATER he is in Auxonne. He shows Louis round the barracks of the regiment of La Fère, where he must report to Colonel Monsieur de Lance, and the Pavillon de la Ville, where they will live. He puts his brother in a servant's room adjoining what will be his own room.

On the church square, as he is showing Louis the bookseller's shop, the two brothers are surrounded by a group of officers. They greet Napoleone coldly. During his seventeen months on leave, the kingdom and the royal army have undergone great trials. Word has it that Buonaparte sided against the royal garrison and Monsieurs de Barrin and La Férandière in Corsica. Why didn't he follow Monsieur Massoni's example and choose the King's camp?

When he presents the affidavits from the district of Ajaccio to the colonel, Napoleone is nervous. These documents not only attest that he has been trying to rejoin his regiment since October, but also that he has 'been motivated by the purest patriotism, as witness the indubitable proof he has given of his attachment to the Constitution since the start of the Revolution'.

The colonel is understanding and supports Napoleone's request for back pay from 15 October to 1 February. He is reassured, but nevertheless still waits impatiently for ministerial confirmation. He needs those two hundred and thirty-three livres, six sous and eight deniers, for now two people are living on his pay. He buys the meat, milk and bread himself, argues bitterly over the price of foodstuffs and sewing, and brushes his own uniform. He never complains to his comrades, but later he will reveal, 'I deprived myself of everything to pay for my brother's schooling, even the bare necessities.' However, he still goes regularly to the book-seller's shop and buys notebooks, books and newspapers.

The newspapers are awaited just as impatiently in Auxonne as in Corsica and Napoleone gives instructions for articles on events in Paris to be read out to those non-commissioned officers and soldiers who espouse revolutionary thinking.

At night, however, when Louis sleeps, Napoleone continues working with a passion undimmed by the political upheavals which he follows, comments on and is involved in, both in France and Corsica. He reads Machiavelli, a history of the Sorbonne and another about the nobility. Sometimes, next morning, he shows Louis the lists of words he has made to expand his vocabulary. He copies out turns of phrase and expressions. He wants to take full possession of this French language which he writes in a fever of excitement. 'The southern blood that flows in my veins,' he scrawls at the bottom of a letter to his friend Naudin, who is a war commissary in Auxonne, 'runs with the speed of the Rhône. Forgive me then if you have difficulty reading my scribbles.'

He rereads the works of Rousseau. and makes notes in the margin alongside certain passages: 'I do not believe that.' Sometimes he vigorously strikes out something he has written, no longer just the pupil taking notes. He is forging his ideas in complete freedom, but they are always marked by passion. 'The nobility is the scourge of the people,' he writes. 'The Pope is only the legal head of the Church. Infallibility belongs to the legitimately assembled Church and not to the Pope.'

Sometimes he works fifteen or sixteen hours a day. And once his own work is done, he turns to Louis.

'I force him to study,' he says.

He often flies into a fury and slaps his brother. Their neighbours indignantly remonstrate with him. 'Wretched bully,' they cry. But when Louis does well in mathematics or French tests, Napoleone relaxes. He smiles and flatters his young brother.

'He will be the best of us all,' he tells Joseph. 'All the women round here love him.'

He listens delightedly when the thirteen-year-old talks, and watches how he enters a drawing room, insouciant and elegant. 'He has quite the proper French manner,' he writes. 'When he goes into company, he bows gracefully and asks the usual questions with as much gravity and dignity as if he was thirty.'

Napoleone's attentiveness to his younger brother never falters. He feels responsible for him, teaches him everything he knows and tells Joseph, with a sense of fulfilment, 'None of us will have had so fine an education.'

'LET'S GO,' says Napoleone. This is how one schools a younger brother. It is three thirty in the morning and Louis's teeth are chattering. He dresses hurriedly, eats a bit of bread, and off they go through the country lanes in the icy blackness, with a wind blowing for good measure.

Napoleone takes the road to Dole. There, at number 17, rue de Besançon, lives Joly, the printer, who has agreed to print the *Letter to Buttafuoco*. This is easily worth the four leagues' walk there and as many back, and the necessity of repeating the journey several days running.

One morning Napoleone arrives dressed in the revolutionary sans-culotte uniform: a short, buttoned jacket and striped white linen trousers. In his curt, staccato way, he tells the surprised printer that he is on the side of all who defend liberty. That is the only cause there is.

He never spends any time in Dole. He instantly tells Louis to set off again. They have to be back in Auxonne before midday. Napoleone uses their walk back as an opportunity to give Louis a geography lesson and again tell him that one should never let one's time just pass aimlessly.

One day, when they reach the Saône river, not far from Auxonne's barracks, two officers of the regiment of La Fère accost them.

So, here is this Lieutenant Buonaparte!

A spirited discussion ensues. The officers reproach him for having newspaper articles sympathetic to the Assembly's decrees read out to the soldiers. He has even read out the address sent by Ajaccio's patriotic club to the Constituents, and told the men that his elder brother Joseph had written it. Voices are raised. The two officers claim that every nobleman has an obligation to emigrate, since this is the only way to stay loyal to the King.

'Long live the nation!' Napoleone replies. The country is above the King.

The two officers jostle him and threaten to throw him in the Saône, but he defends himself and soon soldiers come out of the barracks and the argument ends.

Napoleone may not be able to persuade the officer corps to embrace the revolutionary ideas, but the soldiers and sergeants are ready converts. The marshal of the camp, Baron du Teil, who has been appointed inspector-general of artillery, writes that, although the regiment continues to show up well under arms, 'the soldiers and non-commissioned officers have acquired an air of villainy and insubordination which shows itself in all manner of ways'. They avert their eyes so that they do not have to salute officers; they fraternize with the citizens of the National Guard; they present arms to the officers of the militia.

ONE EVENING, when Napoleone accepts an invitation to a dinner in Nuits for one of his fellow officers who is lately married, he guesses as soon as he enters the drawing room that he has fallen into a trap. All the gentry of those parts have been invited as well.

They laugh at him derisively. So, is this the sharp-tongued lieutenant who shares the brigands' opinions and fosters indiscipline among the men? He is surrounded, challenged. What are his views about acts of insubordination? Do they reflect any frame of mind that could possibly meet with an officer's satisfaction?

Napoleone defends himself. He is not 'antimilitarist'; he believes in the necessity of discipline and order; but these can only be respected if the officers themselves observe the law and accept the new principles.

The mayor of Nuits arrives, in a crimson coat. Napoleone thinks he has found an ally, but the man mounts an even more vigorous defence of officers who are thinking of emigrating. What can one expect of a regime, he says, which cannot even maintain order in the army?

It is such a bitter tirade that the mistress of the house has to step in and put an end to the discussion.

FROM THEN ON Napoleone is involved in daily confrontations, both in Auxonne and then in Valence, where he is posted as first lieutenant and reaches with his brother on 16 June 1791.

His new regiment – the 4th artillery, the regiment of Grenoble – is as divided as the regiment of La Fère he has just left. The rank and file is in favour of the new ideas, whilst part of the officer corps is considering emigrating or resigning out of loyalty to the King.

'Never leave,' Mademoiselle Bou advises Napoleone who has never contemplated doing so. 'Exile is always a misfortune.'

He has gone back to his old landlady and room, and Louis has become the apple of Mademoiselle Bou's eye. She spoils him like a son and shields him from the ever-demanding Napoleone's fits of anger. However, there's less time in Valence to devote to Louis. He sets him a syllabus each day and then goes out, to the barracks and Monsieur Aurel's reading room.

Everywhere people are arguing fervently.

At the beginning of July 1791, an extraordinary piece of news has the whole town agog: on 20 June Louis XVI and his family tried to leave France and were arrested at Varennes. The Marquis de Bouillé waited in vain with his army to escort them into exile.

'The King,' exclaims a comrade of Napoleone's, 'is three-quarters dead.'

The officers around him protest, but Napoleone agrees. He is willing to sign the new oath of allegiance to the constitution which is being demanded of officers. Which constitution, someone asks. Should the King be granted a right of veto, and if so, which veto? Suspensive or absolute? Why shouldn't the King be put on trial?

On the Place aux Clercs, Napoleone debates endlessly with certain fellow officers. Most are monarchists. Coming to a halt, he forcefully proclaims his position, chin raised: he is a determined Republican, a supporter of Public Safety and not a master's wishes.

He has read the royalists' speeches. 'They exhaust themselves in vain analysis,' he exclaims. 'They make irrelevant assertions that are incapable of proof . . . They take great pains to bolster a bad cause . . . A nation of twenty-five million can perfectly well be a republic . . . To think the opposite is an "impolitic old saw".'

Napoleone can be exasperating. He speaks vigorously and always has an answer to everything. Passions run so high that some officers turn away when they meet him. In the Three Pigeons, where he is again one of the regular customers, people refuse to sit next to that 'frenzied demagogue' who speaks in a way 'unworthy of a French officer educated at no cost at the Military School and shown every kindness by the King'.

Napoleone hears what they are saying, but doesn't look for an opportunity to respond. He doesn't even react when a fellow officer, Lieutenant Du Prat, snaps at a servant who has laid him a place next to Napoleone, 'This is the last time I will tell you, never give me that man as a neighbour.'

A few days later, Napoleone has his revenge. Du Prat goes to the window as a crowd of patriots are streaming past and launches into a provocative rendition of the aristocrats' song, 'O Richard, o my King'. The procession stops, the people rush into the tavern to tear the royalist officer to pieces and it is Napoleone who has to step in and save him.

NAPOLEONE is a familiar figure in the town. He is a member of the Society of the Friends of the Constitution, along with several other officers, soldiers and local notables.

He sees the bookseller Aurel at the revolutionary club and they embrace each other. Napoleone gives a speech denouncing the King's flight and the behaviour of the Marquis de Bouillé, this officer's 'infamy'. He speaks with nervous eloquence in clipped, staccato sentences and there is cheering when he finishes. He is made secretary and Society librarian.

On 3 July, there is a meeting to pass judgement on the King.

'He must be tried,' declares Napoleone. In trying to leave France Louis XVI committed treason. A soldier steps forward and shouts in the name of his comrades, 'We have cannon, arms, hearts. We owe them to the Constitution!'

On 14 July, the entire population of Valence, the regiment, the official bodies, the National Guard, the bishop and the clergy gather on the Champ de l'Union. Napoleone is at the head of the soldiers of the 4th regiment. His brother Louis is in the crowd with Mademoiselle Bou. They sing the '*Ça ira*'. They take the civic oath, shouting 'I swear.' Then the bishop leads a Te Deum, and everyone processes back to Valence.

The most ardent patriots meet in the hall of the Society of

Friends of the Constitution where a table is set for a banquet. At the end of the meal, Napoleone stands up and there is applause. He is one of the best-known and most trusted patriotic officers in the town; he has sworn the oath required of soldiers, he has declared himself a Republican and he has made it known that he thinks the King should be tried.

He calls for a toast, raises his glass to his former comrades at Auxonne and to those who, in that Burgundy city, are defending the rights of the people.

'Long live the nation!' he cries.

That evening he is so exhilarated he cannot sleep. This seething energy of a whole population, of a whole country caught up in the whirlwind of revolution, which every day brings a new reality, forces him to choose afresh every instant. How can one rest?

He writes to his brother and to Naudin, his friend who is still in Auxonne. The writing, as he says apologetically, is a 'scrawl'.

'To go to sleep with one's head full of great public questions, and one's heart stirred by companions whom one respects, and from whom one is sincerely sorry to have parted, is such a pleasure as only great Epicureans can enjoy.'

He cannot stop questioning the future.

'Will there be war?' he wonders. He doubts it. The sovereigns of Europe, for fear of the revolutionary contagion, would rather wait for France to be torn apart by civil war — but in that, they are mistaken. 'This country is full of zeal and enthusiasm,' judges Napoleone. Even the regiment is very sound: 'The men, the sergeants, and half the officers are in favour of the new principles.'

Shall he go to sleep, once he has sealed and addressed the letter?

Impossible.

NAPOLEONE takes out his notebooks.

He is undertaking his first genuine piece of writing. The Academy of Lyon is offering a prize of twelve hundred livres to the author of the best essay on, 'What truths and sentiments is it most important to inculcate in men for their happiness?' He decided to enter the competition the moment he heard about it.

Didn't Rousseau win the same prize once for his *Discourse on Inequality?*

So, in the Valence night, Napoleone starts to write.

Man is born for happiness, he says, but 'where kings are sovereign, there are no men, only the oppressing slave more base than the slave that is oppressed'. Therefore everyone must resist oppression. 'The French have done so.' They have won liberty 'after twenty months of struggle and the most violent shocks ... After centuries the French, brutalized by kings and their ministers, by nobles and their prejudices, by priests and their impostures, have suddenly awakened and marked out the Rights of Man.'

He writes as if this is a revolutionary speech. He extols liberty and equality. Two words often recur: *strength* and *energy*: 'Without strength, without energy, there is neither virtue nor happiness.'

He writes as if giving orders. There is no sympathy for the tyrants, but no pity either for those who accept tyranny, for the weak: 'All the tyrants will doubtless go to hell, but their slaves will too because, after the crime of oppressing a nation, that of suffering this oppression is the greatest.'

His hand trembles from writing so fast.

This Lyon essay – which the Academy will judge 'too ill-arranged, too disparate, too vague and too badly written to hold the attention' – is a mirror for Napoleone. He looks in it every night. When he praises 'souls as ardent as the furnace of Etna', it is himself he is talking of – and here he is painting a silhouette 'with pale complexion, wandering eyes, hurried gait, stiff movements, a sardonic laugh'. He sees it approach, points it out and denounces it. It is 'ambition', a form of madness.

He sees a second silhouette, just as alarming. It is 'the man of genius. The unfortunate soul! I pity him. He will be the admiration and envy of his fellows, and the most miserable of all. His equilibrium is broken: he will live unhappy.'

Napoleone wants happiness. Besides, isn't that the subject of the competition? But he concludes, 'Men of genius are meteors destined to burn to illuminate their age.'

He is twenty-two year old.

There, that is that night's work.

IN THE MORNING, in the dazzling sunshine that seems to set Valence ablaze, Napoleone emerges from his dream and sets about organizing his future.

He listens to the patriotic officers in his regiment. Most dream of being put in command of a volunteer battalion; that way a lieutenant, for instance, can become a colonel.

Why not me?

But Napoleone could only stand a chance of that in his country, Corsica, where he could rely on the backing of Ajaccio's *Globo Patriottico*. Joseph would be a valuable supporter too: he is one of the city's representatives and aspires to become a deputy in the Legislative Assembly, which is about to take over from the Constituent Assembly.

Admittedly, there is Pascal Paoli's coolness towards him to consider.

Napoleone picks up the letter his hero has written him. Napoleone had asked Paoli for certain documents that would be useful for writing a history of Corsica, but Paoli's reply was as terse as the advice he had vouchsafed when Napoleone had sent him his *Letter to Buttafoco*.

'I am not able at present to open my packing-cases and search through my papers,' he replies to Napoleone. 'Besides, history is not best written in the years of one's youth. Allow me to recommend that you plan the work on the model which the Abbé Raynal gave you and in the meantime you will be able to concentrate on collecting anecdotes and the most salient facts.'

Napoleone grits his teeth. He has to convince himself that Paoli is still the hero he should follow. He is still young, so he must accept the scornful tone and the rebuff and return to Corsica, since he is Corsican and it is there that he has acquired a little of the renown and influence over men without which nothing is possible.

And yet, he feels a citizen of this French nation which has freed itself from its chains in so many ways now. He no longer hates its people; on the contrary, he is surprised and full of admiration for these 'peasants firm in their views' and this whole country 'full of zeal and enthusiasm'.

But he must return to Corsica and his family that needs support. He must follow Paoli.

A pragmatic rather than a heartfelt decision.

So NAPOLEONE requests another leave, but he is refused by Colonel Campagnol, the commander of the 4th artillery regiment. The situation does not permit first lieutenant Napoleone Buonaparte a third furlough when his first lasted twenty-one months and his second seventeen!

Napoleone does not admit defeat.

One day in August he sets off on the road to the Château de Pommier in Isère, the family home of the marshal of the camp and inspector-general of artillery, Baron du Teil.

The officer is not an adherent of the new ideas, but nor does he envisage emigrating, although that has not stopped him being threatened as an 'aristocrat'.

When, at about ten in the evening, Napoleone knocks on the gate, the servants are slow to open up for him, so he shouts his name several times. He is finally shown in and is instantly glad to have made the journey. Du Teil is pleased to see this lieutenant again who had astonished him at Valence with his doggedness and talent. They speak about their profession, bring out maps.

Napoleone is Du Teil's guest for several days, at the end of which Du Teil grants him a leave of absence for three months, on full pay.

As he is signing the permission, he looks benevolently at Napoleone. 'You have great powers,' he says. 'You will make a name for yourself.'

But everything depends on circumstances. That is what war is.

ON 29 AUGUST, Napoleone is back at Valence, quivering with impatience.

Louis must get ready, quick. He has to run to the barracks, be paid by the quartermaster treasurer, settle up his debts, and pay his dues for the regimental banquets.

The quartermaster gives him one hundred and six livres, three sous and two deniers.

When he gets back to the Bou house, Napoleone berates Louis

for being slow, and Mademoiselle Bou intervenes. Why this urgency? They can leave Valence tomorrow.

Tomorrow?

Who knows what tomorrow holds?

XI

ON THAT 15 SEPTEMBER 1791, Napoleone walks alone through the streets of Ajaccio. He stares at everyone he passes, forcing them with his gaze either to greet him or to look away. He wants to know how many Corsicans the Buonapartes can count on.

Since he disembarked with Louis, not much more than a few hours ago, this is the main question he has been asking himself. He has listened to his brothers and sisters distractedly and wondered out loud, more than once, 'Where is Joseph?'

First Lucien, and then Letizia explain that he is in Corte, where the 346 electors have gathered to appoint deputies to the Legislative Assembly. Joseph is a candidate, as planned, but everything depends on Pascal Paoli. He controls Congress. Not a single decision will go against him. The six deputies will only be elected because he wishes them to be. In Ajaccio, Joseph has Pozzo di Borgo and Peraldi for rivals.

'He will prefer them to Joseph,' murmurs Letizia.

Napoleone is silent. He remembers the times already that Paoli has rebuffed him.

'My sons are too French,' adds Letizia.

Napoleone flies into a rage, leaves the room, stalks across the garden, and then walks slowly along the rue St Charles.

Late that afternoon, the sun is still hot but the shadows have reached the peaks and the sea breeze is slipping through the alleys, soft and light. Napoleone heads towards the Place dell'Olmo. He knows every house, every paving stone; he can put a name to almost every face; he is at home. This intimate familiarity with places, people, scents, the colour of this twilight gives him a feeling of strength, but he also feels a sense of misgiving.

He has only been in Ajaccio for several hours and yet it feels as if he is wandering in a labyrinth. Nothing is foreign to him — he has walked every street, he knows all the detours, all the traps — and yet he is afraid he won't be able to find a way out, as if the very familiarity of this country renders him powerless here.

He rebels. That cannot be. This is where he must apply his energy, this is his first stage, this is where he must play his part.

He will go to Corte.

HOWEVER, a few days later, when he sees the city of Corte built on a mountain peak, dominated by a rock at whose summit stands the citadel, when he walks his horse through the cobbled alleys and hears the echo of its hoofbeats, when he has to force his way through the crowds of delegates of Congress, that feeling of powerlessness comes over him again.

He senses the delegates' indifference and especially the hostility in the haughtiness of some of them. They call him 'the Frenchman', 'the officer', and whisper that his father, Charles Buonaparte, went over to Monsieur de Marboeuf and betrayed Paoli. This climate of contempt makes his blood boil. He clenches his jaw. He grows paler than usual and seems even thinner. Loud enough for him to hear, someone says that this *ragazzetto* playing at soldiers doesn't even seem to be fifteen.

They'll see who Napoleone Buonaparte is!

He meets up with Joseph, who wavers between despondency and delight, and their friends. Paoli and his associates dominate Congress. He chooses who he wants and he mistrusts the Buonapartes, but he hasn't rejected them outright. He thinks them young. He wants to observe them, assess their loyalty. He is prepared to have Joseph elected a member of the Directory of the department, and even allow him onto the Executive Committee. For a young man of twenty-four, isn't this an unhoped-for appointment?

Napoleone remains reserved. Do they have a choice? Can anyone break with Pascal Paoli? He decides to greet him respectfully, and renew his offer to serve him in any way he can. When the election is over and he meets Peraldi and Pozzo di Borgo, who have been elected to represent Ajaccio in the Legislative Assembly, he congratulates them.

Once back at home, however, he paces endlessly about his room. This double election is a defeat for the Buonapartes. Their influence in Ajaccio is reduced to their rivals' advantage, and Joseph has to stay at Corte to work in the department's administration. Paoli has played his hand skilfully.

Napoleone feels alone in a hostile predicament, but it is as if, simultaneously, the energy within him is increasing tenfold.

HE GIVES orders to everyone, to his brothers and sisters, in an abrupt, imperious tone.

'You can't argue with him,' Lucien complains to their mother.

Lucien is the only one who tries to resist him, but Napoleone loses his temper instantly; he will not tolerate anyone answering back or making observations. He is like a wild cat, tense, watchful, pitilessly lashing out with its claws at whatever comes within reach.

His desire for action, his wish to find a way out of a situation he thinks is temporary, his ambition and his desire to show what he is capable of find expression in an irritable, surly impatience that is palpable in every gesture.

ON 15 OCTOBER 1791, Napoleone is the first of the Buonapartes to enter the room where his great-uncle, Archdeacon Lucien, is dying slowly and peacefully.

He goes and stands at the foot of the bed, and is soon joined by his brothers and sisters and his mother. Joseph has come from Corte. When Uncle Fesch, the priest of the family, appears with his surplice and stole, Archdeacon Lucien sends him away. He doesn't need any help from the religion that, in principle, he has served all his life!

Napoleone stands stock still, watching and listening to the dying man facing him.

The archdeacon takes Letizia Buonaparte's hand. She is sobbing. He is the one who, since her husband's death, has managed the family's estate. The archdeacon murmurs, 'Letizia, stop your crying, I die happy seeing you surrounded by all your children.'

He breathes with difficulty.

'They do not need me alive any more,' he adds in a lower voice. 'Joseph is at the head of the country's administration. He can direct your affairs.'

The Archdeacon turns towards Napoleone.

'*Tu poi, Napoleone, sarai un omone.* (And you, Napoleone, you will be a great man.)'

He repeats the last word, *omone*.

Everyone turns to look at Napoleone; he doesn't lower his gaze. This is not the first time he has been invested with a glorious and singular future. It is as if all those who have marked out a destiny for him have made it beholden upon him to attain it. It is his duty to become what they hope he can be.

When he returns to the house in rue St Charles after the archdeacon's funeral, he is even more impatient to act.

HE BEGINS by tallying up their finances.

Letizia Buonaparte is heiress to the archdeacon's modest fortune, but she chooses to put it at her sons' disposal and, since Joseph has returned to Corte, Napoleone is the one who will manage this sum that has been found in a leather purse tucked under the dead man's pillow.

As he stacks those gold coins in columns on the table in the ground floor parlour, he shows no emotion: there is no gleam in his eyes, his hands do not tremble. First and foremost, this money is a means of gaining security for the future. For that, he must enlarge their estate. Uncle Fesch is a valuable adviser, because he knows which Church land is being put up for sale as national property.

At the start of December 1791, Napoleone and his uncle pay a visit to the estates of St Antoine and de Vignale in the suburb of Ajaccio, and to the beautiful house of La Trabocchina, which is in the middle of the town. These properties once belonged to the chapter of Ajaccio: on December 13, they become the joint property, in equal shares, of Napoleone and Fesch. On several occasions at the end of that year, 1791, Napoleone goes walking his land. Sometimes he stops before the Trabocchina house. *It is mine.*

Rather than assuaging his desires, these acquisitions are even greater spurs to action. Owning land and property is not what will fulfil him. Quite the opposite: this security only encourages him to press on.

Money is also a way of gaining power over men.

Pozzo di Borgo and Peraldi are influential because they are

rich. They 'buy' clients, do favours for their friends. With the rest of the gold, Napoleone thinks that he will be able to strengthen the Buonaparte party.

He starts to entertain in the house in rue St Charles, extending his network of friendships, but he can feel his impatience mounting.

AN OPPORTUNITY is not slow in presenting itself.

At the beginning of 1792, he travels around Corsica in the company of Monsieur de Volney, a *philosophe* and former member of the Constituent Assembly who dreams of moving to Corsica. He is a man of influence in Paris and considerable fame. Napoleone does not leave his side for a moment, confirming him in his impression of Corsica as a place where the 'people are simple, the soil rich, the spring perpetual'. Volney is not merely a disinterested traveller. Whilst conversing with Napoleone and telling him, his voice aglow with passion, of his voyage to Egypt, of that country's beauty, its readiness for a revolution, Volney is looking for land to buy. He knows that there are enormous properties to be had that once belonged to the monarchy and have since been trans-ferred to certain families at no cost. Napoleone makes recommen-dations to Volney, especially the property of La Confina, an estate of six hundred hectares, which is to be sold at auction. Good land and a good price! In return for his role as intermediary, does Napoleone demand a share of this property from Volney? Or do the *philosophe* and the young officer who is not yet twenty-three enter into some form of partnership?

When he returns to Ajaccio, Napoleone doesn't reply to his mother's questions; he seems even more determined and impatient.

These long conversations with one of the most prominent figures in contemporary life, an author whose works he has read, have made him even more certain that everything is possible. Volney has set him dreaming of the Orient, Egypt, far-off lands, of Paris, too, but Napoleone also finds himself thinking: is that all a *philosophe*, a writer, a traveller and a deputy in the Constituent Assembly is? Napoleone admires and respects Volney, but he also feels the scales have fallen from his eyes. He feels the equal of Volney now – a man who, after all, wants to do a good land deal just like anyone else – but, more than that, Napoleone is certain that within him lie an energy and strength – these two words from his Lyon essay spring to mind again – that Volney has never possessed.

Who else has such reserves of power to draw on?

At the start of that year, 1792, Napoleone begins to believe that he alone among all those he associates with, or is pitted against, can count on such inner resources. He remembers all the challenges he took up at school at Brienne, when he was just little *Paille-au-Nez*.

When he wants something, he can get it.

HE WANTS TO be promoted and play his part, at a more senior level than lieutenant, in one of the volunteer battalions that are now being formed. The adjutant-majors of these units can be officers in the regular army, and their rank is the equivalent of captain. This is his goal then: to become an adjutant-major. He goes to see the brigadier, Antoine Rossi, who is effectively the commander of Corsica's army and is a distant cousin of the Buonapartes. He needs competent officers to supervise the peasants who make up the volunteer battalions, and eagerly accepts Napoleone's request. He will appoint Lieutenant Buonaparte adjutant-major of the Volunteers of Ajaccio and Tallone.

This is a victory for Napoleone, and yet Letizia notices that her son is worried. He writes innumerable letters to France and asks one of his friends, Sucy, a war commissary posted to Valence, for advice. He has learnt that any officer absent from his corps during the review of January 1792 will be struck off the army lists and lose his officer's rank if he is not on leave or able to provide exceptional grounds for absence. He does not want to be discharged. He values his rank. He values France.

'Overwhelming circumstances have forced me, my dear Sucy,' he writes, 'to stay in Corsica longer than the duties of my employment would have allowed. I know this and yet I have nothing with which to reproach myself: dearer and more sacred duties justify me.'

A few days later, trying to explain his absence again, he writes,

'In difficult times the honourable place for a good Corsican is his own country. For this reason my friends have demanded that I stay among them.'

'You do not want to lose what you have gained in France,' murmurs Letizia.

She is pleased with her son.

Neither lose France, nor renounce Corsica; keep every door open. This is what Napoleone chooses, this tactician who is not yet twenty-three.

When, in February 1792, Rossi tells him that he cannot in fact appoint him adjutant-major because the law obliges officers choosing this rank to return to their corps by 1 April, Napoleone thinks he either has to return to France instantly or resign from the army, neither of which he wants.

Then he discovers that the law makes an exception for first and second lieutenant-colonels of volunteer battalions. These officers will be allowed to remain at their posts in Corsica and retain their rank in the regular army.

But one is elected, not appointed to these ranks

Napoleone immediately makes his decision: he will be a lieutenant-colonel of the 2nd battalion of the Corsican volunteers, the Ajaccio and Tallano battalion, as it's known.

He will have to be elected, because he has no choice, but he will be a lieutenant-colonel, whatever the cost.

THIS IS HIS first great battle, he knows he must win it.

He shuts himself in his study. He reads the newspapers that come from France. He takes notes. When he goes down to the salon, he is taciturn and pensive, his face the unreadable mask of someone locked in thought.

However, as soon as he leaves the rue St Charles, his manner changes. He is an assured figure in his artillery officer's uniform, resolutely striding through the streets, his chin held high. He speaks plainly to whoever approaches him, and they go away captivated or astonished by the boldness of this 23-year-old lieutenant whose looks are still an adolescent's and yet who knows everything that is happening in Paris.

He has five rivals, all from influential Ajaccio families. He allies himself with one of them, Quenza, agreeing to be his second lieutenant-colonel on condition that Quenza's followers vote for him, and vice versa, and on these terms they conclude a pact.

However, his opponents, Pozzo di Borgo and Peraldi, refuse to be reconciled.

'I am not afraid so long as I am attacked head on,' Napoleone says to those who put him on his guard. 'One might as well do nothing as do things by halves.'

He is told of Pozzo and Peraldi's threats, the way they insult him. He restrains himself. They laugh at his overweening ambition, his diminutive stature, his diminutive fortune, his *petulanza*.

One day in March, he cannot control himself any longer; he challenges Peraldi to a duel and waits for him all day in front of the Greek chapel. Peraldi backs out, but even so makes it appear he has come out of it best.

Napoleone clenches his fists. He assembles his supporters at his house, delivers speeches, lodges them, feeds them. Volunteers from the four companies of the Tallano district sleep in the passages, on the stairs and in the bedrooms of the family home. Napoleone spends freely, keeping a permanent open house. Sometimes at night, as he steps over the bodies, he remembers the hours he used to spend in his rooms at Auxonne and Valence, making notes on Rousseau or Montesquieu. Political struggle obeys different rules, and demands constant vigilance. It is as exciting to him as a woman. It is an alcohol which, as Napoleone discovers, goes to one's head. He loves this tension, this duel that calls into play both looks and speed of thought, the body as much as the mind. When the moment of decision comes, it will be a release, an almost physical liberation.

ON 30 MARCH 1792, Napoleone hears that the three departmental commissioners who are going to monitor the ballot, which is to be held the following day, have arrived in Ajaccio. Two of them are staying in Buonaparte family houses, so they are Napoleone's, but the third, Murati, has seen fit to accept the Peraldis' hospitality.

Napoleone stays shut in his room all that day. He anxiously

throws himself into a chair, then paces about, worrying. Without the third commissioner's support, the result of the election is uncertain.

Napoleone wants to obtain this position of lieutenant-colonel. He cannot tolerate any setbacks, any room for doubt. He opens his door, calls one of his men and gives his orders: they are to arm themselves, force their way into the Peraldi house, kidnap the commissioner and bring him back.

The operation runs its violent, brief course.

Napoleone calmly welcomes the commissioner. 'I wanted you to be free,' he says. 'You were not free with the Peraldi; here, you are at home.'

The following day in the church of St Francis, despite Pozzo di Borgo and Peraldi's protests, Quenza is elected first lieutenant-colonel and Buonaparte second lieutenant-colonel.

That evening the house on rue St Charles is full of people feasting and singing. The regiment's band plays. Napoleone stands aloof, silent, staring.

Victory is what counts.

This is the law he has just learnt.

It doesn't matter what the means are. Everything lies in the plan and the goal.

BUT TO BE VICTORIOUS is also to be hated.

When Napoleone visits the volunteers quartered in the seminary, he feels looks of hatred boring into him. Peraldi and Pozzo's supporters mutter as he goes past. During the voting, friends of Napoleone's had knocked down Mathieu Pozzo as he was making a protest, and dragged him off the tribune in St Francis's. If Napoleone had not intervened, Pozzo would have been killed, but still, to the Pozzi, Napoleone is the leader of these brigands. 'Amongst men of good sense, the only reputation the Buonapartes will ever have is of excellence in crime,' his enemies are fond of repeating.

Peraldi and Pozzo di Borgo, moreover, are deputies in the Legislative Assembly and behind them is the one who has had them elected: Pascal Paoli. Napoleone knows that this hatred will pursue him from now on, but that is how it is. He must live with it. What matters is that he has carried the day and, in the process, discovered a new and exhilarating source of joy: commanding men.

Soldiers have answered to him before, but only when he himself was obliged to obey a superior's orders. Now, when he goes to the seminary and musters the national volunteers, there is only one leader. First lieutenant-colonel Quenza has no experience and little more desire – it is Napoleone who draws up, in minute detail, the regulations of the battalion which from then on is known not as the Ajaccio-Tallano battalion but as the Quenza-Buonaparte battalion. Everyone in the army and the city knows that it is Napoleone who is in command.

In a few days, he measures his power. He inspects the men, speaks to them, gives orders. The more he acts, the more he feels the need to act. So, he wanted to be a lieutenant-colonel, did he? Well, he is one now – but what good is that if he does not use it to go further? This victory gives him fresh impetus.

Clearly, to gain control of the town, one would need to gain a foothold in the citadel where Colonel Maillard's Limousin regiment is stationed. Napoleone studies the fortress, inspects it at close quarters; that is where the cannon are. Gaining control of them might also be a way of convincing Pascal Paoli that he is someone who knows how to act, to set affairs in motion. There are risks. Any action would constitute a rebellion against the legal authorities, so precautions have to be taken; one must portray oneself as acting to safeguard the law and defend the new principles from the supporters of despotism.

In those first days of April 1792, Napoleone is constantly on the move, criss-crossing the city, reviewing the volunteers. His body pulses to the rhythm of his thoughts, always on the alert, always searching for the perfect moment, the ideal strategem.

ON 2 APRIL Colonel Maillard reviews the Quenza-Buonaparte battalion on the parade ground. They have a martial air; Napoleone wheels on his horse in front of his men. But when Maillard requests that the battalion leave the city, Quenza, prompted by Napoleone, refuses and, on various pretexts, demands that they be allowed a longer stay.

The people of Ajaccio grow concerned. What are these 'peasants' doing in town? Napoleone is cursed, the circumstances of his election denounced. Certain families, the richest, pack their bags and leave for Italy. Brawls break out here and there between the National Guard and sailors from the port.

On 8 April, the priests who have refused to swear an oath to the civil constitution of the clergy celebrate a mass in the Convent of St Francis and announce that they will lead a procession the following day.

'They are declaring a schism!' exclaims Napoleone. 'These people are ready to commit any folly!'

That evening, another brawl breaks out in front of the cathedral and Napoleone and the officers around him are fired on. Lieutenant Rocca Serra is killed. Cries ring out from all sides, '*Adosso alle spalette!*' 'Down with the epaulettes!'

The hunt is on for national volunteers and they all have to flee. Napoleone takes refuge in the seminary with his soldiers.

There is rioting from 8 April to the 13th. Napoleone is everywhere. He organizes resistance, blocks the ways in and out of the city, incites the citadel's garrison to revolt, pulls the wool over Colonel Maillard's eyes, negotiates, and delivers a stream of harangues and orders. 'We shall not relinquish the sword,' he says, whilst adroitly continuing to negotiate with the authorities, since he does not want to appear the cause of the troubles, a rebel.

He rides from post to post, rallying his supporters. On several occasions he orders houses to be fired on, and his men pillage in different parts of the town. Everyone is swept along by this torrent he unleashes and then controls: guiding, curbing or exacerbating it as he pleases until bringing it to a halt.

Then, once a truce has been established, he hastily drafts a report to justify himself.

The words ring out, distorting events, but that doesn't matter; all that matters is to be convincing. 'The inhabitants of Ajaccio are cannibals,' writes Napoleone. 'They have maltreated and assassinated volunteers,' he continues. 'In the terrible crisis in which we found ourselves, what was needed was energy and audacity. It needed a man who, if he was asked after his mission to swear that he had never transgressed any law, would have been able to respond like Cicero or Mirabeau, "I swear that I have saved the Republic!" '

He signs the report without a moment's hesitation. He has discovered that there are successive truths. Writing and telling are also forms of action, which one must know how to mould to the necessities of the moment, how to adapt them to circumstances – but how many people are there who can understand this? 'Spirits are too narrow to rise to the level of high affairs,' Napoleone writes.

HE GOES TO Corte to see Paoli and obtain a new command, but once again Paoli rebuffs him. Napoleone knows that Paoli accuses him of having used his name during the riots.

Back in Ajaccio, Napoleone realizes the depth of the hatred he will encounter from now on. People walk away from him in the street. They are afraid of the volunteers. He is accused of having put the city at risk. Peraldi and Pozzo di Borgo, the Corsican deputies to the Legislative Assembly, slander him constantly. According to them he is 'the bloodthirsty tiger' who mustn't be allowed to 'enjoy his barbarism'.

He laughs disdainfully. Only those who stand out from the crowd are hated. Talk of him having caused another Saint Batholomew does not worry him at all. He reassures his anxious mother, telling her that he will leave the island in mid-May for Paris, to defend himself against Pozzo di Borgo and Peraldi's slurs in the Legislative Assembly, and to secure his rank in the army, since he has been struck off the list on the grounds of 'expired leave'.

These events in Ajaccio have been a revelation. Everything in him has changed. Everything is changing in France. On 20 April 1792, war has been declared against Austria.

He feels in tune with this world in motion.

Nothing will stop him, he is certain of it.

XII

On 28 May 1792, as the afternoon is drawing to a close, Napoleone is slowly walking through the narrow streets of the Tuileries district. He is looking for the Hotel of the Dutch Patriots, in rue Royale-St-Roch. He knows that this is where all the Corsican deputies to the Legislative Assembly stay and he has decided to follow suit.

Joseph is astonished when he discovers his brother's choice of lodgings. Pozzo di Borgo and Peraldi are Buonaparte's adversaries; why would he want to associate with them? There is scorn in Napoleone's voice as he answers, 'One must never run away; one must always go and meet one's enemy head on.'

He has already walked past the hotel entrance twice, but each time the spectacle presented by these streets around the Assembly has kept him outside, on the pavement, transfixed. Not far away, in the Palais-Royal, women are plying their trade the same as ever, but there is more of a scrum of people in the arcades and the crowd is noisier and rowdier than it used to be when he'd steal through these galleries as a shy young eighteen-year-old.

He stops. A fellow standing on a bench is bellowing, 'We're all going to get our throats cut. Monsieur Veto and his Austrian wife are going to surrender Paris to the Brunswick armies. What are the officers doing, the generals? They're betraying us! They're emigrating!'

'Death to the traitors!' shouts a voice.

Napoleone walks on. He passes hordes of National Guard with tricolour cockades pinned to their white lapels. No one pays him any attention. He looks at himself in a window, a short, thin officer in a dark uniform, with a bilious complexion but a proud bearing. He continues on his way, alone, his eyes full of defiance. This indifference is a spur; he will emerge from the shadows.

The longer he walks through those streets, the more this ill-assorted and, for the most part, raucous and tattered crowd exasperates him. Is this the populace of a capital? Who will impose order on this rabble?

In rue St Honoré, he stops outside the Feuillants Convent and the Capuchins church, which, together with the Manege at the end of the Tuileries gardens, now house the Legislative Assembly; this is where the deputies hold their consultations.

Napoleone enters the courtyard of the Feuillants. Here it is, the centre of power. Is this all it amounts to? A mob is chaotically milling about, heckling the deputies as they pass and darting forward to force its way into the chambers. Men with loud voices and threatening gestures denounce the government's incompetence.

'Bring the traitors to trial! Try Monsieur Veto!'

Napoleone is fascinated. How can a regime tolerate this anarchy, this rebellion, this criticism from the street, when a constitution exists that all reasonable people should accept? He moves away, mulling over a thought that he will formulate that evening: 'The people are like waves stirred by the wind. Under a bad impulse, all their passions are unleashed.'

He decides to return to his hotel, and on his way in, he runs into Pozzo di Borgo, who starts when he sees him. Napoleone hesitates, and then greets the deputy. He is a man of influence; people say he is on excellent terms with the minister of war.

Once he is in his room, Napoleone immediately begins a letter to Joseph. He needs to share his impressions. 'I am too expensively lodged,' he writes. 'I'll change hotels tomorrow. Paris is in great convulsions . . .'

He breaks off and goes back outside to look for a hotel where he can live more economically.

NIGHT HAS NOT emptied the streets. Battalions of National Guard are heading towards the Tuileries Palace where the King and his family are in residence. Idle onlookers cheer on the soldiers and call for the disbanding of the Swiss and Royal Guards who are protecting the sovereign.

'They have their pistols trained on the heart of Paris,' someone shouts.

Napoleone carries on walking.

In the narrow little rue du Mail, he comes upon the grey façade of the Hôtel de Metz where Bourrienne, his old schoolfriend from Brienne, is staying. The rooms are reasonable because, as a rule, deputies prefer to lodge as close to the Assembly as possible.

That evening, after supper at the Three Posts, a little hostelry in the rue de Valois, Napoleone quizzes Bourrienne, who has been living in Paris for several months, about everything.

Bourrienne speaks at length and Napoleone only intervenes with the occasional, brief question. Bourrienne is well up on life in the capital. His elder brother, Fauvelet de Bourrienne, owns a furniture storehouse in the Hôtel Longueville where he sells movable property left by the émigrés. Some people have lost everything, while other good citizens are speculating and making fabulous fortunes.

'Why not us?' asks Bourrienne, who's short of money. Napoleone pats his uniform pockets. They laugh like two young fellows of twenty-three who, as they roam the streets, are constantly thinking up schemes to get rich. They could become landlords, rent out apartments, why not?

Suddenly armed men pass. Their pikes gleam in the lamplight. The streets are kept constantly lit, Bourrienne explains, to reassure people and stop them killing one another at every turn.

'Anarchy,' says Napoleone.

He is not laughing any more.

NEXT DAY he moves into room number 14 on the third floor of the Hôtel de Metz. After leaving Bourrienne the night before, he had returned to the Palais-Royal and inhaled the heady fragrances of women.

On 29 May, early in the morning, he goes to the War Office and sets about securing his reinstatement in the army.

He produces testimonials from Rossi, who was in command in Corsica, and affidavits from the directories of Ajaccio and other departments. He explains why he was not present at the review of January 1792. He was serving as second lieutenant-colonel in the National Guard and the troubles that broke out in Ajaccio forced him to stay in Corsica.

He senses that he is getting a sympathetic reception. More than two thirds of all artillery officers have deserted; there is a critical shortage of commissioned and non-commissioned officers.

He is asked questions. Did he used to know Lieutenants Picot de Peccaduc, Phélippeaux, and Des Mazis? All émigrés. The Military School of Paris's register for the year 1784–5 is produced; he sees Laugier de Bellecourt, Castres de Vaux and many other familiar names: all émigrés too.

As he returns each day to the ministry, Napoleone grows convinced that he will recover his commission, but the ministry's clerks and the officers examining his case reveal that he has a stubborn enemy.

Who? A Corsican deputy, who sends letter after letter to the ministry denouncing Lieutenant Buonaparte and his part in the riots in Ajaccio. It is Peraldi.

'That man is an imbecile and more insane than ever,' exclaims Napoleone. 'He has declared war on me! There'll be no quarter now! He is lucky that his elected office renders him inviolable. I would have taught him manners!'

He is reassured: the commission's report to the minister will be favourable; but although he is not overly worried, Napoleone doesn't want to leave anything to chance. He attends the sittings of the Legislative Assembly, makes himself known to the other Corsican deputies and strikes up courteous or amicable relations with them – for he has not renounced the idea of playing an important role on the island one day. France is so divided it is impossible to predict its future; he must keep the Corsican card up his sleeve.

'This country is torn in all directions by the most desperate parties,' Napoleone writes to Joseph. 'It is difficult to grasp the thread of so many different projects. I don't know how it will turn out, but it is taking a very revolutionary turn.'

ON 20 JUNE, Napoleone has arranged to dine with Bourrienne at a tavern in the rue St Honoré, near the Palais-Royal. While he waits for his friend, he watches the lissom women passing under the galleries. The weather is mild.

Bourrienne has hardly sat down, when Napoleone sees a crowd of five or six thousand coming from the direction of the markets, marching towards the Tuileries. He grabs Bourrienne by the arm and drags him up out of his chair: he wants to follow them. They draw closer – a mob of men and women, carrying pikes, axes, swords, muskets, spits and sharpened sticks. When they reach the gates of the Tuileries garden, they falter for a moment, then throw them down and enter the apartments of the King.

Napoleone watches from a distance. He sees the King, the Queen and the Dauphin put on the red cap. After hesitating, the King raises a glass and drinks with the rioters. Buonaparte turns on his heel. He says to Bourrienne, 'The King has lowered himself – and in politics, whoever lowers himself does not pick himself up.'

Then he grows indignant, 'That disorderly crowd, their clothes, their language – that is everything that is most abject about the people.' He grumbles as they walk along. He is an officer, a man of discipline and order. Liberty and equality, certainly – but without descending into anarchy; due respect for hierarchies and authority must be maintained. There have to be leaders. He has been thinking about his experiences during the riots in Ajaccio, he explains: efficacy presupposes that there is someone, a leader, who will take decisions, impose them on others and see that they are carried out.

'The Jacobins are fools without any common sense,' he exclaims. He praises Lafayette whom, sure enough, the Jacobins paint as an assassin, a beggar, and a wretch. The Jacobins' attitude and their language are dangerous, unconstitutional.

LATER, IN HIS room at the Hôtel de Metz, he writes to Joseph. 'It is hard to foresee what will become of the country in such stormy circumstances . . .'.

This is another reason to stay close to Paoli. Perhaps Lucien, their young brother, could be his secretary. As for Joseph, he should try to be elected deputy to the Convention. 'Otherwise you will always play a sorry role in Corsica.' He says it a second time: 'Don't let yourself be trapped: you must be in the next legislature, or you will never cut anything but a sorry figure!'

He hesitates. Then, pressing so hard his quill gouges the paper, he adds, 'Go to Ajaccio, go to Ajaccio to become an elector!' and underlines it.

He stands up. He must choose: this is the first law of politics, and of life; and yet the future is uncertain.

One of the Corsican deputies to the Legislative Assembly has told Napoleone that the director of fortifications, La Varenne, has declared in a report to the military committee of the Assembly that keeping Corsica in the French state is neither possible nor of any real purpose.

Napoleone takes up his quill again and, in that tone of command he always uses with his elder brother, he writes, 'Keep in close relations with General Paoli. He can do everything, is everything and will be everything in the future. In all likelihood this will end with our independence.'

Therefore he must attend to Corsican matters.

He frequents the island's deputies more and more regularly and pays them court. He attends to the family's affairs as well, growing impatient that he hasn't received the necessary papers about the plantation, and then turns to his sister Elisa, who is a boarder at St Cyr. This institution is about to be shut down. What is to be done with this young girl of fifteen? Take her back to Corsica, to the family – which would mean Napoleone having to make the journey as well? How could he get out of it?

He goes to visit Elisa at Versailles and passes battalions of Marseillaise federates who are hollering at the tops of their voices the Army of the Rhine's new marching song, repeating its vengeful chorus, 'To arms, oh citizens!'

'Everything points to violent events,' Napoleone writes, 'and many people are leaving Paris.' The thought doesn't cross his mind personally, apart from to take Elisa to Ajaccio. He keeps calm and alert and observes, like a scientist studying 'a moment of combustion'.

SOMETIMES, going into his room in the Hôtel de Metz, Bourrienne finds him working out calculations, plotting trajectories. He is surprised, and Napoleone shows him the path of the stars he has drawn. 'Astronomy is a fine recreation and a superb science,' he says. 'With my mathematical knowledge it does not take much effort to master it. It is another important attainment.'

He smiles at his companion's astonishment.

He likes to observe and understand, he adds. Astronomy, mathematics: aren't they ultimately more fascinating than human behaviour? 'Those at the top are poor sorts,' he continues. 'It must be admitted, when you see things at first hand, that the people are not worth the trouble taken to win their favour either.'

He uses the same phrases in a letter to his brother Lucien who, at seventeen, is passionate about politics and a harsh judge of Napoleone. He has just written to the eldest brother, Joseph, that 'Napoleone is a dangerous man ... He seems to have strong leanings towards tyranny and I think he would become one even if he was a King, and to posterity and any patriot of feeling his name would be a name of horror ... I think him capable of turning his coat.'

Napoleone doesn't lose his temper when Joseph informs him of the gist of this judgement: Lucien is young. Seventeen years old! He needs to be restrained. 'You know the ways of Ajaccio?' he writes to him:

> Those of Paris are exactly the same. Perhaps men here are even pettier, nastier, more slanderous and more censorious ...
> Everyone seeks his own interests and wants to succeed, whatever the horror and calumny he must peddle; intrigue is as vile as ever. All of which destroys ambition. People pity those who have to play a prominent part, especially when they have a choice; to live quietly and enjoy one's family and one's own life, that, my dear brother, is the life one should lead if one has an income of 4,000 or 5,000 francs and one is between twenty-five and forty, that is to say when one's imagination no longer troubles one.

Words from an elder brother to a younger brother he wants to protect.

But often, in that period from June to August 1792, when Napoleone sees violence running wild in the streets, chaos ruling, and the mob ebbing and flowing, seemingly uncontrollably, he feels a mixture of disgust at anarchy and anxiety at not being able to master this storm where the 'rabble' alone seems to rule.

ON 12 JULY, Napoleone finds at his hotel a letter dated the 10th informing him that the Ministry of War has decided to restore him to his 'employ in the 4th artillery regiment . . . to serve there as captain'.

His reinstatement with this rank takes effect from 6 February, 1792, with arrears of pay.

Napoleone immediately writes to his family, wanting to share his joy with them, and Joseph replies enthusiastically. At twenty-three, a captain of artillery on an annual salary of 1,600 livres! What success! Letizia Buonaparte is beaming with joy, she sends her *omone* her congratulations. He should join his regiment and stay in France.

This is perceptive of her. Napoleone is still hesitating: now he is entered in the lists of the regular army again, why shouldn't he try to act in Corsica once more? After all he is still lieutenant-colonel of a volunteers battalion in Ajaccio!

'If I had consulted only the interests of the family and my inclination,' he writes on Tuesday, 7 August to Joseph, 'I should have come to Corsica, but you are all agreed in thinking that I ought to go to my regiment. So I shall go.'

In the days that follow, he prepares for his departure. His regiment is in action on the frontier, but he cannot join them yet because he has not received his captain's brevet.

He walks about the streets where, at every moment, groups form to discuss the news. The Court is denounced; they accuse it of conspiring with Marshal Brunswick whose Austro-Prussian troops are advancing. Roars go up when a speaker reads out Brunswick's Manifesto to the Parisians. The Marshal promises to deliver Paris 'to military execution and complete destruction, the revolters will be hung if the Parisians do not submit immediately and unconditionally to their King'.

Madness, Napoleone thinks.

The city's 'combustion' is growing fierce. Fights break out between federates from Marseilles who sing the 'Marseillaise' and Parisian National Guards.

IN THE NIGHT OF 9–10 August, Napoleone is startled awake. All Paris's bells are sounding the alarm. He throws on his clothes and rushes out into the street to go to Fauvelet de Bourrienne's, whose shop in the Carrousel, is an ideal vantage point.

On rue des Petits-Champs, he sees a troop of men carrying a head on a spike coming towards him. He is surrounded, jostled. He is dressed like a gentleman. They demand that he shout 'Long live the nation!' He does so, his face drawn.

At Fauvelet de Bourrienne's, he watches events from the window as the insurgents come out onto the place du Carrousel and head towards the Tuileries. He is simply a mesmerized spectator, opposed to 'these groups of hideous men', to this rabble.

He knows he is risking his life, but at the start of the afternoon, when the Tuileries Palace has been overrun and sacked by the rioters and the King has taken refuge in the Assembly, Napoleone enters the gardens and the palace. More than a thousand lie dead in this small space, blocking the stairs and strewn through the rooms. He feels disgust and horror. This is the first battlefield he has been on. The Swiss Guards fought to the bitter end, and then they were massacred.

A few paces away from Napoleone, a native of Marseilles is preparing to kill one of these Swiss.

Napoleone goes up to him.

'Southerner,' he says, 'let's reprieve this poor man.'

'Are you from the South?' asks the federate.

'Yes.'

'Very well, let's spare him.'

Napoleone carries on walking round the gardens and the rooms of the castle. He wants to understand.

'I saw well-dressed women inflict the grossest indecencies on the corpses of the Swiss,' he tells Bourrienne a few hours later. 'The women mutilated the dead soldiers, then brandished their bloody organs. Vile scum.'

He goes into the neighbourhood cafés. All are full of people singing, shouting, raising glasses and congratulating each other. Napoleone senses the hostile stares: he is too calm, his reserve is suspect; he beats a retreat. Everywhere violence and 'rage show on every face', he says. His anger bursts out. 'If Louis XVI had shown himself on horseback,' he tells Bourrienne, 'victory would have been his.'

He despises this *coglione* sovereign who capitulated on 20 June – and has been doing so ever since – instead of sweeping the mob away with the cannon. This King is no soldier. He hasn't given himself the means to reign; disorder and anarchy have triumphed. His opinion of the revolutionary days of 20 June and especially 10 August is that of a man of order, an officer. Whatever the principles he believes in himself, he considers that power cannot be left in the hands of the street, the mob, the rabble. The law must be imposed. Therefore there must be a leader who can take decisions. There must be a man of energy, strength, daring. He can be that man.

On the evening of 10 August, he makes up his mind. He will return to Corsica, rather than rejoin his regiment. It is on the island that he has a chance to distinguish himself. He is nothing here, but over there he is a Buonaparte, a lieutenant-colonel.

The Legislative Assembly has just suspended the King and declared that elections to the National Convention will take place on 2 September. He must fly to Corsica, and urge Joseph on so that finally he can be elected.

'Events are hurrying apace,' he writes at the end of August to his uncle Peravicini. 'Let our enemies talk, your nephews love you and they will be able to carve out a place for themselves.'

FIRST HOWEVER, he must take his sister Elisa out of St Cyr. He busies himself all day on 1 September, as bands begin appearing on the streets of Paris, railing against an aristocrats' conspiracy, demanding punishment for the 'plotters' who are crowding the prisons and hoping for the arrival of Brunswick troops to avenge them and slit the patriots' throats. As the day comes to an end, at last Napoleone is able to help his sister into a shabby hackney carriage.

Then everyone has to go into hiding as the alarm sounds and the news spreads that Verdun has surrendered to the Austro-Prussian armies; the enemy is going to enter Paris and subject the city to 'complete destruction'.

Crowds mass outside the prisons, force the gates, summarily try the prisoners and then massacre them. The rabble seems to have broken loose from all control. It is whispered that Danton is letting the revenge-seekers have their heads. Robespierre is nowhere to be seen. The prisons and streets are in the hands of '*massacreurs*', whipped into a frenzy by Marat with his articles and posters.

On the 5th, the killing stops, and on 9 September, Napoleone can at last leave Paris with his sister. In the diligence and then on the boat down the Rhône, he senses the fear of his fellow passengers, some of whom are fleeing Paris, and say as much in veiled terms.

In Valence, he pays a visit to Mademoiselle Bou, who tells him that there have been massacres all along the valley as well. Then, a few hours later, Napoleone and Elisa set off again with a basket of grapes which Mademoiselle Bou has given them. It is the end of September when they reach Marseilles.

Just as they are entering their inn, some men and women start shouting and crowding round them. With the feathers in her hat, Elisa looks like a young girl of the nobility.

'Death to all aristocrats,' the shout goes up. Anything can happen.

Napoleone tears off his sister's hat and tosses it into the crowd.

'We're no more aristocrats than you are,' he yells.

Applause rings out.

That same evening, he enquires after a boat bound for Ajaccio, but he has to wait until 10 October before setting sail from Toulon. By then he has heard that his brother has not been elected to the Convention. Joseph received only 64 votes out of a possible 398, and in the second round he didn't get a single one. Bad news. He has also learnt that the monarchy has been abolished and the Republic declared by the Convention on 21 September, 1792. The day before that, the French army of which Napoleone is an officer carried the day at Valmy under the command of Kellermann and Dumouriez, and while he is at sea, the Prussians evacuate Verdun on 14 October.

He has played no part in any of the events that, according to Goethe, 'initiate a new era in the history of the world'.

On 15 October, he lands at Ajaccio with Elisa, and, seeing his family gathered on the dock, Napoleone is happy.

But it is far away to the north, on the border at Valmy, that glory has brushed the army with her wing.

What can he do here, on this island?

XIII

HE WATCHES HIS MOTHER in the main room of the family house. She seems to have grown heavier, but she is as animated as ever and, on that evening at the end of October 1792, she is radiant. She goes from one child to the next. She often stops in front of Elisa, whom she still calls Marianna. She gives her a kiss, and then goes over to Napoleone and caresses his cheek with her fingertips.

This is the first time in so long, she says, that all her children have been together at home. A moment of peace and happiness like this must be enjoyed to the full.

He gets to his feet and moves away from the group.

For several days now he has been waiting for a sign from Paoli. Is *Il Babbo* going to leave him idle? Napoleone wrote to him on 18 October, declaring that he was coming to resume his post as second lieutenant-colonel of the volunteers' battalion, but there has been no reply from Corte where Paoli resides – with his Court around him, Lucien adds, bitterly. Paoli did not want that *giovanotto* as a secretary.

'He has no love for us,' Lucien tells his elder brothers. Napoleone has returned from France with another stripe. 'That makes you too French for Paoli, and therefore suspect,' Lucien continues. 'He fears us.'

Napoleone has persisted nonetheless, and has also informed his battalion's companies garrisoned at Corte and Bonifacio that he will join them. 'From now on I will be there and everything will go as it should.' He is going 'to put everything in order'.

He has had no reply. He waits. He cannot break with Paoli, who holds all the power in Corsica and enjoys the support of the peasantry, the majority of the population. So, despite his family's happiness, his mother's joy and her manifest gratitude to him, he is growing impatient in that house in Ajaccio.

It is pouring with rain; he opens the door, goes out into the garden and comes back several minutes later, his hair stuck to his face, his uniform soaked. His mother goes up to him but he brushes her aside and starts talking.

'There's the Indies,' he says. 'Out there they need artillery officers. They pay well.' He could serve under the English in Bengal, or else organize the artillery of the Hindu resistance. The camp doesn't matter. What is he doing here except wasting his life away? His comrades have marched into Mayence, Frankfurt. He cannot tolerate this inaction, when the world is on the move: France is victorious and he could have been a part of the conquering Army of the Sambre and Meuse, but he has not rejoined his regiment. He has come here, to Corsica, where everyone refuses to employ him.

He will go to the Indies. 'Artillery officers are in short supply everywhere,' he says, 'and if I should choose this course, I hope that you will hear tell of me.'

He clasps his mother to him. This display of tenderness is unusual for him. Most of the time he is on his guard, and Letizia Buonaparte is surprised by this impulsive gesture, this sensitivity suddenly finding expression.

'I will return from the Indies in several years,' Napoleone whispers.' I shall be as rich as a nabob and will bring you fine dowries for my three sisters.'

Lucien protests that Napoleone's must indeed be a demanding nature if he isn't content with being made a captain at twenty-two.

'Ah, you are too kind if you imagine that my promotion – which has certainly been rapid, I admit – stems from any merit I may or may not possess. Napoleone shrugs his shoulders. The reason I am a captain, you know as well as I, is because all the senior officers of the La Fère regiment are émigrés. You will see now how long I will be left a captain. I was close enough to the heart of it over there, in Paris, to know that one gets nowhere without influential supporters – women, especially; they are the true and powerful machinery of patronage, and I, as you know, am not their type. One is not pleasing to them if one cannot pay them court, and that is what I have never known how to do and probably never will.'

'He won't leave,' Letizia says simply.

But suddenly, in a brutal voice, Napoleone declares, 'I'm going to Corte.'

HE SETS OFF the next day on horseback across the Gravone valley.

When he reaches Bocognano, the peasants and shepherds welcome him with open arms. They are loyal men, and their respect and the marks of affection and devotion shown him on all sides calm Napoleone and strengthen him in his resolve. He will wrest from Paoli the command which is his by right. He will not let himself be cast aside.

Some of the shepherds from Bocognano accompany him until the walls of Corte come into view. Again they tell him that they are ready to die for him, a Buonaparte. He needs them, he says. He will remember their friendship for ever.

This is what being a leader is: building up a clan around oneself, drawing men together, binding them to you and rewarding them for it.

He is learning.

PAOLI REIGNS in Corte; Pozzo di Borgo is his close adviser and he has appointed his cousin Colonna-Cesari as commander of the army. Napoleone insists on an audience with, as he calls him, 'General' Paoli.

But Paoli makes him wait.

Every day Napoleone visits the companies of volunteers who are billeted around Corte. These men greet him joyfully but Paoli's circle lets him know that they have no need for another lieutenant-colonel. First Lieutenant-Colonel Quenza is there already. What use would Buonaparte be?

Napoleone listens. He goes for long walks alone through Corte's narrow streets and remembers all the mortifications, the rebuffs he has accepted from Pascal Paoli. When the Convention has just solemnly declared 'that it will extend fraternity and assistance to all peoples who wish to recover their liberty', when Dumouriez's troops have just won the great victory of Jemappes over the Austrians and occupy Belgium, must he remain in Paoli's shadow?

Other Corsicans – members of the Convention, Saliceti, Chiappe and Casabianca – have chosen to be overtly on the side of France and the Republic. Napoleone, and the Buonaparte clan in general, have always been on friendly terms with them, especially with Saliceti. So why continue under Paoli?

'Paoli and Pozzo di Borgo are a faction,' Napoleone tells Joseph in confidence. When his brother reacts cautiously, he adds, 'An anti-national faction.'

In his battalion's quarters, when the volunteers gather around him, Napoleone delivers rousing speeches extolling the armies of the Republic: 'Our men are not sleeping,' he says. 'Savoy and the Comté of Nice have been taken.'

He looks at each volunteer in turn and repeats, '*Our* men.' The French, in other words. Then, pausing for impact, taking a step back, he adds, 'Sardinia will soon be attacked.'

The volunteers raise their weapons.

'The soldiers of liberty will always triumph over the hired slaves of a few tyrants,' he concludes.

The words have come out naturally, brooking no caution, welling up after months of hesitation and reflection, and having made this choice, Napoleone feels liberated. He brushes past Paoli's entourage and finally manages to come face to face with the figure whom he now thinks of as an old man requiring no special precautions. He is simply an obstacle, which he can continue using as a shield or overcome. He just has to choose his moment.

Napoleone addresses him forcefully, and so sharply that some of Paoli's inner circle start to mutter amongst themselves.

He lays out his demands. He wants his command, he is entitled to it. The Corsicans must intervene in the Republic's war. If his requests are refused, he concludes, he will leave and write to Paris from Ajaccio to denounce the delays, petty annoyances, not to say treachery of an anti-national faction.

Paoli listens, his eyes half-closed, and then in a calm, firm voice, says simply, 'You can leave, if you wish.'

PAOLI CONTROLS Corsica. This is all Napoleone can think on the way back to Ajaccio and in the weeks that follow. His hold on power must be broken and, for that, Napoleone must become still more French.

In the house on rue St Charles, he entertains Admiral Truguet, a young and brilliant officer who is in command of the flotilla that has been assembled for the attack on Sardinia. There is dancing and the Admiral pays court to Elisa, and completely turns the heads of Pauline and Caroline.

Then comes Huguet de Sémonville, a diplomat on his way to Constantinople who, during his stay in Ajaccio, co-hosts the parties given by the Buonapartes. He also speaks to the city's patriotic club, and Lucien, with an authority belying his eighteen years, acts as his interpreter and soon his secretary. Napoleone even offers Sémonville and his family one of their country houses in Ucciani.

He shows his guests around Ajaccio, but he senses the population's hostility, because the Buonaparte clan is becoming the French clan.

When, in December, sailors from Truguet's fleet and recently arrived volunteers from Marseilles provoke fights with the Corsican volunteers in Ajaccio and kill some of them, Napoleone denounces the aggressors: 'These Marseillais are anarchists who spread terror wherever they go, who ceaselessly hunt for aristocrats or priests and thirst for blood.'

But whatever he says, he knows that from now on, in the eyes of Corsicans, he is the one who has chosen France. He has to see this thing through now.

HE CORRESPONDS with Saliceti who has just voted in the Convention for the King's death, and at the same time realizes how serious a breach this sentence has opened between the majority of Corsicans and France.

He is told of Paoli's speech condemning Louis XVI's death. 'We do not want to be the executioners of kings,' *Il Babbo* has declared. Pozzo di Borgo is at his side, advocating with great skill an alliance with England.

'The King of England funded Paoli for years,' Lucien tells Napoleone. 'He is still in his pay.'

Napoleone is more measured, but on 1 February 1793, the

Convention declares war on England and Paoli, the former exile in London, only becomes more suspect.

One evening, later that month, Napoleone confides in a low voice to Huguet de Sémonville. 'I have thought carefully about our situation,' he says. 'No doubt the Convention has committed a great crime in executing the King and I deplore it more than anyone, but, whatever happens, Corsica must always remain united with France. It cannot exist except on these terms. I and those around me, I give you fair warning, will defend the cause of that union.'

THREE DAYS LATER, Napoleone is in Bonifacio. His volunteer battalion has regrouped there to launch a raid against the isles of La Maddalena, which belong to Sardinia and command the channel between it and Corsica. Admiral Truguet's flotilla has set sail with the federates from Marseilles and is heading for Cagliari, the Sardinian capital. The attack on La Maddalena will serve as a diversion.

Napoleone is simultaneously calm and in a fever of anticipation. At last he is going to fight. Several times a day, he walks to the end of Bonifacio's promontory. From there he can see the greyish coasts of Sardinia. Then, returning to the house he occupies in rue Pizzalonga, he summons a former clerk of the court and dictates his orders to him in short, trenchant sentences. He makes sure he sees all reports and examines them in detail. He wants discipline, regularity and precision, he says. He wants to supervise everything in person.

Very early each morning, he washes with a sponge and cold water, dries himself vigorously, and then dresses with care, taking pains to ensure that his uniform is clean and beyond reproach. 'One only fights well with clean men and clean uniforms,' he says, but around him, despite his orders, slovenliness is the rule. Watching his men he wonders: how many of them truly want to fight?

WHEN HE LANDS from *La Fauvette* on the little island of Santo Stefano, he immediately establishes a battery of two of his four guns and the mortar. He starts to bombard the town of La Maddalena, but his soldiers are inexperienced and frightened, and the commander of the expedition, Colonna-Cesari, Paoli's man, has been ordered by Paoli not to attack 'our Sardinian brothers'. The crew of La Fauvette mutiny and want to return to Bonifacio. In the south, in Cagliari, the volunteers from Marseilles have fled the minute the firing began.

Biting his lips with rage, Napoleone is forced to evacuate his position and scuttle his cannon which the sailors refuse to take on board.

On the bridge of La Fauvette, he keeps a scornful distance from his fellow officers. It feels as if every day he is losing another of his illusions: about Corsica, about men, about Paoli. 'So much perfidy enters the human heart, and this fatal ambition leads an old man of seventy-eight astray,' he says of the man whom he has so admired.

Shortly after landing at Bonifacio, as he is walking through Doria Square, sailors from La Fauvette mob him, shouting, 'String up the aristocrats' and intending to kill him. He defends himself, and then volunteers from Bocognano rush up, set about the sailors and send them packing.

This is what men are, even those who declare themselves patriots and revolutionaries. So little can be expected of the majority!

HOWEVER, does to be relieved of his naive beliefs in this way does give Napoleone a feeling of liberty and strength. He can count only on himself. He must act only for himself. Men are only worthwhile in so far as they are his supporters, his allies. The rest are enemies who must either be won over to his cause, persuaded to change their views, or crushed.

As soon as he gets back to Ajaccio, Napoleone starts writing, drafting a protest against the manner in which Colonna-Cesari conducted the expedition against La Maddalena – which is a way of attacking Pascal Paoli, since Colonna-Cesari is his liege man. Then he suddenly learns that the Convention has dispatched to Corsica three commissioners with unlimited powers, of whom Saliceti is one, and that they have landed at Bastia on 5 April. Napoleone prepares to join them, since their appointment is a show of no confidence in Paoli.

But the breach is not yet complete.

He puts Saliceti on his guard: 'Paoli bears kindness and gentleness on his face, and hatred and vengeance in his heart. He has the unction of human feeling in his eyes, and gall in his soul.'

Negotiations begin. Napoleone counsels caution and Saliceti agrees. Paoli is still master of the island and the Corsicans remain loyal to him. They must play a clever game.

Napoleone observes and listens to Saliceti. He learns the art of the ruse, of the political manoeuvre such as he has already attempted in Ajaccio, the year before. Saliceti is a master who goes to Corte and engages Paoli in long conversations. Napoleone admires his unwitting teacher. Then, on 18 April, as negotiations are continuing, news spreads through Corsica from town to town and from village to village.

NAPOLEONE is in the family house on rue St Charles, when one of his supporters puts two documents in front of him. The first is a copy of a decree by the National Convention ordering the arrest of Pascal Paoli and Pozzo di Borgo. The decree is dated 2 April 1793. On the day before, Dumouriez had defected to the enemy. In Paoli's case, the Convention is not waiting to see who will make the first move.

The second document is a copy of a letter that Pozzo di Borgo's men are circulating around Corsica.

Napoleone reads it several times. The letter is signed by Lucien Buonaparte, who has been living in Toulon for the past few weeks, having followed Huguet de Sémonville there, and is addressed to Joseph and Napoleone. It has been intercepted by Paoli's men and is being used to destroy Napoleone's reputation once and for all.

'Following an address from the city of Toulon, proposed and drawn up by myself in the council of the club,' Lucien Buonaparte has written, 'the Convention has decreed that Paoli and Pozzo di Borgo be arrested. Thus I have delivered a decisive blow to our enemies. The newspapers will already have informed you of this news. You cannot have been expecting it. I am impatient to know what will become of Paoli and Pozzo di Borgo.'

Napoleone closes his eyes. This letter and the Convention's decree mean open war with Paoli – and thus between Corsica and the Republic – and exile and ruin for the Buonapartes. And all of it without Napoleone having had a chance to prepare his future. His eighteen-year-old brother has decided to intervene with all the insolence and posturing of a *bricconcelle*, a good-for-nothing.

Napoleone calls his mother and reads the two documents to her. 'If Archdeacon Lucien was still alive,' he says, 'his heart would bleed at the threat to his sheep and goats and cattle and his prudent nature would seek to avert the storm.' Therefore he is going to try to delay Paoli's vengeance, he explains. He goes to Ajaccio's club and draws up an adresss to the Convention demanding the Assembly revoke its decree.

But he knows it is too late.

In Corte, the Corsican delegates gathered around Paoli denounce the Buonapartes, 'born in the mire of despotism, nursed and raised under the gaze and at the expense of a generous governor who commanded the island ... Let the Buonapartes be abandoned to their inmost remorse and public opinion which has damned them now and forever to perpetual execration and infamy.'

Napoleone does not imagine for a single moment that his adversaries will stop at these shows of contempt. He tells his mother, '*Preparatevi, questo paese non è per noi.*' Get ready to leave, this country is not for us.

BUT HE MUST try everything first: attempt to seize the citadel of Ajaccio and then, with Saliceti, take the city and stir France's supporters to rise up.

It is all in vain; no one budges. Finding himself in the Capiteu Tower, at the tip of the Bay of Ajaccio, where he has taken refuge with a few men, Napoleone looks down on the city of his birth. He knows that this is the end of a part of his life. He is going to be twenty-four, and from now on his destiny can only be bound up with France: his family have no other means than his captain's wage. Joseph and Lucien will only be able to find a job in France, perhaps with Saliceti's help.

This is where his Corsican illusion comes an end.

'Everything has given way here, my presence is useless,' he tells Saliceti. 'I must leave this country.'

Throughout May and the start of June 1793, he will resist, however, and elude his pursuers. Unable to catch him, Paoli's men turn on Letizia Buonaparte and her young children.

When he learns that his mother has had to go into hiding to escape the Paolist bands who have ransacked, looted and burned their family house, Napoleone does not make a gesture or say a word; anger seems to have turned him to stone. Later he will say that Paoli is a traitor, and that the Corsicans are rebels, counter-revolutionaries, like the Vendeans who have been in revolt against the Republic since March.

This family house in flames – this is his Corsican past turning to ashes. He is French. He can no longer be anything but that.

SOME CORSICANS arrest him, lock him in a house in Bocognano and prepare to take him to Corte to be tried and sentenced, but loyal shepherds help him escape through a window. He has never experienced this before. He slips through lanes at night, evades his pursuers. He hides in a cave, then in a house in Ajaccio which is searched by the gendarmes.

He is imperturbable. He never loses his composure. This is what politics and war are: men whom one flatters or fights against, whom one buys or kills. He reassures the shepherds from Bocognano who escort and protect him. He will never forget, he says, as they head for the coast to pick up the French ship which is carrying Paris's envoys.

On 31 May, when the commissioners' ship, with Napoleone and Joseph on board, sails into the Bay of Ajaccio, a group of fugitives signals to it from the shore. Napoleone goes to the prow, then leaps into a launch, taking Joseph with him. They land on the beach and rush to Letizia Buonaparte and her children, who have walked all night through the maquis to escape Pascal Paoli's men. Napoleone helps them into the boat one by one. His mother does not utter a word of complaint.

The ship takes them to Calvi, where Napoleone decides to ask his godfather Giubega to put them up. Then he sets off again as soon as his family is settled, and returns to Bastia with the commissioners. He is agitated and fretful. The French only retain control of three towns in Corsica – Calvi, Bastia and San Fiorenzo.

Can he leave his mother, his brothers and his sisters on the island at the mercy of their enemies?

On 10 June he sets out from Bastia alone, on horseback, to rejoin them and put them aboard a ship bound for Toulon. For several days he rides an emaciated, broken-winded old mount which, nonetheless, instinctively knows the dangers of these paths that snake along the mountainsides, barely distinguishable amongst the thick scrub.

He inhales the scents of the Corsican countryside, which have so often made him nostalgic and which, each time he has returned to the island, have filled him with such ardour and joy.

This has come to an end too, he knows. His destiny is elsewhere – in France, his homeland from now on, his nation. He has reverted to the choice his father made on his behalf. He has not been offered any other. To live, he must break away.

He must break with Corsica.

On 11 June 1793, Napoleone Buonaparte and his family embark for Toulon.

PART FOUR

Better to be the one that eats than
the one that is eaten

XIV

IN THE DISTANCE, out at sea in the bay of Toulon, the cannon
boom.

Napoleone leans out of the door of the carriage which is driving
slowly through the olive groves.

That morning of 20 June 1793 has the luminous brilliance of a
summer's day, but the air is thinner, there is more of a tang in it.

He makes out, between the dark massifs that hang over the
roads of Toulon, the silhouettes of ships with their periodic crowns
of white smoke as a cannon is fired. They are shelling Toulon's
forts.

'It is the Spaniards,' says a fellow traveller. He tells how, since
the Marseillais rose up against the Convention, Spanish boats have
been waiting in the bay, ready to land troops to come to the
rebels' aid. The entire Rhône valley is at war with Paris. Avignon,
Nîmes, and even Marvejols and Mende, are in the hands of the
federates and royalists. Since the Convention decided to arrest
the Girondist deputies, Vergniaud, Brissot and Roland, on 2 June,
uprisings have broken out everywhere – not just in Provence, but
also in Bordeaux, in Normandy, and in La Vendée of course,
where the rebels have chosen as head of 'the Catholic and royal
army' a former pedlar called Cathelineau. The Mountain and the
Jacobins are going to have the utmost difficulty regaining control
of the country.

Napoleone has shut his eyes.

He is thinking of his mother and the brothers and sisters he
has left in a little house in the village of La Valette, at the gates
of Toulon. He has since been told that this town is a hotbed of
royalists and aristocrats and the English fleet is cruising a few
cables off the coast, just waiting for a signal to enter the roads.
Perhaps they will have to flee again, range further afield.

Before setting out for Nice to rejoin the 4th artillery regiment's
five companies that are garrisoned there, Napoleone had tried to
reassure his mother.

She had barely looked up from the stove. Jerome and Louis were chopping wood. Elisa and Pauline had gone to the fountain to fetch water and wash linen. In the week he had spent with his family, Napoleone had obtained financial assistance and bread rations from the authorities at Brignolles and St Maximin. The Buonapartes, he told all and sundry, are patriotic refugees, exiled from their country by the yoke of the English and their accomplices.

He had explained to his mother that she wouldn't have to live in those wretched conditions for long. Joseph and Lucien were going to speak to Saliceti, representative on detached service in Provence with the revolutionary army that was charged with fighting the Girondist federates and nobles. As for him, he should get back pay at Nice of almost three thousand livres, and he should receive his brevet of captain with command of an artillery company.

He has left La Valette, but he is still worried. What if Toulon falls into the hands of the royalists, if the the English enter the roads, if the armies of the Republic don't take Provence and the whole country in hand, what fate will await his family? And him, what destiny?

The Convention must succeed; the Republic must be victorious.

AFTER A FEW DAYS spent in Nice, Napoleone is even more determined to array himself wholly on the side of the Convention.

He says so to the general of artillery of the Army of Italy, Jean du Teil, the brother of the marshal of the camp whom Napoleone knew at Auxonne and Valence.

'An officer at the nation's service,' is all du Teil replies.

Napoleone is enthusiastic when du Teil puts him in command of the coastal batteries, and is quick to make thorough inspections of each position. On 3 July, he writes to the minister of war requesting a model of a reverberating furnace for forging cannon-balls 'so that we shall be in a position to have them constructed on our coasts and burn the ships of the despots'.

He signs himself Bonaparte.

He has no recollection of any hesitancy any more, as if all the thoughts, all the plans that had pointed him towards Corsica had never existed. This 24-year-old captain is now Napoleon Bonaparte, French, Republican, a supporter of the Mountain and the Convention against all those who would endanger the unity of the Republic. He admits that heads are rolling, that 'Doctor Guillotine's machine' carries out its duties every day. The King was beheaded on 21 January 1793. The Mountain governs. 'The Terror' is underway. Bonaparte accepts this. He has made his choice: the only choice that allows him to imagine his future as open, there to be made his own.

SEVERAL DAYS later, he crosses the Provençal countryside again.

He rides alone under an already scorching July sun. He loves this dry heat, these colours, broom here, lavender there, and the ochre villages perched on hilltops. He is going to Avignon to organize, on General du Teil's orders, convoys of powder and material destined for the Army of Italy.

But his horse keeps rearing. There's shooting in the countryside, and soon he hears the rumble of cannon, but only a few guns. Avignon is in the hands of the Marseillais federates and it is holding out against General Carteaux's Revolutionary army.

Napoleon rides through the billets of an army which is more than four thousand strong. He recognizes a Côte d'Or regiment, the Allobroges dragoons, a Mont-Blanc battalion, and then suddenly he sees a familiar face.

Captain Dommartin, who is in command of a company of artillery, was promoted to second lieutenant in the same year, 1785, as Napoleon; he came 36th, Napoleon only managing 42nd. They embrace one another.

Listening to Dommartin, Napoleon is overcome by a wave of discouragement. He would like to fight like Dommartin, and yet all he is is an officer in charge of arranging a convoy of powder! 'A fine job that is,' he curses, growing more and more impatient.

When the army moves off after Carteaux's troops enter Avignon, and he watches Dommartin go by 'in the finest military carriage you can imagine', he rebels against himself. He cannot accept this situation. Nor should he.

HE HAS STAYED on in Avignon to organize his convoy. Wretched convoy!

Sometimes he goes to Beaucaire and listens to the merchants' conversations in the cafés around the fairground, as they discuss the situation in the south. He is desperate for an idea! How is he going to get out of this impasse in which he feels he is trapped?

When he hears that the French garrison in Mayence has been forced to surrender to the enemy, he immediately takes up his pen and addresses to the citizen minister a request to be transferred to the Army of the Rhine with the rank of lieutenant-colonel. He must go where there is danger; to shape his destiny, all his actions must be forceful and for all to see. The minister should consider it the 'offer of a patriot'.

A patriot: that is what he must be. Since he finds himself in a particular camp, he must proclaim his loyalty to it and do everything in his power to ensure it is victorious. 'If one must belong to a party, sooner it were one that triumphs, better be the one that eats than the one that is eaten.'

The minister is slow to respond, however, and Napoleon is bored to tears in Avignon, waiting for delivery of the guns and munitions he must take to Nice.

How can he force his way in, make it known that he exists, that he is a resolute supporter of government and that he can be singled out for distinction and promoted? What if he writes something? That could be the way to emerge from the shadows.

Napoleon sits down at his desk and writes in the heat of night at the end of that Avignon July. His quill moves faster than usual, the writing is terse, emphatic.

First the title; that comes to him immediately: *Supper at Beaucaire, or the dialogue between a soldier of Carteaux's army, a Marseillais, a Nîmois and a manufacturer from Montpellier, on the events which have taken place in the former Comtat at the arrival of the Marseillais*. Then follow twenty pages in favour of the Convention, against the federate insurrection. He invents a conversation which allows him to put into the mouth of the Marseillais, who supports the revolt, arguments which the soldier can then refute.

'Don't you realize that the struggle between patriots and despots is a fight to the death?' he asks.

He reasons dispassionately. At times the writing catches fire, but it remains an analytical tool. Point by point, Napoleon proves that the revolutionary forces are going to crush the rebels and that, good or bad, the latter's intentions are of no relevance.

'It is no use playing with words any more, one must analyse actions.' And it is not enough to wave the tricolour. Didn't Paoli brandish it in Corsica when he 'was dragging his compatriots into his ambitious and criminal undertakings'? Napoleon sums up in a firm hand, 'The centre of unity is the Convention; this is the true sovereign, all the more so when the people finds itself split.'

He rereads it and then, without even having slept, as soon as it is dawn, he takes the manuscript to the printer Sabin Tournal, who publishes the *Avignon Courier*. He puts it on the printer's desk and Tournal picks it up and glances through it. He is a patriot. He will print it in the same typeface and on the same paper as the newspaper.

'Who is paying for this?' he asks.

Napoleon takes out some coins.

'I am.'

Tournal makes a note on the original: 'At the author's expense.'

Napoleon agrees. One has to know how to stake a bet. He wants the proofs by the end of that afternoon, 29 July 1793. He will personally send them to the representatives of the people attached to Carteaux's army, Saliceti and Gasparin.

A FEW DAYS later, there is a knock on the door of the hotel where Napoleon is staying.

He opens it. A soldier hands him a package containing a dozen pamphlets entitled simply *The Supper at Beaucaire*, published by the army's printer, Marc Aurel.

The soldier explains that the troops are distributing these pamphlets in their march.

Napoleon knows he has gained a victory. He is no longer just a simple artillery captain charged with convoying barrels of powder and material to Nice. He has acted on the political stage – politics, as he discovered in Corsica, is the great spring setting the fates of men in motion.

And whoever wishes to advance must take sides. He has chosen to be against the factions, and for 'the centre of unity that is the Convention'.

It is not a question of ideas, but the fruit of a conviction, forged as much by the tragic spectacle in Paris of 10 August 1792 as by the experience he gained in Ajaccio. Power must be *one*. The Convention is this power. It is what is conducting the war.

I am with this power.

AT THE START of September 1793, Napoleon has finally assembled the munitions and material. He writes repeatedly to the administrators in Vaucluse, requesting six waggons for their transport. The Army of Italy, he says, needs powder to fight 'the tyrant of Turin'.

He is kept waiting. Carteaux's army, which liberated Marseilles on 25 August, is living off requisitioning, since Toulon, where the royalists and Marseillais federates have taken refuge, has delivered its roads to English and Spanish ships.

Napoleon chafes at the delay. His brother Joseph has been made a war commissary with Carteaux's army by Saliceti. Lucien has been appointed an army storekeeper at St Maximin. Perhaps they can help him find the transport he is lacking.

On September 16 he goes to the headquarters of Carteaux's army, which have been established in Beausset.

THE OFFICERS have taken over several houses in the little market town. As Napoleon goes from one to the next, he hears someone calling him; it is Saliceti, who is accompanied by Gasparin, another representative on detached service like him.

'*The Supper at Beaucaire* . . .' Saliceti begins. Then he breaks off and takes Gasparin to one side. They exchange a few words and Saliceti turns towards Napoleon.

'Captain Dommartin, who was commanding one of the companies of artillery, has been wounded in the shoulder and evacuated to Marseilles. We need a trained officer.'

Gasparin cuts in. 'The English must be driven out of Toulon at all costs,' he explains.

'Before, when I'd wait for the boat to Corsica,' Napoleon says, 'I used to study the town's fortifications. I haven't forgotten anything.'

On a corner of the desk, Saliceti composes the order which attaches artillery captain Napoleon Bonaparte to Carteaux's army at the siege of Toulon.

Then he writes the date, 16 September 1793.

At last, for the first time I am going to show on French soil who I am.

XV

IT IS GETTING DARK. Napoleon is standing, with his arms crossed, in the doorway of the house which is going to be his quarters and watching the soldiers around him nonchalantly going about their work. Some of them, unarmed, are returning from the nearby orchards. They are carrying baskets of fruit, their arms round each other's shoulders, and their lips are stained with figs and grape juice. Others, further off, are making bivouac fires, tossing the doors and window frames of the farmhouses they have looted into the flames. A group of tattered men, also unarmed, are settling down for the night, stuffing barrels with straw and then squeezing into them.

This! An army?

Napoleon would like to grab each of these soldiers by the lapels and shake them and shout that this is not how one wages war! He is sure he knows how it should be done. It's only been a few hours since Saliceti and Gasparin put him in command of the artillery — but what does that matter. He knows. He doesn't feel a shred of doubt. He knows — and he has to know, because this is where he must succeed.

He hears laughter from the house opposite. Through the window he can see the large candlesticks on the table. This is where General Carteaux is quartered with his wife. The general is giving his officers dinner.

Napoleon had seen him earlier in the day.

'I am a sans-culotte general,' Carteaux announced, looking about him with an assured air. He stroked his long black moustache and tilted his head back; he cut a haughty figure, with his blue frock coat. Looking Napoleon up and down with a mixture of contempt and suspicion, he spoke of Captain Dommartin. 'It is a great loss for me,' he said, 'to be deprived of his talents.'

Then he added that he would take all the forts of Toulon, held by 'these English, these Spaniards, these Neapolitans, these Sicilians, these aristocrats', by the bayonet.

Napoleon listened in silence. 'He is an ignoramus, this general,' he thought, and declined his invitation to dinner.

He has other matters to attend to: war. His war. He is not going to have dinner, or sleep. Until Toulon has fallen, nothing counts except war, nothing.

He hails a soldier who doesn't know where the artillery park is. Eventually Napoleon discovers the six cannon which comprise it. The sergeant in charge has neither ammunition nor tools.

This! An artillery?

Napoleon walks away. So, these are the cards he has to play with: an indisciplined army, a non-existent artillery, an incompetent and suspicious general whose sole source of pride is having persuaded his fellow gendarmes on 10 August 1792 to join the people ('The rabble,' Napoleon murmurs), a general who, for years, has done nothing but paint little pictures!

And this is the game in which his life is at stake!

But that is how it is.

IT'S DRIZZLING and there's a cold wind blowing as Napoleon climbs a path up to one of the hilltops from which one can see the roadsteads and forts of Toulon. He will wait for dawn up there. This first night has been a night of resolutions.

When the sun finally rises, stripping away the last of the low cloud, he is soaked to the skin, but he sees all the forts dominating the roadsteads which are occupied by the English and their allies. He sees Fort La Malgue, the large tower and forts of Balaguier and Malbousquet, and others.

His gaze comes to rest on the one which has lodged itself in his memory. Fort de L'Eguillette commands the narrow channel between the larger and smaller roadstead.

It is the key.

Napoleon is sure of himself. It is as if nothing existed in him any more except this certainty. This fort must be taken, and everything must be organized so it can be. Under fire from L'Eguillette's cannon, the enemy ships will be forced to leave the roadsteads and Toulon will fall.

The sun is hot when Napoleon goes back down the hill.

The goal has been set and he has become calm. All that is

needed now is for people and circumstances to bend to fit the goal, and for the obstacles that oppose this design to be overcome. If anyone doesn't understand the plan, don't let them be involved — that should suffice.

He goes to see Saliceti and Gasparin, who have only just woken up. He strides into the room and begins, 'Every operation must follow a system, not chance.' Then, turning to the window and jerking his chin towards General Carteaux's house, he adds 'It is the artillery that takes fortresses, the infantry does no more than help.' In a few sentences spoken in a calm voice but charged with a body's entire nervous energy, he outlines his plan.

'An orthodox siege of Toulon is impossible. The city is impregnable to frontal attack. The allies' ships must be driven out of the roadsteads and for that they must be brought under artillery fire, bombarded with red-hot cannonballs that will set the sails and hulls on fire and blow up the holds. And for that,' Napoleon stretches out his arm as if they could see the fort, the key to the whole plan, 'and for that L'Eguillette must be taken. Storm L'Eguillete and you will be in Toulon within a week.'

In the doorway as he is leaving, he enjoins, 'Do your job, citizen representatives, and let me do mine.'

HE DOESN'T SLEEP, he barely eats, but the activity sustains him and the certainty of being right is an inexhaustible source of energy. The feeling one can change things and people is a spring that winds tighter with each success.

He organizes.

Every day I need a thousand bags to fill with sand. I need an arsenal with twenty-four smiths. I need wood and pile. I need oxen and other draught animals.

Let Marseilles, Nice, La Ciotat and Montpellier provide me with what I need.

A battery must be erected here, another there. This one will be called the battery of the Convention, that one the Sans-Culotte battery.

Napoleon stands on the parapet of one of the batteries that the English General O'Hara's cannon are concentrating their fire on. The cannonballs fall thick and fast. Napoleon does not bat an eyelid. 'Watch out,' he says simply, 'there's a shell coming.'

The men around him hesitate to run away, to protect themselves. A roundshot whistles past.

I am not moving. Nothing can hit me. There is something driving me forwards. How could my path come to an end? So long as I advance, I cannot fall.

The blast throws him to the ground. He picks himself up.

'Who can write a good hand?' he asks.

A sergeant presents himself.

'This will be called,' Napoleon announces, 'the battery of Men Without Fear.'

The sergeant starts to write and then a cannonball crashes into the ground a few metres away, showering his piece of paper with earth.

'That'll save me having to blot the ink,' says the sergeant.

'What is your name?'

'Junot.'

Napoleon gives this young sergeant a long look. He feels he is compelling men to surpass themselves: convincing them; seducing them; sweeping them up; giving them no choice but to follow. At every moment, Napoleon discovers these intense, burning pleasures. For his part, there'll be no ducking when the cannon open fire; he'll bed down in his coat on the bare ground amidst his men; lead the charge in a hail of bullets; get back up when his horse is shot under him; and when the men bravely, furiously launch themselves at the enemy, he'll cry – even if they are wrong – 'The wine is drawn, it must be drunk,' and if a frightened general orders the retreat, he'll call him 'a good-for-nothing'.

NAPOLEON has never felt such fulfilment in his life. He observes Saliceti and the other representatives of the people – Gasparin, Barras, Fréron, Ricord and Augustin Robespierre – and tries to get the measure of them. Augustin Robespierre is the brother of Maximilien Robespierre, the man who is the driving force of the Committee of Public Safety. Saliceti is an old friend by now.

These are the men who have power. They are the deputies of the Convention. They are the ones who have to be convinced.

One evening Napoleon persuades Saliceti to accompany him to one of the batteries. Suddenly bullets whistle past and the representative's horse is killed. Napoleon rushes up and helps Saliceti to his feet. They have to hide, then work their way round to the next battery in silence because the English patrols are very close.

Just before they get there, the gunner is killed. Napoleon grabs the ramrod and, like any ordinary ranker, helps load ten or twelve rounds. The other soldiers stare at him; one starts trying to explain that the dead gunner ... Then he stops and just scratches his hands and arms. The gunner had scabies and no one had been touching his ramrod in case it was infectious. Napoleon shrugs. Can one stop for that, even if in the days that follow the illness starts to take effect? There is no time to get himself treated.

ON 29 SEPTEMBER, the representatives promote him to major — fresh impetus, fresh energy, fresh conviction that he can go further, faster.

Napoleon visits Saliceti every day. He drums out his message: his plan is the only one that can make Toulon fall, but obstacles remain. He repeats his views. Speaking is like a cannonade. As he tells his gunners, 'You must not let yourself get discouraged when you fire; after a hundred rounds to no effect, the hundred and first strikes home and produces a result.'

He senses that Saliceti and Gasparin, and later Ricord and Augustin Robespierre, and even Barras and Fréron, are not against him.

What a thrill it is, this ascendancy one has over men! What intoxication! What woman could fill one with such a feeling of drunkenness and power?

He is discovering this for himself.

Saliceti and the other representatives have General Carteaux replaced. 'Captain Cannon' has won, but General Doppet, who succeeds Carteaux, is a former doctor. He only lasts a few weeks.

Napoleon, his face bloody from a wound received at the front, gallops up to Doppet after an attack has ground to a halt. 'So you are the good-for-nothing who had the retreat sounded,' he yells at him. The general walks away and Napoleon looks at the soldiers who have gathered around him. They are abusing the general, shouting, 'Shall we always be commanded by painters and doctors?'

Napoleon remains silent. His faith in himself is taking root: he is the one who can command men.

HE REQUESTS an audience with Saliceti; he must be heard, now that he has proved himself. He has been fighting, planning and organizing for more than two months now.

'Will we always have to struggle against ignorance and the base passions it breeds? Always have to argue and lay down the law to a pack of *ignorantacci*, to overcome their prejudices and make them take action which theory and practice alike have shown to be axiomatic to any trained artillery officer?'

Saliceti bows his head in agreement.

ON 16 NOVEMBER, General Dugommier arrives at Ollioules to replace General Doppet, and two hours later General du Teil joins him. At the end of the afternoon, Napoleon goes to see them. He knows du Teil. Dugommier listens to him and invites him to dinner. During the meal, he passes him a dish of sheep's brains. 'Here,' he says laughing, 'you need them.'

When, on 25 November, he walks into the little room where the council of war meets, Napoleon knows he has overcome all obstacles. Generals Dugommier and du Teil nod approvingly as, bent over the map, he summarizes his plan: 'Capture Fort de L'Eguillette, expel the English from the roads, and simultaneously mount an attack on Fort Mount Faron.'

Saliceti, Augustin Robespierre and Ricord give their consent.

As he is leaving the room, Napoleon turns towards Dugommier. The general smiles and passes his hand across his throat. If the plan fails, it's the guillotine for him.

THESE ARE the final days before the goal is reached.

No fear; Napoleon even has a sense of invulnerability which does not surprise him.

On 30 November, after the English have taken the battery of the Convention by surprise, he leads the counter-attack in person.

The English commander-in-chief O'Hara is taken prisoner. Napoleon approaches him slowly. O'Hara is sitting glumly, his elbows on his knees.

He straightens up when he sees Napoleon.

'What do you want?' asks Napoleon.

'To be left alone and to owe nothing to pity.'

Napoleon walks away, looking at the English general. This is what men of war are. In defeat they should act with pride and reserve.

Napoleon stops for a moment.

He is a man of war. He is twenty-four years and four months old.

LEADING HIS horse by the reins, Napoleon marches in the middle of his drenched soldiers. It is 16 December 1793, and the rain is falling in torrents; no one can see more than three paces in front of them. The attack is set for that night. Only long flashes of lightning break the darkness, lighting up the columns of men.

Napoleon finds Dugommier and the representatives gathered in a tent that is leaking like a sieve. Everyone turns towards him, and on their faces he sees hesitation and anxiety.

He is sure of himself. It goes beyond reason, his confidence in his 'system'. He says simply that the bad weather isn't necessarily unfavourable. Their expressions change. This is how men are. A strong conviction directs them, moulds them, sweeps them along.

Dugommier gives the signal.

Napoleon mounts up, the infantry set off, then battle is joined. The second column breaks up in the downpour amidst cries of 'Every man for himself,' 'Treason.' The other columns march on yelling, 'Victory, at bayonet point!'

Napoleon feels his horse collapse, dead. He gets up and carries on; he's aware of a stabbing pain coursing through his thigh, as an Englishman catches him with a bayonet thrust. He breaks into a run. His friend Captain Muiron is at his side; further down, Marmont and Sergeant Junot are also in the front line.

Fort Mulgrave is carried, its guns turned on the enemy, and as they surge, Fort de L'Eguillette is finally taken. The English have abandoned it, cutting their horses' and mules' throats before they leave, and the corridors are littered with corpses.

Only then does Napoleon feel the pain of his wound and have

it dressed. The English, he says, are good soldiers, and then, scorn in his voice, he adds, indicating the prisoners, 'All this rabble, Neapolitans, Sicilians, are worth very little indeed.'

He stands up and limps to the parapet, 'Tomorrow or, at the latest, the day after, we shall sup in Toulon.' He is calm and does not show his joy. He attends to the final preparations, his mind already elsewhere.

Reports come that 'the English are in flight', and the Neapolitans are deserting the forts. He shows no surprise. These are the expected consequences of his system.

In the harbour, frigates explode. The English and the Spanish are blowing up ships with cargoes of powder.

In the glow of fires he sees dozens of small boats and *tartanes* full of inhabitants of Toulon trying to get out to the ships of the Anglo-Spanish fleet. Launches are capsizing, women are screaming before they drown – dragged under, so it will be said, by their bags full of jewels. The batteries open fire, shattering the flimsy hulls of the feluccas.

It is over.

On 19 December 1793, the Republican troops, the 'Carmagnoles', enter Toulon.

NAPOLEON keeps out of things now. Without even turning his head, he passes the tireless firing squads, the looting, the two representatives of the people who doubted victory most, Barras and Fréron, and yet who today are posting proclamations on every wall warning that they are going to raze the town and therefore need twelve thousand masons.

He sees men pointing the soldiers towards particular houses. They are Montagnards, followers of the Mountain, just released from the hold of the *Thémistocle*, and hunting for the men who informed against them, their torturers, their jailers. Now it's their turn to inform, to massacre.

Sometimes nausea seizes him. Whatever flag it waves, the people remains a ferocious beast.

That is none of his affair.

He returns to his quarters. Some women are waiting, to plead with him. He does not utter a word of pity, but he does intervene.

He sends Junot or Marmont or Muiron, those officers that have become his family, to save some victim or other from death.

What else can one do?

Men are like this. Politics is like this.

He feels so cold, so clear-sighted that the joy of having achieved his goal evaporates.

What does he do now?

ON 22 DECEMBER, he is summoned by the representatives of the people. They are sitting around a table which has glasses and bottles set out on it.

'What uniform do you call that?' Saliceti asks as he sees Napoleon come in. Then he reads out a short order that the representatives have just drawn up. They have promoted Major Napoleon Bonaparte to brigadier-general, 'because of the zeal and intelligence of which he has given proof in contributing to the reduction of the rebel town'.

'You must change,' Saliceti goes on and laughs as he embraces Napoleon.

How drab everything is, when the race is run.

XVI

IT IS 4 JANUARY 1794, and Napoleon is sitting opposite his mother. The little table they are leaning their elbows on takes up almost the whole room. His brothers and sisters are standing behind Letizia.

He jumps to his feet and, in a few strides, crosses the three tiny rooms that make up the apartment. He feels as if he is suffocating. He opens the window but despite the cold, damp wind that is blowing he feels even shorter of breath. He has been having trouble breathing since he came up this alley, ruelle du Pavillon, near the port in Marseilles. The stench of rotten fish, oil and rubbish had made him feel sick. Despite the rain he had stopped for a moment to look up at the grey façade, number 7.

This is where his family lives, on the fourth floor.

When he entered the apartment, his brothers and sisters had rushed towards him and then, intimidated, they stopped. Louis touched his general's uniform.

Letizia Bonaparte came forward slowly. These months of poverty and anguish have aged her.

Napoleon put a leather bag full of bacon, ham, bread, eggs and fruit down on the table. Then he held out a bundle of paper money and a handful of coins to his mother. Finally he opened another bag and out spilled a mass of shirts, dresses and shoes.

He is a brigadier-general, he explained. He is paid twelve thousand livres a year. He has received a field outfit allowance of more than two thousand livres. He is entitled to a general's daily rations.

Letizia Bonaparte, unflappable, tells him how they lived in La Valette, in fear of the royalists, and then in Meonnes.

Napoleon listens. 'It's over,' is all he says.

He is thinking of Barras. Since the taking of Toulon, this representative of the people has proved to be one of the most rabid terrorists. Yesterday, as he was leaving the town, Napoleon again saw men lined up against a wall and soldiers were pointing muskets at them. An officer was moving from one to the next, lighting their faces with a torch and in the shadows an informer was whispering. Barras was making his horse wheel and cavort nearby.

There's a rumour whispered at Dugommier's headquarters that during his missions to the Army of Italy in the Comté of Nice Barras has amassed a personal treasure – 'in the name of the Republic' the joke goes. It's the same with plenty of representatives and officers and even soldiers; they are all pillagers when they get the chance. Some pilfer a handful of figs, others silver dinner services. The smartest and most senior in rank steal gold coins and works of art and buy properties at a good price.

A fine lesson!

Only a few, such as Augustin Robespierre, remain honest and call for the 'national razor' to purify the Republic and institute the Reign of Virtue!

'It's over,' Napoleon repeats, standing up and interrupting his mother.

He must win this war as well, against poverty, or perhaps simply mediocrity.

He does not want to be anyone's dupe. Let's have Virtue, by all means, if it's one rule for everybody, but who thinks that's possible? So he must, and he will, be the equal of those who have the most, because it would be unfair, immoral even, if he and his family lived like paupers, if his mother should find herself in the same situation she has just described to him: only with a bit of ration bread and an egg to feed each of her children.

In the revolutionary upheaval, the Bonapartes have lost everything. Justice demands that they have their share of the spoils.

Money, money! That word rings out like Napoleon's heels on the cobbles of the ruelle du Pavillon.

They must not be poor, because that would be another exile – and because in the meantime all the poeple like Barras in the Republic are getting rich with all their might.

Are they worth more than me?

Money is another Fort de L'Eguillette, a key that has to be seized to gain control of those roadsteads: his life, his destiny.

I want that too.

He returns to Toulon.

In his quarters there is a bustle of activity. He loves all this movement around him. He has chosen Junot and Marmont as his aides-de-camp. They are devoted, efficient and admiring. He watches them.

This is being a leader, becoming the centre of a group of men who are like the planets of a solar system.

Napoleon remembers those astronomy books he was fascinated by in Paris when the monarchy was crumbling. Societies, governments, armies and families are like the heavens. They need a centre around which to organize themselves. It is this heart that determines the trajectory of the satellite planets. If its pull should be missing, each star breaks away. The system disintegrates until another force appears to stabilize it around a new centre.

As he inspects the forts of Marseilles and Toulon, having been appointed to bring their artillery up to strength, Napoleon plays with these ideas.

January is an icy month. The mistral blows, lashing one's face. War and terror spread. In La Vendée, General Turreau's 'infernal columns' devastate the countryside and massacre the inhabitants. In Paris, the factional struggles grow more brutal, Saint-Just and Robespierre turn on the '*enragés*' of Jacques Roux, and the '*indulgents*' of Danton.

Napoleon often looks out to sea from the roof of a fort and, on two or three occasions, at dawn, he thinks he can see Corsica. On 19 January, Pascal Paoli appealed to the English to land and they have begun to establish themselves in the Gulf of San Fiorenzo.

Paoli is not a centre any more. The system turns around the Convention, the Committee of Public Safety, and Robespierre, who is its driving force.

Napoleon often sees Augustin Robespierre, Maximilien's brother, representative of the people with the Army of Italy, but he tends to listen more than talk. Augustin Robespierre is keen to know his views on political events, but Napoleon, his face rigid, mumbles that he is wholly at the Convention's orders.

It is Augustin Robespierre who tells him that Lucien Bonaparte, 'your brother, citizen general', is a fervent Jacobin. On Lucien's suggestion, St Maximin has taken the name of Marathon and he has changed his name to Brutus! 'Look, this is what he wrote to the Convention in the first days of January 1794 after the capture of Toulon.'

Augustin Robespierre hands Napoleon a sheet of paper. Napoleon reads without a flicker of expression:

Citizen Representatives,
    It is from the field of glory, marching in the blood of traitors, that I announce with joy that your orders have been carried out and that France has been avenged. Neither age nor sex has been spared. Those who had only been wounded have been dispatched by the sword of liberty and the bayonet of equality.
    Greetings and admiration,
        Brutus Bonaparte, sans-culotte citizen

Napoleon gives the paper back to Augustin Robespierre. He senses that Maximilian's brother is scrutinizing him, waiting for him to comment, but Napoleon is not going to say anything about that young madman Lucien, who has not understood that the systems are changing and that as long as one is not at the centre of one of them, one must be cautious, keep on one's guard.

Hasn't he, Napoleon, seen Louis XVI, the sovereign of the greatest of kingdoms, put on the red cap, drink with his former subjects, and then, on 10 August 1792, flee like a gutless coward?

Who can say that tomorrow Robespierre won't suffer the same fate? As virtuous, energetic, pitiless as he may be.

Augustin Robespierre folds up the piece of paper.

He intends, he says, with the agreement of the other representatives of the people, Ricord and Saliceti, to appoint as artillery commander to the Army of Italy a general whose abilities are proven and whose Jacobin and revolutionary sentiments have been vouched for.

Napoleon remains impassive.

'You, Citizen Bonaparte.'

His appointment to the Army of Italy comes through on 7 February 1794 and it only takes a few days before Napoleon feels the looks of jealousy or almost bitter hatred that the envious give him.

A general who isn't yet twenty-five years old in charge of an entire army's artillery! It's a political nomination, people imply. Bonaparte is a robespierrist.

In Nice, entering the rooms near the port occupied by General Dumerbion, Napoleon overhears a discussion and pieces together these insinuations.

General Dumerbion looks tired, drawn. He offers Napoleon a chair and quizzes him. 'This citizen Robespierre . . .' he begins.

Napoleon doesn't respond, letting Dumerbion tie himself in knots until finally the latter explains that he is ill, that he's suffering from a hernia that prevents him riding and that he's giving Napoleon carte blanche. What's called for is an overhaul of the artillery and fresh plans of operations: they must drive the Sardinian armies out of the towns they're holding in the north-east of the Comté of Nice, towards Saorgio and the Col di Tende and push them back on the coast, past Oneglia as well.

HE MUST GET organized, set to work, take action. Napoleon curtly dictates his orders to Junot and Marmont, and then sets off through the town. It is 12 February.

On one of the squares, which he can still make out used to be called place St Dominique, the guillotine has been erected. With an escort of dragoons, Napoleon crosses this place de l'Égalité, as it is now known, and carries on past the port to the east of town. He chooses as his lodgings a fine house in rue de Villefranche, to which the erstwhile Count Laurenti gives him an amicable welcome.

When he sees the young Emilie Laurenti, Napoleon stops.

She is not yet sixteen. She is dressed in a white dress and wears her hair up. He goes towards her, greets her awkwardly.

Suddenly he feels dirty, muddy – as he is, because it is raining.

Napoleon follows Laurenti as he shows him to his room. He looks back: Emilie Laurenti is watching.

It's been weeks since his eyes have met a woman's. Sometimes, during the siege of Toulon, Napoleon had dined at Controller Chauvet's table, with that officer's daughters, but the cannon boomed and he had to go and sleep in his coat, on the ground, under the parapets.

In this house in Nice, he rediscovers the gentleness, grace and delicacy of a young girl.

His uniform feels heavy. The fabric is rough, the leather of his boots stiff.

In his room, Napoleon opens the window. Under a low sky, the sea looks black. Imprisoned between two little headlands, the port is no more than a natural cove. *Tartanes* and fishing boats are pulled up on the beach. It is like a vision from his childhood, part of the Corsican coast, although less rugged, more tender perhaps.

Suddenly Napoleon feels a desire to let his guard down, to surrender to a wave of emotion, feelings, love. Rousseau's words he had read when he was younger come back to him. He thought he had forgotten them, but they're there, quivering.

Love, women – these exist. They are at the heart of life, like war and money.

He wants them too.

IN HIS OFFICE at headquarters, he has the maps laid out and with thick black lines marks up the routes the battalions are to take to capture Tende, Saorgio, Oneglia, and hustle the Sardinians out of their positions. He meets Masséna, who has also just been appointed a general and whose eight thousand men, after distinguishing themselves in the siege of Toulon, march through the streets of Nice.

Napoleon watches the parade. He sees the enthusiasm of Nice's revolutionaries and the fear of most of its inhabitants. But isn't fear what governs men?

Then, with Junot and Marmont, he rides by precipitous paths up into the high valleys. They look over at Saorgio, that village whose houses seem to merge into the mountain, but they cannot get closer because the Sardinians are bombarding the La Roya valley from the peaks. Napoleon spends the following days inspecting the coastal fortifications, which are sometimes approached by the English fleet sailing out of the Corsican ports that are now in their hands.

In Antibes, as he is leaving the Fort Carré on one of the few fine days at the end of February, Napoleon notices on a hill a private house with a faded tile roof and closed, bright green shutters.

He climbs up to it and walks into a garden planted with orange trees, palms, laurels and mimosas. From the flower-decked terrace, there is a view over the Cap d'Antibes, the Gulf Juan and the Baie des Anges. It looks down on the Fort Carré and its angle towers built by Vauban.

'This will be it,' Napoleon says to Junot.

A WEEK LATER, he is waiting for his family on the threshold of this house which he has had requisitioned. It is known locally as the Château Sallé. Napoleon still has his residence in the Laurenti house in rue de Villefranche in Nice, but he wants his mother and his brothers and sisters near him, under his protection, where he can best provide for them. He needs his family. His mother's gaze, his siblings' admiration and envy are ways for him to measure his progress, his success.

Look, here they are, flanked by Junot's cavalry, because the roads between Marseilles and Antibes are not safe.

In the three days they have been travelling, Junot says, they have often been followed by 'Children of the Sun', the royalists waging guerrilla warfare in the Var who have gone into hiding in the Estérel and Maures forests.

Without order or peace within its borders, what is a nation?

Napoleon shows his mother round the house, pushing back the shutters himself.

'Here it is,' he says. 'It's yours.'

It is not the family house in Ajaccio, of course, but it seems to him as if he has started rebuilding its walls.

He greets Louis, his brother and former pupil in Auxonne and Valence. He has just had him appointed to his staff, even though he is only sixteen. Then he asks after Lucien; Letizia reports that he is set on marrying his landlord's daughter. Joseph, meanwhile, has a good introduction in Marseilles to the Clarys, a rich merchant's family in rue des Phocéens. Their eldest daughter, Julie, has a dowry of one hundred and fifty thousand livres.

Napoleon listens. He is the centre of this Bonaparte 'system'.

HE BECOMES a regular visitor at the Château Sallé. He dines there with Marmont, Junot, Muiron and Sébastiani. Masséna is also to be seen there, and sometimes Representative Ricord's wife, and even Maximilien and Augustin Robespierre's sister, Charlotte, meet at the house of the one they call 'the ardent republican'.

After entertaining at the château, Napoleon returns to Nice in the morning, often with his aides-de-camp. The horses race along the beach, their hooves spraying foam into the air. They ford the Var and reach the quays of Nice's port as the sun is rising.

Then he immerses himself in work on the plans and maps, and in meetings with General Dumerbion. Napoleon is surprised by how fast time passes. His imagination, prompted by the maps, catches fire. He anticipates the troops' movements, the enemy's responses. Everything organizes itself in his mind like the terms of a mathematical proof, of a system.

When he speaks to Augustin Robespierre or General Dumerbion, he feels that nothing can resist his thought.

ONE DAY in April Augustin Robespierre talks to him at length, leading him down to the port and telling him that he has written to his brother Maximilien to praise this 'Citizen Bonaparte, a commander of artillery of transcendent merit'.

The Army of Italy has followed Napoleon's plans. Saorgio, Oneglia, the Col di Tende have fallen and in a note to the Convention Dumerbion has acknowledged what he owed 'to the expert combinations of General Bonaparte which have secured our success'.

'Why not,' continues Augustin Robespierre, 'play a still greater role, in Paris?'

Napoleon stops, acts as if he doesn't understand. He has prepared a plan which he wants to submit to Maximilien Robespierre, he says. It is a plan of operations for the entire Army of Italy, which would force the Austrians to defend Lombardy and Tessino, and thereby enable the Army of the Rhine to attack a weakened opponent.

Augustin Robespierre listens and is impressed, but says that is not what he means.

'Besides to attack on all fronts would be a tactical error,'

Napoleon carries on as if he had not heard the representative's remark. 'One must concentrate one's attacks, not disperse them. The principles of war are the same as those of a siege. Fire must be concentrated on a single point, and as soon as the breach is made the equilibrium is broken, everything else becomes pointless and the place falls.'

'Very well,' says Augustin Robespierre. He will pass on this plan of attack – but does Bonaparte know Hanriot, the head of the revolutionary army's staff in Paris and guardian of the Convention and the Committee of Public Safety?

Napoleon lets a moment pass in silence, then says, 'Strike at Austria, weaken it by a wound in Italy, set the army in motion from Oneglia and the Col di Tende – there, that is my plan.'

THAT EVENING, as he gallops back to Antibes alone, far ahead of Junot and Marmont, he analyses Augustin Robespierre's proposal: to put himself at the heart of the robespierrist system. Should he expose himself prematurely to coups?

Yesterday he had had another example of the jealousy he provokes. He was summoned to the bar of the Convention to defend himself against a charge of repairing guns at Marseilles for the benefit of aristocrats! The representative of the people defended him, but the sword of a conviction is still hanging over his head.

One must be able to open fire at the right moment, otherwise the blade falls.

NAPOLEON leaps off his horse in the garden of the Château Sallé and his brothers Lucien and Joseph come to meet him. He takes them down to the bottom of the garden; the weather is mild. He looks at the sea and thinks out loud. It is up to him whether he goes to Paris or not tomorrow, he says. If he did, he would be in a very good position to set up all the Bonapartes.

He turns round.

'What do you say to that?' he asks, but does not wait for his brothers to answer.

'It's not a matter of putting on a show of enthusiasm,' he carries on. 'Saving one's skin in Paris is not as easy as it is in St Maximin. The younger Robespierre is honest but his brother is not trifling.

One would have to serve him. Me, support that man? No, never! I know how useful I would be to him replacing his imbecilic commander of Paris, but that is what I do not want to do. It is not time. Today, the only honourable place for me is in the army: be patient, I will command Paris later.'

He goes off a few paces.

He had already made up his mind but putting into words what he was thinking on the way back from Nice, and even when Augustin Robespierre was actually talking, convinces him that there is only one possible choice, the one he has made.

He turns round and calls to his brothers, 'What would I do in that hell hole?' But still he stays looking at the sea for a long time.

He is sure of something, and Augustin Robespierre's offer has given rise to this certainty: as he said, one day it will be time to command Paris.

SUMMER COMES suddenly, and with it, painful news.

On 21 June, acting on behalf of the council, Paoli has proposed to George III, King of England, that he accept the crown of Corsica – and the sovereign has agreed!

In Paris, more heads roll and the terror becomes frenzied, even as the victory at Fleurus on 26 June makes this cruel repression useless.

Often, in those June and July days of 1794, Napoleon repairs to the garden of the Laurenti house in rue de Villefranche. He doesn't speak much. He looks at Emilie. He grows calm – but he cannot remain still for long.

The atmosphere at headquarters is oppressive. The army's coffers are empty, there's a shortage of uniforms and out of a full strength of forty thousand, sixteen thousand men have been declared sick!

When Napoleon answers the summons of Representative Ricord on 11 July he still has in mind the words he has just written to one of those officers who were complaining about the state of the army, 'It will end badly for those who are raising the alarm amongst the people.'

He feels caught up in this climate of violence and anxiety himself. What does Ricord want?

The representative reads out two long, confidential instructions he has drawn up with Augustin Robespierre. 'General Bonaparte is to go to Genoa, inform himself of the state of the fortifications, collect powder there that has already been paid for, assess the civic attitude of the French representatives and discuss with the government of Genoa ways to combat the "hordes of brigands" to whom Genoa is allowing free passage.'

It is a secret mission, insists Ricord, at once diplomatic and military.

How is one to slip out of that?

Ricord and Robespierre still hold the power. Augustin Robespierre is to go to Paris and defend Napoleon's plan of operations against Italy before the Committee of Public Safety.

'I will set off immediately,' says Napoleon.

HE RIDES ALONE, in civilian clothes, along the coastal roads that hug the cliffs.

The country is not safe, but at intervals there are French posts and cities held by Italian revolutionaries. In Oneglia, Napoleon dines with Buonarroti, who he knew in Corsica and who has been appointed commissary of the Convention by Ricord and Robespierre.

They talk about the past. In Corsica, Buonarroti used to publish *Il Giornale Patriottico di Corsica*, for which Napoleon had written an article. Then, on the terrace looking over the port, Napoleon listens in silence as Buonarroti speaks of the equality that must reign and that Robespierre may perhaps contribute to creating.

Napoleon does not answer at first. Equality? How can Buonarroti, who's over thirty years old, keep such faith?

'The equality of rights,' begins Napoleon, 'that which the law can establish . . .'

But Buonarroti interrupts him passionately. 'No, the equality of wealth,' he says, 'of riches, in order to establish the true equality of rights.'

One would have to cut every second man's head off, and that still wouldn't be enough, murmurs Napoleon. Who wants to be poorer than he already is?

ON HIS WAY back from Genoa, Napoleon does not stop at Oneglia and when he arrives in Nice on 27 July 1794, he gives a report of his mission to Ricord, and then goes back to the Château Sallé with Junot.

The house is empty. Letizia and her children have left Antibes to go to the wedding of Joseph Bonaparte and Marie-Julie Clary, the daughter of Marseillais silk and soap merchants. Joseph has chosen the one hundred and fifty thousand livres dowry!

Napoleon feels alone; he returns immediately to Nice, to the Laurenti.

ON 4 AUGUST, Junot appears in the morning, nervous and pale. 'Robespierre has been beheaded,' he blurts out as soon as he sees Napoleon. Maximilien was arrested on 27 July and executed the following day with his brother Augustin.

Napoleon bows his head.

Laurenti comes up and asks for the news to be repeated. At last! The prisoners will be set free; Doctor Guillotine's machine will be dismantled.

Napoleon leaves the house without saying a word. He has seen too much hatred in people's eyes, sensed too much jealousy quivering in their hearts to imagine that he will not be denounced.

'They are going to take their revenge,' he says.

He thinks of the streets of Toulon. Then he adds, loudly, so that the officers around him will hear, 'I have been a little affected by the catastrophe of Robespierre, whom I liked to a degree and thought honest, but had he been my brother, if he aspired to tyranny I would have stabbed him myself.'

He waits.

He bumps into Saliceti in the street, and Saliceti cannot look him in the eye. He tries to sees Ricord, but is told that he has fled. He will be in Switzerland by now.

On 9 August, when the gendarmes present themselves at the Laurenti house to inform him that a writ has been issued for his arrest by order of Representatives Saliceti and Albitte, Ricord's replacement, Napoleon shows no emotion.

Laurenti steps in and offers to pay a bond enabling Napoleon to remain there under house arrest.

Napoleon is told that he is suspected of being an associate of Robespierre. Why did he go to Genoa? Commissaries of the Army of the Alps even claim that a million livres were put at his disposal by émigrés in Italy to corrupt him. Saliceti adds, 'There is with Bonaparte strong grounds for suspicion of betrayal and peculation.'

He is taken to Antibes's Fort-Carré under a heavy escort. From the window of the room where he is locked up, he can see the Château Sallé.

AT FIRST he turns in on himself.

He thinks about Saliceti denouncing him, betraying him to save himself. The cowardice of men. He thinks of his destiny that has already raised him so high, in so short a time, and now brings him crashing to the ground, condemned to the guillotine before his twenty-fifth birthday.

Should he accept this destiny or get to his feet, like one does when one is charging, and fall over? He requests a quill and paper. He is going to write to the representatives of the people. He is going to stand up.

> You have suspended me from duties, arrested me and declared me suspect. I am disgraced without having been judged or else judged without having been heard. Since the start of the Revolution, have I not always been attached to its principles? I have sacrificed the home of my *département*, I have abandoned my property, I have lost everything for the Republic. I have since served at Toulon with some distinction and earned some title to the laurels which the Army of Italy has acquired. My claim to the title of a patriot cannot therefore be disputed.

> *Saliceti, you know me! Have you ever seen anything suspect in my conduct for the last five years which might be suspect to the Revolution?*

> Hear me, destroy the oppression which surrounds me and restore me to the esteem of patriots.
>   An hour after, if the wicked want my life, I shall give it to them, I value it so little and have scorned it so often! Yes, nothing but the thought that it may still be useful to my country makes me bear the burden of it with courage.

He gives the letter to the sentry.

Napoleon is on his feet. He hears the sea pounding against the rocks that surround the fort.

In the night, a soldier passes him an escape plan that Junot, Sébastiani and Marmont have devised.

He picks up his quill again:

I recognize all your friendship for me, my dear Junot. Men may be unjust to me, but it is enough for me that I am innocent; my own conscience is the tribunal before which I bring my conduct.

When I examine it this conscience is calm. So do nothing, you would only compromise me.

Goodbye, my dear Junot, regards and friendship.

Bonaparte, under arrest in the Fort-Carré, Antibes.

He does not sleep.

Some men betray one. Others remain loyal. Depending on whose actions one hears of, one despairs or takes fresh heart.

But one must only rely on oneself. Only trust oneself.

HE KNOWS that in Nice his aides-de-camp are badgering the representatives of the people and General Dumerbion.

At the front, in the high valleys, the Sardinians are attacking, taking advantage of the disorder that has afflicted the Republic and its armies since the fall of Robespierre.

Napoleon is needed. Saliceti retracts his accusation. 'Nothing definitive' has been discovered against Bonaparte, he writes on 20 August to the Committee of Public Safety.

That same day, the sentry opens the cell door and smilingly presents arms.

'Citizen General . . .' he begins.

Napoleon walks slowly past him.

He is free.

One mustn't depend on a system. One must be one's own system. He has been twenty-five for five days now.

XVII

NAPOLEON ENTERS the offices of General Dumerbion, who is sunk in his chair, legs outstretched, his body heavy and slack. He seems to have trouble raising his arm in greeting. A number of officers are standing around the table which is covered with maps.

Napoleon stares at each in turn. They look at the floor. He has seen these men every day for months, but still not one of them dares make a friendly gesture or congratulate him on regaining his freedom. Everyone is silent. This is how it's been since Napoleon has resumed his position at the Army of Italy's headquarters in Nice.

General Dumerbion clears his throat and sighs.

Finally he points his finger at the map and asks Napoleon to approach. The other officers step aside. Napoleon wants to touch them and yell, laughing, 'I am plague-ridden. Fear for your liberty and your life!' But what would be the use? He has discovered since his imprisonment that cowardice and fear are widespread.

Dumerbion has asked him to draw up a new plan of operations in the region of Dego and Cairo, in Piedmont, beyond the Cols di Tende and di Cadibona, but he feels surrounded by suspicion. He is watched, spied on and everyone shuns him. They mistrust the new representatives of the people. They fear the purges ordered by the Convention and the Committee of Public Safety – hunting down officers suspected of Jacobinism, docking 'Robespierre's tail' in the army. Some officers have been transferred; others have been imprisoned. More than a hundred people have been guillotined since the fall of the one they now call 'the tyrant'. The prisons are crowded with yesterday's rulers, and sometimes the crowd smashes down the gates and puts them to the slaughter. The Companies of Jesus and the Companies of the Sun are hot on the Jacobins' track, claiming thousands of victims, and they are spurred on by royalist émigrés or the new representatives of the people.

Napoleon knows that Lucien has been arrested as a Jacobin and thrown in Aix prison. He has written to one of the administrators of the city, 'Help my brother, that young madman, and have the solicitude of friendship for him.'

But what can one expect of someone when fear has him in its grip? What can one expect of a country, when the centre of power swings in this way from one hand to another and the Jacobin terror is succeeded by the white terror?

Napoleon does not look at the map while General Dumerbion is talking.

He knows every fold in the ground: he has written so many notes on what sort of campaign should be fought in Italy! Each time he has suggested the same lines of advance to isolate the Austrians from the Piedmontese. He has explained that the troops must be disposed as skirmishers. Everything he read when he was garrisoned at Auxonne and Valence – the books by Guibert and Gribeauval, du Teil's treatises – has come back to take its natural place in these documents. So why listen to Dumerbion, this helpless general who has no imagination at all?

If only Dumerbion and these cowards knew what confidence he has, if only they had a sense of the ideas he juggles with.

There needs to be a country whose centre is a rallying point, a fixed axis, he thinks, and where every citizen would be certain of the place he occupied in that system – neither red terror, nor white terror, but method and order, an almost mathematical organization.

He answers Dumerbion without listening – yes, he is ready to lead the battalions into the region of Cairo and Dego. He will set off today to join them.

He knows what General Schérer has written about him: 'This officer knows his army well but he has a little too much ambition.'

But what is a man without ambition?

A barren land.

HE IS IN THE FIELD. It is raining in these high valleys and on these Piedmontese hills that fall away to the Lombard plains in long serried spines. Down there, in the fertile alluvial soil, the opulent cities of Milan, Verona and Mantua are drowsing on the banks of the Po. As the Sardinians retreat, and the Republican troops, poorly clothed, underfed and sick with dysentery and typhus, win victory at Dego and Cairo, Napoleon studies the rich Italian provinces through his field glass. Lombardy. It would only need a little audacity to seize control of it – but he is not commander-in-chief, and what can one do when one has to obey men who are one's inferiors?

Thin, body arched forward, he paces around the house in Cairo where the headquarters have been set up. Everything is too straightforward, too slow. He is becoming impatient. He won't be able to live like this for long. He pushes open the door of the office belonging to Turreau, a member of the Convention who has been posted to the Army of Italy, and stops in his tracks. A woman is sitting in the office. Turreau is not there.

'I am Citizeness Turreau,' she says.

Her long dress, pleated and tight-waisted, brings out the curve of her hips and her breasts.

She does not lower her eyes.

He is attracted by this body, this blonde hair, this languid attitude. They are like a plain to be conquered, to be taken by brief, brutal assault.

He leans towards her, utters a few words; she replies. Citizen Turreau, she says, is on a tour of inspection, he will return tomorrow.

He sweeps her away.

In the morning, as he and Junot are riding to Nice, he murmurs, 'Blonde hair, wit, patriotism, philosophy.'

HE RETURNS to headquarters in Nice.

One woman, one night: can they appease this need to act, this yearning to be what he knows he can be?

Félicité Turreau spends a few days in Nice and she allows herself to be taken again, but if the nights are short for Napoleon, the days stretch endlessly before him.

All the talk at the headquarters is of an expedition to Corsica to dislodge the English. Troops and ships are being assembled at Toulon. He must be a part of it – but he has the feeling that every time he asks someone about it they change the subject. One morning he learns that Buonarroti has been stripped of his post as

Commissary of the Convention at Oneglia and was driven through Nice at night, flanked by an escort, on his way to the prisons of Paris, suspected of robespierrism.

Napoleon realizes that Buonarroti's arrest will make him the object of even more suspicion and he grows furious and indignant: this means he won't be part of the Corsican expedition. Even worse, on 29 March, he is recalled from the Army of Italy.

He is rough on Junot, Marmont and Muiron, who try to calm him. Nothing soothes him. He receives a letter from his mother. 'Corsica,' she writes, 'is nothing but a barren rock, an insignificant, wretched little plot of land. Whereas France is large, rich, well populated. It is ablaze. This is a noble conflagration, my son. It is worth the risks of being burnt.'

But how is one to throw oneself into the fire?

Suddenly, during that March of 1795, it seems that, for lack of a target to aim at, the bowstring has gone slack and the arrow has fallen from his fingers.

HE GOES TO Marseilles.

When he rides through Draguignan, Brignoles and the little towns of the Var, he feels the hostile looks that follow him. The royalists of the Companies of Jesus have taken over the countryside and are running rampant in the Rhône valley. They are hunting down Jacobins and, in Lyon, massacring them in the prisons. In Paris, the Muscadins are beating them unmercifully; the Jacobins Club has been shut down.

What is one to do without support, when one is a 25-year-old general suspected of Jacobinism, isolated, deprived of a command, dependent on the good will of hostile or indifferent strangers, who preside all-powerfully over their departments in the War Office, have never seen one charging at the head of one's men and are ignorant – and perhaps afraid – of all the strength, energy and desire for victory you possess?

Perhaps the age of mediocrities is beginning?

Where is my place in this country?

HE ENTERS the prosperous salon of the Clarys in rue des Phocéens, and Joseph comes forward to greet him, stout and smiling, holding his wife Julie Clary by her plump and dimpled arm. Then Joseph steps aside and pushes towards Napoleon his sister-in-law, Désirée Clary, a young brown-haired girl with a round face and slender figure. She has the intermittent shyness of all sixteen-year-olds and is playful and admiring and gentle. She offers herself without affectation, like a fortress which gives itself up in a rush to an advancing warlord.

Napoleon sits beside her. She says little. She waits. He dreams of being like Joseph, that calm old bird, contentedly married, enjoying a regular diet of rich food, without enemies or desires, aspiring only to a mundane happiness at his family's side.

The dream persists and grows stronger as the days pass, first March, then April 1795.

If he married Désirée Clary, it would spell the end of his days on the prowl, of that raw-boned cat who is always alone.

He seizes Désirée's wrist. Her skin is cool. She lets him take her hand and grip it tight.

Each night, lay siege to this fortress, possess it definitively.

Why not?

She is only sixteen, she says, but he will only be twenty-six in four months. He woos her. He devotes as much vigour to turning this dream into a reality as he would to constructing a battery.

On 21 April, under the benevolent gaze of their respective elder brother and sister, Napoleon and Désirée Clary are declared engaged.

Everything is fine.

On 7 May, Junot gives Napoleon a form, which he recognizes instantly from the colour of the ink. He tears it out of Junot's hands, reads it and swears. He has been appointed commander of an infantry brigade in La Vendée. Infantry! Him, general of artillery, 'Captain Cannon' of the siege of Toulon, commander of artillery of the Army of Italy! It is a degradation, not a promotion! And in La Vendée!

He has fought the English, the Sardinians – him, fighting the Chouans!

He brushes Junot aside, pushes past Joseph and then sees Désirée.

He stares at her. His dream is sitting there, in that salon, demurely, her hands on her knees.

He is leaving for Paris tomorrow, he says.

Do they think he is going to let himself be stifled, packed off out of sight, exiled, humiliated? What is happiness if not acting, fighting?

PART FIVE

My sword is at my side,
and with it I shall go far

MAY 1795 TO 11 MARCH 1796

XVIII

'YOU ARE NOTHING!'

No one has actually flung these words in Napoleon's face since his arrival in Paris in mid-May 1795, accompanied by Junot, Marmont, his aides-de-camp and his brother Louis, and yet he feels this judgement, contemptuous or indifferent, as a matter of established fact, at every moment – in a look, an attitude, a comment.

When he complains that the furnished apartment he is renting in the Hôtel de la Liberté, rue des Fossés-Montmartre, is meagrely furnished and the linen dubious-looking, the hotelier simply says, 'Seventy-two livres a month, seventy-two livres.' And indeed, what more can one ask for that price?

But Paris is dripping with money. Twirling their stout, knotted walking sticks, the dandies of the moment, the 'incroyables' in their powdered wigs, accompanied by their belles, the 'merveilleuses', strut along the boulevards and give the Jacobins and sans-culottes a thrashing.

Napoleon curses, 'And it is on such creatures that Fortune confers her favours!'

He is nothing.

He claims his travel expenses, 2,640 livres, and presents himself at the War Office to collect his pay and daily rations for six, but money can lose ten per cent of its value in less than a day! What are these bundles of notes they give him? Paper that goes up in smoke before one's eyes!

At the War Office, they barely pay him any attention and he waits for Aubry, the minister, to deign to receive him. Aubry! An old captain of artillery who has made himself a general, an inspector of artillery and who decides men's careers! An officer who owes his position to political intrigue and looks at Napoleon with an insufferable air of superiority.

Napoleon pleads his case: he is an artilleryman, brigadier-general, he cannot accept this command of an infantry unit.

'You are too young,' Aubry reiterates. 'One must let one's elders go first.'

'One grows old quickly on the field of battle, as I have found out,' he ripostes.

Hot blood is inappropriate, when one is nothing, when one has no support, when one only has a worn-out uniform on which the silk bands of one's rank are almost indiscernible.

The streets, offices and salons are thronged with swells who don't even see this officer with uncombed, badly powdered hair falling to his shoulders like dog's ears. His hands are long and thin, his skin sallow. He has a stoop, and wears a shabby round hat jammed down over his eyes. He walks clumsily, uncertainly. There is only his gaze, which sometimes takes people unawares, unprepared for the piercing look in his grey eyes. Then they notice his features, the fine mouth, the wilful chin, the resolute expression, the energy that emanates from this youthful and yet chiselled, almost emaciated, face.

Napoleon knows that there is nothing indulgent about the way people look at him. They turn away after having sized up at a glance his clothes, his dusty boots that are worn down at the heel, his sickly complexion.

The poor are suspect that spring of 1795. They demonstrated on 1 April, and again on 20 May, only a few days before Napoleon arrived in Paris. They stormed the Convention, beheaded the deputy Féraud and, like in the days of the Revolution, paraded his head about on a pike. The army, commanded by General Menou, restored order, but the *faubourgs'* cries of 'Bread!' and 'The Constitution of 1793!' have sent a shiver down people's spines. The boot-heel must be pressed down harder on the mob's throat.

'A country governed by property owners belongs to the social order, whereas that governed by those who are not property owners is in a state of nature, in other words, barbarism,' declares the Member of the Convention Boissy d'Anglas.

Napoleon knows that the taint of robespierrism still clings to him and that, at this time, there is no worse a mark of infamy. He roams around Paris trying to understand which are the seats of power determining the order of things. He is sure that everything is decided here, in the capital. There is no use blustering on the battlefield if one has not first gained supporters among those who hold power. If he agreed to go to the Army of the West, it would not only be an unfair loss of standing, but it would also mean losing all possibility of advancement and of finally being recognized for what he is, for what he is worth.

This straining towards the future is such a powerful drive that it exhausts him. He is constantly on the hunt, watching without knowing exactly what he is on the lookout for, where the prey will come from or how he will leap on it. He feels worn out by this uneasy quest.

'I am unwell,' he writes to Joseph, 'which forces me to take two or three months' leave. When my health is better, I will see what I will see.'

HE TRULY is ill; feverish, haggard, and at times overwhelmed with despair.

He takes up his quill and writes letter after letter to Joseph. Often he is on the verge of tears: 'I feel, writing these words, an emotion I have seldom known in my life. I feel we shall not see each other again soon, and I cannot go on with my letter.'

He is alone despite the presence at his side of Junot. Marmont has rejoined the Army of the Rhine, Louis has been accepted into the artillery school at Châlons-sur-Marne. He needs his family. 'You know, my friend,' his letter to Joseph continues, 'that I only live by the pleasure I cause my family.'

Nostalgia for a different life comes over him. 'Life is a flimsy dream that fades away,' he says. Why not choose a 'respectable house', a country life?

He writes to Bourrienne, 'Look for a little property in your beautiful Yonne valley. I will buy it as soon as I have the money. I want to withdraw there, but don't forget that I don't want a national property.' He is as prudent as a bourgeois who fears that one day the émigrés will come and demand the return of their property!

As he is imagining burying himself in the peaceful comforts of family life, he suddenly bursts out to Junot, 'That Joseph is a lucky rogue!' and his thoughts turn to the days he spent with the Clarys. He dreams of Désirée.

He becomes impassioned and writes a short novel in a few nights, which he entitles *Clisson and Eugénie*. He reveals himself in the person of a young man of twenty-six already covered with the laurels of many battles, but in love with a seventeen-year-old girl called Eugénie. Clisson is very cut and dried about things, with qualities Napoleon ascribes to himself: 'Clisson could not accustom himself to petty formalities. His ardent imagination, his fiery heart, his stern reason, his cold mind could only grow bored with the wheedling of coquettes and the ethos of the lampoon. He had no understanding of intrigues, and wordplays completely passed him by.'

To devote himself to his love for Eugénie, Clisson leaves the army, but returns to the battlefield when he is summoned by an urgent order from the government. He wins victory after victory, but discovers that Eugénie does not love him anymore. So he renounces life, writing a last letter to her:

> 'What is left to me for the future but society and ennui!
> At twenty-six I have exhausted the ephemeral pleasures of reputation, but in your love I tasted the sweetness of human life. Kiss my sons, may they not have their father's ardent soul, otherwise like him they will be the victims of men, of glory and of love.'
>   Clisson folded his letter, gave orders to an aide-de-camp to take it to Eugénie instantly and straightaway put himself at the head of a squadron, threw himself headlong into the mêlée and died run through by a thousand cuts.

Napoleon is twenty-six and his soul is too ardent like Clisson's, his hero.

He is in his room in the Hôtel de la Liberté, and he hasn't slept all night. It is swelteringly hot in this early August. Junot is sleeping in the next-door room.

It is so early in the morning! What should he do? Napoleon rereads the novel he has just finished, edits it and rewrites the first pages three times. Then he begins a letter to Joseph: 'I believe that you have on purpose avoided speaking to me about Désirée . . . If I stay here, it would not be out of the question for the marrying folly to seize me; to this end I would like some words on this subject from you.'

Napoleon wants Joseph to raise the question with Désirée's brother. He forms the words in his angular, swift hand: 'Continue writing to me in detail, see about arranging my affair in such a way that my absence will not prevent something I desire.'

He writes another few lines, and then, in conclusion, asks a brutal question: 'The matter of Désirée must conclude or break off, must it not? I await your reply impatiently.'

WRITING A NOVEL, looking at oneself in it as if in a mirror, trying to make a young girl a long way away marry one – these are ways of struggling against the emptiness of uncertainty, the anxiety that comes from getting nowhere.

Napoleon tries to open every door. He haunts the ministry. He climbs to the sixth floor of the Pavillon de Flore in the Tuileries Palace, the office of a member of the Committee of Public Safety, Doulcet de Pontécoulant, who is responsible for military operations. Napoleon has been given a letter of recommendation by Boissy d'Anglas. He would rather draw up plans of operations in an attic in the War Office than be a forgotten general at the head of an infantry brigade hunting Chouans. General Hoche is carrying out that task perfectly well, and the representative of the people, Tallien, has just given orders for seven hundred and forty-eight émigrés, who landed at Quiberon and were taken prisoner, to be shot. What is to be gained from that war? Much better to join the throng of petitioners.

His clothes provoke amazement and scorn in Pontécoulant's office. People look at him as if he is half-crazed. He senses the astonishment and alarm his passion arouses, and he is dismissed with the same phrase he has heard again and again: 'Put down all you have told me, present it as a report and bring it in.' Napoleon turns on his heel. He is not going to write up his notes, he thinks. When Boissy d'Anglas insists, however, he drafts a plan of operations for the Army of Italy, and Monsieur de Pontécoulant employs him for a few weeks at his side in the topographical department.

Napoleon's section are astonished by his prolificacy, and by the originality and talent of his work. He imposes himself on Pontécoulant, and once a relationship of mutual respect has been established and his qualities have been recognized, he requests to be reinstated as a general of artillery. Why not send him to Constantinople to reorganize the Turkish army? Pontécoulant supports his demands. Perhaps leaving for the Orient will be a way out, but he has to wait for Letourneur, who is in charge of personnel, to decide – and he is only a captain of artillery at forty!

Well then, he must seek other goals, because impatience is gnawing away and he knows how much damage inaction can do.

MONEY FIRST. What can one do without it? There's his pay, certainly, but the men who lord it in Paris have millions to juggle with. They dress in extravagant creations of silk and brocade, surmounted with turbaned hats, and when Napoleon manages to gain entrance to their salons, he is just a black silhouette squeezed into a badly cut uniform.

Money first, then.

Joseph has some, since Julie Clary has brought a hundred and fifty thousand livres with her.

'Yesterday I visited the estate at Ragny,' Napoleon writes in haste to his brother. 'If you want to do a good deal you should come and buy this estate for eight million assignats; you could put down sixty thousand francs of your wife's dowry. That is my wish and advice . . .'

But interesting deals are snapped up because everyone is in a rush to convert the devaluing currency into decent land and property

'Yesterday was the auction of the land I had intended to acquire, nine leagues from Paris; I had decided to give one million five hundred thousand, but, unbelievably, it went up to three million . . .' This is what this world is like! A world of money, intrigues, luxury, lechery, power and factions!

Napoleon noses out this world, examines it. It is the corrupt nouveaux riches who meet at the house of Madame Tallien, *Notre*

Dame de Thermidor, who allow one to enter the realms where destinies are settled!

He must be part of this world, or else not be at all.

This discovery undermines Napoleon's health.

He acquires an invitation to the Luxembourg Palace, where Barras, the so-called King of the Republic, reigns, and enters the drawing room of the Chaumière in the Queen's Walk, on the corner of the allée des Veuves and the Champs-Elysées. Here Madame Tallien entertains as the official mistress of Barras, who has so many others including, it's said, several young favourites.

Barras! Napoleon remembers this representative of the people who, with Fréron and Fouché, cleared Toulon of royalists. All that crowd have made a fortune supplying the armies, misappropriating public funds, and pillaging left and right. It is a world of debauchery, corruption, luxury and lechery which attracts Napoleon because he is a wolf ravenous for glory, women and power, and because he has understood that that is where everything is decided, but he also doubts his ability to conquer this world, to make a reputation for himself in it. Yet none other exists. Who concerns themselves with the poor any more? Every day more of them throw themselves and their children into the Seine to escape hunger and destitution. This is how the world is. Equality is just a chimera. Woe betide the poor and defeated!

'LUXURY, pleasure and the arts are reviving here in an astonishing way,' Napoleon writes.

He goes to the Opera and watches a performance of *Phèdre*. He roams about town. 'Carriages and the fashionable are reappearing, or rather they only remember as a long dream that they ever stopped glittering.'

He is still consumed by a yearning for knowledge. 'Libraries, history, chemistry, botany, astronomy lectures succeed one another,' he notes, but what animates the whole city is a desire to forget the months of Revolution in pleasure. 'It is as if everyone has to make up for the time they suffered and the uncertainty of the future means sparing nothing of the pleasures of the moment,' Napoleon explains to Joseph.

This is what this age is. Anyone who doesn't understand this, or wishes it were different, is mad.

'This town is still the same: everything is devoted to pleasure, to women, theatres, balls, promenades, artists' studios.' Can one be nothing in this world, the only real world there is? One might as well die.

Bitterness and despair abruptly overwhelm Napoleon. He no longer replies when Junot speaks to him. He hunches over and retires within himself, shut away in his thoughts.

He has spent that morning waiting to be seen first by Barras, then by Boissy d'Anglas, then by Fréron. He went to the War Office, where they allot active officers cloth for their uniform coats, frock coats, waistcoats and breeches. Napoleon put in his request and read the Committee of Public Safety's decree setting down the criteria of eligibility. Then he was sent away. They asked who he is. Even for a uniform, one needs influence.

This is what a man such as him is reduced to!

He takes up his quill. During that night of 12 August 1795, he lets his pain come flooding out. There is an abyss between what he would like to be and what he is, between the battles he dreams of fighting and this swamp he is floundering in. It is as he said of his character Clisson – he 'could not accustom himself to petty formalities ... He had no understanding of intrigues, and word-plays completely passed him by.'

That is all Thermidor Paris is! Napoleon feels disarmed, powerless, unable to force his way in.

So that night he gives way to despair, for the duration of a letter to Joseph.

I feel very little attachment to life. I watch it without great concern, perpetually feeling as one does on the eve of a battle, convinced that since death may finish everything at any moment, there is no sense in worrying. Everything prompts me to brave fate and destiny. And if this continues, my friend, I shall end up not getting out of the way of a passing carriage. This attitude sometimes astonishes my reason, but such is the inclination that the moral spectacle of this country and the hazards of war have engendered in me.

Sealing the letter, Napoleon leaps up and calls Junot. Junot's family has been sending him money which he stakes at cards and then gives any winnings to his general. Napoleon shares out the coins and notes, and they go to the Palais-Royal.

He is twenty-six, Junot twenty-four. They walk, hungry-eyed, through the women. Their bodies, their perfume and their eyes, when they meet his, instantly make Napoleon forget his near-suicidal despair. Desire reawakens the enjoyment of being alive. If one is to impose oneself on this world as it is, then one must first conquer and possess a woman.

'WOMEN ARE everywhere,' writes Napoleon to Joseph, 'in the theatres, out driving, in the libraries. In the scholar's study you see great belles. Here, alone of all the places on earth, they deserve to govern: plus the men are mad about them, think of nothing else and live only by and for them. A woman needs six months in Paris to know what is her due and the extent of her empire.'

So one must go where they go, these beautifully dressed, powerful, intelligent, witty, sensual women. If he wishes to gain the support of Barras, the King of the Republic, he must find some way of approaching *Notre Dame de Thermidor*, Thérésa Tallien.

Look, here she is in the salon of the Chaumière, which is decorated like a Greek temple. Napoleon is the most shabbily dressed of all the guests. The Muscadins wear blond wigs, woven, so they say, from the hair of victims of the guillotine. They sport extravagant ensembles in green, yellow and pink, and their coats have long tails which they play with. There isn't one of them who seems to notice this 'black' general, this 'puss in boots' with piercing eyes.

Napoleon threads his way through the officers covered with medals and the members of the Convention with their broad tricolour belts. He greets Fréron who, in Marseilles, paid frequent and insistent court to his sister Pauline. Barras strolls through the salons with Thérésa Tallien on his arm, like a sovereign in his gold-embroidered army frock coat. It has been a long time since Viscount Barras de Fox d'Amphoux, deputy for the Var, left the royal army and he dreams of higher ranks. On 1 August, he had himself made a brigadier-general! This is the sort of general one must defer to! He parades about, showing off Thérésa Tallien like a jewel.

She is dressed in a simple muslin shift, that falls in long folds like the tunics in Greek statues; it is draped over the bosom and the sleeves are gathered on the shoulders by clasps set with classical cameos. She is not wearing gloves. One can make out her breasts, her hips.

Other perfumed, tantalizing women mill around her in similar forms of undress. A voluptuous creole looks every man intently in the eye, as if inviting them to try their luck. That is Citizeness Hamelin, and over there is Citizeness Krudener, a pale, blonde Livonian. Here is Madame Récamier, and that young brunette who smiles without parting her lips, that is Josephine de Beauharnais, the widow of a general beheaded under the Terror. People say that she knew Madame Tallien in prison, that she was Barras's mistress before her, and that she still is from time to time. All these women are credited with several lovers, dissolute lives and fortunes.

Fascinated, Napoleon deferentially approaches Thérésa Tallien. He seems to attract some sort of attention and Barras whispers a few words in her ear. Perhaps he mentions the siege of Toulon.

Napoleon plucks up his courage. These near-naked women make him bold. In an instant, the thin, drab officer becomes a flamboyant, conquering, imperious figure. Making fun of himself, he petitions her – he hasn't got a uniform any more, look! Can Madame Tallien help him get the material he is entitled to? Can she, the Queen of Paris, grant him this favour?

He has played his card. She deigns to look at him and is struck by the energy that radiates from him. This officer's silhouette is not up to much, it's rather absurd, but his eyes are very arresting. She listens, and then replies magnanimously that Lefeuve, under whose jurisdiction this falls and who, furthermore, is in her debt, will provide the cloth for the uniform.

As she is talking, Barras walks away, smiling, a bored look on his face.

Their conversation continues. Napoleon pounces on every remark and turns each into an opportunity for him to shine. Suddenly he is at his ease, as if he had been learning all his life to pay court to her, as if this world was his own. Full of self-assurance, he takes her wrist and declares that he can see a person's fortune in the palm of their hand. A circle of women forms around him and he makes them laugh with his extravagant fancies, the allusions embedded in his prophecies. He is Corsican, almost Italian, isn't he? A civilization that can predict the future. General Hoche holds out his hand. Napoleon announces that the general will die in his bed, 'like Alexander'.

He exchanges a few words with Josephine de Beauharnais, who looks at him, trying to get a sense of this short, thin, wiry man, whose mind and conversation are so nimble they make one forget his wretched appearance.

She is looking for a husband.

Napoleon strides out of Thérésa Tallien's Chaumière. That is all Paris is. At last, at the beginning of September, he feels that for the first time he has managed to establish outposts on the terrain he has to conquer. He must see her again and, through her, approach Barras and Fréron whose only response to his overtures until now has been courteous, friendly, blunt refusals.

Coaches pass. In the corners of gateways, poor are huddled together, asleep, their children swaddled in rags.

The night is still mild.

In his room, he starts to write to Joseph, 'Whatever happens, you need have no fear for me; I have all the right people for friends, whatever their party or opinion ... Tomorrow I shall have three horses, which will enable me to drive about in a cabriolet and attend to my business. I foresee only agreeable matters in the future, and if it were otherwise, then one would just have to live even more in the present: the future is an object of scorn for a man who has courage.'

IN THE DAYS that follow, Napoleon feels buoyed up by this certainty that, at last, he has given himself the means to act. He writes to Barras and he makes sure that Pontécoulant still supports his plan to obtain a post in Constantinople.

The decree authorizing his appointment is ready, Pontécoulant assures him; his travel expenses are fixed, he will be leading a full delegation. So he will escape the upheavals he senses are about to shake Paris. The royalists are mobilizing – they have mixed feelings about the new Constitution of the Year III, with its two assemblies, the Council of the Ancients and the Council of the Five Hundred – but the decree the Convention issues on 28 August seems to them nothing short of a coup d'état.

The Convention has decided that two thirds of any future assembly will be drawn from its membership – a way of avoiding seeing either royalists or moderates winning the forthcoming elections. The Barras, Talliens, Fouchés and Frérons do not want a return of the monarchy.

Napoleon is too marked as a Jacobin, too suspect to hope for anything from the monarchists or the Convention, so every day he waits for the appointment that will allow him to leave France with a good salary and a prestigious position.

Then, on 15 September 1795, the Committee of Public Safety issues the following decree:

> The Committee of Public Safety decrees that Brigadier-General Bonaparte, formerly requisitioned to serve under the orders of the Committee of Public Safety, is struck off the list of employed general officers on account of his refusal to take up the post assigned to him.
>
> The 9th Commisssion is charged with the implementation of this decree.
>
> 29 Fructidor, Year III of the Republic
> Cambacérès, Berlier, Merlin, Boissy

Napoleon is dismissed, purged.

Victory, talent, determination, all his efforts to convince the members of the Convention, the Barras and Frérons and their women – all of it has been useless.

He is just an unemployed general, one of many; seventy-four suspects have been struck off like him.

He is twenty-six years old.

'You are nothing, Napoleon!'

XIX

So he must start again.

Napoleon does not feel weary. Quite the opposite. This unexpected blow, just as he thought he was reaching his goal, spurs him on.

Either I launch myself into the fray again or I give up.

He lifts his head and watches Junot, who is storming up and down the room, roundly abusing Letourneur, head of military personnel, Cambacérès, Barras, Fréron, all those profiteers, all those bureaucrats who think they can decide the future of General Napoleon Bonaparte!

Why add his voice to Junot's? What's the good of resentment? Why waste that energy?

He must hold his head up high, as if a spur has been furiously dug into his side.

Come on.

Outside he strides briskly towards the Palais-Royal. He doesn't reply to Junot's questions. The evening is a mild one, the twilight flushed by a blood-red sunset.

Suddenly there is shouting and men running past, yelling, 'Down with the Two Thirds!' They have collars in the Comte d'Artois's colours and their *cadenettes*, those locks that hang down to their chests, dance around their shoulders. They storm into the cafés on the square and the Théâtre-Français, forcing the customers, audience and passers-by to take up their chants condemning the Constitution and the decree of the Two Thirds. From time to time a voice yells, 'Long live the King!'

Word has it that the Lepeletier section, which contains the Stock Exchange, has sent an address to all the communes, urging them to challenge the decree of the Two-Thirds and demand its repeal. It has appealed to General Danican to take command of the National Guard of Paris so that, if need be, they can rise up armed against the Convention.

The Assembly meets. In the entrance hall, resting the paper on his knees, Napoleon writes a letter to Barras, and another to Fréron. He recognizes this atmosphere, this wind getting up – a storm is on its way. He remembers 20 June and 10 August 1792. He was a few paces from the rioters then, not far from here, a spectator convinced that he could have changed the course of events. He would be even better equipped to do so now, but he is off-stage. So, if he cannot play the leading role, he might as well walk away from the theatre. He must secure that appointment that apparently has already been drafted. He must go to Constantinpole.

A few days later, he is in a position to write to Joseph, 'My journey is more likely than ever; in fact, it would already be decided if there were not such a ferment here. Things are boiling up at the moment and there are some very inflammatory developments; it will all be over in a few days.'

HE CANNOT stay in his room. He goes to the theatre. He needs that clamour and laughter around him: it isolates him and at the same time stimulates his mind. He feels Junot looking at him, anxious and surprised; when the entire audience collapses in hysterics, only Napoleon remains impassive.

Outside, in the galleries of the Palais-Royal, groups are shouting, indignantly protesting against the referendum which has endorsed the Constitution, with a little over a million votes for, barely fifty thousand against, and more than five million abstentions. As for the decree of the Two-Thirds, which will allow much of the Convention to form part of the two new assemblies, it has only won 205,498 votes, with more than 100,000 against! It's a farce, they yell. The crack of musket shots ring out. An army patrol is being fired on. Youngsters come past, armed. Some are wearing the emblem of the Vendeans, a heart and a cross combined.

A thousand émigrés, with two thousand Englishmen, have landed on the island of Yeu. Thirty of Paris's forty-eight sections, under the leadership of the Lepeletier section, are calling on the people to rise against the Convention and take up arms. Now that the sans-culottes have been crushed and the army purged of its Jacobin officers, the moderates and royalists think it will be easy for them. They have thirty thousand National Guard in uniform and the Convention can only count on eight thousand men.

VOICES, SHOUTS, uproar, gunfire, the tramp of National Guard under arms, the occasional echo of a galloping horse – Napoleon listens to all of these like a hunter waiting for the right moment. But he is nothing. He can only watch, wait. 'For what?' asks Junot.

They have just heard that the Convention is anxiously appealing to such generals and officers as have been disgraced on the grounds of Jacobinism to rally round to its defence. It has even formed three volunteer battalions, 'the Patriots of '89', from members of the anti-royalist sections. To protect Barras, Fréron, Tallien and Cambacères! Napoleon laughs derisively. He takes Junot by the arm, 'Oh,' he mutters through clenched teeth, 'if the sections would only put me at their head, I'd give them my word that within two hours I'd have them in the Tuileries and driven out every miserable member of the Convention!'

But the sections have chosen General Danican, and the Convention's army is led by General Menou, the same officer who broke up the sans-culottes' hunger riots on 20 May.

What's the difference between Danican and Menou? Let's go to the theatre instead.

DRUMMERS are sounding the alarm in the streets. Troops pass – infantry, gunners, cavalry – heading for the rue Vivienne to occupy the Lepeletier section which is where the central military committee of all the insurgent sections meets under the leadership of the royalist Richer de Sérizy.

It is nine o'clock in the evening. Napoleon keeps in the background. It starts to rain and his uniform lets in the water. His long, shoulder-length hair gets soaked. No one notices him in the darkness. Battalions of National Guard advance with drummers at their head, and take up position on rue du Faubourg St Honoré. Why is General Menou waiting to disperse them?

It seems the complete opposite is happening; the sections' troops are gradually cordoning off the whole capital, as the rain becomes torrential.

NAPOLEON makes his way towards the Convention. Someone calls out to him. Has he heard that General Menou has been placed under arrest for parleying with the sections and withdrawing the army, so that the streets have been left in the hands of the insurgents? Thirty thousand of them! All the generals on Menou's staff have been dismissed with him and Barras has been appointed commander-in-chief, charged with protecting the Convention.

You are wanted, Citizen General.

Napoleon feels no emotion. He does not hurry. Look, here's Fréron coming towards him, suddenly familiar, talking about Pauline with whom he is in love, whispering that he suggested Bonaparte as second-in-command to Barras, and that Barras took his suggestion very seriously. Carnot mentioned other names besides Bonaparte's — Brune and Verdières, for instance — but Barras replied, 'Generals of manoeuvre are not what's needed here; we need an artilleryman.'

Barras approaches and signals to Fréron to leave them. He is grave. The royalists must not be allowed to overthrow the regime. That would leave the way open to the enemy, to the English who have forty ships off Brest, and to the Austrians who are mustering forty thousand men before Strasbourg. It would mean renouncing the annexations, giving up Belgium, which has been French since 1 October. Barras breaks off. He offers Napoleon the post of second-in-command.

Napoleon is impassive, eyes set, complexion even sallower than usual. Has the time come to declare himself? Is this the point when he emerges from behind the parapet to face the grapeshot? When he gives the order to engage? Declare himself, expose himself — to defend what exactly? Barras, Fréron? France? The Republic?

What do these men who have sent for him care about? Their power, the treasures they have amassed, and the fact that they never want to have to account for what they have done: they are regicides, terrorists, souls of corruption ordering soldiers to fire on the faubourgs. They are Thermidoreans who just want to digest in peace and enjoy themselves to the full!

Must he, in their name, become a scapegoat for so many crimes he has been a stranger to?

Who for? What for?

For me.

'You have three minutes to make up your mind,' says Barras.

He must grab this chance by the mane as it passes like a horse at full gallop.

'I accept,' says Napoleon in a calm, curt voice. 'But I warn you . . .'

He stops. How simple everything is when the action starts.

'If I draw my sword,' he continues, 'it will not return to its sheath until order is restored, whatever the cost.'

IT IS ONE o'clock in the morning on 5 October 1795, 13 Vendé-miaire. He has seized hold of the mane: now he has to tame the horse carrying him off.

When Napoleon inspects the men or questions the officers, he senses their astonishment at 'the disorder of his appearance, his long, lank hair, his decrepit old clothes'. He overhears people whispering amongst themselves, 'Bonaparte is in command? Who the devil is he?'

First understand the situation. General Menou is sitting in a guarded room. In a brief, sympathetic conversation, Napoleon gains the necessary information.

Then give orders. No superfluous rhetoric; terseness, clarity. The troops are not to be put at risk, but used to defend the Convention. The insurgents have superiority in numbers, but they will be advancing in separate columns which will be vulnerable to cannon fire.

Napoleon beckons over a young cavalry major, Murat, who is swaggering about with a conceited air. The officer approaches, slightly contemptuous. The words cut like a knife, 'Take two hundred horses, go to Les Sablons immediately. Bring the forty guns from the park. We must have them! Use your sabres if you need to, but bring them.'

Murat prepares to speak.

'You will answer to me for this. Go,' concludes Napoleon.

In the drumming of hooves, Napoleon cannot hear the members of the Convention who are pressing round him and bombarding him with questions. When the cavalry have gone, he looks at these men whose faces are distorted with fear and worry, 'Arm them,' he says. 'Let them form a battalion and get ready.'

He is so calm, so sure of himself. One decision connects to the next like a piece of machinery. He anticipates the sequence of moves in the game that is about to begin. The sectionaries must have thought about the cannon as well, but they won't get there before Murat, and these forty pieces of ordnance will be the trump card – the one Louis XVI did not play in June '91 or in August '92, the one that must be played to clear the streets, because the use of cannon in the city will take their opponents by surprise and cancel the balance of power at present in favour of the royalist sections.

He leaps on his horse and goes from one position to another, only stopping at each for a few minutes. He loves the briskness of the lieutenants coming to report. He senses the soldiers turning to look at him. He only says a few words, but he sees the attitudes changing. They trust him. He moves off again. He knows that being in command also means being seen. Everyone must know he is here with them, under fire. They must hear him giving orders unhesitatingly.

Right arm outstretched, he places the cannon at the corners of all the streets leading to the Convention. If the sections' columns attack, they are to open fire. The guns will rake the streets with enfilade fire; grapeshot will be used; a few minutes will be enough to sweep aside the enemy troops.

Barras listens and then says that *he* is the one who is going to give the order to engage. He is the commander-in-chief, Napoleon the second-in-command.

Why challenge his authority? The time hasn't come for that. Napoleon has nothing to say; he is the one the officers come to, around three in the afternoon, to announce that the rebel columns are closing in on the Convention. It is his orders they await. Barras gives a signal; Bonaparte advances and commands the gunners to open fire.

THERE'S A general stampede in the streets amongst the bodies mown down by the grapeshot. Gunsmoke hides the road and the façades. Sectionaries are rallying on the steps of St Roch, others are gathering at the Palais-Royal. Napoleon mounts his horse. He must be where the fighting is. He approaches the Feuillants Convent in rue du Faubourg St Honoré, but his horse falls, killed. Napoleon picks himself up unharmed as the soldiers pour forward. He orders them to open fire on the mustered sectionaries, and the steps of St Roch are soon blood-spattered and covered in bodies.

The streets are empty. It needed less than two hours to gain victory.

IN FRONT of the Convention, Napoleon sees the deputies coming up to congratulate him. He ignores them and heads towards the Tuileries Palace where the wounded have been brought. They are lying on mattresses or thick, fresh straw. Deputies' wives are looking after them. Napoleon bends down and salutes the wounded, as the women flock to him. He is the victor and the saviour.

He hears Barras in the chamber of the Assembly orchestrating the cheers as his name is mentioned.

He walks away. He knows that he will have to pay a price for his victory. The three hundred dead his cannon have stretched out in the road are nothing among all those who have already been carried off in the revolutionary upheaval, but he will never be forgiven for breaking the royalist movement. He will have dedicated political enemies from now on. Whatever he does, he belongs to a camp now, the one that contains Barras, Fréron, Tallien and all the regicides, as well as Robespierre.

That is the truth of it – but only a man who acts can become anything.

HE DOES NOT sleep the night of 5–6 October, 13–14 Vendémiaire. He gives orders for patrols to be carried out in Paris all the following day, then he writes to Joseph, because he needs to tell what has happened: 'At last everything is finished, my first instinct is to think of you and send you my news.' He rapidly details the principal events of the last hours, then he adds, 'As usual, I have not been wounded. PS Happiness is mine: regards to Désirée and Julie.'

XX

ON 6 OCTOBER 1795, as troops patrol Paris without encountering any resistance, Napoleon feels and sees and knows that everything has changed, but he does not show any surprise.

One of those uniforms of good wool which he had petitioned for unsuccessfully is brought to him. He puts it on slowly. His body clothed in the thick fabric and his face framed by the high collar with its gold braid no longer seem quite the same. His gestures are less jerky, his skin which is inflamed by scabies seems smoother, even his complexion isn't as sallow.

An officer approaches him. He waits, arms crossed, leather boots polished to a brilliant shine. Letters are deferentially handed to him. The expression of the courier, a lieutenant, is at once admiring and fearful. Napoleon looks at him. The man instantly drops his eyes, as if he has done something wrong and is afraid of being reprimanded.

Napoleon says nothing.

This is power; this is victory. Even Junot is not as familiar as he was; he hesitates before speaking, hangs back a few paces, respecting Napoleon's silence.

Newspapers are brought, Junot scans them and then presents them to him.

This general they talk of, this name that keeps coming up, Bonaparte, Bonaparte, it is me.

Every feature of Napoleon's face is suffused with surprise and joy. In an address to the Convention, Fréron has eulogized 'this general of artillery, Bonaparte, who was appointed on the night of the 12th and 13th and only had the morning of the 13th to make the expert arrangements of which you have seen the effects'.

Barras has intervened to have Napoleon's promotion to second-in-command of the Army of the Interior confirmed. On 16 October, he is made general of division, and then, on the 26th, before breaking up, the Convention appoints him commander-in-chief of the Army of the Interior.

At last.

HE SITS in a large carriage drawn by four horses and flanked by an escort. The guard salutes as he drives into his headquarters, rue Neuve Capucine, his official residence. He walks through the salons. People get to their feet as he approaches and click their heels. He summons his aides-de-camps: Marmont, Junot, his brother Louis, and five other officers who are, as he writes to Joseph, 'his captain aides-de-camp'.

He reads the list of those who are waiting in the antechamber to see him. These petitioners whose lives he can change with a word or a sentence are proof of what he has become.

The walls are hung with mirrors with gilt frames. Napoleon looks at himself for a long time when he lifts his head and waits for the first of these importunate fellows to be shown in. He is the same as he was a month ago. The same as the man who was locked in the Fort-Carré, discharged from the Army of Italy, purged from the forces. The same man who would be answered with a hasty note, the same man whose boots took in water.

But he is here, identical and yet completely different. He commands forty thousand men, and the people who come into this room, who do not dare sit down in his presence, see him in the light of power.

He is not intoxicated, or surprised. He remembers the child he once was, who often, to get to the top of the hill quicker, left the path and ran through the bushes. The brambles caught on his clothes, scratching his hands, his arms and legs. Sometimes the branches would whip him in the face, and the undergrowth would clutch onto him, holding him back. He'd fall to his knees, then think he'd reached the top and fall down again, or else a thicker bush, a higher rock would rear up in front of him. When his efforts had finally been rewarded, he would stand facing the horizon, free to move about on that platform wherever he chose, not knowing how far it stretched nor what new dangers it contained, but able at last to take a deep breath.

He is finally able to be himself.

He gives orders. There is to be no revenge, no executions or even arrests of yesterday's insurgents. The sectionaries are to be shown clemency.

He sees Barras, Fréron and Tallien. He pleads for General Menou's acquittal. They listen to him, ask him questions. He answers in clipped sentences. He observes. He gauges the anxieties of these men who, until so recently, kept him at arm's length and treated him with condescension, irony and a little contempt. So, they are simply this, are they – fearful there'll be a royalist victory at the next elections, whispering amongst themselves about calling them off, if there is no other alternative, and inciting a coup d'état. For the moment they are organizing the Executive Directory, of which Viscount Barras de Fox d'Amphoux is to be the prime mover, the plumed director, the 'King of the Directory', hated, scorned, envied and feared:

> Purple is the reward they wear
> Wear wear wear
> For the crimes of the Vendémiaire
> Fox just says 'D'amn You!'
>
> Paris does not think it fair
> Fair fair fair
> Another thing to grin and bear
> Fox just says 'D'amn You!'

Junot tells Napoleon the pendant to this song that can be heard everywhere in Paris, clinging to Barras's coat-tails:

> He's not yet forty but like all damned souls
> The crimes don't wait for the criminal to get old.

Nevertheless, these are the men in power, and from now on Napoleon sees them every day, as a guest in their houses or as a host in his.

HE ENTERS Thérésa Tallien's salon. He doesn't have to thread his way through the throng to her any more. She comes up to him, takes his arm. He is surrounded by all these perfumed women, whose diaphanous dresses brush against him, who leave their hands in his for a long time. He is the new man in their little world, their saviour, this vigorous, lean fighting man who is so different from the men they have known for years, whose fat bodies and vices they know intimately, who they have shared and swapped so often they no longer hold any surprises. But then, neither can they surprise these men who they try to hold onto but who have grown blasé and need ever stronger stimulants.

Besides, none of them talk any more; they play cards, and sit staring around little tables piled with vast bets. They pass their nights at whist, faro, vingt et un, *bouillotte* and *creps*.

But this Bonaparte, this general-in-chief presiding over the army in Paris who everyone says is a coming man – he does not join them.

The women ask him questions. He looks at them without lowering his eyes. One of them, with a dark complexion and bare arms under the gauzy sleeves fastened at her wrists by little gold clasps, tilts her head back slightly. He sees her breasts, her bared neck. He senses an invitation. Her movements are slow. Sometimes her fingertips brush her hair, which is pinned up by a gold clip except for a delicate fringe of curls that frames her forehead like a diadem. She smiles as she speaks, her face expressive, her eyes shining.

'Tell me everything,' she seems to be saying.

He complies. Gradually the other women drift away as if she, Josephine de Beauharnais, had acquired a right over this general who is not yet twenty-seven.

She invites him to pay her a visit, rue Chantereine, number 6.

He knows who she is.

That night, in his vast bedroom on rue Neuve Capucine, he cannot get to sleep. He walks up and down, as he usually does. He goes into his study. Writing is the only way to calm himself. He begins a letter to Joseph. 'I am excessively overworked,' he writes, 'my health is good. I am here, happy and content.' He stops.

He knows who she is.

Widow of General de Beauharnais, two children, Eugène and Hortense. Mistress to Barras. Of aristocratic, West Indies stock, born Marie Josephe Rose Tascher de la Pagerie. Part of the *ancien régime* and the new one. A woman. So different from Désirée Clary. Perhaps she is even rich.

A life behind her already. Probably over thirty. But that body, that skin, that way of moving, as if she were dancing, like a climbing flowering plant entwining itself around a tree.

She is friends with everyone. She is the woman at the centre of the world he has entered.

He knows who she is. That is why she attracts him.

HE TAKES up her invitation. The little town house she lives in is set in a park in the chaussée d'Antin, a recent neighbourhood which is still mainly countryside, and to find it he has to go through gardens until he comes upon a semi-circular pavilion, in the neo-classical style. Four tall windows topped with a fan-light fill the ground floor with light. Josephine is sitting on a bergère. She seems barely dressed; the diaphanous folds suggest every curve of her body. A Roman frieze runs round the salon, above its pale wooden panelling. Armchairs and bergères are dotted about, and a harp in front of one of the windows rounds off the stage design. Josephine has rented the house from Julie Carreau, the wife of the great actor Talma.

With a languid wave, she invites Napoleon to come and sit next to her.

He knows who she is: she is the sign of his victory.

He hesitates. He could embrace her, sweep her off her feet, win her, he is sure of it, desires it. He sits on the bergère, but he still preserves a distance between them.

ON 28 OCTOBER, when he is surrounded by his aides-de-camp, a soldier brings him a letter. The officers move away as he opens the envelope.

He does not recognize the rounded writing, with thick down strokes, that seems hesitant and painstaking. The letter is signed 'Widow Beauharnais'.

> You no longer come and see a friend who loves you. You have completely neglected her; you are most wrong, because she is tenderly attached.

Come tomorrow and lunch with me; I need to see you and
talk with you about your interests.
Goodnight my friend, with love
Widow Beauharnais
6 Brumaire

Napoleon folds up the letter and dismisses his aides-de-camp.
A woman, at last.
This woman who is offering herself.
To me. If I want.

WHEN JUNOT returns to go through the police reports, which
suggest that 'decent people' consider Bonaparte 'excessively Jacobin' and nickname him 'General Vendémiaire', Napoleon stands
stock-still, an inscrutable look on his face. 'I'm fond of the title
General Vendémiaire,' he says. 'In the future it will be my first
title to fame.'

Then he takes the bundle of reports and starts to read them.
While the royalists are criticizing him, attacking the Directory and
plotting, the Jacobins are reorganizing. They have founded the
Pantheon Club. Napoleon starts; amongst the names he does not
know – Babeuf, Darthé – suddenly there's a familiar one, Buonarroti, still faithful to his ideas of equality and now supporting
The Tribune of the People, the newspaper that Babeuf is secretly
publishing.

What do these men hope for? One cannot share everything
with everybody. Life selects those who are capable of taking and
owning, and those who accept being dominated by others. That is
how it is. At every moment one must defend what one has won
and add to it, look after one's intimates – one's family, one's clan.
Napoleon sits down and writes to Joseph.

Taking from some and giving to others – this is what being in
power is.

Ramolino has been appointed Inspector of Transports, Lucien is
a war commissary with the Army of the Rhine, Louis is with me
. . . I cannot do more than I am for everybody . . . The family
lacks nothing; I have sent them money, assignats . . . I have
received, only a few days ago, four thousand francs for you;

Fesch who I have given them to will explain . . . You should not concern yourself about the family at all, it is well provided for. Jerome arrived yesterday, I am going to put him in a college that will suit him . . . I have lodging, table and a carriage for you here . . .

Later he adds a last message to repeat that 'the family lack nothing. I have sent them everything they need . . . almost sixty thousand francs, silver, assignats, frills and furbelows . . . So don't be at all worried.'

Give what one has to one's family, share with them. What else can one do in this world of ours?

NAPOLEON walks the streets surrounded by his staff. He needs to see for himself; the maintenance of order is one of his responsibilities. Strikes are breaking out, the price of bread is soaring. Food is scarce. It is cold and there's a shortage of firewood.

He sees what is happening, he understands. He organizes bread and firewood to be distributed, but crowds still form in front of the bakeries. A woman shouts at him. She is misshapen, her voice is a piercing screech. 'All these epaulettes make fun of us,' she yells, pointing at Napoleon and his staff. 'Just as long as they eat and get nice and fat, they don't care a scrap that the poor people are dying of hunger!'

The crowd murmurs. Napoleon stands in his stirrups, 'My good lady, take a look at me and tell me which is the fatter of us two?'

The crowd laughs. Napoleon puts his horse into a gallop, followed by his staff. From high on one's horse, just as from the height of one's power – that is how one leads men.

But as he urges his horse through the slow-moving crowd, Napoleon feels fettered once more, for the first time since Vendémiaire. What is this command of the Army of the Interior except being a policeman to the men who hold true political power – Barras, the five directors, and now Carnot as well?

They are the ones who give the orders and Napoleon is at the head of the troops that force their way into the Pantheon Club because the Directory has decided to shut it down. It is too successful: nearly two thousand people at each meeting to acclaim

Buonarroti and read *The Tribune of the People*. One does not leave a fuse burning when the citizens are cold and hungry.

Napoleon yanks hard on the reins as his horse stamps on the cobbles. He is not a gendarme. He is a soldier. On 19 January 1796 he has submitted, for perhaps the tenth time, plans for an Italian campaign. Schérer, the commander of the Army of Italy, has rejected them and they have outraged Ritter, the government commissioner attached to Schérer's headquarters. He has written to the Directory, and to Carnot first, since he is responsible for military matters. What is this plan they have been sent? Who has drawn it up? 'One of those lunatics who think that one can seize the moon with one's teeth? One of those individuals gnawed by ambition and greedy for positions beyond their capability?'

As the soldiers lead off the Jacobins under arrest, Napoleon dreams of a genuine, substantial command.

Carnot has told him that the reactions of Generals Schérer and Ritter were sceptical, or downright hostile, and have effectively ruled out his plan of operations – but at the same time Carnot gave him the impression that there was a chance he could be put in command of the Army of Italy.

Once again Napoleon curses himself for showing how certain he is, what his ambitions are. 'If I was there,' he had exclaimed, 'the Austrians would have been swept aside!' Carnot had murmured, 'You shall go' – but since then nothing, apart from rumours and more rumours, and scraps of envious gossip. Napoleon listens to the latest batch from Louis, who culls them in the ante-rooms, where they are indignantly retold by his loyal aide-de-camps.

People are saying that Napoleon is Barras's protégé. The director is looking to shuffle his old mistress Josephine off onto a husband with a nice dowry. Why not Bonaparte, and put him in charge of the Army of Italy at the same time?

Napoleon is infuriated.

'Do they think,' he exclaims, 'that I need patronage to succeed? They would all be overjoyed if I gave them mine. My sword is at my side and with it I shall go far.'

'This woman . . .' murmurs Louis. 'This planned marriage.'

Napoleon stares at his brother, who flinches, then goes out of the room.

HOW CAN anyone else understand what I feel?

He has pulled Josephine towards him and felt her mould herself to him, so supple, offering her hips, her sex, arching her back, and he has carried her like that to bed.

She is his, this woman with expert hands and long fingers; this woman who is silk and honey and whom he clasps with such passion, such intense desire that it seems she will faint and she tries to push him away, until suddenly she yields and abandons herself to him with immeasurable tenderness – and yet he has the feeling that she is always slipping from his embrace and just when he thinks he catches her, when he takes her, she is gone, she is somewhere else.

What can anyone know of those nights when he goes to her, when he brushes aside her clothes without even taking off his uniform or his boots? She is the woman for this moment in his life when he can finally be himself. She is his victory made flesh and delight – a living victory, which does not lose its allure as soon as it's attained, but on the contrary, arouses new reserves of passion.

He writes to her:

> I awake full of you. Your portrait and the intoxications of last night have left no repose to my senses; sweet, incomparable Josephine, what a strange effect you have on my heart! If you are angry, if I see you sad, if you are worried, my soul is broken with grief and there is no rest for your friend. But will I ever rest when, yielding to the innermost feeling that masters me, I drink a burning flame from your lips, from your heart? Ah, this night has shown me that your portrait is not you. You are leaving at midday, I shall see you in three hours. Till then, *mio dolce amore*, a thousand kisses, but do not give me any, for they set my blood on fire!

He thinks constantly of that body, that woman. He wants to keep her prisoner in his arms, as if that would assure him not only of her but also of all she represents – her past, her friendships, her fortune perhaps, and her place in Parisian society where, as he well knows, he is just one of the ones hovering in the doorway.

With her on his arm, he would incontrovertibly be a part of that world he came into on a night of civil war, in the storms of 13 Vendémiaire. Thanks to this woman, he wants to proclaim his victory, his new-found standing. He wants to be certain he can have her any night, whenever the desire might take him, because she is his wife.

Josephine is evasive. Waiting for her in the antechamber of a notary, Maître Raguideau, whom she wanted to see, Napoleon listens at the door. He hears the notary grumble, 'What, marry a general who only has his cape and sword, a pretty business that would be! What does he own this Bonaparte? A poky little house? Not even that! Who is he? A petty civil war general, no future, not fit to be mentioned in the same breath as the great generals of the Republic! Better to marry an army contractor!'

Napoleon controls himself. He would like to storm into the notary's office, but he moves away and goes over to the window. He will have this woman. He knows who she is. He knows what she brings him, how she makes his blood run hot. He knows her body. It is the first woman's body that he has held like that, that he can caress and make love to as he wants. No woman has ever touched him the way she does, without restraint, with a gentleness and assurance and skill that exhilarate and transport him and arouse him, even at the very moment he feels all his desire is spent.

And they would like him to give her up!

HE SEES her every day. He discovers that the span of a day can include, besides military matters, seeing her, loving her, thinking of her, writing to her – as well as meetings with Barras, Carnot and La Révellière-Lépeaux, one of the five members of the Executive Directory.

Far from draining his energy, his desire for her gives him new strength.

On 7 February 1796, the marriage banns are published and, over the next few days, the Directory decides to put him in command of the Army of Italy.

'Barras's dowry,' the envious are quick to say.

Louis and Junot are outraged by this tittle-tattle, but he tells them to be quiet. Must he explain that they are putting him in charge of the Army of Italy because Generals Schérer, Augereau, Sérurier, Masséna and others are not winning decisive victories and the Directory wants success, it wants booty, the coffers are empty and Napoleon must secure the victories that will fill them?

On 23 February, the decree appointing him to the head of the Army of Italy is drawn up, and on the 25th, the Directory appoints General Hatry commander of the Army of the Interior.

These are feverish days. Napoleon organizes his succession, chooses his aides-de-camp and prepares his plans of operations.

In the evenings he spreads out his maps in Josephine's salon and boudoir in rue Chantereine. Her dog Fortuné, a ribbon tied around its neck, scampers about barking when Napoleon takes Josephine in his arms and pushes her to the bed, imperious and passionate.

Sometimes he thinks she is half-hearted, just submitting to him, and he is worried. She will be his wife in a few days. He kisses her ardently. Can she imagine the passion he feels? She smiles without parting her lips.

He presses her. She will be his wife.

They must have a marriage settlement. When it comes to giving their ages, Josephine loses four years, he notes, and he gains eighteen months, but what do details like that matter. He wants this marriage.

When Maître Raguideau reads out that the future spouse 'declares that he possesses no movable or immovable goods other than his clothes and *equipages de guerre*', Napoleon stands up, rereads the sentence, and demands that it be struck out. Under the settlement, husband and wife will administer their separate properties. In the case of Napoleon's death, Josephine will receive fifteen hundred livres. She remains the guardian of her children, Hortense and Eugène. The contract gives a list of her trousseau: four dozen blouses, six petticoats, twelve pairs of silk stockings . . . Ostensibly, Napoleon isn't listening, but he freezes when two black horses and a calash are mentioned among Josephine's possessions. Barras had arranged for this carriage to be sent over from the national stables, as compensation for property General Beauharnais had lost under the Terror.

THE WEDDING day is 9 March 1796 (19 Ventôse Year IV), with the ceremony at nine in the evening in the town hall on rue d'Antin. Napoleon has assembled his aides-de-camp, and is allocating each of them their duties. Promotion to the head of the Army of Italy has been officially confirmed on 2 March, and departure for the headquarters town of Nice is set for 11 March. The aides-de-camp must prepare the stages, Napoleon's lodgings, and send word to the generals.

Suddenly Napoleon looks up and jumps. It is after nine. Barras, Tallien and Josephine must be waiting at the town hall.

Followed by one of his aides-de-camp, Le Marois, Napoleon rushes out. He has already given Josephine the little sapphire ring which will be their wedding ring. Inside are engraved the words, 'To Fate'.

It is ten o'clock when he reaches the town hall and he takes the steps at a run.

They are all there and the mayor, Le Clerq, is drowsing in the candlelight.

Napoleon shakes him. The ceremony begins; it does not last long. Josephine murmurs her consent. Yes, Napoleon says in a ringing voice.

Then he takes Josephine away.

She is his for two nights.

On 11 March, accompanied by his brother Louis, Junot, and Quartermaster-General Chauvet, Napoleon sets off for the headquarters of the Army of Italy.

Josephine stands on the steps. He waves to her.

She is mine.

As Italy will be.

PART SIX

I saw the world receding beneath me . . .

27 March 1796 to 5 December 1797

XXI

IN THE MAIL COACH, Napoleon is silent. At each of the relays, he signals to Junot to bring him paper, ink, a quill and leaves the room where dinner is to be served.

He sits down at a little table and writes.

It wrenches him to be apart from Josephine. He needs her. He would like her body to be next to his. He feels mutilated and rebels against his state.

He wants everything.

Her *and* the command of the Army of Italy.

Why must going towards one mean going away from the other? It is stupid, unfair, unacceptable.

And this journey to Nice is interminable! They are only due to arrive at the end of March! The coach stops at Fontainebleau, Sens, Troyes, Châtillon, Chanceaux, Lyon, Valence. He will spend two days in Marseilles seeing his mother.

Every time they stop, he is tempted to go back to Paris, tear Josephine away from her boudoir and her friends and force her to come with him, but it is not the right time. She will come on later. First he has a task to accomplish, a difficult one, because the Army of Italy is the most deprived of the Republic's armies. It is only meant to play a minor role, tying up a part of the enemy forces to enable the larger and better equipped armies of the Rhine, under Generals Moreau and Pichegru, to win a decisive victory over Austria.

For him to conquer, with the Army of Italy's thirty thousand men – that is the challenge he has to take up! The thought of it brings him out in a fever; he feels lifted as if he were being carried by a wave.

He calls Junot and asks for the document Carnot gave him on 6 March: *Instructions for the General-in-Chief of the Army of Italy*. He reads it again, and recognizes the ideas he has explained on so many occasions to Augustin Robespierre, Doulcet de Pontécoulant, to Carnot himself: 'Only to attack Piedmont would not accomplish the goal the Executive Directory needs to set itself, that of driving the Austrians out of Italy and concluding a glorious and lasting peace as quickly as possible ... The general-in-chief should not lose sight of the fact that it is the Austrians who should principally be done harm.'

He cannot read the conclusion without chuckling: 'The Directory must insist before concluding the present instruction on the necessity of making the Army of Italy subsist in, and by means of, the enemy territories and of providing it with all it may need from the resources which will be presented by the districts it occupies. It will levy sizeable contributions, half of which will be deposited in the office of the army paymaster in order to pay the subsistence allowances and wages of the army.'

Take whatever one can from the Italians, seize whatever one wants by force: that is what the *instruction* means, and with the booty feed, pay and arm the soldiers, and fill the Directory's coffers.

So be it. Such is war. Such is the power of arms.

He folds the directive back up – and instantly it is as if he has slid from the crest of a wave to its trough, from exaltation to despondency.

He takes up his quill again and visualizes Josephine.

I wrote to you yesterday from Châtillon ... Each moment takes me further away from you, adorable friend, and each moment I find less strength to bear being separated from you. You are the perpetual object of my thoughts; my imagination exhausts itself picturing what you are doing. If I see you sad, my heart breaks and my grief grows more acute; if you are gay and frolicking with your friends, I reproach you for having forgotten our painful separation so soon; you are fickle and cannot be touched by any profound feeling.

As you see, I am not easy to please. I regret the speed with which the distance between us grows ... May my guardian spirit which has always kept me safe in the midst of the greatest dangers surround you, cover you, and I will give myself openly. Ah, do not be gay but a little melancholy ... Write to me, my tender friend, write at length and receive these thousand and one kisses of tenderest and truest love.

He seals the envelope without rereading the letter, then he writes the address, 'To Citizeness Beauharnais, rue Chantereine, no. 6, Paris'.

He hands it to Junot without a word, and already he longs to write again, but he must wait for the next stopping place.

THEY ARRIVE in Marseilles and the carriage proceeds at a walk through the narrow, crowded streets which lead down to the quays of the port. Napoleon leans out. He recognizes the tang of brine, the musty stink of rotten fruit, and it is as if the past – still so recent – is being brought back by these smells and cold winds that are just like those that blew through the ruelle du Pavillon when he came to visit his family.

He has changed their life. It was his duty and it is the source of his pride. His mother, his brothers and his sisters have been able to leave the wretched apartment in the ruelle du Pavillon, just as they had done the Hôtel de Cypières before that. The carriage passes this imposing, austere building which is the first port of call for Corsican refugees. Letizia Buonaparte lived there for thirteen months, surviving on assistance from the departmental Directory. She will never have to do that again.

The carriage stops outside number 17 rue de Rome, a few metres from the Hôtel de Cypières. Napoleon gets out and looks up at the façade of this imposing, prosperous town house. This is where his mother lives now, in one of the finest, largest apartments in Marseilles. It is he, her son, who has made this possible.

His sisters, Pauline and Caroline, rush to the door, elegant young women now, thanks to him. They ply him with questions. This marriage? His wife? Letizia waits sternly for him to come to her and be kissed. He does so tenderly, deferentially. She looks at him. He feels her suspicious, inquisitive maternal gaze, as if she is searching for signs of a compromise of his conscience, a betrayal even. He knows that she does not approve of this marriage with 'that woman', who her sons have already told her has two children, is six years older than Napoleon and has had many lovers, no doubt including Barras – a hussy who has been able with a courtesan's wiles to seduce, trick and steal her son.

But Letizia Buonaparte does not say anything. She takes

Josephine's letter which Napoleon holds out to her. Naturally she will reply, she murmurs, jamming the Other Woman's letter into her pocket.

'So here you are, a great general,' she says, taking Napoleon by his shoulders and pushing him over to the window so she can have more light to see him by.

He loves this look of admiration his mother gives him. He tells her what positions he has secured for Jerome, Lucien, Joseph and Uncle Fesch. Did his mother and sisters get the money, did they like the 'frills and furbelows'?

She kisses him. 'My son.' She begs him not to lay himself open to danger.

He hugs her. May she live a long, long time. He needs her.

'If you died, I should only have inferiors in this world,' he murmurs.

HE ESTABLISHES his headquarters in the Hôtel des Princes, rue Beauvau. The local authorities come to see him. When an officer – or even Fréron, the representative of the people, Fréron whom he has petitioned so often – approaches him, he looks them in the eye and, just with this look, makes them stand still.

At Fréron's, where a dinner is given that night in his honour, he remains silent, a severe expression on his face. He is the general-commander-in-chief. With a disdainful shake of his head, he compels Fréron, who is being over-familiar and telling everyone of his intention to marry Pauline, to be quiet.

The next day, before he leaves, Napoleon reviews the troops of Marseilles' garrison. He sees a look of ironic surprise in the eyes of the soldiers, sergeants and captains. Who is this general? An artilleryman. They call him a 'mathematician and dreamer', an intriguer; General Vendémiaire. What can he do? Give the order to fire grapeshot into a crowd? He should come and take a look around a proper battlefield!

He stops in front of some of these men and forces them to look down. They are his inferiors – not just because he is their general-in-chief, but because his mind contains them, they are parts of his plan, whereas he is a mystery to them. They cannot begin to grasp who he is, what he can do. They are his inferiors because he is the one who imagines their future, he is the one who will decide what they will be, dead or alive, depending on whether he sends them into battle or not.

How can one live without commanding men?

The entire Army of Italy must lower their eyes before him; they must obey.

But when he gets out of his carriage on 27 March 1796, in rue St François-de-Paule in Nice, the soldiers on duty in front of the Nieuwbourg house where he is staying do not even salute him.

Napoleon stops dead.

The house is beautiful. It has a pale staircase supported by marble columns, and stained glass in its tall windows. An officer approaches, presents himself; Napoleon stares at him and repeats his name, 'Lieutenant Joubert'. The officer explains that this is one of the most comfortable houses in Nice, opposite central adminis-tration. Napoleon turns, points to the ragged soldiers whose shoes have holes in them, and says, his voice rising, that they look like 'brigands'.

Joubert hesitates. Napoleon begins to climb the staircase.

'The army is given no money,' Joubert calls out, 'and left at the mercy of the rogues who administer it. Our soldiers are citizens. They have indefatigable courage and patience, but they are dying of hunger and sickness. We are not treated like the good gentlemen of the Army of the Rhine.'

Napoleon enters the apartments which have been prepared for him on the second floor. Sun pours in through every window. To the east, the dungeons of the fortress guarding the Bay of Angels merge into the rocks. The sea glitters.

Joubert waits in the doorway.

'The government is expecting great things of this army,' says Napoleon. 'We must accomplish them and extricate the fatherland from the crisis in which it finds itself.'

Now – to take command of these men, and make an army out of this wretched mob. He immediately settles down to this task, dictating to Junot, communicating with Paris, giving orders.

'It may be that I will lose a battle one day, but I will never lose a minute though overconfidence or idleness,' he says.

There is no use complaining, regretting the state of the troops, or that he hasn't better ones at his disposal. These are the men he must conquer with. There are never any excuses for defeat, as there is no forgiveness for those who fail.

'A soldier without food commits excesses which make one blush to be human,' he snaps. 'I am going to make terrible examples or I will relinquish command of these brigands.'

The satchels containing the two thousand gold louis the Directory has given him to conduct his campaign are put on the table. It is a pittance – the rest of the money will have to come from his conquest.

Have the troops fall in.

The officers are astonished. Now?

'I shall never lose a minute,' he repeats.

He watches the generals come in. He stands with his legs splayed, his bicorne hat on his head, sword at his side. They look at him with a mixture of jealousy, recrimination and haughtiness. Each of these men, Sérurier, Laharpe, Masséna, Schérer and Augereau – the latter most of all, with his height and wrestler's build – thinks he has more right than Napoleon to occupy the post of general-in-chief. They have all proved themselves. Who is this 27-year-old general who has never been a commander-in-chief, apart from of an army of police guarding the Convention? Augereau looks him up and down.

Napoleon takes a step forward. These men are merely round-shot. He is the gunner who directs the fire.

He looks at each of them in turn. Each time, it is a test of strength and a hot, quivering joy rises up in him when first Masséna, then Schérer lower their eyes. The others yield in turn but Augereau holds out a few moments longer. He must convey with his expression: 'My five feet six inches can have you shot this instant' – and feel resolved and ready to carry it through. This is what it is to command.

Augereau looks away.

The generals leave and Napoleon hears Masséna exclaim, 'That little bugger of a general thinks he can crush you with one look, he thinks people are afraid of him.'

I will crush them.

Napoleon sits at his desk, facing the bay. Commanding men also means writing, because words are acts.

'You can have no idea of the army's administrative and military situation,' he writes to the Directory. 'It is undermined by troublemakers. It is without bread, without discipline, and in a chronic state of insubordination . . . Grasping administrators reduce us to a state of absolute destitution . . . The six hundred thousand livres I was promised have not arrived.'

He breaks off his letter.

Being commander-in-chief, in these conditions, with almost seventy thousand Austrian and Sardinian troops stationed in Piedmont and Lombardy – this is the first big test.

If I am what I feel I am, then I will be successful and another stage will have been reached. On the way towards what? Towards more. Once again there is no other choice than to advance, to act with what one has at one's disposal.

He takes up his quill, 'We must burn here, have renegades shot.'

Then he adds, grinding his quill into the paper, forming the letters with thick downstrokes, 'Despite all that, we shall go on.'

To work. Act. Act.

NAPOLEON does not even wait for Berthier, his new aide-de-camp, to be ready before he starts dictating. It feels as if he is reading a document that is unscrolling before his eyes – as if his thoughts become words without even needing to be formulated in his mind.

There needs to be a factory here with a hundred workers, for artillery and arms. Fresh meat must be issued every two days. Sums of money still in the possession of several war commissaries must be deposited in the army's coffers. There must be no reduction in rations for men or horses without his express authorization. Major-General Berthier is to report the officers and men who have distinguished themselves.

Napoleon stops walking up and down. Suddenly he appears pensive.

'It is only a step from triumph to failure,' he says. 'A trifle has always decided the greatest events.' Then he goes over to the table on which maps and plans have been laid out. 'Prudence, sagacity,' he murmurs. 'It is only with attention to detail that one attains great goals and overcomes all obstacles, otherwise one succeeds in nothing.'

He looks at Berthier, who has stepped forward.

'I have decided,' Napoleon says, and with his finger, he indicates the lines of attack he has chosen.

It has taken an entire night without sleep to formulate this plan, a night magnifying 'all the possible dangers and disasters', a night of acute agitation. Now everything is forgotten and he knows what needs to be done for the undertaking to be successful.

He keeps his finger on the map, arm outstretched, frozen, as an excitement as keen as that he used to feel solving a mathematics problem seems to make every part of his body quiver, without any of it showing. Then he goes to the window. 'The secret of great battles consists in knowing when to extend one's line and when to concentrate,' he says without looking at Berthier. As he dismisses him, he murmurs, 'These are the axes which must be used to plot the curve.'

Suddenly he is assailed by fatigue, strain, this cold night that is falling, solitude, the impossibility of sleeping because his mind is still racing, carried along by the momentum of his thought. Only pleasure, the confidence of a body offering itself, could quieten this whirl of questions for a few moments; he has to voice them, write them to Josephine: 'What is the future? What is the past? What are we? What magic fluid surrounds us and hides from us the things it is most important for us to know?'

Desiring her, he is finding it so hard to be apart! Why this divided life? 'One day you will no longer love me. Tell me; at least then I will know why I deserve my misfortune. Truth, frankness without limits . . . Josephine! Josephine! Do you remember what I have told you: nature has made me a strong, determined soul; it has fashioned you from lace and gauze. Have you stopped loving me? . . . Farewell, farewell, I go to bed without you, I must sleep without you. I beg you, let me sleep. For several nights now I have felt you in my arms. Happy dream, but it is not you!'

He walks up and down his room, as if to shake himself free

from this obsession which clings to him, torments him. What is she doing? Is she thinking of him?

His skin is on fire again.

He opens the door and sends for his aides-de-camp.

THERE IS a parade next morning. As he approaches he hears a murmur and sees the ranks rippling as the soldiers lean forward to catch a glimpse of him. Their uniforms are shabby, ill-assorted. Even the officers standing in front of their men look like brigands.

The hubbub does not stop when he approaches the front ranks. This is a fresh test of strength. He pulls on the reins of his horse and it rears up on its hind legs. He towers over this sea of men who turn their faces towards him. This crowd must become an army. He had to effect the same transformation in Toulon, but here the task is tougher, bigger. He is the commander-in-chief.

'Soldiers,' he cries. 'You are naked, starving; the government owes you much, it can give you nothing.'

The clamour grows louder. He is launched on this sea and he must take the helm.

'Your patience and the courage you show in the midst of these rocks are admirable,' he resumes, 'but they bring you no glory, none is reflected on you.'

The hubbub quietens. They listen.

'I shall . . .' He looks around the soldiers, their muskets glinting in the sun. 'I shall lead you into the most fertile plains on earth. Rich provinces, great cities will be at your disposal . . .'

He repeats, 'At your disposal.'

There is silence now on the square, between the houses with ochre façades.

'There you will find honour, glory and riches.' He pauses.

'Riches,' he says again.

'Soldiers of Italy, will you be wanting in courage or stead-fastness?'

His horse stamps. The silence, all of a sudden, is broken. The sea erupts in a confused uproar within which it is impossible to distinguish support from dissent.

That evening, sitting opposite General Schérer, he listens to his predecessor give a detailed account of the situation on the different fronts. Then Schérer comments on this morning's proclamation. 'The men reacted well,' he says.

How can one content oneself with any measure of uncertainty? An army must be bound to its commander as the planets are to the sun. How can one depend on it if every man, every unit, every officer goes their own way, and thinks of themselves rather than obeying? That night does not give Napoleon peace of mind.

In the morning, when Berthier brings word that the 3rd battalion of the 209th demi-brigade, encamped on the place de la République, has mutinied, he springs to his feet. Followed by his aides-de-camp, he rushes down the stairs, runs through the streets and comes face to face with those mutinying soldiers and their wavering officers.

He'd rather die than accept insubordination.

An old soldier who dares not look at him cries, 'Does he think we're bloody idiots he can make fun of with his fertile plains! What about giving us shoes first, so we can climb down to them!'

Napoleon walks forward, alone in the soldiers' midst. He is like a sharp blade slicing through soft flesh.

'The grenadiers responsible for the mutiny will be court-martialled,' he orders. 'Put the commander under arrest. Any officers and non-commissioned officers who have remained in the ranks without speaking out are culpable.'

The mutterings cease, the soldiers form up. The officers bow their heads.

Now, I can conquer.

ON 2 APRIL 1796 he sets off for Villefranche. After several hundred metres, he stops in front of a house which is set in a garden. The troops carry on past, marching at a good pace. He has taken these men in hand. They will fight and they will go to their deaths willingly. Yesterday he had marauders shot and brandy and gold louis distributed amongst the generals.

The door of the house opens and there stand Count Laurenti and Emilie. Only eighteen months have passed since Napoleon was arrested here, in this house. What will be able to check his progress now? Only death and that seems impossible to him. He is not yet twenty-seven.

Officers crowd around him. The coast road he has chosen is exposed to the cannon of any English vessels that come within range of the shore. It is reckless to take it, they say. He seems not to have heard, and kisses Laurenti and his daughter goodbye.

A leader must set an example and not hesitate to march under fire. He leaps nimbly onto his horse and takes the coast road at the head of his staff. The white cliffs fall sheer into the calm sea and there is not a sail on the horizon.

Napoleon turns to Berthier, who is riding a horse's head behind him.

'Temerity,' he says, 'wins as often as it loses: for it, the odds of life are even . . . in war, fortune is half of everything.'

He is silent for a few minutes, then goes on, 'In war, audacity is genius's finest tactic . . . It is better to abandon oneself to one's destiny.'

On 3 April, the headquarters are at Menton, on the 5th, at Albenga.

The generals are all gathered around him, in a large white room, in front of a table on which the maps are laid out. Their bodies, their faces, their weapons, their uniforms emanate strength and power.

And yet they dare not look at me.

'Hannibal crossed the Alps,' says Napoleon. 'We have out-flanked them.'

The Italian campaign can begin.

XXII

NAPOLEON WATCHES THE BATTALIONS of grenadiers start briskly up the narrow road that leads to the Col di Cadibona. They have a steep climb ahead of them. The mountain rises up from the sea like a slender, towering barrier separating the Mediterranean coast from Piedmont and Lombardy beyond.

He pulls on the reins of his horse. The staff officers' mounts whinny. It is dawn on 10 April, and a cool wind is blowing off the mountain, bringing the scents of forests and high pastures and shaking the laurels and the flowers running down to the sea shore. Here there is peace – on the other side of the pass, war.

The Austrians of Generals Beaulieu and Argentau are waiting close to the pass, in Montenotte and Dego. The Piedmontese of General Colli are slightly to the west, at Millesimo, and further into the mountains, at Mondovi.

Napoleon rides out into the road. The officers follow him and the soldiers mark time and then start off again behind the general staff.

Napoleon does not nod to the men as they get out of his way, opening their ranks to let him through.

He has to learn how to send these men to their deaths by the hundreds, the thousands. The success of his plans depends on their agreeing to make this sacrifice.

All that last night at Albenga he has let himself be carried away by his imagination. He sees the Austrians driven back towards Lombardy, the Piedmontese beaten and forced to sue for peace. For that, he must strike at a point between them, separate them, fight them individually and, once the Piedmontese have been brought to their knees, pursue the Austrians into the Po valley, to Lodi and on to Milan.

Everything depends on these men who are marching on the verge of the road. They must be willing to accept death. They must march day and night to get from one point to the next faster than anyone else, to surprise the enemy where they are not expected. Always outnumber the enemy when they attack. What does it matter if there are seventy thousand Austrians and Piedmontese in total, if, at the actual moment of battle, the soldiers of the Army of Italy sweep down and overwhelm smaller units!

Napoleon urges on his horse and signals to his officers and non-commissioned officers who are marching at the side of their men. They must hurry.

As he rides off, he hears the order to quicken the march.

Marching to die, marching to kill.

Commanding men is knowing where one is going to have them die, where one is going to kill others. Commanding is knowing how to die. Knowing how to order men to perform a sacrifice. And for that, one's mind must be as taut as a bow and one's words must fly like arrows.

FIGHTING has broken out to the south of Montenotte. Who's there? Colonel Rampon, who is holding out against Argenteau's Austrians.

Napoleon comes out of his tent. The battlefield is wreathed in smoke. Now is the moment of decision. He orders General Masséna to outflank the Austrians, and General Laharpe to mount a frontal attack. The aides-de-camp race off.

One must know how to wait.

ON 12 APRIL, the Austrians are beaten at Montenotte, and on the 13th, they are defeated again, at Millesimo and Dego.

Napoleon is sitting on a chest covered with a dark red carpet. There are two thousand six hundred Austrian prisoners, around eight thousand dead, a thousand or so French.

Rampon comes forward, covered in blood and mud. War means forgetting the dead, congratulating the living. Napoleon embraces Rampon, and promotes him to brigadier-general.

Then, on the march, hands behind his back, he listens to the reports. Units have broken ranks to find food and drink. Masséna has had to rally these men, many of whom were fleeing the fighting around Dego.

There has been pillaging.

How is one to fight, kill and die if discipline breaks down?

Napoleon calls Berthier and dictates, 'The commander-in-chief sees with horror the fearful looting committed by perverse men, who only join their corps after the battle ... Divisional commanders are authorized to have shot officers or soldiers who, by their example, incite others to pillage, thereby destroying discipline, spreading disorder through the army and compromising its glory and safety.'

He goes on, 'These men will be stripped of their uniforms and branded cowards in the opinion of their fellow citizens ...'

Then he bends over the maps and marks in arrows with a steady, precise hand. Three victories in four days. He is surprised by how little joy he feels. Defeat would have been unbearable, but success is not a wild intoxication because there is always another battle. One only stops acting when one stops living.

'Now it's the turn of Colli's Piedmontese,' says Napoleon.

He barely sleeps, only a few minutes, waking up fresh yet paler, and even more curtly spoken, as if the night has honed his ideas.

On 21 April, Colli is defeated at Mondovi, but again joy eludes him.

Again troops have broken ranks to pillage. They must be dealt with severely: shot, reduced to the ranks if they are officers. If the iron fist of discipline does not bind men together like a bundle of sticks, how will they agree to march to their deaths?

He takes a walk through the camp. Suddenly soldiers and officers start shouting, 'Long live General Bonaparte!' Envoys of General Colli have presented themselves asking for an armistice.

From me.

He feels a flicker of joy.

ON 25 APRIL, envoys of the King of Savoy, Victor-Amedeo, present themselves before Napoleon at Cherasco – two digni-fied, respectful Piedmontese aristocrats, La Tour and Costa de Beauregard, whom Napoleon invites to sit opposite him. The aides-de-camp stand in a row behind their commander-in-chief.

Napoleon speaks.

The Piedmontese are to hand over three fortresses, Coni, Tortona and Valenza. They are to furnish the French army with all necessary supplies. The terms of peace will be discussed in

Paris since, *at the moment*, he is only the commander-in-chief of the Army of the French Republic. The two Piedmontese noblemen bow, but then begin to discuss the proposals Napoleon has made.

'Gentlemen,' he says, barely parting his lips. 'I should advise you that the general attack is set for two o'clock and will not be delayed for a moment.'

Then he crosses his arms and waits. He is powerful through the strength of arms and his resolve, and the fear that both of these inspire.

Before daybreak on 26 April, the Piedmontese sign the armistice, and again he hears the soldiers' shouts: 'Long live General Bonaparte!'

How simple it is to impose one's law on men when one is a victorious general.

IT IS SILENT at dawn. He leaves the house which contains his headquarters, followed by several officers.

The streets of Cherasco are crowded with carriages and carts covered with fresh hay on which wounded are resting. Some are moaning, their limbs bloodstained stumps. Soldiers are slumped on the paving stones, leaning their backs against the house fronts.

Reaching the end of a street, Napoleon walks along a promontory which overlooks the countryside. The hills and confluence of the Tanaro and Stura rivers are shrouded in a bluish haze. In a field, the dead are laid out in rows. Stooped figures are moving amongst them like carrion feeders and when they straighten up they are carrying armfuls of sabres and satchels full of ammunition. What has been accomplished, what is dead no longer exists. All that counts is what is still to be done.

He strides briskly back to his headquarters. Thoughts swarm in his head: dead, wounded, runaways, marauders, cowards, battalions that panicked, the looters that have been shot. This has all been the bloodstained, mud-grimed reality.

He stops for a moment in front of a cart where three wounded men crowded on top of one another are slowly dying. Cowards, shot in the back? Thieves, caught by an officer and sentenced to death? Or heroes? Who knows?

He goes into the house and begins to dictate to Berthier the proclamation which the officers will read to the troops and which will then be printed and distributed to everyone.

This will become the truth of what happened in those days of battle. There will be no other reality than this,

> Soldiers! In fifteen days you have gained six victories, captured twenty-one standards, fifty-five guns, several fortresses, conquered the richest part of Piedmont . . . Devoid of everything, you have supplied everything: you have gained battles without guns, passed rivers without bridges, accomplished forced marches without shoes, bivouacked without brandy and often without bread. The Republican host, the soldiers of freedom alone were capable of enduring what you have endured. Thanks be to you, soldiers! But soldiers, you have done nothing because you still have more to do.

Then he bends over the table where the maps are still outspread. He traces with his finger those lines that form in his mind which he knows that no one else thinks of or imagines. Beaulieu's Austrians are there, at his fingertips.

'Tomorrow . . .' he starts.

He stops, and with a gesture indicates to Berthier that he should take down a note for the Directory.

'Tomorrow I shall march against Beaulieu, force him to cross the Po, cross straight after him and seize the whole of Lombardy. Within a month, I hope to be in the mountains of the Tyrol, where we shall find the Army of the Rhine and we will carry the war together into Bavaria.'

Everything is still to be done.

XXIII

NAPOLEON STANDS IN his stirrups and looks back.

Cherasco is no more than an ochre shape on the horizon, receding into the dense fog in which the brigade of grenadiers has been marching since dawn. He has confidence in these men whom he has chosen personally and put under the command of General Dallemagne, the officer who commanded the grenadiers at the siege of Toulon.

But it is Napoleon who leads the march.

A great struggle is underway for the possession of Lombardy and the jewel at its heart, Milan, and he wants to experience it from the front, with his feet in the mud of battle. He feels no fear. Death is not for him. He wants to be the first to cross the Po. He looks at it constantly, that long trail of silver that emerges, vast and majestic, when the fog clears, guarded by tall, motionless poplars like halberdiers. In this plain, a few leagues to the north, around Pavia, François I was defeated and taken prisoner in 1525 by one of Charles V's generals.

Here, the French kingdom lost a hand. Now it's the rematch and I am playing.

HE PRESSES ON. During the night of 6–7 May, they reach the Po at Piacenza. There is an exchange of fire; Napoleon races forward, the grenadiers follow; the enemy falls back. Napoleon doesn't stop.

When day breaks, he sees Lombardy before him. The sun plays on the surface of the marshes and ponds. The soil is rich. The farms vast, massive. There they are, the fertile plains!

In the distance another glittering ribbon can be seen, the Adda, the tributary of the Po. The cities silhouetted against the plain look like ships, with spires as masts: there is Lodi and there Cremona.

In the middle of the morning of 9 May, as they are advancing by forced march on Lodi and its bridge which will enable them to cross the Adda, an aide-de-camp suddenly appears, his uniform white with dust, and announces that the Austrians have counter-attacked. General Laharpe's troops have panicked in the night and Laharpe has been shot by his own soldiers who have confused him with a troop of enemy cavalry.

Forward, quicker.

ON 10 MAY, Napoleon enters Lodi. Thousands of troops are there already from Masséna and Augereau's divisions, tramping through the narrow streets, and Napoleon, followed by his brigade of grenadiers, makes for the river banks which are swathed in smoke.

Twenty or so Austrian cannon are raking the bridge over the Adda with grapeshot. The roadway is littered with dead and wounded and he can hear the whistle of musket balls. Cannon are firing from both banks.

It is up to me. A movement of his whole body carries him forward, pushing him onto the bridge, with drawn sabre, amid the hail of bullets and grapeshot.

They must get across. The future is at the end of this bridge, on the other side of the river. He hears nothing, only his heart which, as he runs, feels as if it will burst in his chest. The grenadiers are following and the cavalry fords the river, upstream. The enemy has to fall back.

The grenadiers catch their breath, leaning on their muskets, standing in the middle of the bodies stretched out on the ground. Napoleon looks around. They come up to him. He has been able to accept the risk of dying like them, like an ordinary soldier. The grenadiers raise their muskets and start shouting. They are alive. They are victorious. Long live General Bonaparte!

He has fought like a 'little corporal', a grenadier says. Long live the little corporal!

Here on the Po plain, where François I was defeated, he has been victorious.

HE ENTERS Cremona and demands a contribution of two million gold francs from Parma, and the provison of seventeen hundred horses.

The farms open their granaries, the cities their coffers and museums. The Parmesan is delicious with wheat bread and Lambrusco, their sparkling wine. The houses, castles and churches are overflowing with pictures which they load into waggons and send back to Paris.

The soldiers sing and laugh, their mouths red from the foam of the wine. Italian patriots come to meet Napoleon and he listens to the crowds shouting, *'Viva Buonaparte, il liberatore dell'Italia!'*

Saliceti, commissary of the Army of Italy, the sly, corrupt former informer, encourages this explosion of support for Italian unity and Milan gives itself to Napoleon.

This city, these triumphal arches, on this Ascension Day 1796, these women who come towards me with armfuls of flowers, this Serbelloni Palace which opens its gates, this cheering – all of it is for me.

Napoleon moves into one of the large panelled rooms of the palace. He has just learnt that in Paris the treaty of peace has been signed with Piedmont. Nice and Savoy have become French. It is he who put the King of Piedmont in their hands.

He writes to the Directory, 'If you continue to have confidence in me, Italy is yours.'

Theirs? Or mine?

This sudden thought dazzles him. Perhaps he can do everything?

'I can see the world receding beneath me,' he murmurs, 'as if I have been carried up into the air.'

He calls Marmont and tells him, 'They have seen nothing yet.'

The reddish-brown, polished parquet floor creaks under his boots.

Napoleon goes through the papers tossed haphazardly across a marble table. He lists in a voice hoarse with scorn, 'The province of Mondovi will give a million in contributions. I have put two million in jewellery and silver ingots, plus twenty-four paintings, Italian masters, at the Directory's disposal. And the directors can count on twelve million more.'

Are they satisfied?

Marmont holds out a message which a dispatch-rider has just brought from the Directory. With a brusque gesture, Napoleon unseals the letter and reads it. The directors advise him to make for the centre and south of Italy, Florence, Rome, Naples, while General Kellerman takes his place in Milan and Lombardy.

He stops dead in the middle of the room as if he has been hit. He sags forward for a moment, hunching his shoulders. So, they want to dispossess him, send him away, perhaps ruin him in some military and political adventure.

Do they think he is blind?

He starts pacing up and down again.

One is never finished with fighting. One can never be free in one's actions unless one decides on one's own, at the top.

Do they think he will submit? He who is filling the Directory's coffers? He who is winning victories whilst the Armies of the Rhine mark time in Germany? 'I have waged this campaign without consulting anyone,' he begins, telling Marmont to write. 'I should have achieved nothing if I had to reconcile myself with the viewpoint of another,' he dictates. 'I have gained the better of superior forces whilst in a state of absolute deprivation. Because I have been convinced that I had your confidence, my movements have been as swift as my thought ... Everyone has their way of making war. General Kellermann has more experience and will do it better than I; but the two of us combined will do it very badly. I think a bad general alone is worth two good ones together.'

Marmont mumbles with emotion and anger.

Napoleon shrugs his shoulders. *They will back down. They will tremble at the thought of my resignation.*

'Fortune has not smiled today for me to disdain her favours now,' he declares. 'She is a woman and the more she does for me, the more I shall demand of her.'

Marmont should not worry.

'Up to now no one has conceived of anything great. It is up to me alone to set an example.'

He walks over to the window and opens it. Milan the Great is there in front of him, its paving stones glistening in the light spring rain.

Murat comes in, talking away, and suddenly says, 'People say you are so ambitious you'd like to take the place of God the Father.'

Napoleon slams the window shut.

'God the Father? Never, it's a cul-de-sac!'

MURAT AND Marmont leave.

He is alone.

A long way away, such a long way away, he hears carriages rolling over the cobbles, church bells ringing. This hollow of the night is a chasm into which he plunges. Everything is too quiet. The Serbelloni Palace is a deserted island in a sea of silence.

A battlefield is always reverberating with the boom of guns or shouts and screams or the crackle of bullets. One's head is full of the furies of war. One must act without pause. One forgets that there is this void in oneself.

Only Josephine can fill these nights here, in Milan.

He has written to her so many times. The moment the explosions of grapeshot die away and silence descends, she obsesses him. One cannot live solely on high ambition. It takes time for the order of things to change, even when one turns them on their head as he does.

He has just decided to pay the wages of the troops in good, hard cash and he has been cheered by the men.

He has just signed armistices with Parma, Modena, Bologna, Ferrara and the papal legations, and in each case obtained contributions of several million and donations in kind such as paintings, manuscripts.

The Directory, naturally, capitulated before his threat to resign, and it has done so again, when he circumscribed the powers of the government's commissioners. 'The commissioners have no business in my policies,' he said. 'I do what I want. That they involve themselves in the administration of public revenues is well and good, at least for the moment, but the rest does not concern them. I count on their not remaining in office long and that replacements will not be sent to me.'

I do what I want.

With men, with the Directory, but not with her!

When villagers and then the inhabitants of Pavia attack his soldiers and resist requisitioning, 'I do what I want.' The city of Lugo, in which five dragoons have been killed, is subjected to military execution. Hundreds of people are sabred, buildings pillaged, hostile inhabitants put to death.

I do what I want.

But her? What can one do with a woman who is always slipping away, whose silence is torment, whose absence is a torture and whose memory haunts one in the solitude of the night?

Write to her again, write constantly, implore her to come here, to Milan. And fear her in every way.

The glass of her portrait has cracked. An omen. She is sick or she is unfaithful.

'If you loved me, you would write to me twice a day, but you have to chatter away to all your precious little gentlemen visitors from ten o'clock in the morning and listen to their idle talk and nonsense until one after midnight. In countries where there are such things as morals, everyone is in their homes by ten in the evening, but in those countries a wife writes to her husband, and thinks of him, and lives for him. Farewell, Josephine, you are a monster whom I cannot understand . . .'

How can he free himself of this passion, when he needs passion to live and when, even if he wins six battles in two weeks, these empty nights stretch out between the fighting?

Napoleon confides in his brother Joseph, 'You know the love I feel, you know how ardent it is, you know that I have only ever loved Josephine, that Josephine is the first woman I have adored . . . Farewell, my friend, you shall be happy. I have been destined by nature only to be brilliant in appearance.'

Well then – submit, acknowledge one's weakness, confess one's servitude: 'Recapitulating the wrongs done me every day, I make desperate efforts not to love you – bah, look, I only love you more . . . I will tell you my secret; make a fool of me, stay in Paris, take lovers, let the world know, never write – and I will love you ten times more! Is that not madness, fever, delirium? And I shall never recover from it! Oh yes, of course I shall . . .'

He doesn't know anything, but he suspects; he is devoured by jealousy. He is told that Josephine, who is now called Our Lady of Victories, dines at Barras's house; that Murat and Junot, the aides-de-camp he has sent to Paris to ask Josephine to join him, have become her lovers; that she takes her latest conquest, her

'Punchinello', everywhere – Lieutenant Hippolyte Charles, an 'amusing' man with ornate, tight-fitting uniforms that show off his young Lothario's build.

Napoleon doesn't want to hear, he doesn't want to know, but he writes, 'Without appetite, without sleep, without interest in friendship, glory, country, you and the rest of the world no more exist for me than if they had been annihilated.'

Suddenly he cannot contain his pain. 'Men are so contemptible,' he says. 'You alone used in my eyes to erase the shame of human nature! I do not believe in the immortality of the soul. If you die, I shall die immediately, but of the death of annihilation.'

For several days he cannot send her these letters that all too often go unanswered.

HE RETURNS to his maps and his war. He leaves Milan and rides towards Mantua, the impregnable fortress which controls the whole of Lombardy and stands at the gates of the Veneto. It commands the roads which, running alongside Lake Garda, lead to the Tyrol and the passes which debouch on Austria. Vienna conquered like Milan? Why not?

He imagines what it would be like. Only a few days before he has addressed a proclamation to his soldiers, congratulating them on their victories: 'Soldiers, you dashed like a torrent from the summit of the Apennines; you have overthrown and scattered all who opposed your march.' Tomorrow, with him at their head, why should they not be able to swarm down the Alps to the Danube?

He lays siege to Mantua. He attends to every detail. He leaps down from his horse, chooses the gun emplacements, calculates the angles of fire. Then suddenly he goes white in the face, staggers and faints, exhausted. He is carried to his tent, but he gets up, shoos his aides-de-camp away and picks up his quill again: 'I shall show you my pockets full of letters I haven't sent you because they are too stupid . . . Write me ten pages, that alone can console me a little.'

He is in pain, a throbbing, oppressive ache in his stomach.

'Fatigue and your absence, it is too much all at once . . . You are going to come out, aren't you? You are going to be here next to me, in my heart, in my arms, on my lips! Take wing, come, come. A kiss on your heart and then one lower, much lower!' He wants her – 'A thousand kisses on your eyes, on your lips' – and his desire is made all the more acute by the jealousy that obsesses him.

He even writes to Barras, 'I am in despair, my wife doesn't come, she has some lover who detains her in Paris. I curse all women, but I embrace my good friends.'

He knows. And he does not want to know.

'You know that I will never be able to think of you as having a lover, still less suffer you to have one; seeing him and tearing out his heart would be one and the same thing for me; and then if I could raise a hand to your sacred person . . . No, I will never dare, but I will leave this life if that which is most virtuous should deceive me. I am sure and proud of your love.'

He blinds himself.

He does not want to think of all the gossip that follows him around, the lists of Josephine's lovers, so they say, names he recognizes: Barras, before him Hoche and perhaps Hoche's groom, a big strapping lad, and Murat and Junot and Hippolyte Charles. He longs to kill and die.

Then he learns that she has finally set off for Milan.

The explosion of gaiety and fervour in him brushes aside everything else, all resentment and suspicion.

He enters the room where the aides-de-camp are standing waiting, and goes from one to the next. Marmont receives instructions to gallop to meet Josephine de Beauharnais with an escort of honour. He organizes her arrival like a military operation. He goes through the Serbelloni Palace, room by room, rearranging the furniture, choosing ornaments, pictures, rugs. She loves luxury. He assuages his impatience by giving orders: the vast bed, here, the blue canopy with the gold braid.

Word reaches him that Junot, who he sent to Paris to take the enemy flags they had captured to the Directory, is returning with Josephine and Lieutenant Charles, but what does that matter? This is not the time for jealousy any more.

She arrives and her coach, surrounded by the escort of dragoons, draws to a halt in the courtyard of the Serbelloni Palace.

He rushes forward.

She is there, smiling, holding her dog Fortuné in her arms. He embraces her in front of the officers. He sees neither Junot nor Charles. He drags her away. He wishes she would hurry, but she tiptoes along, worrying about her luggage, talking about Fortuné, who has been worn out by the long journey, just as she has. He shuts the door of the bedchamber behind them.

She laughs at his passion. She lets herself be loved.

Two days, he has only two days to explore every dimension of pleasure, every dimension of this body which he almost crushes, he holds it so tight, which is submissive most of the time, amenable and patient, but then is suddenly daring and provocative and free in a way that fascinates and terrifies Napoleon, as if he is standing before an abyss the bottom of which he will never know.

Then, one morning, Napoleon girds on his sabre, buckles his general's belt and puts on his bicorne. Josephine looks calm. He has never noticed those two little lines at the corner of her mouth; under the mask of her smile, they look like signs of indifference.

HE HAS ONLY JUST parted from her, and yet already he is missing her, feeling he has lost her. He hasn't assuaged anything. He would like to hold her again, but the horses are pawing the ground, the orders are ringing out. War is raising its hollow clamour again.

Würmser, the Austrian general, is on the march at the head of twenty-four thousand men. He is coming down the east bank of Lake Garda, towards Verona and Mantua. General Quasdonovitch is following the west bank.

The dice are rolling again. A victory is never permanent.

He must leave Josephine.

Does she know what war is? Can she imagine what I feel?

Her body consents to a final embrace, and then pulls away.

He must throw himself into war. It fills the void.

On 6 July, Napoleon writes, 'I have beaten the enemy. I am dead with fatigue. I beg you to come immediately to Verona, for I think I will be very ill. A thousand kisses. I am in bed.'

But can one stay in bed when one is in sole command of thousands of men who are marching to their deaths?

So he fights.

And in the evening he writes.

'Come to me, so that at least before dying we can say, "We had so many days of happiness!"'

The cannon roar.

'We have taken six hundred prisoners, and we have captured three pieces of ordnance. Seven bullets tore holes in General Brune's uniform without one wounding him; that is being lucky.

'A thousand kisses as burning as you are cold.'

XXIV

HE IS ALONE.

And yet a crowd of men surround him.

Soldiers shout his name, 'Long live Bonaparte!' Others greet him familiarly as 'our little corporal'. Aides-de-camp leap from their horses, bringing him dispatches: the white coats of Austrian infantry have been seen in the suburbs – 'We must leave Verona, General' – Würmser's van has already pushed up to here. Other riders announce that further to the west the troops of General Quasdonovitch have reached Brescia; Masséna and Augereau's divisions have fallen back; uhlans are venturing far forward – they are in the neighbourhood of Mantua, they are attacking the convoys and isolated carriages.

Napoleon senses in the officers' attitude, and sees on the soldiers' faces, worry and anxiety, the fear of defeat and the temptation to take flight. In a few hours, everything he has won since the start of the Italian campaign might be lost.

He longs to be able to let down his guard for a moment, find some support, ask for advice. He feels crushed by the weight of all the decisions he must take. He doubts himself.

He sends for all the generals under his command. Perhaps the reports are wrong? But no, Würmser and Quasdonovitch are still advancing, victorious.

Augereau, Masséna and Sérurier enter the room and Napoleon knows immediately that he can expect nothing of them.

To be a commander-in-chief is to be alone.

So he calmly explains, as if he did not feel a gnawing anxiety inside, that an army's strength, 'as Guibert has taught us', is the product of its speed multiplied by its mass. The troops must be moved with every possible dispatch. They must march day and night to take the enemy by surprise and beat them. Then march again, keep marching to another goal.

He has decided, therefore, to raise the siege of Mantua, which will astonish and unsettle the Austrians, go north with all his men to beat Quasdonovitch, and then return to confront Würmser, who will think he has won a great victory by liberating Mantua, 'which we shall have deliberately abandoned'.

'Raise the siege of Mantua . . .' Sérurier starts to object.

'Raise the siege,' repeats Napoleon. 'And march.'

He is alone; it exhausts him. If he could only confide in someone, be reassured, consoled, loved. To be able for one moment to shed one's armour, not be alone any more – what peace that would be!

But he is alone.

'IT HAS BEEN two days since I heard from you.' He forces himself to write clearly so that Josephine can read it without growing too impatient. 'This is the thirtieth time today I have had this thought. I sent for the dispatch-rider and he tells me he has been to your house and that you told him you had no instructions for him. For shame! Evil, ugly, cruel, tyrannical, pretty little monster! You laugh at my threats and my nonsense! Ah, you know that if I could lock you in my heart, that would be the prison I would confine you in.'

This idea of holding onto Josephine, of not being alone any more, is starting to obsess him. If he could at least possess that – a beloved wife who does not flee, who is not unattainable, like final victory – it seems to him that he would feel more peace.

He tells her.

'I hope you will be able to come with me to my headquarters and never leave me again. Are you not the soul of my life and the sentiment of my heart?'

The next day, 22 July 1796, he insists, 'You tell me that your health is good. In consequence I beg you to come to Brescia . . . I am sending Murat this very moment to prepare lodgings for you in the city, just as you like them . . . Bring your silver-plate and some of your necessities. Travel in short stages and in the cool of morning and evening so as not to tire yourself . . . I will come as far as I can to meet you on the 7th.'

To write to Josephine and express his passion allows him not to feel alone and, for as long as he is writing, to forget the war, as if suddenly all that existed was this woman and this love. He opens letters that come addressed to Josephine, as if he is violating a fortress. Then he apologizes and humbles himself and promises it is the last time he will do it. The same man who brings Würmser's Austrians and Quasdonovitch's Croats to their knees begs for forgiveness: 'If I am guilty, I will make it up to you.'

He feels better for having spoken of his feelings for a few minutes, and for having committed himself, as if he truly were just a young man who will celebrate his twenty-seventh birthday on 15 August 1796.

To horse, forward march.
Marching, battles.

At Lonato, on 3 August, Quasdonovitch is crushed and Würmser, who has entered Mantua in triumph as anticipated, sallies forth to help his defeated deputy.

So Würmser must be beaten.

Napoleon rides through the streets of reconquered Brescia. The soldiers are washing in the fountains, quenching their thirst with that clear, cascading water which supplies each street. Carts filled with muskets looted from armaments factories bump over the cobbles of the busy town.

Napoleon enters the Municipio on the Piazza Vecchi – this is where he has set up his headquarters – and Josephine appears, surrounded by officers, including Murat, who is making a display of himself, and that young captain, Hippolyte Charles, who is holding her dog Fortuné in his arms. Napoleon bluntly dismisses them and they leave. She is here now, mine, 'little white shoulder, little springy, firm white breast, little face, as pretty as a picture, with her creole headscarf, and that little black forest'.

He leads her into the bedroom with a sort of fury.

On the other side of the closed door, there is barking but Napoleon stops Josephine going and letting Fortuné in. She gives up.

Later at dinner, during which she keeps her dog on her knees, Napoleon cannot help pointing at the animal and whispering to Arnault, a writer friend of Josephine's, with a combination of bitterness and merriment in his tone, 'You see, that gentleman is my rival. He was in occupation of Madame's bed when I married her. I wanted to get him out: vain hope. I was told that I would have to sleep elsewhere or agree to our sharing. This vexed me a fair amount, but it was a question of take it or leave it, so I resigned myself to the arrangement. The favourite was less accommodating. I bear the proof on my leg.' He is immediately angry with himself for this confidence. He has already finished eating. Time spent at table always seems wasted to him. He obliges the other guests to leave the room, and at last he is alone with Josephine. The dog growls.

HE HAS A day and a half with her. Only one night. Then there is the sound of galloping horses, a cannonade in the distance. Würmser's troops are advancing; uhlans are reported at the gates of Brescia. Josephine bursts into tears, afraid. She should go back to Milan, with an escort led by Junot.

'Farewell, my beautiful and good, peerless, divine one. Würmser will pay dearly for the tears he makes you shed,' says Napoleon.

He beats Würmser at Vatiglina on 5 August, and on the 7th, after having retaken Verona, he lays siege to Mantua again.

I took the decision on my own. Victory is mine.

But for how long? Würmser is reforming his forces, receiving new troops, and Davidovitch is replacing Quasdonovitch. Everything can be thrown into doubt at any moment. This uncertainty is hard for him to bear. It wears him out.

Junot asks to see him. He tells how a party of uhlans attacked Josephine's coach on the way to Milan. There was a fight, two horses were killed and the coach's wheels smashed by a cannonball. Josephine travelled on in a peasant's *carricolo* and took refuge in Peschiera before regaining Milan.

He must hide his anxiety, congratulate Junot, and accept that Josephine stays in Milan and lavishly entertains in the Serbelloni Palace like the royalist aristocrat she is, surrounded by men dancing attendance.

Can I really tolerate that?

Napoleon flies into a rage. Captain Charles is to be dismissed, and driven out of the Army of Italy. Napoleon questions Junot:

are the reports true that Josephine has been seen, on several days in succession, walking by Lake Como with Charles? Junot is silent. Junot knows. They all know.

Must I acknowledge that I am an unhappy deceived husband?

'You are unkind and ugly,' he writes to Josephine, 'as ugly as you are frivolous. How perfidious to deceive a poor husband, a tender lover. Must he lose his rights because he is far away, burdened with work, fatigue and trouble?'

But what is the use of beseeching and repeating, 'Without his Josephine, without the assurance of her love, what is there left him on this earth, what should he do here?'

Will she listen?

Then he speaks of the war, 'We had a very bloody affair yesterday, the enemy lost many men and was completely beaten. We took the faubourg of Mantua from them.'

But what is war for her? he asks. Why would she understand what these fresh victories mean? These decisions taken on one's own and that incommunicable joy when the enemy falls into the trap? Davidovitch has been crushed at Roverdo on 4 September, he writes, when we fell on him en masse. Then we turned back on Würmser, who was defeated on 7 September at Primolano and on the 8th at Bassano. The only choice left to the helpless Würmser has been to retreat back into Mantua.

Can Josephine imagine what I demand of my soldiers?

In six days they have marched, fighting all the way, one hundred and eighty kilometres. Würmser's second offensive has been broken in a fortnight. Who will lead the next one?

This work, war, is insatiable, it devours me. It would need a woman's love to protect me from this carnivore.

'But your letters, Josephine, are as cool as a fifty-year-old's, they make it seem that we have been married for fifteen years. They display the friendship and sentiments of that winter of one's life. It is very cruel, very malicious, very treacherous of you. What is there left for you to do to make me truly pitiful? Not to love me any more? Ah, that has happened already. To hate me? Well, I wish it were so; everything is degrading apart from hatred; but indifference, with its pulse as cold as marble, its fixed stare, monotonous tread . . .'

So, war on her too . . .

'I don't love you any more; on the contrary, I detest you. You are a vile, gauche, beastly, sluttish wretch . . . What, then, Madame, do you do all day? . . . Who can he be, this *merveilleux*, this new lover who engrosses your every moment, dominates your days and prevents you attending to your husband? Josephine, take care: one fine night, the doors will be thrown open, and I will be there!'

HE HAS moments of rage in the dead of an autumn night as the rain falls on Lombardy; the damp seeps into his uniform and the fog shrouds the marshes surrounding Mantua. Fatigue turns into exhaustion; a stubborn cold that becomes a fever and a recurrence of his scabies all besiege his thin, sallow body that, nevertheless, he must get on its feet and hold steady in the saddle as they go from one city to the next, from Bologna to Brescia, from Verona to the faubourgs of Mantua. News comes from Vienna that the Empire is mustering fresh troops, in greater numbers, more seasoned, better armed, under the command of General Alvintzi. He is going to have face up to the enemy once again.

Napoleon inspects the troops, listens to their complaints: this fellow was insulted in town, that one was attacked, the roads are no longer safe. 'The population are against us,' the men repeat. A convoy of paintings bound for Paris has had to return to Coni because bands are attacking army transports and patrols in the Piedmontese countryside. 'These peasants are dogs who hate us,' the men explain to Napoleon.

Once again he is alone, facing the future.

With an army of barely forty thousand men, threatened by superior and seemingly inexhaustible forces drawn from Croatia, Hungary, Germany and Austria, can he hold Italy, Piedmont and Lombardy, Bologna and Verona?

He calls in Miot de Mélito, the Republic's representative in Tuscany. This small, eloquent man, explains the situation. Napoleon questions him and as he does so, senses his surprise. The diplomat was expecting to find a general like Masséna, courageous and hot-tempered.

'You are not like the others,' he says to Napoleon. 'Your military and political views . . .'

He falters, and then whispers, as if he dares not admit it, 'You are the furthest from the Republican forms and ideas of anyone I have ever met.'

'We must make friends,' says Napoleon, 'to protect our rear and flank.' He moves away, his back hunched, his lank hair falling either side of his pale and still gaunt face. 'Coalitions are forming against us on all sides. The prestige of our troops is fading. Our days are numbered. Rome's influence is incalculable. She is arming the people and arousing their fanaticism.'

He breaks off. 'We must adopt a system that can give us friends, among the people as much as among the princes.'

Then he crosses his arms and remarks sardonically, 'One can do everything with bayonets except sit on them.'

So they must work with other arms: 'Politics,' he says, 'institutions.'

He remembers his reading. He could recite all the notes he took in Paris or Valence when he steeped himself in history. He remembers the *Institutes of Justinian*. Why not create allied republics here, in the heart of Italy, like those ancient Rome established around herself?

'The Executive Directory . . .' interjects Miot.

Napoleon gestures irritably. What do the directors know? What are they doing? He has written to them. He has called for 'troops, troops if you wish to keep Italy'. They have only answered with advice, urging him to be prudent and telling him that the cause of Italian patriots must not be helped.

'On the contrary,' Napoleon continues, 'a congress must be convened at Bologna and Modena, drawn from the states of Ferrara, Bologna, Modena and Reggio. This congress would form an Italian legion and constitute a sort of federation, a republic.'

Miot panics. These are not the goals of the Directory.

Napoleon shrugs.

On 15 October, the congress meets in his presence at Modena and its one hundred deputies proclaim the Cispadena Republic.

POWER, POLITICS, diplomacy: he is beginning to enjoy these fruits, which victory allows him to pick and, as general-in-chief of this conquering army, taste.

The Commander d'Este, brother to the Duke of Modena, asks to see him. Saliceti, the schemer, the tempter, sidles closer and whispers in Napoleon's ear that this envoy from Modena is carrying four million in gold in four chests.

'I am from your country,' says Saliceti. 'I know your family's affairs. The Directory will never acknowledge your services. What you are being offered is yours by right, accept it without scruple and without publicity; the duke's contribution will be reduced in proportion and he will be very pleased to have acquired a protector.'

'I want to stay free,' says Napoleon.

Not long afterwards a representative of the government of Venice offers him seven million in gold.

What are these sums they are offering him, compared to the immense desires and ambitions he feels rising in him? He doesn't want these crumbs from the high table. He wants power itself. He wants to use politics and diplomacy for purposes other than filling his own purse. In any case, it will be full if he is successful. At what? When he tries to pin down what he desires, he can never define it. He wants greatness, he wants more. He does not envisage limits. He is beginning, now that he has spent time in the company of men who include small states, duchies, counties and principalities among their possessions, to think that no one can coerce him, because he feels stronger than everyone he has met. Hasn't he beaten the Austrian generals?

He writes in a tone of command to the Emperor of Austria:

Your Majesty,

Europe desires peace. This disastrous war has lasted too long.

I have the honour to inform Your Majesty that if plenipotentiaries are not sent to Paris to enter into peace negotiations, the Executive Directory orders me to fill up the port of Trieste and to ruin all Your Majesty's establishments on the Adriatic. Up until now I have refrained from carrying out this plan in the hope of not increasing the number of innocent victims of this war.

I hope that Your Majesty will be aware of the misfortunes

threatening your subjects, and restore peace and tranquillity to the world.

    I am, with respect, Your Majesty's,
      Bonaparte

The signature rings out like a challenge at the bottom of what is, he knows, a veritable ultimatum.

REMEMBERING this letter, in the great, chilly rooms of the Scaligeri Palace in Verona, Napoleon is gripped by uncontrollable anxiety. On the walls, the Scaligeri's coats of arms show the emblem of the medieval family: a ladder. Hasn't he, the little Corsican, tried to climb too high? Alvintzi's men are advancing, outnumbering his armies by three to one. Thousands of his men are in hospital, wounded or exhausted after months of uninterrupted marching and fighting.

DURING THE first clashes with Alvintzi, on 6 November and the 11th, at Caldiero near Verona, Napoleon has to fall back. He has been beaten.

He does not hang his head, despite the unbearable pain of this reverse. He marches at his soldiers' side across the muddy ground. Tomorrow he will fight again and he will win, because he senses that if a black wave of defeat swamps the Army of Italy again, then all the weaknesses, the accumulated fatigue, jealousies and resentments will drown his men – and him, their general-in-chief, especially.

He writes to the Directory: 'I beg you to have muskets sent to me as soon as possible; you can have no idea of the rate our people go through them . . .'

The Directory must know the situation. 'The inferiority of the army and the loss of the bravest men fill me with fear.'

How is he to feed his men? 'When they left, the Germans committed all kinds of horrors, felling fruit trees, burning houses, looting villages . . .'

He is the general-in-chief, but the directors above him must shoulder their responsibilities, as he assumes his, 'The destinies of Italy and Europe are being decided here, at this moment. The whole Empire has been on the move and still is . . . It is rare that a day passes without five thousand more of their men arriving; and it has been obvious for two months that we need reinforcements . . . I do my duty, the army does its duty. My soul is ravaged, but my mind is calm. Help, help . . .'

BUT WHEN he marches through the Alpona marshes, on 14 November 1796, he is no longer thinking of help. One makes do with what one has.

He advances at the head of his troops, on narrow causeways that cross the marshes. The village of Arcola is hidden by fog and the water in the marshes is icy, rank. Alvintzi's Austrians are dug in on the other bank. Officers fall at Napoleon's side; marching crowded together on these banks of earth, they offer an easy target to the enemy.

Here is a wooden bridge, just as at Lodi, and Napoleon feels the same reflex in his body. One must risk everything every time if one wants to win.

Napoleon rushes onto the bridge, accompanied by a drummer who sounds the charge. He does not look behind him. He seizes a flag from a sergeant and brandishes it above his head, shouting, 'Soldiers, are you no longer the victors of Lodi?'

Forward! He stumbles over bodies, gets jostled out of the way. Grenadiers run in front of him, the enemy guns fire a salvo and they are all stretched on the ground. He is alone, exposed. What is death if it comes like this, in combat? Muiron, his friend from the siege of Toulon, Muiron the best aide-de-camp he has, places himself in front of him. A tremor. Muiron is dead. His body slumps against Napoleon's.

He *has* to keep moving forward. He slips, bangs into one of the bridge's uprights, topples over and everything vanishes. Night enfolds him . . .

WHEN HE OPENS his eyes, he listens in silence to his brother Louis explaining that he fainted and was snatched from the marsh just as the Croats were about to seize him.

He stands up. That was the test. The dark hour. He is alive and Alvintzi is defeated.

'Send the cavalry after the Austrians,' he says. An officer murmurs that that is a perilous manoeuvre which is never used.

'War is using one's imagination,' he says, closing his eyes.

He thinks of Muiron, of the men floating face down on the surface of the Alpona marshes like dead trees. He could have been one of them, like Muiron who gave his life for him, but since he is alive, everything is possible. Death has grazed him, as if to let him know that it didn't want him, that he was the stronger of the two of them.

He is weary but resolute in the carriage that takes him to Milan. His limbs feel broken with fatigue, and he coughs constantly, but only death can stop him acting. There are still so many things to do. The Directory has sent out General Clarke to negotiate with Vienna.

They mistrust me, the conqueror, the one whose success Paris applauds.

The rue Chantereine where Josephine lives has been renamed rue de la Victoire, and a theatre is showing a play glorifying Napoleon entitled *The Bridge of Lodi* – every evening, the audience gets to its feet to applaud the victorious and heroic general – but the directors fear him. There is never an end to rivalry between men.

Let my wife console me.

ON 27 NOVEMBER, Napoleon enters the Serbelloni Palace. He doesn't need to go beyond the steps. This palace is empty, dead. Where is she? In Genoa, invited by the Senate to preside over festivities. She has gone with Hippolyte Charles. 'Have that man shot,' he shouts. Then he pulls himself together. What reason could he give? Jealousy? Which is more ridiculous – the husband or the lover? All there is is despair, like a small death that echoes in private his fall into the marshes of the Alpona from the bridge at Arcola. He writes to her:

I arrive in Milan, I hurry to your apartment, having left
everything to see you, to press you in my arms . . . You are
not there: you are gadding about every town where there's a
celebration, you leave as soon as I arrive . . . Habituated to

dangers, I know the remedy to the troubles and ills of life. The unhappiness I feel is incalculable: I was entitled not to expect it.

I will be here until the 9th, when I will leave in the daytime. Do not trouble yourself; immerse yourself in every pleasure; happiness is made for you. The whole world is only too happy if it can please you, and only your husband is very, very unhappy . . .

The night is interminable. When will the day come? He will not gain this victory over Josephine. This time he has given orders that Hippolyte Charles be dismissed from the Army of Italy by order of the general-in-chief, but he has already demanded that once before. Josephine had wept and implored, and he had gone back on his decision.

Surrounded with pleasure, you would be wrong to commit the least sacrifice for me . . . I am not worth the trouble, and the happiness or unhappiness of a man you do not love has no right to interest you . . . When I expect from you a love like mine, I am wrong: why should I wish that lace weighs as much as gold? I am wrong if nature has not given me the charms to captivate you, but what I deserve from Josephine is consideration, esteem, because I love you madly and only.

He leaves Milan.

He is in a hurry to return to the war. That isn't unfaithful.

On the plateau of Rivoli, in the night of 14 January 1797, the fires of General Alvintzi's outposts can be seen. He has returned with fresh troops. Opposite, only a few hundred metres away, those fires girdling the hilltops like a belt of stars are Joubert's and Masséna's divisions.

They spend the night preparing for battle. Now, there to the left, in reserve, is Masséna. To the right, towards the Adige, is Joubert's division. Berthier and his men are in the centre. Dawn comes quickly. He must walk along the line of troops with Murat and his aide-de-camp Le Marois.

A regiment falls back. A counter-attack is launched. Officers dash forward, having taken their orders.

The battle is indecisive. Suddenly, bands playing, flags unfurled, reinforcements appear. It is the 18th regiment, and Napoleon goes to meet them. His words resound like the rolling of a drum: 'Brave 18th, you have yielded to a noble impulse; you have added to your glory. Now to make it complete and to reward your conduct, you will have the honour of being the first to attack those who have had the temerity to turn us.'

He is answered with cheers; men charge with bayonets and bowl over the Austrians who start to surrender in their hundreds, shouting, 'Prisoners! Prisoners!'

One only has time to command and act.

Night comes and several dozen officers pile into the two rooms of a house. Napoleon is at the centre of them. They eat stale bread and rancid ham.

He jokes about the quality of this 'sustenance'.

'Immortality's sustenance is always good,' proclaims Captain Thiébaud. Then the officer looks down, suddenly intimidated, even though he has fought all day, with drawn sabre. Napoleon feels even more certain that he has been given the gift which allows one to command men.

He chooses his place on the straw. He is going to sleep among his officers. He shares their lot, but he is alone.

IN THE MORNING he must talk to the soldiers who have frozen overnight. Commanding them does not mean dwelling on their suffering, but demanding that they march on to defeat Würmser who is trying to help Alvintzi and another Austrian general, Provera.

'Do you want glory, General?' cries a soldier. 'Well, we'll damn well give you glory!'

They move off at a brisk pace.

They defeat Würmser at La Favorita and Provera surrenders with his troops. Würmser capitulates on 2 February and evacuates Mantua.

HE BECOMES different when he wins like this and hears men cheering who would die when he gives the order; when twenty-two thousand Milanese have been taken prisoner and they come through the town, flanked by soldiers, and march off towards

France; when he returns to Verona surrounded by guides carrying unfurled more than thirty flags taken from the enemy at Rivoli.

He speaks and he writes in a different way when he can say to the soldiers, 'You have won victory in fourteen pitched battles and seventy actions. You have taken more than a hundred thousand prisoners, five hundred field guns, two thousand heavy guns ... You have enriched the Museum of Paris with more than three hundred objects, masterpieces of ancient and modern Italy ...'

And the directors would like to give me orders from Paris?
Politics, diplomacy – these are my domain too.

NAPOLEON receives the envoys of the Pope and jointly they sign the Treaty of Tolentino: in addition to the sixteen million already promised, the Pope must pay a further fifteen million and relinquish Avignon.

I am changing the map of France.

AND NOW, here is the sea.

On 4 February 1797, Napoleon occupies Ancona. He walks to the end of the harbour's jetty on his own and looks straight ahead.

'One can reach Macedonia in twenty-four hours from here,' he says to Berthier when he rejoins him on the quay.

Macedonia, birthplace of Alexander the Great.

Suddenly all the victories he has won seem dusty, far in the past.

'I am still in Ancona,' he writes a few days later to Josephine. 'I am not sending for you, because everything is not finished yet. Besides, this country is very gloomy and everyone is afraid. I am leaving tomorrow for the mountains. You don't write to me at all ... I have never been so bored as in this wretched war.'

XXV

THE MOUNTAINS LIE BEFORE NAPOLEON.

He has stopped at the beginning of the road which runs from Treviso to the first river they have to cross, the Piave. After that there are two other valleys, the Talgliamento and the Isonzo.

The soldiers march ahead of him with a slow, heavy tread. The road is narrow and steep, even here. These men are tired, like him. He has written to them, 'There is no other hope of finding peace than to seek it in the hereditary states of the House of Austria' — but first they must fight again and face a new Austrian general, the Archduke Charles, who has massed his troops in the Tyrol, around the Col di Tarvis, at the source of the rivers and beyond them, and for that, they must push on through these stony valleys, cross the Piave, Tagliamento and Isonzo and march between scree-covered slopes in the shadow of whitish blue limestone massifs with lacerated sides and peaks, as if the mountain were nothing but a giant skeleton stripped of every shred of flesh.

It is on the other side, in Tyrol, Friuli and Carinthia, around Judenburg and Klagenfurt, that they will find meadows and forests again, but here the rocks are splintered and sharp.

NAPOLEON is worried.

'The further I advance into Germany,' he says, 'the more enemy troops I have on my hands ... All the Emperor's forces are on the move and in all the states of the House of Austria preparations are underway to oppose us.' He thinks of those French forces who are waiting, arms at the ready, over on the Rhine. 'If we are slow crossing the Rhine, it will be impossible to hold out for long.'

Moreau's armies are stationary on the banks of the Rhine. The Army of the Sambre and Meuse, which has been taken in hand by Hoche, seems to want to attack, but when? And if they were to gain victory over Austria, the principal enemy, and if they make

Vienna sign a treaty of peace, what would remain of the Army of Italy's glory and that of its general-in-chief?

This question has been tormenting him for nights.

At Ancona and at Tolentino, while waiting for the Pope's envoys, in the damp fog of the final days of a rainy winter, he meditates in private, pacing up and down his chamber and sending away any aides-de-camp who present themselves.

Who is he fighting for? For whom has he won these victories? For the members of the Directory, those barristers, those 'idlers', or for himself?

During those nights in February, his skin breaks out in pustules and scurf again. He has tried to write to Josephine but the words won't come, as if the questioning going on within him is too strong to allow for the expression of another passion.

His life is at stake. The cards he is playing are his. Why should he let the game be controlled by men who are inferior to him? What qualities do they have? They are greedy, they think only of their power. Have they ever risked their lives in battle? Do they know what it feels like to cross a bridge under grapeshot? By what right do they impose their will? Because they are elected by the people? Apparently so, but in fact they have drafted a constitution to enable them to hold on to their seats and possessions, and they turn cannon on anyone who challenges it. Are they the ones who will scoop the pot? In the name of France, in the name of the French?

Haven't I already done more than they will ever do?

I will play for myself.

The Archduke Charles must be defeated and negotiations entered into with Vienna, so that he can be not just a victorious general but also the man of peace.

He must act fast, because one cannot bring Austria to its knees with forty thousand men, especially when one has to keep a close eye on the Italian cities and countryside, where most of the people detest the French.

NAPOLEON and his armies march north-east.

He crosses the Tagliamento on 12 March and Joubert is at Bouzen and Brixen, Bernadotte at Trieste.

On 28 March, Napoleon enters Klagenfurt and the vanguards

soon reach Leoben, in the heart of Styria. From the heights of Semmering, he looks down on the great Danube plain and, a hundred kilometres away, he imagines as much as actually sees, in the mists on the horizon, the domes and roofs of Vienna.

He must not let himself be intoxicated, but keep to the 'system' he has defined: victory and peace as fast as possible.

In his tent, on 31 March, he composes a message intended for the Archduke Charles. He is very explicit with the aide-de-camp who is going to ride to the Austrian lines: the letter must be put into the hands of the Austrian general-in-chief. Then he watches for a long time as the officer rides away through the streets of Klagenfurt.

The words he has written and which echo in his head have little chance of being heard. Archduke Charles is unlikely to want to take liberties with the authorities in Vienna, but the Emperor of Austria is no 'barrister' or 'idler' like those who govern in Paris. One day the people will hear this message, one day they will have to reckon with Napoleon.

'Our brave soldiers make war and desire peace,' he wrote to the archduke. 'Have we not killed enough men and done enough harm to suffering humanity? It cries out on all sides ... Are you resolved to earn the title of benefactor of humanity and saviour of Germany? As for myself, if this approach which I have the honour to make to you saves the life of a single man, I shall be prouder of any civic crown I may thereby deserve than of such sad glory as may result from military success.'

HE WAITS and pushes further into Styria, reaching Judenburg and Leoben.

These new victories — Neumarkt, Unzmarkt — give him no pleasure. They are insipid after Lodi, Arcola, Rivoli. Perhaps he has exhausted the strongest emotions of war itself? At first it made him feverish with excitement, but now he has dedicated himself to it every day for almost a year; he has seen enough dead to make his gorge rise; he has seen the best fall — especially Muiron at the bridge of Arcola, saving his life. Now that he is almost twenty-eight, he knows that war is only a means, a tool whose facets he is well acquainted with. Can it still surprise him? It is what one gains from it that attracts him: glory and influence over men, not just those who march in step but all men in their daily round, over their institutions and their pleasures.

He watches the officers, aides-de-camp and generals – Joubert, Masséna, Bernadotte – around him. They are good soldiers, courageous, talented, but he has moved beyond them, into circles where people do not limit themselves just to leading an army, even as generals-in-chief, but make decisions for all the armies, where they hold political power.

Circles of people or just one person?

If he wishes to join them or – and why not dare think it – be the only one, he must confront the holders of power in Paris.

HE KNOWS the five directors: Barras, Carnot, Reubell, Barthélemy and La Révellière-Lépeaux. Since 13 Vendémiaire, he has been Barras's military arm. These men barely trouble themselves with the law. Napoleon has lived through the Revolution and knows that, just as on a battlefield, the sword is what makes the difference, in other words the balance of power.

He calls one of his aides-de-camp, Lavalette. The officer bows and Napoleon recognizes these respectful without being obsequious manners, this 'society air'. This is a mark of aristocrats, former royalists.

Lavalette is loyal, intelligent. He would be an excellent agent; Napoleon invites him to sit down.

He wants Lavalette to see Carnot. With Barthélemy, he is close to the royalist circles in the Clichy Club. For the sake of stability, would Carnot be prepared to dissolve the Republic? Napoleon must know what he is thinking and planning. Elections are scheduled to take place in a few weeks. Everything suggests the royalists will win them. Faced with that prospect, the triumvirs Barras, Reubell and La Révellière-Lépeaux have no doubt decided to repeat Vendémiaire.

Napoleon paces up and down. The game excites him; he feels a talent for it. It is a form of war, but underground, stealthy: a game of chess, a confrontation just like on a battlefield but with more complex rules, more skilful players, more squares and more pieces. If war is a game of draughts, politics is chess.

But the chessboard itself could be subjected to other forces that are suddenly unleashed and sweep aside the pieces and the players. Napoleon remembers the scenes in the courtyard of the Tuileries, those women on 10 August mutilating the dead bodies of the Swiss in a frenzy.

'Democracy can be maddened,' he whispers, 'but it has a heart and one can move it.'

He wants Lavalette to set up newspapers, to meet writers and journalists, people who influence opinion. Let it be broadcast everywhere who Bonaparte is, what he does and what he wants: peace. These orators, novelists, poets and painters must speak of the exploits of General Bonaparte.

Lavelette agrees.

'The aristocracy is still unresponsive, isn't it?' continues Napoleon. 'It never forgives.'

Then he gives his instructions. Lavalette must see Carnot, he repeats, and Carnot must be reassured, lulled.

'Tell him, as your own personal opinion, that I will withdraw from public affairs at the first possible opportunity and that I will offer my resignation if it is slow in coming. Pay attention to the effect that has on him.'

On 13 Vendémiaire, he had been Barras's man. This time he is only playing for himself.

THE ELEMENTS are falling into place. On 13 April 1797, in the little town of Leoben, the two Austrian plenipotentiaries ask to be received.

Napoleon has them wait; these stiff, elegant aristocrats, these two 'gentlemen', General Count Merveldt and the Count de Beauregard, must understand that they are not masters of the negotiations.

Thinking of them growing impatient under their impassive expressions, Napoleon feels the pleasure of the player who anticipates several steps ahead. He has learnt, and is still learning, how to put men off-balance, however alert they are. Everything counts in this struggle of man against man, power against power that goes on in negotiations.

He wants Austria to give up Belgium and the left bank of the

Rhine. He will offer the Venetian States in exchange; he is not in control of them yet but he only needs a pretext to overthrow the Doge. France will keep the Ionian isles.

These offers must remain secret. What would the Venetians think? And how would the directors react who have already let it be known that, in any negotiations, Lombardy must be ceded to Austria?

Napoleon slowly enters the low-ceilinged room where the two plenipotentiaries are waiting. He is going to win, because he knows what he wants. What constitutes a man's strength, whether he is a general or a head of state, is being able to see further and faster than his adversaries.

On 18 April, the Preliminaries of Leoben are signed by Napoleon and the emissaries of Vienna.

I have moved my piece.

ANOTHER NIGHT of insomnia, but he must not neglect any of the squares. So now he must send a courier to the Directory with the text of the Preliminaries and threaten, with great humility, to resign if the Preliminaries are not accepted. He must find the words to give these men no chance to refuse, even if they do not believe a word they read – to snare them in his trap and not allow his critics any loopholes. He calls an aide-de-camp and dictates:

> As for myself, I ask to rest. I have justified the confidence you invested in me . . . and acquired more glory than is necessary to be happy . . . Calumny will endeavour in vain to attribute treacherous intentions to me, but my civil career will be the equal of my military career in its simplicity. However, I have no doubt you feel that I ought to leave Italy and I beg you to include, with your ratification of the preliminaries of peace, orders as to the direction I should give to affairs in Italy and leave for me to return to France.

REST? What is rest?

During that night of 19 April 1797, breathless officers, their faces drawn with tiredness, enter headquarters. Napoleon stops them with a look. Commanding men is keeping them at a respectful distance.

'Four hundred . . .' one of them begins.

Four hundred French soldiers, the majority of whom were wounded and confined to hospital, have been killed by bands of peasants in Verona — stabbed, sabred or their throats cut.

In Venice a French boat has been attacked in the roads of the Lido and its captain killed.

Napoleon dismisses the officers. Vengeance is a necessary part of order. One must answer violence with even greater violence. He has learnt this law at every stage of his life — as a child, at the Military School at Brienne, in Ajaccio, his first command, his first battles — but one can also use vengeance as a pretext for an action that one has already decided upon. If one's adversary exposes himself and does not see the impending attack, so much the worse for him. Strike fast and hard.

'Do you believe,' Napoleon writes to the Doge of Venice, 'that my Italian legions will suffer the massacre you have incited? The blood of my brothers in arms will be avenged.'

A pitiless repression falls on the *massacreurs* of Verona, and French troops enter Venice. This is the end of the Republic of Venice, with its thirteen centuries of independence. It will be handed over to Austria in exchange for the left bank of the Rhine and Belgium — after long debates, the Directory has ratified the Preliminaries of Leoben.

I am drawing a new map of Europe.

A FEW DAYS later, Napoleon opens the first letter his aide-de-camp Lavalette sends him from Paris: 'Everyone, my dear General, has their eyes fixed on you. You hold the fate of France in your hands. Sign the treaty of peace and you change its complexion, as if by magic. Should you have to do so on the sole basis of the preliminary treaty of Leoben, then conclude it . . . And then, my dear General, come and enjoy the blessings of the entire French people who will call you their benefactor. Come and surprise the Parisians with your moderation and philosophical nature.'

Napoleon rereads the letter.

He is enjoying this spring of 1797.

XXVI

HE IS TWENTY-EIGHT. He is learning to rule.

He has decided to install himself and his entourage, his family who have come from Marseilles, his staff, his guests – the crowd that surrounds him now – in the Château of Mombello, twelve kilometres from Milan, a sumptuous villa which he has chosen in order to escape the heat of summer in Lombardy.

Josephine is at his side. Finally!

He sees her at every moment, whenever he wants. Everything changes, even with a spouse, when one rules. She no longer goes to the Corso – that promenade for the elegant women of Milan, who parade up and down in their low carriages, the *bastardelle*, receiving the admiring attentions of gallants, who ride alongside, then stop to eat ices at the *Corsia de Servi* café.

He does not like her court and its insistent officers. They are always around her here, at Mombello, but they are afraid of him.

He loves to see Josephine presiding over the dinners they give every evening in a great marquee pitched in the park. The table is set for forty places.

Napoleon talks and everyone turns towards him, and listens religiously. He is the master. He prescribes the frugal menus: soup, boiled meat, an entrée, salad, fruits, and just one wine.

He presides over his world: his sisters Pauline and Caroline, his brother Jerome, Eugène and Hortense de Beauharnais. Often he feels his mother's gaze resting on him or darting glances at Josephine. She does not like her, but Josephine is in her element here, surrounded by Austrian or Neapolitan diplomats, all of them aristocrats. He watches her. She has the grace and elegance of the viscountess she once was. Sometimes he feels a sudden wave of desire and he leads her away. What does it matter what the other guests think? On an excursion to Lake Maggiore with Berthier and the diplomat Miot de Melito, he sees their embarrassment when he embraces Josephine. What's that? She is his wife and he sets the rules.

It is a long time since he felt this happy and light, perhaps he never has before. His body is recovering. He has never been short of energy, but gradually he is shaking off his tiredness and that scabies which recurs less and less frequently.

He makes decisions about the lives of others and this is a profound source of joy to him, perhaps one of the strongest he has ever felt. His sister Elisa has married a modest Corsican captain, Felix Bacciocchi, in Marseilles. So be it. He disapproves but he was given no choice. The marriage will be celebrated in the château's chapel, along with the one he wanted, between his youngest sister Pauline and General Leclerc. The English having left Corsica in October 1796, Bacciocchi will be put in command of Ajaccio's defences. Since Paoli's followers have left in the train of the English, Joseph has been elected deputy for Ajaccio in the Council of the Five Hundred, one of the few thought to be Jacobin amongst a monarchist majority. Joseph will become the Republic's ambassador to Rome, another favour the directors cannot refuse. Louis Bonaparte is already a captain, Lucien – the independent, ambitious Lucien – is a war commissary attached to the Army of the North, of the Rhine, and he is then sent to Corsica, but he spends most of his time loafing around Paris. As for the black-clad Letizia Buonaparte, to whom everyone bows respectfully, a return journey fit for a queen is being organized for her, because she wants to go back to Corsica.

This feeling of power, this certainty one is influencing the destiny of others, what confidence they give one in oneself!

HE GOES out onto the steps. In the distance he sees the peaks of the Alps, which are still snowbound. Generals Berthier and Clarke stand a few paces behind him, with Lannes, Murat and Marmont a little further away.

They wait for him before sitting down to eat.

A crowd of Italians, local peasants or townsfolk from Milan, is being kept at a distance by some of the three hundred Polish legionaries who guard the château. These soldiers are giants, recruited by Prince Dombrowski, exiles like him from their divided, occupied country. They are devoted to Napoleon body and soul.

To reign is to inspire admiration and devotion.

Napoleon thinks of Muiron on the bridge at Arcola. When men sacrifice themselves for the one they have chosen as their leader, they legitimize his authority.

The Italians push forward. They are going to be spectators at the dinner, as used to happen in Versailles under the Sun King.

Now the Marquis de Gallo is being announced, the ambassador to Vienna from Naples.

They are coming to me now, all those from before, from the royal and imperial courts.

They rub shoulders with the likes of Lannes and Murat, commoners, soldiers of the Revolution.

This woman walking beside Josephine is Saint-Huberty, an actress who had her moment of glory before the Revolution and is said to be married to the Count d'Antraigues, a royalist agent supposed by army intelligence to be in Venice, where he serves the Austrian Court, London and Louis XVIII.

Take care of that, order him found.

Now here is the ambassador of France, Miot de Mélito, who stops and waits for a gesture from Napoleon to approach in order to talk to him of the imminent peace, no doubt; Gallo is here and other Italian diplomats are on their way. He congratulates Napoleon on the creation of a Cisalpine Republic and a Ligurian Republic. He questions him about his future role.

Don't hesitate to confide at times, because this is how ideas acquire shape and vigour. They force one's interlocutor to make up his mind, they make him tremble or dream and they organize the future. Confide half-truths, question one's ambitions as one partly reveals them.

'I would only want to leave the Army of Italy,' says Napoleon, 'if it was to play a role more or less similar to the one I play here, and the moment has not come yet ... Perhaps the peace is necessary to satisfy the desires of our "idlers" in Paris and if it must happen, then is up to me to do it. If I leave and allow another to assume the merit for it, this good deed would place him higher in public opinion than all my victories.'

Enough serious talk, let us eat.

Napoleon takes his seat. He tells stories, mostly drawn from history. All eyes are turned towards him.

LATER, he signals that dinner has ended, and walks alone in the shade as the Italians cheer and hail him as 'the liberator of Italy'. He waits for the Marquis de Gallo and tells him that after the peace is signed his ambition is to resume his studies of astronomy or mathematics. He could live in a house here, far from the clamour of the city, merely serving as a justice of the peace for the local population.

Josephine has joined them.

'Don't believe a word of it,' she says to Gallo in her cooing voice. 'His is the most restless mind, the most active, fertile brain in the world, and if he were not occupied with great affairs, he would turn his house upside down every day. It would be impossible to live with him.'

She laughs and he silences her with a look. He can do that now.

He leans towards the Marquis de Gallo. 'Do you know the Count d'Antraigues?' he asks. Then he walks away without waiting for the marquis to reply.

BERTHIER waits for him in one of the château's reception rooms which, with its heavy sculpted ceilings, dark velvet hangings and plethora of furniture, has a stifling atmosphere. On one of the tables which he uses as a desk, Napoleon sees a large red portfolio, with a gilt lock.

He looks questioningly at Berthier. This portfolio has been found on the person of Count d'Antraigues whom General Bernadotte has arrested on his orders. The royalist agent was in the company of the Russian ambassador, Mordvinov, and carrying a Russian passport, which allowed him to get out of French-occupied Venice and through the first checkpoints. Bernadotte caught him in Trieste. The prisoner has been transferred to Milan.

Everything has a dark, hidden side – that is where the explanation often lies – but few people know those secrets. The rest – the crowd, the people – only find out afterwards that their hero was just a puppet whose strings were being pulled. Napoleon thinks of Mirabeau, so admired until the discovery of his iron safe at the Tuileries, which revealed that he had been paid by the King, just like any second-rate agent.

Using a dagger, he breaks the red portfolio's lock and begins to leaf through the pages covered in fine writing. He stops. He recognizes names: particularly General Pichegru, who has just been elected president of the Council of the Five Hundred and is now head of the royalist faction, one of the most active members of the royalist Clichy Club.

He reads the thirty-three pages. It is a report from a royalist agent, Montgaillard, to d'Antraigues, which gives overwhelming proof of General Pichegru's treachery when he was commanding the Army of the Rhine and Moselle. Agents of the émigrés of Condé's army and of the Austrians made contact with Pichegru after he harshly suppressed a sans-culotte riot in Paris on 1 April 1795. Taking that as a good sign. Montgaillard, speaking for Condé, proposes he leads a coup d'état with his army which will lead to a restoration of the monarchy. In return for his treachery, he will receive a marshal's baton, the cross of the commander of St Louis, the Château of Chambord, two million in cash and one hundred and twenty thousand livres pension, revertible half to his wife, a quarter to his children, and even four cannon!

Napoleon reads it again. It is as if a breach were opening in enemy lines. With these proofs, he can influence the situation in Paris. He can provide Barras with the means to denounce and break Pichegru and the election-winning royalists, by accusing them of treason.

He has stopped reading. When he resumes, he recoils. Montgaillard writes to d'Antraigues that he can 'soon obtain a result from Eleonore as positive as that I had obtained from Baptiste'.

Baptiste is the pseudonym used for Pichegru, and Eleonore is the code-name for Bonaparte. Montgaillard reckons that Bonaparte can be bought for thirty-six thousand livres.

Napoleon pushes the sheets of paper away. The fact that his name is in this document weakens the case against Pichegru, so every reference to the Army of Italy must be suppressed, and d'Antraigues must sign the pages concerning Pichegru. One cannot deprive oneself of a weapon like this.

'Have d'Antraigues brought to the château,' says Napoleon.

IT IS NIGHT. The room is dark. Napoleon watches d'Antraigues come in. The man is elegant and sure of himself, but his face betrays a certain anxiety. He sees Berthier first, then recognizes Napoleon. He protests vehemently. He has a Russian passport. He is a diplomat.

'Passports – fiddlesticks! Why should anyone trust passports?' says Napoleon. 'I only let you have a passport so I could be surer of catching you.'

'We are not conversant with this new political right in Russia,' says d'Antraigues.

'You will be. The Emperor may take this event as he pleases, it is all the same to us. If I had been at Trieste, his ambassador would have been arrested, his effects and papers seized, and I would have sent him back alone to take the news to Russia. You are my prisoner, I do not wish to release you.'

He must deal this man a stunning blow, unhorse him, so that he can break his resolve.

'Let us talk of something else now.' Napoleon ushers d'Antraigues over to a large sofa and sits next to him as Berthier brings up a little table on which are laid the papers from the red portfolio.

Sizing up a man, knowing what flattery and threats it will need to make him give in – this is how one acquires the power to influence, guide and lead other men.

'You are too enlightened,' Napoleon begins, 'and too gifted not to realize that the cause you have championed is lost. The people are tired of fighting for imbeciles, the soldiers of fighting for cowards. The revolution is irreversible in Europe. It must run its course. Look at the Kings' armies: the soldiers are good, the officers dissatisfied, and so they are defeated.'

Napoleon gathers the papers together.

'A new faction exists in France,' he says. 'I want to crush it. You must help us, you will not be displeased by our response . . . Here, sign these papers, I would advise it.'

He hands him the expurgated documents but d'Antraigues protests. His portfolio has been opened. He does not recognize these papers.

Napoleon gets to his feet and exclaims, 'Heavens, you are making fun of me! All of this is mad, it has no common sense. I opened your portfolio because it pleased me to do so. Armies are not courts of law. I am not asking you to recognize your papers: I am asking you to sign these four notebooks . . .'

As quid pro quo, Napoleon offers him the recovery of his properties in France and even the position of ambassador to Vienna.

'I want nothing you propose, sir,' replies d'Antraigues.

What does this naïf think? What world does he think he is living in?

'Proofs, proofs! Ah! Very well, if we need them we will make them!'

This man must yield.

A FEW DAYS later, Napoleon meets d'Antraigues's wife as she is coming with her five-year-old son to visit Josephine, and strides towards her: one must be able to exaggerate the anger one feels.

'Perhaps your husband will come out of prison at six o'clock tomorrow, and I will send him to you at eleven with ten bullets in the stomach,' he says.

Saint-Huberty hugs her son to her. She is screaming and the child is crying.

'Isn't my son old enough to be butchered as well?' she yells. 'I would advise you to have me shot, because I will murder you wherever I can . . .'

Josephine comes in and takes Saint-Huberty away, who says loudly, 'You told me Robespierre was dead, Madame, but here he is, brought back to life. He is thirsty for our blood. He will be wise to spill it, because I am going to Paris and I will obtain justice . . .'

Robespierre?

Remembering Maximilien's brother as he walks away, Napoleon wonders – perhaps those men, the terrorists, were primarily naïfs, even if they ruled by the guillotine.

On 9 June 1796, d'Antraigues eventually agrees to copy out the sixteen reworked pages and sign them, and the red portfolio is sent to Barras. The triumvirs of the Directory now have a decisive weapon against Pichegru, the royalist armies and the members of the Clichy Club.

'My handiwork,' says Napoleon.

He orders that d'Antraigues be allowed to move about freely if he promises not to escape. Let him live. Let him escape even, if he wants. The traitor cannot do anything else. Or rather, he can try – his correspondence is opened and his letters passed to Napoleon.

One evening, walking slowly around his office, Napoleon reads d'Antraigues's portrait of him. He stops often, as if before a mirror.

This destructive genius, perverse, atrocious, cruel, resourceful, irritated by obstacles, counting existence nothing and ambition everything, wishing to be master and resolved to perish if he shall not succeed, unbridled, considering vices and virtues just as means and only feeling the most profound indifference to all and sundry – he bears the very stamp of the Man of State. Naturally violent to excess, he restrains himself by the exercise of a more reflective cruelty which makes him suspend his rages and adjourn his revenge; physically and morally incapable of existing for a single moment in a state of repose . . . Bonaparte is a man of small stature, puny figure, ardent eyes, something heinous, dissembling and perfidious in his look and mouth, who says little but speaks out when his vanity is at stake or offended. His health is very poor, due to an acridity of the blood. He is covered in patches of dry skin, and these sorts of maladies increase his violence and activity.

This man is always occupied by his projects and this without distraction. He sleeps three hours at night, and only takes remedies when his ailments are unbearable.

This man wants to become master of France and through that, Europe. Everything else seems, even in his successes, to offer only means. So he steals openly, pillages everywhere, amasses an enormous treasure of gold, silver, jewels and precious stones. But he is only interested in that to put it to use. This same man who will rob an entire community will give a million without hesitating to the man who can be of use to him . . . A deal is struck with him in two words and two minutes. There you have his means of seduction.

Am I like this?
Napoleon goes out into the park of the Château of Montebello. He walks. The wind has freshened into gusts, as it often does

in the evening after the violent heat of the afternoon. The storm does not always break, but the air is so thick with thunder that it crackles and sometimes seems to tear itself apart. Lightning illumines the blackish sky in the distance, towards the lakes and mountains.

They see me like this. My enemies.

To want to become something, to want to make one's mark is to arouse calumny, the hatred of envious people, rivals. One cannot be without enemies. Those who are not hated are nothing, and they do nothing.

Am I like this?

I am.

XXVII

IT IS RAINING. The Tagliamento valley is filled with low cloud. It is the end of August 1797. Napoleon is on the steps of the Château of Passariano, and at the end of the grand alley of poplars he can see the carriages of the Austrian plenipotentiaries driving away. They are staying nearby, in Campo Formio, others have chosen to stay in Udine, but they are coming to negotiate here, in the château. Neither Count Louis de Cobenzl, a seasoned diplomat, nor the Marquis de Gallo, nor General Count Merveldt seem in any hurry to conclude the peace. They are still discussing the Preliminaries signed at Leoben.

They indulge their frivolity and elegance, their arts of conversation, to make the days pass. They pay court, in their affected aristocratic fashion, to Josephine. They even join in the games of cards or dice she organizes to relieve the tedium.

Napoleon walks into the château, slamming doors as he goes. He is not fooled. These diplomats are waiting to see what turn affairs take in Paris. They hope that, in the struggles dividing the Directory, Pichegru's supporters, the royalists, the members of the Clichy Club, will triumph. In which case, farewell peace. The monarchy would return in Paris.

It is out of the question. What would my destiny be then?

NAPOLEON has taken action. Proclamations and newspapers have been distributed in their thousands to the soldiers of the Army of Italy: 'Soldiers, you owe yourselves entirely to the Republic ... Soldiers, as soon as the royalists show themselves, that will be the end of them. Implacable war on the enemies of the Republic and the Constitution of Year III!'

It is a complicated manoeuvre. He must not lower his guard too much. As he keeps telling Lavalette, 'See everybody, guard against being infected by party spirit, give me the truth and give it to me free of all passion.'

How can one choose a strategy if the fog is not dispersed?

Lavalette explains: Barras and La Révellière-Lépeaux have appealed to General Hoche to mount an anti-royalist coup d'état with his army, but, having committed himself at first, the general has recoiled at the in-fighting and intrigues. The directors are looking for another sword.

I will not be General Vendémiaire any more.

But there is Augereau, whom Napoleon has dispatched with three million livres for Barras. He will act. Napoleon received a letter from him soon after he arrived in Paris: 'I pledge to save the Republic from the agents of throne and altar.'

Lavalette advises Napoleon to keep out of the way himself, so as not to compromise his glory as a victorious general by being embroiled in the imminent crackdown in Paris.

'Have they received d'Antraigues' papers?' Napoleon asks.

'They will be the pretext for the repression, and the *coup de grâce*,' explains Lavalette. 'The victims have already been chosen. They are already secretly printing d'Antraigues' confession, which proves Pichegru's treason. Posters have been stuck up, denouncing the foreigner's conspiracy.'

WAIT FOR Augereau's sabre thrust, keep one's distance but not remain idle.

Summoning them to the Château of Passariano, Napoleon badgers the men he has employed to launch newspapers in Paris and Milan, aimed at influential citizens and the army. He leafs through the first editions of *The Courier of the Army of Italy*, *The French Patriot*, *France Seen from Italy* and *The Journal of Bonaparte and Virtuous Men*. He flies into a rage. Too tepid! The attacks of the royalist papers can't go unanswered; they must promulgate strong, simple ideas: 'Have them talk about me, about my exploits,' he says.

One can never praise a leader enough.

He reads out a sentence from the *Courier* in a loud voice, 'He flies like lightning and strikes like thunder, he is everywhere and he sees everything.' That's the sort of thing.

He dictates, 'I have seen kings at my feet, I could have had fifty million in my coffers and I could have laid claim to a great many other things; but I am a French citizen, I am the envoy and senior general of the Great Nation, I know that posterity will do me justice.'

If these sorts of truths are not dealt out in the newspapers he owns, where will they be? There are eighty royalist newspapers peddling outrages and calumnies every day, he exclaims.

'I see that the Clichy Club wishes to trample over my corpse to finish off the Republic. They say, "We're not afraid of this Bonaparte, we have Pichegru." We must demand that these émigrés be arrested and the influence of foreigners be broken. We have to insist that the presses of papers sold in England are smashed; they are more bloody than anything Marat ever wrote.'

When his penmen – Jullien, a Jacobin, Regnault de Saint-Jean-d'Angély, a former member of the Constituent Assembly and the writer Arnault – have left, he calls Berthier. He wants the principal newspapers, French and foreign, to be read to him every morning. The situation in Paris is uncertain. The point? Just as in war, nothing should be left to chance. Opinion counts.

He constantly interrupts, 'The nation must have a leader, a leader renowned for his glory in war,' he says, 'not for theories of government, words and ideologists' speeches of which the French know nothing ... A Republic of thirty million men, the very idea! With our morals, our vices! It is a chimera the French are infatuated with, but it will pass, like so many others. They need the glory and satisfactions of vanity, but they don't know the first thing about freedom. Look at the army: our triumphs have already given the French soldier his true character back. I am everything for him.'

Then he looks at Berthier for a long time. One cannot say everything, even to a loyal supporter, and yet one must hint, so that this man can understand and help the plan take shape.

'A party is rearing its head in support of the Bourbons,' resumes Napoleon. 'I do not want to contribute to its triumph. I am quite happy to weaken the Republican party one day, but I do not want to benefit the previous dynasty in the process, and I definitely do not want the part of Monk, who restored the monarchy in England after Cromwell. I don't want to play it and I don't want anyone else to play it either ...'

It is my 'system': I play for myself.

ON 9 SEPTEMBER, Napoleon opens the letter Lavalette has sent him by special courier. His head is teeming with ideas.

Lavalette writes that on 4 September (18 Fructidor), at three in the morning, Paris has been occupied by Augereau's troops. The royalists have been arrested. Barras is triumphant, Carnot is in flight. Barthélemy, the other director and loyal supporter of the Clichy Club, has been captured. The Council of the Five Hundred and the Council of the Ancients have been purged. Huge copies of d'Antraigues' papers have been put up all over Paris.

'My handiwork,' says Napoleon, folding up the letter.

It was Napoleon who sent Augereau to Paris and unmasked Pichegru's treachery.

Pichegru is arrested.

A few days later, another courier brings news of the death of General Hoche, a long-time tuberculosis sufferer, and of the discharge of General Moreau, suspected of complicity with the royalists.

I am the only one now.

He must reassure those directors who have just grown stronger and may now fear this glorious general whose name is cheered in Paris and is supported by the newspapers.

On 10 October, Napoleon sits at his desk and writes to the directors: 'I wish to merge back into the crowd, take up the plough of Cincinnatus and set an example of respect for the magistracy and aversion to that military rule which has destroyed so many republics and been the ruin of several states.'

Are you reassured, gentlemen?

XXVIII

'FOR MYSELF . . .' NAPOLEON BEGINS.

He is standing in the salon of the Château of Passariano where he usually sees Count Cobenzl. Vienna's plenipotentiary is due to arrive from Campo Formio in a few minutes and Napoleon is determined to conclude the peace negotiations today. Now that the danger of a royalist coup d'état in Paris has been averted, Napoleon must appear to all Frenchmen as the man of peace.

'For myself, I have no ambition,' he continues, looking at Berthier who has just read to him from the Parisian newspapers.

All of them sing General Bonaparte's praises.

'Or if I do,' he goes on, 'it is so natural, so innate, so well anchored in my existence that it is like the blood flowing in my veins, or the air I breathe; it doesn't make me go faster at all. I never have to fight, either for or against it; it is never more urgent than myself, it only accords with circumstances and the ensemble of my ideas.'

What is ambition? He would rather say energy, the desire to forge ahead. He knows that if peace is concluded he will have to leave Italy. He cannot stay in this country he has conquered but which does not belong to him and where he would always be dependent on decisions from Paris. He will have to return to Paris, but what position could he occupy there? Be one of the directors? 'The pear is not ripe,' he has often thought. So – he must look somewhere further afield.

Several times he has thought of the shore of the Adriatic. He has visualized, to the east and south, those jagged coastlines that recall Corsica and anticipate Greece and the Orient. He daydreams, he imagines. It would only take a few hours to reach the Ionian isles, which are now French. From there, in another leap, it would only take a few days sailing to reach Malta, that citadel in the heart of the Mediterranean. Thus, hopping from isle to isle, one could reach the continent of the conquerors of history who made their entrances into the mythical cities – Alexandria, Jerusalem.

But for that one would have to control the sea and subjugate England.

'Destroying England would put all Europe at our feet,' he says to the diplomat Poulssiègue, whom he sends on a spying mission to Malta. When the diplomat expresses his surprise at this remark, Napoleon shrugs his shoulders. Why must he always explain an intuition, a dream? Obviously the diplomat has not read *Journeys in Syria and Egypt* by Volney, his old friend from Corsica.

'The time is not far off,' he murmurs, 'when we will feel that to truly destroy England, we must take Egypt.'

Napoleon stands, eyes fixed on the horizon.

Further afield.

But first, he must conclude this peace with Austria.

COUNT COBENZL sits down elegantly, crosses his legs and begins to propound his arguments.

Napoleon walks impatiently up and down the salon. He cannot listen any more. Who does this aristocrat take him for? Some titled little diplomat you send round and round in circles like a donkey? For days now the negotiations have been making no headway. He feels the fury mounting, but this time no matching inclination to restrain it. Let the storm break, let the lava flow! Sometimes one has to roar.

'Your empire,' he shouts suddenly, 'is an old whore used to being despoiled by all and sundry ... You forget that France is victorious and that you are vanquished ... You forget that you are negotiating with me here, surrounded by my grenadiers.'

He gesticulates and knocks over the pedestal table. The coffee service falls to the floor and smashes. Napoleon stops and sees Count Cobenzl's face twist in fear, surprise and a certain irony. The aristocrat probably considers him a 'madman', as he has already confided to his intimates.

Madman? The victor is never that.

A week later, on 17 October 1797, at Campo Formio, in the name of Austria, Cobenzl signs a treaty of peace with France, confirming the Preliminaries of Leoben. Austria cedes Belgium to France; it gives Lombardy to the Cisalpine Republic. France annexes the Ionian islands of Corfu, Zante and Cephalonia, but in exchange Austria gains Venice and its mainland territories as far as the Adige.

'DO YOU KNOW,' says Lavalette, six days after he has come from the capital, 'that in Paris you are known as the Great Peacemaker? Your name is cheered. Your wife's homecoming was celebrated like a queen's. You are wreathed in the glory of a victorious general and a sage.'

Napoleon listens. He has just received the Directory's congratulations on concluding the Treaty of Campo Formio. The new minister for foreign affairs, Talleyrand, the former Bishop of Autun whom he has not met, has written to him, 'This then is peace à la Bonaparte ... The Directory is happy, the people enchanted. Everything is for the best. Perhaps there'll be some whining from the Italians, but that is neither here nor there. Farewell, General Peacemaker! Farewell, in friendship, admiration, respect, gratitude; one hardly knows where to stop the list.'

'Whining from the Italians': here is a minister who does not concern himself about the Veneto being handed over to the Austrians, a man who seems to understand the nature of politics and diplomacy.

'You will return to Paris in triumph,' Lavalette assures him. 'Every street will be packed.'

'Bah,' says Napoleon. 'The people would be just as keen to see me pass if I was on my way to the scaffold.'

When he is appointed commander-in-chief of the Army of England, charged with preparing an invasion of that island, and again when another message from Paris the following day makes him the Republic's representative at the Congress of Rastadt, where the implementation of the Treaty of Campo Formio is to be organized, he shows no surprise.

He knows that certain deputies, and Reubell of the directors, have not agreed with all the treaty's clauses. Not all have been as realistic as Talleyrand, but how could one reject this peace which has been awaited and greeted with such enthusiasm?

'They envy me, I know,' says Napoleon. 'Even though they shower me with fulsome praise, they won't cloud my judgement. They have rushed to make me general of the Army of England so as to remove me from Italy where I am more a sovereign than a general. They will see how matters fare when I am gone.'

But he leaves without regrets.

He assembles the officers in the Serbelloni Palace and walks slowly along the line of them. Every face conjures up a moment in what has been almost two years of solid fighting. They have changed from the band of 'brigands' he took in hand in the spring of 1796 to these grenadiers who would fight to the death for him, these captains and generals in their iridescent uniforms who enfold him with their admiration in these lavishly decorated halls.

A revolution has taken place in his life. Yesterday, he was only General Vendémiaire, today he is the acclaimed, fêted, lauded General Peacemaker.

He walks away from the officers crowding around him. He remembers Muiron. Muiron is dead, like those thousands of others, young lives like his, full of energy, desire, ambition. He feels that he is the bearer of all that heritage of strength and blood – living through and on behalf of all those dead, answerable to them forever, haunted by their memory.

'In finding myself separated from this army,' he says, 'my one consolation will be the hope of seeing myself back with you soon, fighting against new dangers. Whichever post the government assigns to the soldiers of the Army of Italy, they will always be the worthy upholders of the liberty and glory of the French name.'

I have become that name.

ON THE NIGHT of 17–18 November, he arrives in Turin and the French ambassador, Miot de Mélito, has him to stay at his residence.

Napoleon cannot sleep and paces up and down the main salon, barely looking at the deferential, silent Miot. He primarily talks to himself at this moment, which feels like a parenthesis between a part of his story which is coming to an end and another just starting which he already wishes to explore.

'These Parisian barristers who have been appointed to the Directory,' he says, 'do not know the first thing about government; they are petty-minded. I am going to see what they want at

Rastadt. I very much doubt that we will be able to understand one another or agree on anything for long.'

He breaks off. He seems to have become aware of Miot's presence; without taking his eyes off him, he adds, 'As for myself, my dear Miot, I declare, I cannot obey any more; I have tasted command and I should not know how to renounce it. My mind is made up. If I cannot be the master, I shall leave France; I do not want to have done so much just to hand it all to barristers . . .'

At nine o'clock in the morning, the carriage leaves Turin and he travels through Chambéry, Geneva, Berne, Solothurn and Basle. He looks out at the crowds that cheer him as he passes and sees his face reflected in the window, thin, pale and tired, but when his carriage stops, he jumps down, brisk and energetic as ever. He is surrounded, his advice is asked. He settles the questions put to him, devotes a matter of minutes to a frugal dinner, and is on his way again at dawn. He crosses the Brisgau and reaches the gates of Rastadt in the evening of 25 November.

He orders the carriage to stop there, and the team to be changed: the impression he makes as he arrives must be dazzling. He enters the town in a coach drawn by eight horses and escorted by thirty enormous Veczay hussars, on horses harnessed and adorned as for a parade.

He takes over a wing of the Château of Mombello with his suite, but he immediately feels himself ensnared in these diplomats' negotiations. He is not the master but the subordinate of Director Reubell, who is responsible for the Directory's diplomacy. He no longer has his loyal grenadiers about him, nor his court, and he becomes irritable. It is hard to accept being relegated when one has stood so tall.

In the meeting chamber, he encounters Axel Fersen, the Swedish delegate who was Marie-Antoinette's lover, and looks him up and down. 'The French Republic will not permit,' he says in an imperious tone, 'individuals who are only too well known for their liaisons with the former Court of France to thumb their noses at the ministers of the finest people on the earth.' Then he turns his back on him. He cannot stand the 'diplomatic chit-chat'.

On 30 November, hurrying the diplomats, he exchanges the

ratifications of the treaty, then on 2 December, he summons his aide-de-camp, Murat, and instructs him to go to Paris to prepare for his arrival. On 3 December 1797, he leaves himself, but stops at Nancy on the 4th for a few hours.

The freemasons of the lodge of St John of Jerusalem fête him, but he only says a few words in reply. He is distracted and seems to be daydreaming. He has changed into civilian clothes and it is by mail coach that he arrives in Paris on 5 December 1797, at five o'clock in the evening, accompanied by Berthier and Championnet.

Josephine must still be driving through Italy, since he has instructed her to return to Paris. He does not want to think of her; picturing her only leads to pain and jealousy.

HE GOES to his home in rue Chantereine – except that now it is called rue de la Victoire.

Paris is deserted. No noise, no parades. Silence and discretion when people are expecting cheering – these are further means of taking people unawares.

And how can one govern men if one doesn't surprise them?

PART SEVEN

*Everything wears out
here . . . I must go East*

5 DECEMBER 1797 TO 19 MAY 1798

XXIX

'I MUST MEET THIS MAN tomorrow,' Napoleon is saying.

He has barely arrived in Paris and already he is giving one of his aides-de-camp a note for the Directory's minister of foreign affairs, Charles Maurice de Talleyrand-Périgord. He has no doubt that Talleyrand will see him.

One can know a man's character even if one has never laid eyes on him, and, since his minsterial appointment in July 1797, Talleyrand has made it plain that he is an ally who is ready to be of service and thereby serve himself.

This is all an alliance between men of power ever is.

Napoleon remembers the first letter Talleyrand sent him. 'Justly daunted by an office whose perilous importance I am keenly aware of, I find myself drawing reassurance from the thought of all that your glory shall bring, both in means and prowess, to the negotiations,' he wrote on 24 July 1797.

Daunted, the former Bishop of Autun? The man who in 1790 celebrated mass at the Festival of Federation, who spent several years in exile, in the United States and England, until the guillotine's blade grew still, and who became the Directory's minister of foreign affairs as soon as he returned to France, through Barras's influence and the intrigues of the women he loves so much, especially Necker's daughter, Madame de Staël – could he really doubt his talents? Nonsense! Nothing could scare a man like him. All his letter means is: let us shake hands; we have shared interests. Since then, other overtures have confirmed that first gesture.

When, at eleven o'clock in the morning on 6 December, Napoleon enters the Hôtel de Galliffet's salon, in rue du Bac, he forgets none of that. Talleyrand has given him to understand that he has not taken the directors' supervision well, especially that of Reubell, who is in charge of foreign affairs. This is enough to create a sympathy of feeling between them.

So, this is the man.

He comes towards Napoleon, very tall, pale, hair powdered in an *ancien régime* manner, snub nose. He is clean-shaven and smiling ironically. He has a limp and it is hard to put an age to him.

Guests invited to catch a glimpse of Napoleon have stood up and Talleyrand introduces them with a sort of weariness. Madame de Staël is an eccentric whom Napoleon barely looks at. He mistrusts this woman who devours him with her eyes and has written him impassioned letters. What is a woman who cannot be satisfied with the seductiveness of her sex, but must talk in florid periods and seek to provoke? A woman who is trying to mask her ugliness. Napoleon turns his back on her, salutes the navigator Bougainville, and then follows Talleyrand into his study.

Napoleon observes the minister. He is as he imagined him: high cravat, loose-fitting frock coat, strong, deep voice, stiff bearing, a lordly figure who looks down on things from on high, eyes fixed, illusionless. A man whose words are not for sale. A skilful player, but also one who clearly shows the admiration he feels for Napoleon and who, as the elder man, recognizes that his glorious younger counterpart has the stronger suit. However, there is enough detachment in his attitude to show Napoleon that he feels no obsequiousness nor gives an acknowledgement of inferiority. 'You have the finer hand,' Talleyrand seems to be saying. 'I will second you in this game, but I am not renouncing anything.'

I need partners like this in the game I'm playing.

'You are the nephew of the Archbishop of Reims who has gone with Louis XVIII,' says Napoleon.

He intentionally says 'Louis XVIII', like a royalist.

'I also have an uncle who is an archdeacon — in Corsica,' he continues. 'It was he who brought me up. As you know, to be an archdeacon in Corsica is the same as being a bishop in France.' It is a way of suggesting that, beyond their immediate interests, they have similar origins that bode well for their collaboration.

This first meeting comes to an end. The salon is full now, and a respectful murmur greets Napoleon.

'Citizens,' he says. 'I am sensible to the attentions you show me. I have conducted the war to the best of my abilities and the peace likewise. Now it is for the Directory to profit from this for the good and prosperity of the Republic.'

HE NEEDS to be prudent. Certain newspapers are implying that he wants to be dictator, and ask what he has come to Paris to do. Therefore he must throw dust in the eyes of his adversaries, not appear hungry for glory, please as many people as possible and conduct himself as a humble citizen, who is concerned not with his own interests but with those of the Republic.

He dines with Reubell, the director most hostile to signing the Treaty of Campo Formio, who is Talleyrand's superior and adversary. With him he must be the personification of self-effacement and disinterest.

However, in public opinion, the Directory consists of corrupt men vying with each other for power, so it is important he does not compromise himself with one of the clans, and he must make it clear that he has not become rich from the war. If he is going to entertain in the rue de la Victoire, his guests should primarily be men of science and letters, scholars, members of the Institute, soldiers. He must not be confused in the public mind with the politicians. Berthollet, Monge, Laplace, Prony, Bernardin de Saint-Pierre, Desaix, Berthier: citizens such as these are above suspicion. He talks of mathematics and poetry to Marie-Joseph Chénier and proves a mathematical theorem to Laplace, his old examiner at the Military School.

He knows the gamble has paid off when Laplace exclaims, 'We were expecting anything and everything from you, except a lesson in mathematics!'

He has an idea: he should apply to become a member of the Institute in the place left vacant by Carnot. The newspapers, which Napoleon reads every morning, talk about it immediately. The journalists are astonished: this general seems only to be concerned with this honourable, disinterested candidacy.

On 25 December, Napoleon is elected by three hundred and five votes to the Institute First Class, Physical Sciences, Mathematics, and Mechanical Arts Section, and the following day, at four thirty in the afternoon, he takes his seat between Monge and Berthollet to attend his first sitting. That evening, at dinner, Madame Tallien congratulates him.

Less than three years have passed and he is close to the summit, but it is too soon to show that he knows this. He must still appear to be nothing and to concern himself about nothing.

He has learnt not to let fulsome praise go to his head. During the official ceremony organized in his honour by the Directory at the Luxembourg Palace, he does not turn his head towards those who cheer and shout 'Long Live Bonaparte! Long live the general of the Grande Armée!' The streets around the palace are packed with enthusiastic crowds.

They are there for me. They shout my name.

Hearing them, he looks at the five directors in a different light, with their orangey-red overcoats draped over their shoulders, their big white collars, their lace, their gold-embroidered suits, their black hats turned up on one side with a tricolour plume.

It is not their names the crowd is repeating. It is not for them that the cannon fire, that the altar of the fatherland stands surrounded by statues of liberty, equality and fraternity, and choirs sing 'The Song of Return' to music by Mehul and words by Chenier – it is for me.

But the five directors have the power to organize this, and power is a network of complicities, of insurances and reinsurances, an entire spider's web which binds hundreds of men together.

They still have that.

Talleyrand gives a speech. 'I think of everything he has done to be spared this glory,' he says, turning to Napoleon, 'the classical fondness of simplicity which distinguishes him, his love for the abstract sciences . . . No one can fail to be aware of his profound contempt for fame, luxury, display, those contemptible ambitions of average souls. Ah, far from fearing his ambition, I feel we should petition him one day to tear himself from the comforts of his studious retreat . . .'

Napoleon listens, his face impassive, lips compressed, eyes unmoving. Without need to confer, Talleyrand is being useful.

My modesty must be dazzling.

Napoleon has decided to say only a few words, as befits one who has chosen a retiring role.

'To be free,' he begins, 'the French people had the kings to fight. To obtain a constitution founded on reason, there were eighteen centuries of prejudice to vanquish . . . When the happiness of the French people rests on the best organic laws, the whole of Europe shall become free.'

He is cheered. Has the crowd understood that the country does not yet have 'the best laws'? That he, Napoleon, knows that? He must say it, even if it may be imprudent, since he must embody the wish for change.

Since he has arrived in Paris, people keep asking him the same question. What does he want? They are counting on him to ensure that calm is finally restored in the country, and that there will be an end to the succession of coups d'état. He should therefore at least insinuate that he is of the same mind.

The day after the ceremony, he stays at home in the rue de la Victoire, and Bourrienne pays him a visit. He had been at the Luxembourg Palace. 'A ceremony of icy coldness,' he says. 'Everyone seemed to be watching one another, and I saw more curiosity on people's faces than joy or signs of real gratitude.'

'They are afraid and they hate me,' Napoleon explains.

He shows him a letter that has arrived that morning saying there is a plot to poison him. 'Those who cheered me would happily have choked me with their laurels,' he says.

Prudence, then, must be his watchword. He must veil his glory and pride and concentrate on staying alive.

He asks a faithful servant, a former soldier, to accompany him at all times; it is he who will serve him at table and pour his wine. At the banquet given in Napoleon's honour by the two assemblies, the Council of the Ancients and the Council of the Five Hundred, Sieyès and François de Neufchâteau, who sit on either side of him, express their surprise at these precautions. They have already been taken aback by the sight of him arriving in an 'extremely modest carriage', dressed in civilian clothes but with a pair of spurred boots as if to be able to leap on a horse if necessary.

He answers them with a half-smile. Are they pretending not to know that inconvenient people tend to be killed? He knows it, just as he knows that he unsettles people. The Jacobins suspect him of wanting to establish a dictatorship. The directors fear for their power.

So, even at this banquet for eight hundred people with four courses, eight hundred lackeys, thirty-two majordomos, Cape wines, Tokay, Rhine carp, early fruit and new vegetables of every sort, his personal servant changes his cutlery, plates and glasses, and serves him soft-boiled eggs.

IT IS DIFFERENT at Talleyrand's house.

At ten thirty in the evening, on 3 January 1798, Napoleon enters the reception rooms of the Hôtel de Galliffet, where Talleyrand and almost five hundred guests are waiting.

Craftsmen have spent weeks decorating Talleyrand's town house. Singers, choreographed dancers and musicians perform on stages erected in the centre of the rooms. There are plants everywhere, and on the walls, copies of the masterpieces Bonaparte captured in Italy. In the courtyards, soldiers have pitched their tents. The staircases and rooms are scented with amber. The women, dressed in Roman or Ancient Greek dresses of floating muslin, silk and crêpe, have been chosen personally by Talleyrand for their elegance and beauty.

Napoleon watches Josephine, nonchalant and smiling, a cameo tiara in her hair. She is one of the most beautiful women there. She is his.

He has what he has always dreamed of: this triumph, these women, these powerful men everywhere, crowding round him, but he remains stiff, vigilant. He has chosen to wear not uniform but a simple black frock coat, buttoned up to the neck.

He takes the writer Arnault by the arm and they go into the ballroom where a waltz is in full swing. The orchestra immediately switches to a new tune, a quadrille called 'The Bonaparte'.

He is the centre of this celebration and yet he is irritated. He leans towards Arnault. 'Keep the importunate away from me,' he says. He cannot speak freely. This ball given by Talleyrand is in his honour, but he is not sovereign here. He catches sight of three of the directors amongst the guests. That is the pinnacle of power.

He winces at the thought; this party rings false, it grates on him – too much curiosity and not enough genuine respect. That only comes when one has complete power.

Arnault, who has been separated from him by the crowd, returns accompanied by a woman whom Napoleon recognizes immediately.

'Madame de Staël,' says Arnault, 'claims to need a recommendation to you other than that of her name and wants me to present her to you. Allow me, General, to obey her.'

A circle forms and Napoleon watches this corpulent woman, who speaks emphatically, complimenting and questioning him. Scorn and anger well up in him. He is not someone who lets himself be constrained by a woman he does not desire. This one is not only ugly but also pretentious. They say that she writes, that she has ambitions to political views. Her!

'General,' Madame de Staël asks him. 'Which woman do you like the most?'

'The one I have married.'

'That's very plain, but which is the one you esteem the most?'

She would like him to answer something along the lines of, 'a woman who thinks, who concerns herself with the governance of the city, who writes'. Who does she think she has before her? A literary salon chatterer?

'The one who keeps house best,' he says.

'I can imagine that too, but really, who would you say was the first among women?'

'The one who has the most children, Madame.'

He turns on his heels and goes to the banqueting hall, which is surrounded by a screen of myrtle, laurels and olive trees. The band is playing 'The Song of Leaving'. Only the women are sitting down, and Talleyrand is standing behind Josephine's chair. Napoleon takes the arm of the Turkish ambassador, Esseid Ali.

Lays, the singer, begins a song dedicated to Josephine that everyone is singing:

> Oh beloved companion
> Of the warrior, of the heroic victor
> Who alone apart from the fatherland

> Possesses his heart
> Pay the vast debt
> Of a great people to its defender
> By taking care of his happiness
> You absolve France of its duty

Napoleon looks at Talleyrand, who is leaning over Josephine's shoulder.

This man is a master of the skilful manoeuvre. A precious ally.

TALLEYRAND, however, does not have true power. He is only a protégé of Barras and a subordinate of Reubell, who treats him with sarcasm and contempt. These are the men that Napoleon must be more than a match for, whatever the cost, whilst making sure he does not come to be thought of as one of them.

Napoleon visits them in the Luxembourg Palace. He is working on this plan for the invasion of England. He is the general-in-chief of the army entrusted with this mission, isn't he?

He stands facing the directors and explains the difficulties of the enterprise. He has ordered the readying of the naval armament of Brest, and he has seen Wolfe Tone, the Irish patriot. One plan might be to land in Ireland and stir up a revolt against the English invader.

He feels that he is gradually disarming his critics. The effort is paying off.

EARLY IN January, he is summoned urgently to the palace. Serious disturbances have broken out in Rome. Roused by the clergy, the Romans have attacked the French troops, General Duphot has been assassinated, and the French ambassador Joseph Bonaparte has had to leave.

Napoleon gives his instructions and writes to General Berthier, who has replaced him at the head of the Army of Italy.

But even in dramatic circumstances like these, the looks he attracts are often loaded with political motives. So he takes measures to protect himself; he removes generals he considers rivals: Bernadotte and his former subordinate Augereau, who has written that Bonaparte is 'an ambitious and murderous muddler'. Copies of this letter were circulated amongst the deputies, and Napoleon came to hear of it. Overwhelmed with rage, he scrumpled up the copy of the letter.

One must always be on one's guard.

ON 18 JANUARY, Talleyrand asks to see him.

Napoleon goes to the Hôtel de Galliffet and Talleyrand welcomes him with even more emphatic displays of admiration than usual. He chats about this and that and then finally reveals the reason for their meeting. In the erstwhile Church of St Sulpice, on 21 January, the fifth anniversary of the execution of Louis XVI is to be celebrated. The Directory wishes Napoleon to be present.

Talleyrand smiles and falls silent. Napoleon stares back at him.

'I have no public position,' he says. 'My presence would make no sense.'

The trap is obvious. For weeks he has endeavoured to remain aloof from the different camps; now they are trying to make him choose.

When, three days previously in one of the most renowned cafés in Paris, the Café Garchy near the Palais-Royal, there was a fight between former royalist émigrés and Jacobins which left one dead and many wounded, he protested violently and indignantly denounced vandalism, theft and massacre committed in the name of Jacobinism. He even accused the police of having organized 'this atrocious crime', this 'expedition of cut-throats'. He stands for order and an end to this sort of violence. The old antagonisms between Jacobins and émigrés must cease. There must be a government based on merit, like the ones he established in the Italian republics.

This is what attracts people to him: he is the man who will restore domestic peace. And now the directors are trying to embroil him in this celebration of the death of Louis XVI!

Talleyrand is insistent.

'It is a cannibals' ritual,' Napoleon snaps. 'Appalling nonsense.'

He calms down as quickly as he flared up.

'I do not claim to advance an opinion as to whether Louis

XVI's sentence was useful or harmful,' he says, 'but it was an unhappy incident.'

He considers national festivals should only be held to celebrate victories, he adds, and that only those who have fallen on the field of battle should be mourned.

They both remain silent until, speaking in a slow voice, Talleyrand explains that the country is ruled by the law. This is the point of this celebration. General Bonaparte's hold on public opinion is such that he must attend this ceremony. The directors who have requested it would be astonished by his absence and consider that he had chosen to challenge the Republic.

'Is this the moment?' Talleyrand asks.

He stops, then adds that Napoleon could attend the ceremony in St Sulpice in civilian clothes, among his fellow members of the Institute. 'Appearances would be kept up,' Talleyrand murmurs.

Napoleon does not answer but, on 21 January 1798, he is part of the procession. He listens to Barras's speech, in which he swears an oath of 'hatred of royalty and anarchy'. Then the massed choirs sing the Republican Oath, with music by Gossec and words by Chénier:

> If some usurper wants to enslave France
> May he immediately feel the public vengeance
> May he fall under the sword; may his bloody frame
> Be given over to the devouring vultures of the plain.

Finally an ode by Lebrun-Pindar is read:

> If there are any that want a master
> From all the kings in the universe
> May they go abegging their chains
> These Frenchmen unworthy of the name.

At the end of the ceremony the crowd ignore the Directory and wait, all pressed together. Napoleon hesitates. He wants to slip away but he is seen and cries ring out: 'Long live Bonaparte! Long live the general of the Army of Italy!'

It is hard for him to leave the square.

Whatever songs they sing, these men want a leader.

PERHAPS THIS is the moment to act.

He walks round and round in his house in the rue de la Victoire. He does not even talk to Josephine, who observes him and tries to approach.

He needs to see Barras, who is now president of the Directory. Barras is a supporter of order. He should understand that the institutions have to be reformed, that there must be an end to this government by five directors, which is intrinsically powerless. Napoleon lets his imagination wander. In Italy he drew up constitutions for the republics he created. If he became director, he could dismiss the other three members and establish a genuinely effective executive with Barras.

BARRAS receives him in the Luxembourg Palace with the pomp and ceremony that gives him such delight. He is fat and speaks slowly, as if uttering words was too much of a strain.

Swamped by pleasures, a gourmet and a glutton, a hedonist who is said to indulge in every vice, can this man still have a will at all?

Napoleon hesitates to speak, and then suddenly he begins. 'The Directory's regime cannot last. It was mortally wounded by the coup d'état of 18 Fructidor. The majority of the nation, Jacobin and royalist, reject it.'

He stops. Then, without taking his eyes off Barras, he says, stressing every word, 'The conqueror of Italy and peacemaker must be granted exceptional eligibility. Once in power we two can dismiss the other directors and establish a government of order and tolerance. The moment is right.'

Napoleon goes closer to Barras, who is sitting down and has not moved.

'Public opinion is well disposed,' he continues, 'but the people's favour is like a storm, it quickly blows over.'

Barras abruptly straightens himself. He is sweating. Rolling his eyes he speaks in a thunderous voice – all this is impossible; if the councils elected Bonaparte a member of the Directory, they would be in breach of the constitution; the Directory would reject any decree of the kind.

He raises his voice still more: 'You wish to overthrow the

constitution? You will not succeed and will only destroy yourself. Sieyès has brought you to this with his treacherous advice; you will both come to a bad end.'

NAPOLEON is alone once again, on the brink of his destiny.

One can only trust oneself.

He was counting on Barras, but that fellow would rather let the country rot than take a risk. What should he do? Who should he count on? 'The pear is not yet ripe.' If he acts, he runs the risk of helping the Jacobins, who suspect him and will get rid of him, or else he may play into the hands of the counter-revolution, which he has no wish to see triumph. Besides, the country would reject both of these alternatives and it is not yet time to advocate a third path, which he would like to take with Barras. He cannot do it on his own, not yet.

IN THE DAYS that follow, he remains at home in a sombre mood.

As before, he thinks of leaving.

On 29 January a messenger brings him a report Talleyrand has submitted to the Directory two days before. It is a long document in which the minister of foreign affairs advocates the occupation of Egypt: 'Egypt, which nature has placed in such proximity to us, presents immense advantages with regard to trade, either with India or elsewhere ... Egypt is nothing to Turkey which hasn't a vestige of authority in place ...'

Napoleon rereads the document several times that day. He has dreamt of Egypt so often – in Corsica, years ago, when he listened to Volney's stories about his journeys down the Nile, and then again, only a few weeks ago, at Passariano – so the report seems all too familiar.

When Bourrienne arrives that evening, Napoleon immediately leads him into the little salon, away from Josephine.

'I do not wish to stay here,' he says in an edgy voice. 'There is nothing to do, the directors won't listen to anything. I can see that if I linger, I shall soon lose myself. Everything wears out here, already I have no glory left; this little Europe does not provide enough of it. I must go east, all great glory comes from there. However, first I wish to make a tour of the coast, to ascertain for myself what may be attempted. I will take you, Lannes, and Sulkowsky with me. If the success of an attackn England appears doubtful, as I suspect it will, the army of England shall become the Army of the East, and I will go to Egypt.'

XXX

NAPOLEON stands at the end of the pier at Anvers. It is drizzling and cold. For more than a week now he has been going from port to port, from Etaples to Boulogne and Calais, from Dunkirk to Ostend. He wants to be in Brussels this evening, and then set off again by post coach via Givet, Lille and St Quentin, to be back in Paris around 20 February.

He watches the tide ebb. Everything is grey – the horizon, the waves, the sand, the blocks of the pier. It is all alien to him. These are not his colours, or his reefs, or his sea, but that is not the most important thing. Nothing of what he has seen has been satisfactory. How can one invade England with only a handful of vessels, mainly sloops, when one would need hundreds?

He passes a group of sailors, but only looks at these men whose language he doesn't understand. At Boulogne and Dunkirk he had understood what the sailors were saying: the English are patrolling the coast in large numbers, with frigates, sloops and brigs, some with more than forty cannon.

Those sailors spoke freely to the little general who introduced himself as General Lasne.

Napoleon looks at the horizon one last time. Enough. He gets back into the coach and Bourrienne questions him. Is the general satisfied with what he has seen? Bourrienne adds that the naval forces allocated to the Army of England seem utterly insufficient to him.

What does he think? That I haven't seen that for myself?

'It is too great a risk,' comes Napoleon's brisk, irritated reply. 'I would not sport with the fate of my beloved France in such a fashion.'

That evening in Brussels he is recognized at the theatre, but his sombre air wards off any tiresome intrusions.

On the road to Paris he remains equally grave.

So, he must give up the invasion of England and leave France to embark on this Egyptian adventure he dreams of, but which presents immense dangers and uncertainties. Yet what choice does he have?

He turns to Bourrienne. 'There is nothing to be done with these people. The directors understand nothing of greatness. They have no powers of execution. We should need a flotilla for the expedition and, as it is, the English have more boats than us. All the preparations that would be indispensable to success are beyond our capabilities. We must return to our plans for the Orient; that is where there are great results to be won.'

He retreats into silence again.

He blames Barras, that pleasure-seeker and coward who has refused to help him enter the innermost circle of power. This is why he is compelled to choose Egypt. For he cannot remain in Paris and wait for his glory to rot.

THE EAST, then. Egypt.

When a decision has been made, it must be executed in full.

He meets the directors and Talleyrand, who has drawn up a report on the proposed expedition – but a commander never leaves the organization in the hands of others. He dictates his instructions to Berthier. Loyal troops from the Army of Italy must go to Genoa and be ready to embark.

He requests another audience with the Directory, and looks at these five men with contempt and restrained anger. They have chosen to remove him from France. Very well. Then they will have to accommodate his wishes. He wants twenty-five thousand infantry, three thousand cavalry – without horses, mounts will be found on the spot. He wants five hundred pieces of ordnance, a hundred cartridges per man, and eight to nine million francs for expenses.

Their faces fall. He has not finished.

Napoleon continues in an abrupt voice, 'I want unlimited authority and full discretionary powers, whether it be in Malta's affairs or those of Egypt, Syria, Constantinople or the Indies . . .'

He sees the irony, mingled with incredulity and fear, on the faces of Barras and Reubell.

But they are going to agree to everything, because they want to get me out of the way. They are afraid.

'I want the right of appointment to every position, even that of my successor,' he goes on. 'I want powers provided with all due forms and seals, and the great seal for treating with the Porte, Russia, the various governments of India and the regencies of Africa.'

They think that I am dangerous, singular, perhaps mad. They want to be rid of me.

Napoleon remains silent for a long while, and then he adds, 'I wish to return to France how and when I choose.'

They are looking at each other and imagining me returning to Paris, my forehead wreathed in laurels more glorious than those I acquired in Italy. But they think my chances of coming back are so slim!

They are bowing their heads to hide their hopes. They are accepting my demands.

It is a gamble. The riskiest of my life.

But what other path is there? My life is so constituted that, at its cruxes, I only have the choice of being faithful to myself and taking up the challenge, or denying myself and becoming an average fellow like them.

BUT THEY do rule the country; they still impose their decisions on the people.

Thinking this fills Napoleon with rage. He grumbles and breaks off from drawing up the list of officers and scholars he wants to take on the expedition with him. For Paris must be astonished. He must not only be the warrior and the peacemaker, but also the man who brings to light a vast, forgotten civilization, which thrived in the land where the Pharaohs, Herodotus, Alexander, Caesar and Pompey all once walked.

At the mention of these names, he is swept up by his dream again and his anger evaporates. He becomes impassioned. 'I shall colonize that country,' he says. 'I shall bring artists and artisans of every kind, women, actors. Six years will be enough, if all goes well, to reach India ... I can pass through Asia Minor as its liberator, enter the capital of the old continent in triumph, drive Mahomet's descendants from Constantinople and ascend its throne.'

'Six years,' murmurs Bourrienne, who is listening, fascinated.

'Six years, Bourrienne, or else a few months; everything depends on events.'

He becomes gloomy. What will happen in Paris when he is away from this city where his destiny is at stake?

'Yes,' he whispers. 'I have tried everything. They do not want me.'

He begins walking up and down again, the heavy tread of his feet echoing through the salon of his mansion on the rue de la Victoire.

'I ought to overthrow them,' he resumes in a loud voice, 'and make myself King; but it will not do to think of that yet. The nobilty will never consent to it. I have tested it out. The time is not yet come. I will be alone, Bourrienne, but I will dazzle them afresh.'

HE ARRANGES to leave at the start of May 1798, from Toulon, where ships are being assembled from all the Mediterranean ports under French control, from Trieste to Genoa and Nice.

Indeed, on 25 April, the newspapers announce that 'General Bonaparte has left Paris on 3 Floréal – 22 April – at midnight, after having taken his leave from the directors at three in the afternoon, and having dined at the Director Barras's, with whom he attended a performance of *Macbeth* at the Feydeau Theatre.'

THE REASON Napoleon is unexpectedly facing the directors on 23 April, then, is not to pay his respects to them, but to question the appropriateness of his departure once more.

The previous day, as he was overseeing the final preparations for his journey, a messenger from Venice arrived at rue de la Victoire. His message was brief: General Bernadotte's residence in the capital of the Austrian Empire has been overrun by a mob and ransacked. The members of the French embassy have had to defend themselves and Bernadotte has left Vienna.

Is war with Austria breaking out again? Is this the event that will allow him to act?

Napoleon spends all night considering. He can portray himself as the man capable of preventing a reopening of hostilities. He can go to Rastadt, resume negotiations with Count Cobenzl and return to Paris with the peace consolidated. Better Rastadt than Egypt!

He sends couriers to Italy. The troops are not to embark at Genoa but to wait for him.

He goes to see the directors. They listen to Napoleon giving his undertaking to settle the matter if he is sent to Rastadt with full powers. Talleyrand supports him. Napoleon insists.

Perhaps this is his chance. Perhaps he should risk everything rather than go away. Perhaps he should overthrow the directors and take power now.

On 28 April, Barras visits rue de la Victoire.

Napoleon watches the man, whose measure he has taken, as he flatters Josephine and then comes up and whispers that the Directory wishes him to leave for Egypt without delay. There is no longer any question of a mission to Rastadt.

They have chosen.

After another few hours of doubt, Napoleon makes his decision. He will go.

The telegraph transmits the orders. The couriers dash off and the expedition's momentum resumes.

On 5 May, Napoleon announces to his intimates that he is to leave Paris for Egypt. Servants are already preparing the large carriage covered with a *vache*, a leather tarpaulin which protects the trunks. Marmont, Bourrienne, Duroc and Lavalette will travel in it. Josephine has stepped forward and Napoleon looks at her in silence. She says she will travel too.

Arnault bursts into the salon, furious. 'The Directory wants to be rid of you, France wants to keep you,' he cries. 'Parisians reproach you for being resigned, they are railing louder than ever against the government. Aren't you afraid they will end up railing against you?'

What is there more changeable, more unforeseeable, more untrustworthy than a crowd?

'The Parisians rail but they would never act,' Napoleon replies. 'They are unsatisfied but they are not unhappy.' He smiles and takes a few steps. 'If I were to mount a horse, no one would follow me.'

Then, in a tone of command, he adds, 'We leave tomorrow.'

AT THREE o'clock in the morning of 6 May 1798, they leave Paris. There are storms most of the way.

In the carriage the passengers are silent. The jolting often pushes them against each other. Josephine sleeps. Napoleon, eyes open, seems not to need to.

His life is moving, no one can stop it now.

Suddenly the carriage shudders violently and comes to a halt on a short cut to Roquevaire, which they have taken to bypass Marseilles and get to Toulon quicker.

The berline is high off the road and its *vache* has caught on a branch. They get out and hold up a lantern as Napoleon walks off a little. There, in front of him, are the remains of a collapsed bridge which the storm has carried off into a deep ravine.

'The hand of Providence,' says Marmont pointing to the branch. Without it, the carriage would have smashed to pieces on the rocks.

Napoleon gets back into the carriage. 'Turn quickly,' he cries.

He must carry his decision through without hesitation.

The time for action has returned.

ON 10 MAY, at Toulon, he recognizes the vivid blue sea, the blazing sun, even this early in the year, and the white sails that stand out against a sky so bright it is blinding.

From his window in the Hôtel de la Marine, he watches this vista endlessly, and imagines that land of Egypt beyond the horizon which so many conquerors have trodden since the start of history. He is going to follow in their footsteps. He dons his uniform and goes out to inspect the fleet.

Each time his boat approaches a ship, its cannon fire two rounds to salute him. He is the general-in-chief of this armada, this man who was only an unknown young captain here five years before, his skin still marked by the scabies he had caught there.

That evening the town is illuminated in his honour. Josephine is close to him. He feels strong.

The following day he reviews the troops. Facing the lines of men under his sky, amongst those smells of the sea, pines and olives which are so familiar to him, he rediscovers the energy and drive which he had to keep in check for over a month in the manoeuvrings and tortuous stratagems of Paris.

Everything is simpler here, in action, facing the sea – clear, just like the light of his childhood.

'Officers and soldiers,' he begins, 'it was two years ago that I came to command you. At that time you were in the eastern Riviera in the greatest adversity, lacking everything, having sacrificed everything, even your watches, to stay alive. I promised to put a stop to your sufferings. I led you into Italy. There, everything was granted you . . . Haven't I kept my word?'

That great wave of approval, these soldiers yelling 'yes', stirs him. This is what it is to be alive.

'Well then,' he resumes, 'you should know that you have not yet done enough for your country and that your country has not yet done enough for you. I am going to lead you into a land where, by your future exploits, you will surpass those that already today astound your admirers, and perform for your country the services it is entitled to expect from an invincible army. I promise . . .'

He pauses for a moment, waiting for complete silence.

'I promise every soldier that on his return from this expedition he shall have enough to buy himself six acres of land . . .'

There is a flourish of trumpets and shouts of, 'Long live the Immortal Republic.'

ON 19 MAY, at five o'clock in the morning, he stands on the poop of a boat pulling away from the quay. Josephine is waving goodbye. He looks at her for a long time. Did she really want to embark with him as she implied, or was it only a meaningless offer which she knew he would refuse? He does not want to decide one way or another. He wants to leave with the illusion that she would like to remain at his side.

He turns towards the open sea. The roadstead is covered in ships. One hundred and eighty are waiting to set sail at six. Anchored a few cables off shore, the *Orient*, the flagship, looms up like a fortress, each of its three decks armed with forty cannon.

Napoleon goes aboard and immediately takes up his position on the bridge. Commandant Casabianca gives the order to set sail. The sea is choppy with little waves. The thirteen ships of the line lead the way, upwind, and the transports follow, in a cloud of frigates, sloops and brigs. Some of the heavily laden ships scrape the bottom, and when the *Orient* sets off, it does too, leaning to one side and then pulling clear.

Napoleon has not moved. He stays on the bridge for several hours while the ships make for the high seas.

He is the destiny of these thirty-four thousand men.

He has chosen the divisions, the generals, the cannon. He has personally supervised the selection of the Commission of Arts and Sciences which he wanted to accompany the army.

To succeed, one must try to anticipate everything.

He turns towards Marmont, who is standing near him.

'I steer my dreams by the compass of my reasoning.'

PART EIGHT

⚶

*To be great is to depend
on everything*

19 MAY 1798 TO 9 OCTOBER 1799

XXXI

NAPOLEON IS STANDING ON the bridge of the *Orient*, listening.

They are sailing along the coast of Corsica. The wind has dropped. It is beautiful weather. Cape Bonifacio is already visible and beyond it the peaks of Sardinia are outlined against the horizon. After that they will sail to Sicily, then Malta, Crete and finally Alexandria.

Napoleon has ordered the band to assemble on the foredeck. The musicians have started to play and already trumpets are replying from the nearest vessels. The soldiers have crowded onto their ships' decks and their voices soon join the rolling of drums and the flourish of trumpets.

From one ship to the next, in unison, they strike up '*Le Chant du départ*' 'The Song of Departure', which has been sung in all the services since 1794:

> Victory, singing, breaks down the barriers
> Liberty guides our steps.
> From north to south the trumpets peal
> Announcing the time to fight.
> Tremble, enemies of France.

The men need this communion. They sing the chorus at the tops of their voices:

> The Republic is calling
> Let us win victory or die.
> A Frenchman must live for her,
> For her, a Frenchman would die.

Admiral Brueys comes up and raises his voice to be understood but Napoleon turns his head away. He knows. The admiral has been passing on his concerns for several days. A frigate which joined the convoy off Bastia had spotted an English squadron in the distance. Another message from Genoa contained the same intelligence. The English ships are giving chase, with the *Vanguard* of Admiral Nelson at their head.

Napoleon strolls away.

He has not known such peace for weeks. In the days leading up to their departure, he was racked with anxiety, but since he has put out to sea, he feels a joyful sense of lightness and suspension. He is in the hands of the wind and the sea and chance. There is nothing more he can do. If English sails are outlined on the horizon and battle is joined, well then he will have to decide, make a choice, but for the moment let Admiral Brueys keep his peace, attend to the ships' progress, repair the sails whenever the weather permits and make as good speed as he can by tacking.

NIGHT FALLS. One after another the bands stop playing and only the creak of the hulls and masts and the slap of the sails can be heard. The convoy which, a moment ago, was occupying the whole sea like a majestic city sporting its banners and standards, has disappeared, swallowed up in the darkness. Napoleon looks at the vault of heaven and the milky trail that crosses the sky like an illuminated squadron, a myriad ships that nothing can stop.

This is the certainty that fills Napoleon. He is going from one point of his destiny to another, taking with him this fleet and these tens of thousands of men.

He leaves the bridge. In the vast *salon de compagnie* he has had fitted out near the dining room and his cabin, the officers and members of the expedition whom he has invited to share his table get to their feet.

He has established strict codes of discipline from the first moments aboard. Noting down his instructions, Bourrienne was surprised by what he called this 'Court ceremonial'. But why not? At sea more than other places, and especially in the desert where they will have to fight and march for days, order, discipline and hierarchy are essential. So, the different stages leading up to the summit must be marked and respected. The design, even the luxury of his quarters must be a reminder that the commander-in-chief is exceptional.

The men are crowded together below decks. Every day the food becomes more execrable. Their clothes are impregnated with the stench of vomit, which they add to every day. Almost all of them are sick. Nevertheless the general-in-chief and his entourage have to be spared this – not because of a particular penchant for luxury, but because they are the ones who command and because the privileges they enjoy are the mark of their responsibilities and their role.

Napoleon knows his way of life on board the *Orient* attracts criticism – 'Court practices in a Spartan camp,' he is told they say. When he was walking through the gaming room, someone actually called out, 'One does not acquire fame and reputation through privilege, but through love of one's country and freedom.'

Napoleon stopped, looking for the impertinent fellow, but all he saw were submissive faces and shifty eyes.

He announced loudly, 'Play, gentlemen. Let us see who shall have the privilege and inequality bestowed by chance.'

There was a hubbub. Gold louis were put on the table; the players of faro, that game which used to be played at Versailles, pocketed their winnings.

What is equality in a game? Chance sifts the winners from the losers. And in life?

NAPOLEON takes his seat in the *salon de compagnie* among his intimates. 'Let us talk about equality, and so inequality, among men.'

He looks challengingly at Monge, who is sitting near him, then Bourrienne and General Caffarelli. Junot is already drowsing. Eugène de Beauharnais is dreaming. Berthollet is grumbling. No one, however, would shirk these daily debates which Napoleon has instigated because one's mind must always be active, and because every moment, every look prompts a thought.

'Inequality,' he repeats.

Have they read Rousseau, Caffarelli begins. 'The laws that sanction property sanction usurpation and theft.' The discussion is underway.

Napoleon stands up. 'Let us go to the bridge.' They walk in a group. It is mild and they talk for part of the night. Tomorrow they will continue this meeting of the 'Institutes', as Napoleon calls these jousts.

He asks Bourrienne to follow him into his cabin and lies down. He has had iron castors fitted to the feet of his bed in an attempt to alleviate the rolling of the ship, but nothing helps. Sometimes he has to stay in bed. Berthier reads to him, Monge and Berthollet pay him visits. They speak of God, of Islam, of the religions that are necessary for people. Suddenly Napoleon interrupts them. He wants Bourrienne to continue reading the Koran out loud. The book is filed next to the Bible on the shelf marked 'Politics'.

EARLY IN the morning of 9 June, Napoleon goes up on the bridge and Admiral Brueys stretches out his arm. On the horizon, dozens of sails fleck the sea like white-capped waves. Through his field glass Napoleon recognizes the convoy from Civita Vecchia catching up with the bulk of the fleet. That strip of brown earth that is barely discernible above the sea – that is Malta, and, only a few cables from it, the island of Gozo.

Napoleon asks for his sword to be brought, and then he begins dictating what sounds like an ultimatum to the Grand Master of the Knights of Malta, Hompesch. He desires, he says, permission for the whole squadron to take on water. He also demands the knights' surrender. He knows that he is going to occupy the island, it does not matter what response he will get via these officers who are leaving the *Orient* on two launches. The island must pass into French hands. Taking it is part of the plan, and nothing can stand in its way. It must be taken like an outpost in a charge, a charge that will continue far beyond it.

'General Bonaparte,' he dictates, 'is resolved to secure by force what ought to be accorded him in the name of the hospitality which is the basis of your order.'

Troops can start landing

HE HEARS voices singing 'The Marseillaise'. It is the soldiers of the 9th demi-brigade who are scaling Gozo's fortifications. Napoleon sees them through his field glass. He shouts orders, and in a whirr of ropes, launches are lowered, the infantry embark. Some reach land in a matter of minutes and already smoke is rising from fires in different places. He gives the command for a broadside. He must show that nothing can withstand might.

After several hours, Grand Master Hompesch requests a parley.

NAPOLEON can walk through the streets of La Valette. He slowly explores this city with cobbled streets laid out like a chequerboard. Here, as in Italy, he is walking on history. He is the successor of the crusader knights.

He receives these knights in their own palace, which flies the flag of the Republic. 'Let those who are French and less than thirty years old come and claim their share of glory on this expedition. The others have three days to quit the island.'

Then he continues his tour. He is the master of a state. Nothing can resist his will, and this inflames his imagination. He dictates codes and decrees and reorganizes the entire administration of the island.

When he paces about the great hall of the order, sometimes he stops in front of one of the knights' coats of arms. For several minutes he stops dictating. It had taken centuries to construct this state. It has only taken him a few hours to create a different one, to put in place, in sixteen paragraphs, the entire administration of the island, and put an end to the titles of nobility. He feels his aides-de-camp watching him, frozen in respectful admiration.

A man at the height of power can change the entire order of things; he has sensed this already in Italy when he created the Cisalpine and Ligurian Republics. A man commanding soldiers under arms can do the same, much more than a revolutionary nation, more than a mob and all its chaos. This idea exhilarates him; he is proud of his work.

HE GOES into the cathedral of St John. It has been turned into a foundry; his orders are being carried out. Furnaces have been set up in each of the chapels to melt down the gold and silver of the relics. Ten workers are smashing the precious objects with hammers before throwing in the pieces.

He returns to the knights' palace and orders that the proclamation he has just reread be posted: 'All inhabitants of the island of

Malta have become French citizens and are part of the Republic
... Man owes nothing to the chance of his birth, only his worth
and talents distinguish him ...'

The hours, then days pass. As he strolls through the palace
gardens, he listens to his generals. Lannes complains about the
conduct of some of the soldiers, who have pillaged a convent on
Gozo, tried to rape the nuns and threatened their officers. Others
talk about the hoards of prostitutes only too willing to give the
French a warm welcome.

He listens. What will be remembered? This dross? Ransacked
houses, melted relics, raped women, the soldiers' brutality, the
dead – or else that he came here, the conqueror, on his way to
Alexandria?

What will people remember? The use of force, or that he
has liberated two thousand Muslim slaves from Malta's convict
prison?

He sits down in the garden and a basket of freshly picked
oranges is brought. Under the fruit's thick, bitter peel, there is the
downy freshness of the juicy flesh.

SINCE THE TASK has been done and the winds are favourable,
Napoleon gives Admiral Brueys the order to set sail on 18 June.
The *Orient* puts off as the garrison he has left on Malta salutes the
convoy's departure with several gunshots.

The heat becomes sultrier in a matter of hours, despite the sea
breeze. The coasts of Greece, Cythera and Crete they sail past are
wreathed, in the middle of the morning, in a greyish haze which is
only dispersed by the evening and morning winds. Napoleon stays
on the bridge. Here is the home of Ulysses; these are the coasts
Roman galleys sailed along. Here is the kingdom of Minos, the
home of the myths.

Is he the only one to enter into communion with these
landscapes charged with history? He speaks at length, evoking
the decline of cities and empires, those of Greece and those
of the West and the East. It will take the will of a man the equal of
an Alexander or Caesar to mark out the frontiers of a new power.
Glory is to be won here.

IN THE DUSK on 27 June, Napoleon orders Brueys to call the frigate *Junon* to the stern of the *Orient*. He sees the massed, silent men on the bridge of the frigate which is a yardarm away. They are waiting the way people used to wait for the oracles of a god, but he is the one who pronounces the words they obey. The commander of the frigate listens to his instructions: he is to go to Alexandria and fetch the French consul, Magallon.

They have to wait for the frigate to return, and the weather grows cooler. A north wind hits the convoy, and gradually freshens. The waves are tall, raging, throwing sheets of water onto the bridge. The soldiers are ill, but they assemble for the reading of a proclamation by Napoleon. He looks at them while the officers read it out. These men are having trouble staying upright in the storm but slowly they begin to listen. They must understand. He tells them, 'Whoever rapes is a monster, whoever loots dishonours us.' They have been warned. He won't be able to stop everything, he knows what men are like at war, but he will be able to deal severely with any abuse and he wants to let them know that, and also elevate them, demand they rise above themselves. This is commanding men. He continues:

Soldiers!

You are about to undertake a conquest whose effects on civilization and commerce are incalculable . . .

We shall do some hard marching; we shall fight battles; we shall succeed in all we undertake. Destiny is with us.

The people with whom we are going to live are Mahometans. The first article of their faith is this: 'There is no God but God, and Mahomet is his prophet.' Do not contradict them. Treat them as you have treated the Jews, and the Italians. Pay respect to their muftis and their imams, as you did to the rabbis and the bishops. Show the ceremonies prescribed by the Koran and the mosque the same tolerance you extended to the synagogues, the religion of Moses and that of Jesus Christ.

The Roman legions protected all religions. You will find here customs different from those of Europe. You must accustom yourselves to them.

The first town we shall come to was built by Alexander.
At every step we shall encounter marks of history worthy of exciting the emulation of Frenchmen.

There are only a few cheers: the wind is too strong, the sea too high.

On 30 June, in mid-storm, the *Junon* returns.

Consul Magallon manages to board the *Orient* despite the waves pushing the launch against its hull. He talks to Napoleon, holding onto the wall of his cabin to keep himself steady. An English squadron of more than ten ships has just left Alexandria and is prowling around, waiting for the French convoy.

Napoleon immediately goes up onto the bridge. He gathers from Admiral Brueys's face that he is concerned. Nelson is not far away. The storm makes it impossible to land in the next few hours.

They must wait, Brueys insists.

'Admiral we have no time to waste. Fortune gives me but three days. If I do not make use of them, we are lost. To be great is to depend on everything. For my part I depend on events that a trifle may decide.'

The order is given to land in the Bay of Marabou, west of Alexandria.

From the *Orient*, Napoleon sees launches full of soldiers capsize. He hears the shouts of the men, most of whom do not know how to swim.

It is the most hazardous moment. Napoleon walks on the bridge, his hands behind his back: anxiety has gripped him and he is racked with impatience.

At four o'clock in the afternoon of 1 July 1798, he embarks on a Maltese galley to go in to the coast. Then he jumps into a launch and, at one o'clock in the morning, reaches the shore.

This soil, at last!

He paces it, as he gives his orders. The night is clear and the troops continue to disembark. He feels calm and determined again. He lies down – he is going to sleep on ground where Alexander walked.

At three o'clock in the morning he wakes up and inspects the troops. The soldiers are soaking wet. He examines their faces, and then gives the order to Kleber, Menou and Bou's divisions to march on Alexandria.

What should set the leader apart is not luxury, but courage and daring.

Napoleon briskly takes up his position in front of the column. At his side marches General Caffarelli, who has a wooden leg.

SOON THEY enter the dominion of the sun and thirst and sand and Bedouin and blinding light and heat that is so oppressive it takes their breath away, penetrating their woollen clothes.

Napoleon walks without looking back. Sometimes he hears a muffled cry, then a thud. A man has collapsed with exhaustion, his lips and tongue swollen from thirst.

The wells are empty.

Suddenly, from the top of a dune, they see the fortifications of Alexandria, and Pompey's Column stands a few hundred metres away.

Napoleon sits down by the plinth and an officer brings him some Maltese oranges which he bites into. They are bittersweet.

XXXII

FROM THE FIRST CRACKLE of gunfire in the sweltering heat, Napoleon knows. The dispatch-rider reports that Alexandria's population is receiving Kleber's advance guards with stones and musket fire. Arab cavalry have charged. The defences have been stormed by the troops, but inside the city resistance is continuing. They have been fired on from a mosque and the troops have entered it, punishing everyone inside, men, women and children. The general has been able to prevent it becoming a massacre.

The dispatch-rider leaves. From the city can be heard the shouts of women amongst the explosions. Wounded come past, supporting one another, and then collapse on the scorching ground.

Napoleon knows from that moment.

War's barbarism here will be intensified by the hostility – the hatred even – manifest in the stifling heat, the brilliant light that sears one's eyes, the aridity which parches one's mouth and plagues one's skin. In his aching body, his feet bloody from the night's march, Napoleon foresees that he will have to steel himself at every moment to fight this climate, conquer it and force the men to march and fight.

Everything will be more difficult here. Everything will be pitiless. Whoever weakens will die. Everything must be erased, memories of the Corso in Milan, the Châteaux of Montebello and Passariano, the ceremony at the Luxembourg Palace, Talleyrand's reception at the Hôtel de Galliffet.

Has Talleyrand set off on an embassy to Constantinople to warn the Turks that this invasion of Egypt is not directed against them? Napoleon doubts it. He will have to forget Italy, not think of Josephine. And every soldier will have to do the same.

Will they be able to, these men who have come from the Army of Italy?

Can the Directors Barras and Reubell and all those sensualists who have stayed in Paris imagine what it means to be here, with the sun burning their skin and death surrounding them?

Death will have to be repulsed every day; they will have to be more terrible than death, not let themselves be enticed by it, use death to fight death.

These thoughts brace him. He is inflexible. He could have chosen to hide in the Directory's comfortable intrigues, shuttling between salon and boudoir, between chatterers and women, but war is the labour that since classical times has been imposed as a test on heroes.

The fact that he accepts it proves he is a hero, the equal of those who have trodden this soil, of the man who founded this city, Alexandria.

NAPOLEON delivers an ultimatum to the governor of Alexandria. 'You are either very ignorant or very presumptuous,' he says. 'My army has just conquered one of the leading powers of Europe. If in ten minutes I do not see the flag of peace, you will have to account before God for the blood you have caused to be shed to no purpose whatsoever . . .'

A messenger brings news simultaneously that General Kleber has been wounded by a bullet in the forehead and that a delegation is on its way to swear an oath of loyalty and surrender the town.

He sees it approach surrounded by soldiers under arms. The multicoloured turbans and long silk tunics stand out against the dark uniforms. Camels tower over the band. There is a great crush at the foot of Pompey's Column.

'Cadis, sheikhs, imams, orcadis,' begins Napoleon, 'I come to restore your rights, unlike the usurpers . . . I love God more than the Mamelukes, your oppressors, and I respect his prophet Mahomet and the admirable Koran.'

This is how he must talk. Men need these beliefs and these words.

Discussions begin. The Muslims complain that soldiers have stolen from Arabs who were not obstructing them. Officers explain that they have arrested one of these soldiers, who took a dagger from an Arab.

'Try this man.'

The soldier is brought, stammering, skin puffy with sunburn, his face distorted with fear. He is interrogated and confesses.

Fight death with death.

He is executed a few paces from Pompey's Column.

Bowing, the delegates declare allegiance to Napoleon. He enters Alexandria.

THE ALLEYS are narrow; they seem to trap the heat. Women utter strange, shrill cries. Napoleon rides surrounded by members of the delegation and an escort of guides. Suddenly, just as he hears a report, he feels a blow on his left boot and his horse shies. There is shouting and the soldiers open fire on the house where the shot came from.

Death has grazed me once again.

He takes quarters in the house of the French consul and, while all around him the talk is of the lone marksman who has been found, surrounded by six muskets, and shot, Napoleon begins to give orders.

Tomorrow, 2 July, there will be a review of the troops with the regimental bands and general officers in full dress, then the departure of the first units for Cairo. He calls Magallon, the consul, and chooses the Damanhur road for the troops' advance, so as not to have to cross the Nile which is plied by Mameluke galleys. Already he is harrying the officers, demanding that a workshop to make new, lighter uniforms be set up. Napoleon would like to instil in everyone he talks to his energy, impatience and awareness that every second should be used in activity. He says, 'St Louis spent eight months here praying when he should have spent them marching, fighting and establishing himself in the country.'

How is he to make these men and all the soldiers as keyed up as he is?

Cairo today, and tomorrow . . .?

Further, higher.

HE BEGINS to dictate to Bourrienne a proclamation to the Egyptians, which is to be printed overnight in Arabic, Turkish and French, posted in every town, read out loud and distributed by the armies in their march.

'In the name of God, the clement and merciful. There is no god save Allah: he has no son and reigns without associate.'

Bourrienne looks up.

What does he imagine? That one can speak to Muslims the way one speaks to Christians?

'In the name of the French Republic founded on liberty and equality . . .'

He dictates in a staccato, jerky voice, attacking the Mamelukes, the warlike aristocracy who have been oppressing the Egyptians.

What understanding, what virtues, what knowledge distinguishes the Mamelukes, that they have exclusive possession of everything that makes life sweet? If there is a fine estate, a beautiful slave, a handsome horse, a desirable house – then they belong to the Mamelukes!

But God is just and merciful to the people . . . All men are equal before God. Understanding, virtue, learning alone differentiate between them . . . From now on no Egyptian will be excluded from office and all will be able to rise to the most elevated positions . . . in this way the people will be happy. Cadis, sheikhs, imams, orcadis, tell the people that the French too are true Muslims. To prove it, was it not we who entered Great Rome and destroyed the throne of the Pope, who was constantly calling on the Christians to wage war on the Muslims? Was it not we who went to Malta and drove out the knights who imagined God wanted them to wage war on the Muslims? . . . Happy those Egyptians who promptly rally to our side . . . But woe betide those who go over to the Mamelukes.

May God preserve the glory of the Ottoman Sultan! May God preserve the glory of the French army! May God curse the Mamelukes and bring happiness to the peoples of Egypt.

Headquarters, Alexandria, 13 Messidor, Year VI;

18 Moharram, AH 1213 (2 July 1798)

He sees Bourrienne's smile and the officers poking fun, repeating, 'The French too are true Muslims.' He grows furious. What do they know about governing men? He is trying to revolutionize Egypt, set up a republic, disarm the natives' prejudices and make allies. This proclamation is 'charlatanism', he admits, 'but of the highest kind!' How can one make oneself understood by people if one does not use a language they know? There is only one other way: arms and the fear they inspire.

IN THE EARLY morning of 2 July, Napoleon reviews the troops. The heat is already scorching, and the men must march despite their thirst. They must set out with Generals Desaix and Reynier at their head.

He makes for a group of soldiers who had been taken prisoner by the Bedouin and then escaped or were freed. They hang their heads. Then some start talking; they say what they have seen – torture, mutilations. One of them is crying, his body shaken by sobs. The Bedouin have sodomized him.

'You are in a fine state, you great oaf,' Napoleon reprimands him. 'You have paid for your lack of prudence. You should stay with your brigade. Thank heaven you have got off so lightly. Come now, don't cry any more.'

But the man does not stop sobbing. Napoleon walks away and again passes in front of the troops. Battle must be joined quickly before fear and doubt erode the army. He must drive these men forward so that they remain standing, otherwise they will collapse here. Terror of being caught, tortured and humiliated must drive them to conquer.

ORGANIZE everything, plan everything, manage everything.

In heat that makes every movement laborious, that is so oppressive he thinks he won't be able to breathe any more, Napoleon does not stop moving. He dictates orders while inspecting Alexandria's defences, since he is going to leave and join the army in order to give battle, or while exploring the bazaar, looking at the women, whose faces are all they leave uncovered. He supervises the army's supplies, the number of horses, and sets up a civic administration.

At night the heat is so stifling he does not sleep.

He gets up and calls an aide-de-camp. Can he remember the sergeant who was one of the first to scale the walls and whom he saw fighting from Pompey's Column? Let him be decorated. Then he thinks about the fleet. What orders should he give Admiral Brueys? To stay in Aboukir's roads, go to Malta or Corfu, or else try to enter Alexandria's port? Nelson is clearly going to return with his squadron. Napoleon hesitates. Brueys reckons that he can defend himself at Aboukir if he is attacked. He hasn't enough water to get to Malta or Corfu. As for the port of Alexandria, there is the risk that the ships will run aground.

A flicker of anxiety crosses Napoleon's mind. He feels he is not in control of the squadron's fate, but he is not a sailor. He must trust others. Still, he does not like delegating power or responsibilities.

ON 7 JULY, a reddish haze hides the sun. The air is full of searingly hot dust. The khamsin, the southern wind, has begun, yet they must set off for Damanhur through the desert. Napoleon rides at the head of his staff and his escort and headquarters. The scholars Monge and Berthollet have joined the troop. It is five o'clock in the afternoon. He feels thousands of grains of dust stinging his face. His whole body hurts, just like any of Desaix's or Reynier's soldiers, who have already crossed that stony, blazing desert. Men have committed suicide. Many of the cisterns that punctuated their route were empty because the canal they were marching along had dried up. Blinded by the glare, lips bleeding, sweltering in their woollen uniforms, without water or food because they couldn't find anything in the villages, the stragglers were killed and tortured. Desaix has appealed for help. The men are going mad.

Napoleon rides all night, overtaking the Bona and Vial divisions who are also going to Damanhur.

He sees these men marching in the darkness. He imagines their suffering and fear. He knows they are grumbling, blaming their officers, accusing the directors of having shipped them off here just to be rid of 'their' Bonaparte. They are even starting to blame him. Why hasn't he thought of water bottles? They remember Italy. What the hell do they care about those six acres of land their general has promised them?

These men are with him in the desert; like him they only have one way out: victory. So, they must march. He has to keep them moving. He must ensure discipline is maintained. Saving them now means driving them forward.

At eight o'clock, he is in Damanhur.

He enters the dark hut where the dignitaries are waiting for him, and is given a jug of milk and wheat cakes. He says a few words but his generals' faces are what strike him. Some are furious, others drained and desperate.

First he must keep silent so they can talk. This adventure is hopeless, one says. The men are going mad, another adds. They are going blind, they are killing each other, they cannot fight any more.

Napoleon steps forward. He does not say anything at first, only looks at each of them, and then he announces that they have to march on to Ramanieh on the Nile. Murad Bey's Mamelukes must be broken.

Commanding men is obstinately clinging to what one believes.

They set off on the 9th.

More suffering and then suddenly, after all the mirages, it really is the Nile.

Napoleon sees the ranks break; the dragoons and infantrymen throw themselves fully armed into the water and drink, and then he sees bodies being picked up by the current, dead from having drunk too much, dead from shock and exhaustion. Along the river banks are fields of watermelons which the soldiers gorge themselves on.

He observes them. They have got this far despite exhaustion, disgust, disaffection, melancholy and the utter despair of men whom nothing in the Italian campaigns has prepared for this other world, this violent country.

They have done it because he wished it. Now they must fight.

At three o'clock on 11 July, he reviews them.

A drum roll announces him. He rides slowly. They have brushed their uniforms. Their muskets shine.

Napoleon stops in front of each of the five divisions. He draws himself up. All eyes are on him, lifting him.

'I warn you,' he calls out, 'that we are not done with our suffering: we will have battles to endure, victories to win and deserts to cross. Finally we shall reach Cairo where we shall have all the bread we could wish!'

As he rides away, he hears the voices of the officers, repeating these words to their men. He hears the singing that greets him.

They will fight and they will win.

AT SUNRISE, he gives the order to the bands to play 'The Marseillaise'. He sees the Mameluke cavalry advancing on the horizon. Some are wearing gilded helmets, others turbans. Their opulent tunics gleam. Every Mameluke has a carbine, pistols, a *jerid* – a javelin – and two scimitars.

Napoleon summons his aides-de-camp. He wants the divisions to form battalion squares. The officers are amazed; they say it is the first time this disposition has ever been used.

What do they know? The Russians and Austrians have already used it against the Ottomans; only the French army never has. He repeats his orders. His tiredness has disappeared. He places the cannon at the corners of the squares, each of which is formed from six lines of infantrymen. In the centre they will put the baggage train – 'the donkeys and scholars', someone shouts.

None of these squares must be breached by a charge – and indeed, for a whole morning the Mamelukes dash themselves on those 'hedgehogs' and then take flight.

The dead on the battlefield of Chobrakhyt have purses full of gold under their tunics. They have gone into battle with all their treasure. The soldiers strip them.

Barely three hours pass before Napoleon gives the order to move out.

HE RIDES through that hellish inferno beside the men, who drag themselves along. He sees soldiers collapse; any who stray from the route are beheaded by Bedouin who brandish their heads and then ride off. Villages are burnt, looted. Finally they reach Embabeh, at two o'clock in the afternoon, 21 July, after a gruelling march. The heat is intense. In the distance, Napoleon sees the pyramids to his right and the minarets and domes of Cairo to his left.

At first he stands alone, motionless, looking from the pyramids to the minarets and then to the Nile. He is in the cradle of history.

He remembers those nights at Valence, when he feverishly read accounts of the feats of classical heroes or the history of these founding peoples.

He is here, not as a traveller like Volney and so many others who have set him dreaming, but as a conqueror.

He calls the generals and they gather around him. The divisions will form up in squares, he begins, but while he speaks, he feels he should make these men aware of the significance of this moment.

'Come,' he says eventually. 'Think that from the top of these monuments,' he points to the pyramids, 'forty centuries are looking down at you.'

HE SEES the Mamelukes' first charges break on the squares. He sees the divisions advance to cut the Mamelukes off from Embabeh's fortifications. He hears the cannon firing case-shot, then the shouts of the soldiers as they take the fortifications by storm.

He imagines the carnage. He sees the soldiers rush to the corpses of the Mamelukes and strip them. Over there, in a solitary duel, a French lieutenant is battering a Mameluke with great sabre blows. Here, the Mamelukes are throwing themselves in the Nile and fleeing.

Victory.

He rides past Murad Bey's waggons, which the soldiers are searching. He sees his men fishing Mamelukes out of the river to rob them. Then, all of a sudden, night falls.

He walks alone. He has been victorious. Here, under the gaze of centuries. He watches the city of Cairo in the distance, lit up by the fires started by Bedouin or *fellah* looters. The Mamelukes have set fire to more than three hundred ships and the sky is ablaze. The pyramids loom up out of the darkness, glowing red.

The colour of blood.

He feels weary.

HE DOES NOT go into Cairo yet. He waits calmly, unquestioningly, as if, having achieved this victory, he were standing before an abyss. He goes to Murad Bey's country house at Gizeh and crosses the vast rooms furnished with divans covered with Lyon silks fringed with gold thread. He walks alone in the garden amongst trees of different varieties and sits under an arbour of vines covered with heavy bunches of grapes.

His loneliness weighs heavy on him.

After the impatience, the forced marches, all the tension, he is overwhelmed by melancholy and he thinks of Josephine. He calls Junot; he needs to talk about her, reassure himself, because the old jealousy is returning, he feels doubts, he wants to be shown the light and at the same time left to his blindness . . .

But Junot protests. It is time, on this night of victory, to face the truth. Can a conqueror like General Bonaparte tolerate being deceived?

Napoleon leaps to his feet. Suddenly he sees that officer again, a young man the Arabs had captured on the road to Cairo. They had demanded a ransom for his release. He had refused. The Arabs had instantly killed him with a bullet in the head. Napoleon had watched, then he had continued on his way. One cannot give in to blackmail like that. Now *he* is the officer who has just been seized. With what he says, Junot has blown out his brains. Josephine has betrayed him, he says, and he lists the names of the lovers she has flaunted to all and sundry. Didn't Bonaparte suspect anything?

Napoleon dismisses him and stays in the garden for a long time. Then rage flares up in him. He goes back into the house, knocks all the ornaments to the floor, and crashes into Bourrienne, who has come running. He looks at him. He cannot trust anyone. He is on his own. 'You don't care about me at all,' he cries. 'Women . . .' He gasps for breath. He says in a muffled voice, 'Josephine.' Finally he recognizes Bourrienne.

'If you cared for me,' he resumes, 'you would have told me what I have just learnt from Junot. There is a true friend.'

He is roaring. His voice breaks.

'Josephine . . . And I am a hundred leagues away . . . You should have told me! Josephine betrayed me, she . . .'

He walks away. He'd like to hit somebody.

'Curse them! I will wipe out that race of conceited young puppies and fops! As for her — divorce, yes, divorce: a public, scandalous divorce! I must write, I know everything . . .'

He turns towards Bourrienne.

'It is your fault. You should have told me!'

He vaguely hears Bourrienne talking about victory and glory.

'My glory! What? I don't know what I would give for what Junot has told me not to be true, I love that woman so much! If Josephine is guilty, divorce must part us for ever! I do not want to be the laughing stock of every dullard in Paris. I am going to write to Joseph; he will have divorce declared!'

Some officers come into the garden. They have learnt that there is a vine there and grapes.

Napoleon keeps back as they cheerfully pick them. His mind is blank. He feels nothing now, his anger has drained him.

A COURIER stands in front of him for a long time before he notices. The officer reports that, as planned, two companies of infantry, with drum and bugle band leading, have entered Cairo in the company of the delegation that had brought the city's surrender.

'Not a soul all along the route,' he says. 'Only the ululating of women echoing from the harems.'

The harems? Napoleon lifts his head and brutally dismisses the courier.

HE ONLY takes up residence in Mahomet el Elfi's palace on Ezbekyeh Square in Cairo on 24 July.

People crowd round him; once again he needs to organize. He establishes a Divan, a council, comprised of ulemas, religious leaders, from the mosque of El-Azhar. He dictates instructions all that day, and the following one as well.

He forms units of police from the Ottoman militias.

Sometimes he breaks off in the middle of a sentence, as if the void was opening up again, and then he pulls himself together. There must be an end to the pillaging of the Mamelukes' houses by Egyptians and soldiers. He extends the model of the Divan to all the conquered territories. The hours pass. Merchants present themselves. They are intending to reopen their businesses. It is already the night of 25 July. The void.

HE WRITES to Joseph, 'I may be in France within two months. I recommend to you the care of my interests. I am suffering a great deal of domestic affliction for the veil has been entirely torn from my eyes. You are all I have left on earth. Your friendship is very dear; all that is needed to make me a misanthrope would be to lose it and see you betray me. It is a sad position when one has all one's affections centred in one heart . . . You understand?'

Yes, Joseph will understand. Yes, Joseph must have known where matters stood with Josephine for a long time as well.

'Arrange for me to have a country place when I return, either near Paris or in Burgundy. I intend to shut myself up there for winter.'

He gets up and goes to the window. The night is broken by the constant barking of stray dogs that roam the streets in packs. Napoleon goes back to his desk.

'I am tired of human nature,' he writes. 'I need solitude and quiet. Grandeur bores me. My emotions are dessicated, glory is stale. At twenty-nine I have exhausted everything, and all that is left for me is to become truly egotistical!'

He hesitates.

He thinks of the soldiers whose mutilated, dismembered, burnt bodies he has seen, and those whose heads the Mamelukes displayed, severed with one stroke of a scimitar.

He rereads the sentence and adds, 'I intend keeping my house. I shall never give it up to anybody. I have just enough to live on! Farewell my only friend, I have never been unjust to you!'

HE DOES NOT sleep. He hates these rackety nights, these dogs always howling. He begins a report to the Directory: 'It is hard to imagine a land more fertile and a people more wretched, ignorant and brutish.'

He senses that he won't be able to win over this people. They are too different. These ulemas, he can tell from countless indications, have not been taken in by his declarations of admiration for their religion. He orders the population to surrender its arms. He fears a revolt, and in his anxiety grows tense again. For the moment, whatever his wishes might be for the future, he is in this town. 'Cairo,' he tells the Directory, 'which has more than three hundred thousand inhabitants, has the most wretched populace in the world.'

Every day he must take dozens of decisions, face matters head on. On 31 July, he writes to General Menou, who is in command of the delta, 'The Turks can only be kept in order by the greatest severity; every day I have five or six heads cut off in the streets of Cairo. We have been obliged to treat them gently so far, in order to destroy the reputation for brutality that preceded us. Now, on the contrary, we must assume the tone necessary to make these people obey; and to obey, for them, is to fear.'

BY 13 AUGUST, he is sitting in his tent, near Salalieh, on the edge of the Sinai desert. He is hesitating whether to proceed, and questions his officers. Will they be able to catch up with Ibrahim Bey, who has fled towards Syria and whom they have been pursuing for a fortnight? They have no time to answer because several couriers arrive, panting. On 1 August, they explain, Nelson destroyed Admiral de Brueys's fleet in the bay of Aboukir. Only a few ships have survived the disaster and the sea is still washing sailors' corpses up on the shore. The *Orient* exploded and the noise and shock were heard as far away as Alexandria. Brueys is dead.

A stricken silence follows. 'We are prisoners,' an officer calls out.

Napoleon gets to his feet. In a loud voice, he says, 'Brueys has perished. He has done well.' Then he starts walking up and down the tent, his eyes fixed on his officers.

'So gentlemen,' he continues in a resolute tone of voice. 'We are called upon to do great things!' He approaches them. 'And we will! We are called upon to found an empire – we will found it. Seas of which we are not the master lie between us and our country, but there are no seas between us and Africa, or Asia.'

He scrutinizes them. Most lower their gaze.

'We are numerous, we shall have no shortage of men from which to recruit our commissioned and non-commissioned officers. We shall have no shortage of ammunition; we shall have a great deal and, if need be, we shall manufacture it ourselves.'

The officers laugh nervously as he walks out of the tent and looks into the distance.

XXXIII

He returns to Cairo.

When he enters the great reception room of his palace on Ezbekyeh Square everyone instantly falls silent. All that can be heard is the sound of the water in the vast fountain that takes up the middle of the room.

He guesses the questions that are on the tip of every tongue – officers', beys' and ulemas'. The faces of the latter are impassive, and yet he sees jubilation glinting in their eyes. The disaster of Aboukir is common knowledge.

They watch him. He sits down. He must be serene. He gives a signal.

His servants busy themselves around the seven coffee pots which are on the fire. He offers his guests coffee and sugar, and enquires after the Festival of the Nile, which is to be celebrated starting the following day, 15 August, and the ceremonies marking the anniversary of Mahomet's birth. Did they know that he, Napoleon, was born on the same day, twenty-nine years ago?

As the Muslim notables slowly drink their coffee and observe him, he says, 'I hope to establish a regime founded on the principles of the Koran, which are the only true ones and the source of men's happiness.'

He gets to his feet. The audience is over, and he walks with his visitors as far as the vast staircase of marble and Aswan granite.

Berthier and Bourrienne have stayed behind. They do not dare speak. They follow him as he walks through the rooms of the palace whose owner has fled into Upper Egypt. This palace is the only one in Cairo to have glass in its windows and a bathroom on every floor.

Napoleon stops.

Even his closest officers do not understand him. What do they think? That he has converted to Islam? When he wanted to receive the members of the Divan dressed in Turkish fashion with an Oriental tunic and a turban, Bourrienne and Tallien, who had just arrived in Egypt, protested — and he gave in and put on his black frock coat tightly buttoned to the neck. He had to make a choice between disconcerting his soldiers and possibly winning over the Egyptians. The French did not seem ready, but he does not want to give up altogether. He is considering creating military units of Negros bought in Upper Egypt, Bedouin and former servants of the Mamelukes — an army, in other words, in the image of the country, of the empire which he still dreams of establishing. It would also solve the problem of manpower, since the current army is dwindling, sick are packed into the hospitals and the plague is breaking out in the coastal cities.

He must see to everything. He questions Berthier. Have the men, as he requested, been told that they must bathe daily and attend to the cleanliness of their uniforms? How close is *The Courier of Egypt* to press, the first newspaper which should keep the army informed about just this sort of detail?

He looks at Berthier. He values this efficient, attentive man, and he esteems him for the passion he feels for a woman from Milan, Madame Visconti, whom he has had to leave behind in Italy. Berthier wants everyone to talk to him about her.

'I understand this passion but not this adoration,' Napoleon murmurs.

Berthier hangs his head. He has put in a request to return to Europe — he has made no attempt to hide his reasons — but he knows that the fleet has been destroyed.

'You'll take a frigate,' Napoleon adds, 'and be back with her soon.'

Then he calls on Berthier and Bourrienne to witness that he accuses Admiral Brueys of lack of foresight, and Admiral Villeneuve of failing to fight and, by all accounts, fleeing the roads.

'The empire of the seas now belongs to our rivals, but no matter how great this reverse, it cannot be attributed to the inconstancy of Fortune. She has not yet abandoned us, far from it — she has helped us in this operation far more than she has ever done.'

He sees Berthier's and Bourrienne's surprise.

'All we need now is to organize our conquest,' he explains. 'What I love about Alexander are not his campaigns but his political abilities. It is the mark of a great politician to have gone to Ammon to reign over Egypt.'

Do Berthier and Bourrienne understand?

'My plan is to govern men the way the majority of them want to be governed. This is the way, I think, to acknowledge the sovereignty of the people. If I governed a nation of Jews, I would rebuild Solomon's Temple . . .'

He breaks off. He will attend the Festival of the Nile, then the one in honour of Mahomet; on 21 September, the Festival of the Republic will be celebrated and later, the anniversary of 13 Vendémiaire on 4 October. The bands of the various units, the generals in full-dress uniform and the troops are to be assembled on each of these occasions.

Berthier and Bourrienne leave.

Tomorrow, 15 August 1798, I will be twenty-nine.

AT SIX o'clock next morning when the sun is already blazing hot, Napoleon stand a few paces in front of a group of generals and Cairo notables in Megyas. This is where they are going to open the dyke that will allow Nile water to flood part of the countryside surrounding the city as it sweeps into the canal. The bands play, salvoes are fired. The water finally bursts forth.

Napoleon looks at this torrent and the crowd of spectators and he starts to throw coins. They fight to pick them up, and follow him when he returns to his palace on Ezbekyeh Square.

Then the city celebrates again for the anniversary of the Prophet's birth. Napoleon presides over the military processions. Their might must be displayed. He sits in the midst of the ulemas for the great banquet. He hates that fatty mutton and those overspiced dishes, but he plunges his fingers into the sauce and grabs the bits of meat like all the other guests.

General Dupuy, the commander of Cairo's citadel, leans over to him.

'We are fooling the Egyptians with this show of attachment to their religion, which we don't believe in any more than that of the Pope.'

Why bother to answer him? How many men can manage to live without religion? How could one govern a people who do not recognize the power of God, who do not fear divine retribution? Or the retribution of the sword?

NAPOLEON wants an even greater military presence at the Festival of the Republic in September. On Ezbekyeh Square, he has a vast amphitheatre built with a wooden obelisk in the middle on which are inscribed the names of all the soldiers who have fallen in the conquest of Egypt. A temple is built around this monument, which bears on its frontispiece, in tall gold letters, the inscription, 'There is no God but God and Mahomet is his prophet.' The tricolours and Turkish flags are raised at the same time, the Phrygian cap side by side with the crescent.

To govern, one has to gather together forces, men, ideas and hold them all tightly clenched in an iron fist.

This must have been every conqueror's way of thinking, every emperor, every man who has wanted to make his mark on the history of the world.

He is one of those. He is sure of that now, seeing these soldiers parading around the amphitheatre, these riders straining to win races just like the ones that must have been watched here by civilizations that are now extinct.

He walks towards an altar on which have been placed the *Rights of Man* and the Koran. He is going to address the soldiers, celebrate their exploits and extol the Republic.

He speaks, but he feels that his words are not eliciting any response. No one shouts, 'Long live the Republic!' These men are weary, worried about the war with Turkey they sense is coming, anxious at the prospect of being made prisoners of their conquest.

He raises his arm. The artillery fires a salvo, then fireworks light up the sky. Human enthusiasm is like a punctured hot-air balloon that is always slowly deflating. It must be constantly aroused. Otherwise nothing is possible.

BUT PERHAPS he is wavering as well – is he?

He throws himself into work. He founds the Institute of Egypt, which he enjoys visiting. Isn't he the vice president?

Monge, the president, welcomes him in the palace which used

to belong to Qassim Bey, in Nasrieh, in the suburbs of Cairo. All the expedition's savants are living there, in the buildings that face onto a shady garden.

Napoleon enters the lecture hall which was formerly the main room of the harem, and Monge, Berthollet and Geoffroy Saint-Hilaire sit around him. He listens to them list the innumerable discoveries they have made. At Rosetta, Berthollet explains with great excitement, Captain Bouchard has discovered a Greek inscription on the polished surface of a big block of granite, which seems to have been translated into hieroglyphics and also into a third script which they cannot identify. Perhaps they will finally be able to decipher hieroglyphics by comparing them to other scripts?

Napoleon listens. For a few minutes he can forget his dreams of empire, his idea of marching to India and forming an alliance with Tipoo Sahib, the Sultan of Mysore who is so anti-English that he has agreed to the French creating a Jacobin Club there!

He visits the library which has been installed in one of the buildings. There soldiers, officers and a handful of sheikhs rub shoulders. He crosses the garden, discovers the laboratory, and further on the painters' studio. Sometimes he takes part in the savants' discussions in the Institute's garden. He is caught up by another dream, that of knowledge. To know, to understand – the enthusiasm he felt as an adolescent sweeps over him again. 'The dignity of the sciences,' he says, grasping Geoffroy Saint-Hilaire by the arm, 'that is the only word that exactly expresses my thoughts. I know of no finer occupation of a man's life than to work towards the understanding of nature and all the things in its use and placed by its intent in the material world.'

He carries on speaking vigorously. Egypt must be mapped, they must find the route of the Pharaohs' canal which ran from Suez to the Mediterranean.

'I will go to Suez,' he says, standing up.

Monge and Geoffroy Saint-Hilaire accompany him to the door of the Institute. He looks closely at them. These men seem happy. He questions Geoffroy Saint-Hilaire, who says in an exhilarated voice, 'I am with men who think of nothing except the sciences. I am living in the heart of an ardent seat of learning . . . We passionately attend to all the questions that are of interest to the government and to the sciences to which we have voluntarily devoted ourselves.'

I am the one who has made this possible.

HE RETURNS to his palace. The streets around Ezbekyeh Square have been transformed in the last few weeks. Cafés have opened, run by Cairo's Christians. A teeming crowd mills around street stalls. There are countless soldiers out gallivanting, buying chickens and sheep with what they have pillaged in their operations against the Bedouin. Plenty of them are accompanied by women, of all ages, whom they buy too. The women have put on European clothes and proudly show themselves off.

Around him, in his intimate circle, there is the same quest for pleasure. It exasperates and wounds him. Eugène de Beauharnais appears in the company of a young, graceful, slender black woman who turns every head.

When Napoleon finds himself alone in the middle of the night, the memory of these women haunts him. He feels the need of a body close to him in this humid heat, which is a constant temptation to debauchery. Hundreds of prostitutes solicit around the palace. He cannot get to sleep. The barking of dogs rends the night. He has given orders to destroy all the dogs that roam in packs, and they have been rounded up on the main square, he has been told, and killed by the dozen, but hundreds of others are impossible to catch. Suddenly he has a feeling of powerlessness, and bitterness seeps into his heart. Like his officers and his men, he feels a prisoner too.

The sheikhs have brought women to him, but he has found them too fat and old, masses of oily flesh. He has felt humiliated. The memory of Josephine has rekindled his anger against her.

One evening the Sheikh El-Bekry had pushed a young girl of sixteen towards him, and he spent some nights with her – but what is a woman who only knows how to submit? She satisfied and bored him at the same time, and he felt still more alone. After a few weeks, he dismissed her. He goes out in the evenings with his aides-de-camp who frequent the Tivoli. He wanted this French-style theatre to be opened. It has dance floors, gaming rooms, even a library, and here the handful of women who have followed the expedition vie to be the most attractive as the officers pay them court.

He sits down at a table and looks round at the company. Eugène de Beauharnais and Junot have spoken to him about a young blonde, Lieutenant Fourès' fetching and lively wife, Pauline. She is here. He stares at her all evening. He wants her; she is a necessity. She constantly turns towards him. For the first time in months he feels a desire that obsesses him and wipes out all other thoughts.

He knows everyone has noticed his behaviour. They whisper and point to Madame Fourès, but he is not concerned. He wants something, so he must get it.

He has no doubt she will yield. From the way she has responded to his stares, he knows she is ready. He makes inquiries. She is twenty. She has worked as a milliner. She followed her husband dressed as a soldier. Her blonde hair, people say, is so beautiful and long that she could wear it like a coat.

He dictates an order: 'Citizen Fourès, lieutenant of the 22nd regiment of light cavalry, is ordered to leave for Alexandria by the first Rosetta stagecoach and there embark . . . Citizen Fourès shall be the bearer of dispatches which he shall not open until he is at sea, and in them he shall find his instructions.'

This is how kings act.

Has he not become the equal of a sovereign?

SHE YIELDS. He installs her in a house near the palace on Ezbekyeh Square. He goes driving with her in a barouche. He knows people call her Cliopatra, 'Our Lady of the East'. He revels in her body, her joyous spontaneity, her chatter. She is his Bellilote, since that is her nickname.

And when Lieutenant Fourès returns, because the English captured his ship and then freed him to make trouble for Napoleon, she secures a divorce. All it needs is a word.

She is the first woman to whom he behaves authoritatively. He is no longer the young general whom an experienced woman seduces by her intrigues as much as by her charm and on whom she then imposes her law. He is the one who gives the orders now, and it is as if Bellilote is revealing to him that this is what he likes – that one must behave as a conqueror towards women too. She frees him from that willing submission which for years had made him Josephine's tearful suitor. All that is finished.

Why shouldn't he marry Bellilote, he sometimes thinks. He is going to divorce Josephine. He resents her. It is ultimately so simple and cheerful loving a woman like Bellilote!

If she bore him a child, he wouldn't hesitate to marry her. 'But what do you expect,' he tells Bourrienne. 'The silly little thing can't.'

Would this be the right time, anyway?

This woman diverts him, satisfies him, balances him. She is the guest of honour at his dinner; she is always at his side. His aides-de-camp form an escort, but Eugène rebels at this. He is the son of the legitimate wife, he cries. Napoleon doesn't reply, but he exempts him from this duty. He cannot be angry with Eugène, a good soldier and devoted aide-de-camp.

Napoleon refuses to let his private life encroach upon the duties and responsibilities of his office, however. Josephine has never managed to make him renounce his duty. How could Bellilote? A woman can lighten or darken his destiny but she cannot be the destiny itself.

HE HAS TO put down a revolt by part of Cairo's population. They kill, sack and pillage with a blind fury, and to cow them into submission he has to open fire on the mosque of El-Azhar. General Dupuy is murdered, and so too his aide-de-camp Sulkowski when reconnoitring outside Cairo.

'He is lucky to be dead,' cries Napoleon. An inner fury, betrayed only by his palour and edginess, consumes him.

Almost three hundred French are killed and probably two to three thousand insurgents. Now he must deal severely with Cairo, order that prisoners have their heads cut off in the citadel and their decapitated bodies be thrown in the Nile while the soldiers set about looting, battering and killing.

Then he must restrain the hand of vengeance, officers and soldiers who want to 'send to the scaffold all those, without exception, whose eyes have seen French companies give ground'.

The men are demanding this and this is what he must refuse, because one cannot control a people purely by terror. Haven't they understood that?

Napoleon receives the city's notables the day after the revolt. They kneel; he stares at them. These hypocrites put on a show of submissiveness when it is they who have incited the people to rise up.

'Sherifs, ulemas, orators of the mosque,' he tells them. 'Make it well known to the people that those who lightly declare themselves my enemies will find no refuge either in this world or the next . . . Happy are those who in good faith are the first to join me.'

He bids them rise.

'A day will come when you will be convinced that all I have done, and all that I have ordered done, has been inspired by God. You will see then that, even if all mankind were to unite to oppose the designs of God, they could not prevent the execution of his commands, and it is I he has entrusted with that execution . . .'

'Your arm is strong and your words are like honey,' they tell him.

This is the language he must master and not be carried away by.

AT EVERY STEP history is so close it exhilarates him. In his tent he entertains merchants from Yemen whose caravans go to the Indies. He negotiates with the Bedouin. He visits the springs of Moses, where fresh water gushes from the cliffs of Mount Sinai. He is in the lands where the religions of mankind were created. He too crosses the Red Sea and suddenly the tide catches him and his escort by surprise. Their horses have to swim in the falling light. They are like the soldiers of Pharaoh's army about to be swept away by the flood tide. Finally they reach the shore, amidst the roar of waves, but General Caffarelli has lost his wooden leg.

Napoleon walks to the edge of a promontory that overlooks these waters. This is where myths are born. Where he is standing, this is where his destiny draws sustenance and where, perhaps, his legend will be born.

On the way back, he discovers the canal dug by the Pharaohs. He gets off his horse and walks alongside it for a long time.

Time, like sand, buries the labours of men, but leaves their legend alive.

He rejoins Bellilote and passes days of passion and oblivion with her, for he knows that he is going to have to leave her soon and return to the solitude of action. Already he is letting his imagination lift him up. Turkey is at war now. Its troops are in Syria and are making for Egypt. They must be stopped. He must go to face them, beat them, and then all roads to India or Constantinople will be open.

However, at the start of February, a French merchant, Hamelin, manages to run the English blockade. He brings news from Europe. France is opposed by a coalition, its conquests are under threat. 'If, during March, Citizen Hamelin's report is confirmed and France is in arms against the European Kings, I will cross into France,' Napoleon announces.

The doors of the future are open again. He is going to leave Cairo for Syria.

THREE GRENADIERS of the 32nd demi-brigade are brought before him, accused of murdering two Egyptian women in their homes during an attempted burglary. The Divan wants the general-in-chief to try them.

They are brought before him, coarse fellows, protesting their innocence, listing the battles they have fought in. He questions them. They become flustered. The evidence – a button, a piece of uniform – is damning. He takes the decision on his own. They will be shot.

A few hours later they are executed in front of the whole brigade, after first raising a glass 'to Bonaparte's health'. He listens to the report of the execution. Some soldiers protested, others approve this punishment delivered in the name of order, discipline and justice. He says to Doctor Desgenettes at his side, 'If a man is entrusted by the State with the lives of up to a hundred thousand men, how the devil could one reasonably question his right to curb offences as grave as this as his conviction dictates . . .'

He takes a few paces, and then adds, 'A general-in-chief must be invested with a terrible power.'

XXXIV

IT IS COLD. NAPOLEON looks back. A few hundred metres away, the village is burning. He can still hear a few cries and then, as he rides hard in the middle of his mounted escort, they fade away. Berthier draws near and, at full gallop, enquires after his injuries. Napoleon spurs his mount and stifles a groan. His thigh is aching and there is a ringing in his head. It throbs where he was struck on the temple. He looks back again. The line of dromedary corps hides the flames rising from the village where he could have died, on that 15 February 1799. The peasants, armed with sticks, threw themselves on him when he was cut off with Berthier, having allowed his escort to go on ahead. Suddenly they were surrounding him and beating him. Then the cavalry appeared, sabring, killing and setting the village on fire.

This is another sign. Since he has marched north, at the head of the thirteen thousand men that make up his army, he has been inspired by no feelings of enthusiasm, even though he rides in the biblical lands which the crusaders once occupied. He imagines an uprising of Palestine's Christian population, Arabs rallying to him to take up arms against their Ottoman masters. If that happened he could go to either India or Constantinople, redraw the world map – but still, and he is surprised by it himself, he is sombre.

On 17 February, he arrives at El Arish. General Reynier's men have just taken the fort, and Napoleon slowly crosses the camp where soldiers have lit big fires on which they are roasting sheep and horses' quarters. They have erected large tents and, leaning forward, he catches sight of women's silhouettes, Abysinnians, Circassians. There are mattresses and matting on the floor.

Is this rabble an army that can march to the Indus? The soldiers don't look at him. General Reynier approaches with his officers. The fort of El Arish was well defended, he explains, but he launched a surprise attack. The Ottomans were bayoneted in their sleep. There weren't many losses amongst the attackers, but – he gestures with his arm towards the piles of Turkish corpses on the ground – few of the defenders have survived.

Napoleon steps forward. 'This has been one of the finest military operations one could possibly conduct,' he says. Then he points to the camp. Indiscipline reigns. Why are the soldiers having to fend for themselves? Where are the supplies? Who is distributing the rations?

Reynier suddenly flies into a rage, protesting against the accusation. His officers back him up. General Kleber, arriving unexpectedly, adds that nothing was planned, one cannot maintain an army on the enemy's supplies.

Napoleon stares back at them.

The army shall leave El Arish on 21 February, he says. It will march on Gaza, Jaffa, St Jean d'Acre.

He goes to his tent and, around a fire, sees Monge, Berthollet, Venture the interpreter, Vivant Denon, a painter, Desgenettes the physician and a few other savants whom he wanted to come with the army to Syria.

'Palestine, land of massacres,' Venture says.

Napoleon knows. He thinks of the god Moloch to whom the Phoenicians offered human sacrifice, of the massacres of the innocents ordered by Herod, by the Romans, by the crusaders. Death has been the father of history here.

And today he is history on the march. His head and leg are still giving him pain, but he is alive. His enemies are dead. There has been no other law since the dawn of time.

ON 25 FEBRUARY, he enters Gaza.

The rain falls relentlessly and his horse splashes through the puddles and mud. The camels die of cold on the road to El Ramle. Two monasteries, built of ochre stone, dominate the little town and Napoleon goes to them. One of them is Armenian, the other Catholic. The occupants crowd round him; they kiss his hands and women with very white skin kneel before him. He listens to what they say: he is the first Christian to have reached here for centuries. He walks through the vaulted rooms, followed by Doctor Desgenettes. A military hospital must be set up, he says. As he is leaving the Catholic monastery, he sees the first of the wounded arriving, crammed into carts.

The rain hasn't stopped. The troops he catches up are slowly making their way to Jaffa. He senses their fatigue, their weariness. The men – soldiers and officers alike – are loath to go further away from France, and even from Egypt, where they have settled into a routine. What for, anyway? To crush the Turkish army? Why not wait until it comes to the Nile? Will every town put up a fight before they take it? What's the use of praising Mahomet and calling on the Arabs to join them when everywhere they are rising up in arms, resolute, barbaric, cruel?

IT IS 4 MARCH and here is Jaffa.

Napoleon looks at this town he must take by storm. It stands on a tall, sugarloaf mountain, and the houses rise up the sides in tiers, protected by a surrounding wall flanked by towers. In the cold wind, he draws up the siege plans and then, when the works are almost finished, he goes into the trenches.

The soldiers crowd around him at the foot of this slope they are going to have to climb. He dictates to Berthier a message for the governor of Jaffa: 'God is clement and merciful . . . It is to avoid the misfortunes that will befall the city that General-in-Chief Bonaparte asks the pasha to surrender before he is forced to do so by an attack which is now ready to be delivered.'

Napoleon watches the officer charged with carrying the message. The man approaches one of the gates in the surrounding wall; it is opened and he is pulled inside.

Silence falls on the trenches. Suddenly silhouettes can be seen climbing onto the ramparts. They are waving the officer's head. Shouting erupts and the men launch the attack without receiving the order.

After that they forget their enemies are men.

Napoleon hears the cries, he sees the blood. The soldiers return, their bayonets red, laden with booty, pushing in front of them women and young girls whom they begin to barter.

Napoleon has retired to his tent. He feels empty and his body is frozen. Two or three thousand Turks are still holed up in the citadel, Berthier is telling him, and there seem to be cases of the plague in the town. Pillaging is throwing the army into disorder.

Napoleon seems to snap out of a dream. Two officers are to go and examine the situation. Eugène de Beauharnais steps forward. He wishes to be one of them. Napoleon accepts. A fixed look has returned to his eyes.

After a few hours, Beauharnais comes back. He has induced the Turks to surrender and they are giving themselves up, abandoning their weapons.

Napoleon sits up. He murmurs, pale, 'What can we do with them? What do they expect me to do? What the devil have they done here?'

He convenes a council of war. He stares at his officers. All of them lower their eyes.

'Natives of Egypt must be sent back to their country,' Napoleon says, 'but what are we going to do with the others who have surrendered?'

No one answers. He paces about, his hands behind his back, hunched forward. He remembers the book by Volney he read at Valence, and their conversations in Corsica. A conqueror of Palestine had built a pyramid of severed heads to cow the country into submission. The enemy's death is a weapon one can use.

He gives orders.

The officers leave. He stays rooted to the spot, frozen.

IT HAPPENS in the sand dunes to the south-west of Jaffa. The prisoners are split up into little groups. Some try to escape and throw themselves into the sea. The water turns red. When the soldiers have used up their cartridges, they fix their bayonets.

He hears the screams of the dying as their throats are slit; and after a few hours he smells that stench of death rising from a charnel house of nearly three thousand bodies.

He is a conqueror of Palestine among many other conquerors, now.

He dictates to Bourrienne, who watches him with a sort of terror, a proclamation intended for the inhabitants of Palestine and the people of Nablus, Jerusalem and St Jean d'Acre: 'It is good that you know all human efforts against me have amounted to nothing, because everything I undertake must succeed. Those who declare themselves my friends prosper. Those who declare themselves my enemies perish. The example that has just been made of Jaffa and Gaza should let you know that, if I am terrible for my enemies, I am good to my friends and above all clement and merciful towards the poor.'

Then, with a brusque gesture, he dismisses Bourrienne.

He sits down. Where is he? Who is he? What has he done? Where is he going? He does not know how long he stays there. Perhaps the night has run its course without him moving, since now the sun is high.

DOCTOR Desgenettes is standing in front of him. How long has he been talking about the sick filling the hospitals? They have huge buboes in the groin and on the neck. It is the plague, but Desgenettes has tried to reassure the men. He has dipped a dagger in a victim's pus, then pricked himself in the armpit and groin.

Napoleon stands up and with a resolute step proceeds to the hospital. Some officers of his staff follow him, looking at him with the same dread as when he ordered the execution of the prisoners.

These looks are justification, absolution. He is of another stamp. His actions must not be judged by ordinary standards. The role he plays, the role that he wants to play and will play in history, justifies everything. He has no fear of death: he defies it. And if it does take him, it is because he has been mistaken about the course of his destiny.

The plague sufferers are lying in a half-light, in a foul stench like a sewer. Every smallest nook of the building is full. Napoleon walks slowly. He questions Desgenettes about the organization of the hospital. His officers keep a few paces behind him and try to stop him bending down and talking to and touching each sufferer.

At Reims the King used to touch scrofula.

The King was a thaumaturge.

He must be the equal of those sovereigns. His fear, his feelings don't exist. He is subject to the law of destiny, that is all; he does what this law tells him. He forgets what he feels, to do what he must do.

He goes into one of the hospital's narrow rooms. It is packed with the sick and a dead body is sprawled across a pallet. Suffering has made his face hideous. His clothes are in tatters and spattered with pus from a huge bubo.

He does not hesitate. He takes hold of the body. Officers try to restrain him, but he clasps that dead soldier and carries him out.

What is he afraid of? Only that he will not match up to what he should be. Death – his own, others' – is nothing.

HE DOES NOT catch the plague, but destiny is waiting in Haifa Bay. Two English ships of the line, the *Tigre* and the *Theseus*, are lying at anchor, soon to be joined by gunboats and Turkish craft.

Napoleon occupies Haifa, at the southern tip of the bay. On the other peninsula, to the north, dominating a little port, is the citadel of St Jean d'Acre with its imposing tower.

He contemplates that vast, almost completely open bay for a long time. He knows the men on the other side. The governor of St Jean d'Acre is called Djezzar the Butcher. Napoleon remembers the accounts of Tott's travels which he had read, along with Volney, at Valence: Djezzar the Butcher had shut up hundreds of Greek Orthodox Christians in the wall he was rebuilding around Beirut, leaving their heads uncovered, all the better to enjoy their torments. This is the man whom the Englishman Sydney Smith has come to the aid of. Napoleon first crossed swords with Smith at the siege of Toulon, where Smith had blown up the French fleets in the roads just as the Convention's troops, among them Napoleon, were taking the city. Since then he has not fought France continuously. Napoleon remembers the letter he received in 1797, soon afer 13th Vendémiaire, in which Sydney Smith, imprisoned in Paris, asked to be exchanged for French prisoners. He had not replied. Shortly afterwards he had learnt of Smith's escape with the help of royalist agents, including Le Picard de Phélippeaux.

Phélippeaux! He is in St Jean d'Acre, commandant of Djezzar the Butcher's artillery. This too is a sign.

'Phélippeaux . . .' begins Bourrienne.

Napoleon silences him with a shake of his head. This meeting, here under the walls of St Jean d'Acre, is a turning point in his destiny.

All the confrontations he had with Phélippeaux at the military school come back to him, those kicks under the refectory table, the rivalry, the hatred. Now they will have their denouement.

THEY LAY SIEGE to the town. Approach trenches are dug to sap towards the walls and the enormous towers built by the crusaders. They try to open a breach with mines.

The siege guns coming by boat are captured by Sydney Smith's flotilla. The Turkish cannon sweep their positions. Seeing the crossfire, Napoleon knows that Phélippeaux is giving the orders and applying the lessons they both learnt.

The assaults follow one after the other, useless and murderous. The French camp around St Jean d'Acre looks like a great fair. You can buy wine, brandy, figs, flat bread, grapes and even butter. Women, too. He knows this, but little by little he is losing his hold on the army. Discipline is harder and harder to maintain. He is informed of what the officers are saying, the generals' misgivings, the rank and file's anger. Bourrienne puts on his desk proclamations which Sydney Smith has thrown from the walls into the trenches. Napoleons starts to read one: 'Those of you of whatever rank who wish to escape the danger threatening you should without delay declare your intentions. You will be conducted to wherever you wish to go.'

Napoleon scornfully pushes the proclamation away from him. No soldier will succumb to that temptation, he says. He dictates the order of the day to Berthier. Hundreds of Christians have been massacred at St Jean d'Acre by Djezzar the Butcher. What did Smith and Phélippeaux do? They are complicit. French prisoners have been tortured, decapitated and embarked on plague-infected ships. All diplomatic contact with the English must be broken off. Smith's conduct is that of a madman, he thunders. They must attack again. Caffarelli has been killed. The officers are falling by the dozen at the head of their men.

Kléber murmurs, 'Bonaparte is a ten thousand men a day general!'

He must face up to these reproaches.

Napoleon calls his generals together and Murat takes a step

towards him, 'You are your soldiers' executioner,' he says. 'You must be very obstinate and blind indeed not to see that you will never be able to reduce St Jean d'Acre...'

Listen. Do not fly into a fury. Do not answer.

'At first your soldiers were enthusiastic,' continues Murat, 'but now they have to be forced to obey. Given their state of mind, I wouldn't be surprised if they stopped obeying at all.'

Napoleon turns his back and walks off to his tent in silence.

Why don't these men see what's at stake? In St Jean d'Acre there's the pasha's treasure and enough arms for three hundred thousand men.

Bourrienne has come in with Berthier. He calls to them, 'If I succeed, I shall rouse and arm the people of Syria who are disgusted by the ferocity of Djezzar and who, as you have seen, pray to God for his destruction with every attack we make. Then I shall march on Damascus and Aleppo. Advancing into the country, I shall swell my army with the discontented. I shall proclaim to the people the abolition of servitude and the pashas' tyranny. I shall arrive at Constantinople with huge armies. I shall overturn the Turkish empire and found in the East a new and grand empire which will secure my place in the annals of posterity. Then perhaps I shall return to Paris by Adrianople or Vienna, after having annihilated the house of Austria.'

He sees from Bourrienne and Berthier's faces that they do not share his dream. They must be carried along by a fresh victory every day, and one must keep the final goal to oneself.

Berthier announces that Kléber's troops are in difficulty near Mount Tabor, not far from Nazareth and Tiberias.

Forget the Empire of the East; let's go and defeat the Sultan of Damascus who is attempting to surround the French troops!

Napoleon leads the charge and the Turks take to their heels. Some rush into the Lake of Tiberias, where they are pursued and bayoneted. The water is stained with blood.

VICTORY is complete and Napoleon walks through the narrow streets of Nazareth.

Animals are drinking from the stone basin of a fountain.

Napoleon stops. Perhaps that was there when the religions were born?

The monks of Nazareth's monastery welcome him, and offer him hospitality for the night. He visits the chapel, where the prior gravely conducts him round, pointing out the marble column which the Angel Gabriel broke when he touched it with his heel.

There's laughter amongst the officers and men, but Napoleon restores silence with a look. This is one of the places where history first appeared. The village elders come forward and a Te Deum is sung to celebrate his victories. The monks and the Christian population surround Napoleon. He is the continuation of the crusades. They are happy. The Christians imagine themselves released from their tyrannical masters. He does not disillusion them.

How long will they enjoy their liberty?

WHEN HE RETURNS to camp at St Jean d'Acre, the situation is worse. The besieged have received reinforcements of artillery and men.

Napoleon asks to be left alone in his tent.

Eight assaults have been made, but to no avail. He just needs to walk through the camp to realize the soldiers' exhaustion and, above all, indiscipline. The only good news is Phélippeaux's death.

She has chosen to take him, not me.

A decision must be made. Amongst the papers his aides-de-camp have given him, he finds a letter from the Directory dated 4 November. 'It is up to you to choose, obviously, with the elite of brave and distinguished men you have around you,' it says.

Up to him to decide. He listens to the news a merchant brings after his long journey from Italy. The French have retaken Rome and Naples. The man doesn't know any more, but that is enough. Napoleon feels his impatience mounting. The dice are being rolled again in Europe. If Naples has fallen, Austria has no choice but to declare war on France.

I am here, in this trap, fighting barbarians with weary, dissatisfied men who have the plague snapping at their heels.

He must leave, abandon the siege and get back to France – but first he must give what has happened here a meaning. The sacrifices and suffering must not have been demanded in vain. He needs words to transform the reality and give these men dreams, so that they can be proud of what they have accomplished: 'Soldiers, you have crossed the desert that divides Africa from Asia faster than an Arab army. On the field of Mount Tabor you have scattered that host of men who had flocked from every part of Asia in the hope of pillaging Egypt ... We are going back to Egypt ... The capture of the castle of St Jean d'Acre is not worth the loss of a few days and, besides, the brave men I should otherwise lose here are now needed for more essential operations ... Soldiers, we have a hard and dangerous course to run ... You shall have fresh opportunities for glory.'

The decision is taken.

'We must organize the retreat,' he says, 'and blow up the guns after they have bombarded St Jean d'Acre. Then we will set out, and we will process through every village, enemy flags at the head, bands playing.'

He orders that the wounded be put on horses. All able-bodied men will be on foot.

'General, which horse for yourself?' asks the groom.

'Everyone must go on foot, you rascal – I the first. Don't you understand the order?'

He marches at the head of the army. He has put his carriage at the disposal of Monge, Berthollet and the mathematician Gostaz, all three of whom are ill. The streets of Haifa and Tentoura Square in Jaffa are full of the wounded or plague-ridden. Some are picked up, some abandoned, some ask to be killed.

After revisiting Jaffa's hospital, Napoleon goes up to Doctor Desgenettes.

'Opium,' he simply says.

Desgenettes's whole body recoils.

'My duty is to preserve life,' he says. He will not poison the hospital's sick.

'I am not trying to overcome your repugnance,' Napoleon replies, 'but my duty is to preserve the army.'

He walks away; he will find men who will give the plague-stricken opium.

'If I had the plague . . .' he starts. He would wish to be shown this kindness.

He returns to the front of the march as sappers blow up Jaffa's fortifications. He must march on, listening to the shots of soldiers committing suicide or doing their companions the favour of killing them as they ask.

The fields are in flames. The English ships are firing on the column and the Bedouin are harrying them.

They finally reach Salhiya on 9 June, after crossing the Sinai desert.

Napoleon knows the troops are complaining bitterly. What is an army filled with doubt and rebelliousness? He must take the soldiers in hand again. He has always been an officer. The 'movers' must be punished, if necessary put to death, if discipline breaks down on a forced march or under fire.

ON 17 JUNE 1799, he enters Cairo by the Victory Gate, Bab el Nasr. He has given orders to the commander of the garrison, General Dugua, to organize a triumphal reception. Palms have been strewn on the ground, bands play, the crowds in the streets push forward to see them. The captured enemy flags lead the way.

Reaching Ezbekyeh Square, Napoleon takes up a position in the middle of it and watches these men march smartly past, each carrying a palm frond with the flag.

The fortress of St Jean d'Acre, the screams of those shot at Jaffa, the groans of the plague victims – all that vanishes into what already seems a distant past.

He is alive. His return is a conqueror's return. The future continues.

He walks to the palace.

Pauline Fourès is waiting for him on the steps.

XXXV

HE HEARS THE DOGS BARKING again and gets out of bed. Pauline, his Bellilote, is asleep. He goes to the window and sees the minarets. Can he really stay any longer, now he knows he will not be able to march to Constantinople or the Indies?

He goes down the marble staircase, running his hand over the Aswan granite. He must leave this town where he feels caught in the snare of repetition.

The dogs have returned to haunt Cairo's nights. They will have to be rounded up again on the square and killed. Then, after a few weeks they would be back, running in packs through the streets, howling loud enough to make your skull split.

He must leave, return to France, Europe.

On that 21 June, therefore, he starts to write to Admiral Ganteaume, ordering him to hold the two frigates *La Muiron* and *La Carrière* in Alexandria's roads, in immediate readiness for sea.

Muiron, his death on the bridge at Arcola saved his life.

This is how it is: some fall, others march on.

He goes back to his chamber. Pauline Fourès has not stirred.

LEAVE? But when?

He is on the lookout for an opportunity. Given the chance, he knows he must seize it, jump and not let anything hold him back. It will come, he's sure, because once again this choice is life or death for him, and life pulses so powerfully in him that it will win.

Perhaps his will was not strong enough before the walls of St Jean d'Acre, where his dream shattered? Or did his imagination carry him too far?

'The compass of his reasoning' must decide. He must not give way to impatience, but on the contrary act as if he were going to stay in this country forever, mask his intentions, bequeath an orderly conquest to those who will stay on. As orderly as he can.

He appears before the notables of the Divan, arrogant, well aware his speech must be self-assured.

'I have learnt that enemies have spread rumours of my death,' he says. 'Observe me closely and assure yourselves that I am the genuine Bonaparte ... Members of the Divan, denounce the hypocrites, the rebels! God has given me a terrible power. What chastisement awaits them! My sword is long, it knows no weakness!'

SO THE KILLING will have to go on. That is how it is.

On 23 June, he sees General Dugua, who is in command of the citadel. What are they to do with the prisoners crowding its dungeons? Ammunition should be used as sparingly as possible; they should be executed discreetly, he says.

Dugua hesitates before continuing, 'I propose, General, to call on the services of a headsman.'

'Agreed.'

Death to govern life.

The executioners are Egyptian or Greek, but it is Muslims who drown the prostitutes in the Nile, thereby enforcing the Islamic law forbidding relations between a Muslim woman and an infidel.

Let them have their way. Venereal diseases are rife. The army must be taken in hand, reorganized and protected, because the men and discipline have grown slack, even at the top of the hierarchy. Kléber pokes fun at him. Napoleon looks at the caricatures drawn by Kléber that have been put on his desk for a long time. This thin, sickly man who seems possessed is how Kléber sees him. There's grumbling about him in the ranks of this weary army.

On 29 June, at the first meeting of the Institute of Egypt, Dr Desgenettes gets to his feet in a fury and speaks of the 'mercenary adulation' of 'Oriental despots', accusing Napoleon of trying to make the plague responsible for the outcome of the Syrian campaign, and so laying the blame for their defeat on the doctor.

Do not answer, wait.

Desgenettes, now more composed, says, 'I know, gentlemen, I know, General – since you are here not just as a member of the Institute and wish to be in charge everywhere – I know that I have been driven heatedly to express sentiments that will echo far from here, but I shall not retract a single word ... and I take refuge in the army's gratitude.'

EACH PASSING DAY confirms it: he must leave Egypt, but he needs a resounding victory, otherwise his departure, whatever efforts he devotes to stabilizing the country, will smack of a defeated leader's flight.

He seeks victory in the south first, and sets up his headquarters at the foot of the pyramids to prepare to attack Murad Bey, who is as elusive as ever.

Every day in the cruel heat he marches under the sun, forcing himself to wait until the patrols have found Murad Bey's camp or his signals, since it is said that at night he communicates with his wife who is still in Cairo.

On 15 July, a group of horsemen, their faces burnt by the sand, bring news: an Anglo-Turkish fleet has landed several thousand troops at Aboukir.

No need to hear any more. This is the sign, this is the moment.

Napoleon dictates his orders. This is the battle he was waiting for. They must travel by forced march, rally at Rahminaya, and then converge on Aboukir, where the Turks have entrenched themselves along the shore.

With the back of his hand, he must sweep aside all the counsels of prudence, silence the officers who are demanding they wait for the arrival of Kléber's division.

In the night of 24 July, Napoleon summons Murat. Here is the plan of attack: he must charge, drive the Turks back into the sea. Napoleon has no doubts. This is how they must go about it. He takes Murat by the arm and leads him out of the tent. The night is clear, dawn is taking form.

'This battle will decide the fate of the world,' he says.

He sees Murat's astonishment as he replies, 'At least the fate of the army.'

'The fate of the world,' Napoleon repeats.

He knows he will only be able to leave Egypt if he is crowned with a victory that will erase all the bloody, uncertain episodes, leaving glorious memories in people's minds.

Murat charges at dawn on 25 July, and sweeps the Turks aside. Thousands of bodies turn the sea red, the same sea where so many French sailors died a year before.

When Kléber arrives, the battle ends and Murat is made major-general.

'That is one of the finest battles I have seen,' Napoleon says, 'and one of the most terrible spectacles.'

The reticent, sarcastic, hostile Kléber steps forward but Napoleon seems to tower over his powerful frame. Kléber holds out his arms. 'General, you are as great as the world, and it cannot contain you.'

Napoleon lets himself be embraced.

IT IS 2 AUGUST 1799. The last of the Ottomans holding out in Aboukir's fort surrender in the afternoon: trembling, famished, wounded ghosts whom Napoleon orders to be fed and cared for. Then he sends two officers on board the *Tigre*, Commodore Sydney Smith's vessel – him again, always him – to negotiate an exchange of prisoners.

It is ten in the evening. Napoleon has lain down and is drifting off to sleep, listening to the rhythmical ebb and flow of the sea in the distance. Suddenly he wakes with a start. One of his aides-de-camp enters his tent and announces that Sydney Smith's secretary is here and wishes to speak to him on behalf of the commodore.

Napoleon sits on the edge of the camp bed and watches the Englishman coming towards him. He is a tall, respectful man who puts down a batch of newspapers which Sir Sydney is keen to pass on to the general-in-chief. It includes the French *Frankfurt Gazette* and *London Courier*. Napoleon starts reading, unconcerned by the Englishman's presence. The most recent editions are dated 10 June – Napoleon has not had any news for months.

The contents, the names wound him – French defeats in Italy at the hands of Marshal Suvorov: the Russians! – in Germany, defeats by the Archduke Charles, whom he had defeated – all his conquests swept away – the Directory divided and stumbling from crisis to crisis.

And I am here, powerless to repair the situation, take advantage of it, seize this moment when now everything is possible, when this pear is finally ripe.

Someone else may act.

He questions the Englishman, who confirms the news and hints that Sydney Smith wishes to see the French leave Egypt, and that negotiations can be entered into.

Napoleon escorts him back to his boat, then quickly returns to his tent and resumes reading the newspapers.

That Directory has lost everything he had won. Useless victories and deaths.

He throws the newspapers on the ground.

'Is it possible, those wretches! Poor France! What have they done?' he exclaims. 'Oh, those scoundrels!'

He cannot sleep now. He must leave Egypt, quickly.

IT IS 15 AUGUST 1799; his thirtieth birthday. A stage in his life is ending. Sitting opposite him, Pauline Fourès is carefree, chattering away, dressed in a hussar's tunic and boots, her long, blonde hair loose.

She does not know. No one, apart from the few who will go with him, can suspect he is leaving.

He pretends to listen to Bellilote. She is speaking of the future. When will he bring himself to get divorced? She is free. He promised, or implied, that he would marry her. She says this merrily, without reproach. He shakes his head: 'Power is my mistress. My sole passion, my sole mistress is France. That is who I sleep with.'

The only promise he has ever made is to himself: to be everything he wants to be, everything he feels he can be; but for that he must dissimulate, put on appearances, not let it show that he is already far away, in France, in Paris, imposing his authority on the babblers, the weaklings and corrupt incompetents in the Directory.

As USUAL, he appears before the dignitaries of the Divan. He gives the Muslim form of greeting and prays with them. 'Is it not true that it is written in your books that a higher being will come from the West with the mission of continuing the Prophet's work? Is it not true that it is also written that this man, this envoy of Mahomet's, is me?'

They dare not protest. The victory he has just won has stunned them, crushed them. They are submissive.

Napoleon shuts himself in his palace and begins to draw up the instructions he will leave for Kléber, whom he has chosen as his successor. He writes without respite for hours, explaining the methods that must be used to govern Egypt, but he adds that if the situation becomes critical, due to the plague or lack of reinforcements from France, 'you are authorized to conclude peace with the Ottoman Porte, even if the evacuation of Egypt has to be the principal condition.'

He puts down his quill.

Egypt no longer concerns him.

WHILE HE IS dictating orders, or announcing, as a diversion, that he is soon going on a tour of inspection to the delta, he wonders who shall accompany him. He only needs men he can trust, devoted to him body and soul, and efficient. That is what's indispensable for a leader: his aides-de-camp, then his personal guard. 'Three hundred picked men is vast,' he thinks. Bourrienne, his confidant and a good secretary, will accompany him along with General Berthier his irreplaceable chief of staff, Murat, Marmont, Andréossy and Bessières. They are young, passionate, loyal. Loyalty is what counts most. He thinks of Roustam Raza, the Mameluke whom Sultan El-Bekry gave him on his return from the Syrian campaign, who has since shown the attachment and discretion of a slave. A leader needs a man of this sort who knows everything, can see and hear the most intimate details and knows how to hold his tongue. Roustam will come, as will Monge, Berthollet and Vivant Denon, who have shown courage and loyalty, and who will testify before the Institute of the discoveries that have been made.

No one else.

He sees Pauline Fourès comes in. She doesn't suspect, and he doesn't say anything. She has been a moment in his life. He has been generous to her, and he would be again if they were to meet in the future, but this is his destiny, which is greater than that of others and it will accept no weakness.

Admiral Ganteaume's courier finally arrives on 17 August, in the afternoon. The English fleet has left Egyptian waters, no doubt to take on water in Cyprus. For a few days it is possible to leave Alexandria.

No waiting; decide instantly, inform those who are travelling, give orders.

Go to Pauline Fourès, embrace her, give her a thousand louis and leave immediately, fast. Ride to Boulaq and from there to Alexandria and wait on the beach for night to fall.

He is thirty. The future is opening up again. Anything may happen: shipwreck, capture by an English cruiser, the Directory's condemnation, accusations of desertion – they are capable of it – or else simply arriving too late, after someone – Bernadotte or Moreau, Sieyès or Barras – has already picked the ripe pear and severed with a sweep of the sabre the stalk of that fruit which is power.

He looks at the sea in the gathering darkness. The masts of two frigates and two sloops stand out against a red horizon.

General Menou approaches. He will be the messenger to Kléber, who has been summoned, but they will leave tonight before he arrives.

Napoleon takes Menou by the arm and walks briskly along the shore. The corpulent fellow is out of breath and cannot reply.

'The Directory has lost everything we won, you know, Menou,' Napoleon begins. 'Everything is compromised. France is buffeted by war abroad and war at home. It is conquered, humiliated, close to death.'

He stops and faces the sea. 'I must run the risk of the seas to go and save her.'

He starts walking again.

'If I get there, woe betide the chatter of politicians, the intrigues of the cliques.'

Everyone will be treated as they deserve.

'My presence is superfluous here,' he says, pointing inland to Alexandria. 'Kléber can take my place in all matters.'

He hands his instructions to Menou, then embraces him.

NIGHT HAS abruptly hidden men and ships. No moon. Despite the risks of being discovered, they have to light fires to guide the boats that finally come ashore. The sea is smooth, the ships motionless, as if they had been caught in a black trap.

At dawn on 23 August a little craft comes alongside the frigate *La Muiron* and a supplicant goes aboard. It is a member of the Institute, Parseval Grandmaison, who has understood the purpose of his colleagues' trip and begs to be accepted.

Napoleon looks for a long time at this man imploring him, who has taken matters in his own hands. That deserves a reward. He accepts him on board.

At eight o'clock, at the first breeze, the sails are hoisted and they pull away from the Egyptian coast which is soon no more than a brown line that gradually fades out of sight.

NAPOLEON no longer feels impatient. He sits on a cannon mount. The frigate *Carrère* is bringing up the rear, a few cables behind the *Muiron*. In front of them, acting as scouts, sloops are beating up to windward.

The wind has been slow getting up, but Napoleon feels the calmest of everyone on board. He has said many times, 'Don't fear, we will get through.'

The sails fill and Admiral Ganteaume comes to explain his route. He will go along the Barbary Coast and then cut across and follow that of Corsica.

'I steer by your star,' he says.

Berthollet comes over shortly afterwards, and reports the anxieties of some of the others.

'Whoever fears for his life is bound to lose it,' says Napoleon. 'One must know how to risk and calculate at the same time, and then leave the rest to Fortune.'

He stands up and walks about the bridge. He is in Fortune's hands for the weeks to come. He can do nothing now he has made his choice. 'The future is uncertain,' he says, turning to Berthollet, who has followed him. 'One must only think of the present.'

The present: these days of sailing, one after the other, this wind that slackens or freshens, those sails you think you can see and then they disappear, these books you read.

He listens to one of his aides-de-camp whom he has asked to read *Lives of Illustrious Men* out loud after lunch. He loves Plutarch, that storyteller who can bring events to life. He loves these days when one can let one's mind wander since that is the only thing to do, since the wind and the sea and Fortune decide everything.

'We can do nothing against the nature of things. Children are wilful. A great man is not. What is a human life? The trajectory of a missile.'

'Who loads, takes aim, lights the fuse?' asks Berthollet.

Napoleon strides up and down. The words come. Do they express his thoughts or is he playing with them? He says what he feels. Although at every moment of his life he has made the choice, he says to Berthollet, 'A higher power is urging me towards a goal which I do not know; until it is achieved, I shall be invulnerable and unflinching. The moment I am no longer needed, a fly will be enough to undo me.'

Why does he talk about that with Berthollet or Monge? Do these men of science feel, like he does, that a force is supporting them, do they have presentiments and certainties that cannot be explained?

He knows that the English will not intercept him. He knows that France is weary of these wars between Jacobins and émigrés; it wants peace within its borders and is waiting for a man who can provide it.

Perhaps that man is there already?

That is the only thing that worries him.

ON 30 SEPTEMBER he contemplates the mountainous Corsican coast in the setting sun; he smells the scents of the maquis, and soon Ajaccio's citadel and houses appear.

On 1 October, the *Muiron* drops anchor and immediately craft appear from all directions.

How do they know who it is?

People are shouting, cheering. No one pays any attention to the need for quarantine. They want to see Napoleon, touch him. He is embraced. In the crowd now filling the quay, he spots his wet-nurse, Camilla Ilari, an old woman who hugs him to her. He embraces his childhood – so close and yet so far away now. He learns that Louis, who he sent to France in 1798, came through Ajaccio on his way to the mainland with their mother.

Napoleon goes to the country house in Milelli. He remembers every detail, and yet he feels no emotion. This universe is buried in him like a stage set he has left behind and no longer concerns him. Meanwhile he is surrounded by self-interested attention. 'What a bore,' he says. 'It is raining relatives.'

He asks for the latest newspapers from France and reads them avidly, learning that militarily the situation has righted itself, that Masséna – 'his' Masséna – has won victories in Italy and General Brune is holding out in the Batavian Republic. However, a political crisis is brewing in Paris, where Sieyès is calling the tune.

He must leave Corsica. He must get there in time.

At last, on 7 October the wind gets up and he can sail.

NAPOLEON stands at the prow until the French coast comes into sight.

This is the most dangerous part of the whole crossing. An English squadron is cruising up and down the coast. Off Toulon sails hove into view, but then luckily sail away.

On 9 October, in the morning, they enter the gulf of St Raphael and the citadel of Fréjus opens fire on this unknown naval division. Then, from the bows, Napoleon sees crowds of people rushing down to the quays and throwing themselves into boats and rowing out towards the frigates, shouting, 'Bonaparte!'

Admiral Ganteaume comes up just as the *Muiron* is overrun. 'I have taken you where your destiny calls you,' he says.

Napoleon is picked up and carried in triumph.

'He is here! He is here!' they shout.

He disembarks and a procession forms on the quay. Again, no one thinks of quarantine, of the danger of the plague.

A carriage is made ready for him.

Since he is here, Fortune must have protected him.

Who can stop me now?

PART NINE

❧

Yes, follow me,
I am the God of the hour

9 October 1799 to
11 November 1799 (20 Brumaire Year VIII)

XXXVI

SEVENTEEN MONTHS SINCE he left France! It was spring then, May 1798, and now it is autumn 1799. The weather is stormy and at times the horses have to be reined in, the downpours are so heavy.

Then, he was driving to Toulon and Josephine was at his side, showing him every sign of attachment and ready, so she said, to follow him to Egypt. Now, he knows how things stand with her, with Captain Charles, with her lovers.

Fury and bitterness well up in Napoleon when he is left alone with his thoughts, and the clamour of the crowds that surround the convoy in every village shouting, 'Long live the Republic! Long live Bonaparte!' has faded.

If he should try to forget, he need only look at Eugène de Beauharnais opposite him to remember.

At Avignon, the crowds stop the carriages. They want to salute the victorious Bonaparte, the man of peace. He says a few words: 'I belong to no party, I am of the great party of the French people.' He is cheered, his victory at Aboukir is applauded. News has travelled and, as he had anticipated, the victory is the only thing that has made an impression. He watches the tanned, swaggering figure of Murat, a scimitar dangling by cords from his belt, as he tells the garrison's officers about his charge.

The Mameluke Roustam is trying to push his way through a crowd of people who want to ask him questions and touch his uniform. When he is close to Napoleon, he manages to say that the carriages carrying their baggage have been pillaged, near Aix, and cannot be used. He keeps saying, 'French Bedouin have stolen, French Bedouin.'

Hearing that, the crowd mutters and grumbles. Brigands are harrying travellers, robbing stagecoaches. Peace and order must be restored. 'The Directory is robbing us too!' a voice cries. 'Brigands, the lot of them.'

Napoleon asks the opinions of the local dignitaries, who deplore the situation, flattered by the attention he is paying them. Does

General Bonaparte know the Directory wants to implement forced loans to rob honest people, property owners? And then there are the Chouans, who still hold part of La Vendée and threaten Nantes. Who can assure us that the émigrés are not going to return and demand the restitution of the land that was sold as national property when we bought it? The Republic must be saved, they say.

'I am a national,' Napoleon says as he gets into his carriage, and from the footboard, he adds, 'There must be no more factions; I will not tolerate any. Long live the nation!'

The cries of 'Long live the Republic! Long live Bonaparte!' accompany him through the streets of Avignon, and later, along the road, in every village of the Rhône valley, he is received with the same rapturous demonstrations of joy.

APPROACHING Lyon, he sees tricolour flags in the casement window of every house, and the postilions at the coaching inns sport ribbons in the same colours.

For him.

In Lyon itself all the houses are lit up and decked with flags. There are fireworks and the crowd is so dense that the carriages have to slow to a walk.

He sees grenadiers at the gate of the hotel and, on the steps, his brothers Louis and Joseph.

From all sides cries of 'Long live Bonaparte, who has come to save the fatherland' go up.

He modestly acknowledges the crowd. He feels that this wave carrying him is powerful and profound, but he knows he must avoid any excessive response or impatience. He knows what he wants: to obtain power. He is worth more than all these men who tear each other to pieces. He is thirty. He has commanded tens of thousands of soldiers. He has faced death at their side. He has triumphed. He will brush aside all obstacles – but he must be prudent. The likes of Barras and Sieyès are adroit and devious.

He and Joseph find somewhere private. He would like to ask about the situation in Paris – what does this man plan, or that – but other questions come out: Josephine, Josephine, he repeats.

Joseph begins speaking in a hollow voice, then grows angry. He has stopped paying her the income of forty thousand francs

Napoleon had asked him to. She has made the name Bonaparte ridiculous. She has been living with Captain Charles at Malmaison, the estate she bought. She has continued seeing Barras. She has been seen at Gohier's, the president of the Directory. Is there any powerful man who is not thought of as her lover? She is up to her ears in debt. She has helped Charles in the deals he has made with army contractors.

'Our mother . . .' continues Joseph.

Napoleon stops him. He can imagine his mother's feelings, and those of his sisters. He is going to get a divorce, he says. The word cuts his mouth. He repeats it, hurting himself. He has changed and yet, at every turn of the wheel, he has thought of his wife's body, her scent. He would like to make her submit, like a fort that has held out against a siege a long time and finally gives itself up, and on whom one imposes the law. He has become a man whom the people cheer.

He goes to the window, and sees horse-drawn carriages driving off. He calls an aide-de-camp, who tells him that General Marbot, on his way to take up his command in Italy, had reserved the suite of rooms which the hotel-keeper has now put at General Bonaparte's disposal.

Never neglect anything. A humiliated person, or even someone who has simply been put out, can become an enemy.

Napoleon gives orders. He is going to visit the hotel where Marbot has gone, to pay his respects and apologize. In the game he is playing any man can become a crucial piece.

And any woman.

He thinks of Josephine. Can he afford to make an enemy of her now?

THEY LEAVE Lyon and, despite it being so early, there's another enthusiastic crowd outside the hotel shouting, 'Long live Napoleon, saviour of the fatherland!'

Napoleon has chosen to be alone with Joseph in his carriage. Let us not talk of Josephine any more, he says. He looks at the Forez mountains wreathed in fog. The carriage is going to take the Bourbonnais road, which is narrower and less safe, but will get them to Paris faster, because he has to act quickly. Since his return from Italy, he has never doubted for a single day that he would assume power in Paris, but now this cheering, these cries are transforming what was only an intuition into a reality which he must organize and inhabit.

He leans closer to Joseph, quizzes him.

'One man matters immediately,' Joseph says. 'Sieyès.'

Napoleon remembers this fifty-year-old; he is prudent and determined, a former priest. In 1789, he wrote a lampoon giving his sense of events, *What is the Third Estate?* Then, during the Convention and the Terror, he, as he put it, 'survived'. Joseph explains that Sieyès has struck up conversations with their brother Lucien, who is a Corsican representative on the Council of the Five Hundred. Sieyès wants reform that will increase the power of the executive relative to that of the two assemblies, the Ancients and the Five Hundred, and Lucien has been present at all the negotiations. Sieyès has been looking for a general to enforce this. He had thought of General Joubert, but he was killed at the battle of Novi. General Moreau has been guarded, but can Napoleon guess what Moreau suggested when he learnt of Napoleon's return to France? In Lucien's presence he said, 'There is your man; he will effect your coup d'état better than me.'

'And what of Bernadotte?' Napoleon asks. Hostile, Joseph says, but he is now the husband of Desirée Clary. Perhaps that will make him more understanding. Of course they can count on General Leclerc, their sister Pauline's husband, and many of the troops in Paris are veterans of the Army of Italy. But Sieyès is the most important, Joseph insists. As for the minister of police, Fouché, he is intelligent, like the seminarist and orator he once was. He is a Republican, regicide and terrorist; he massacred Lyon's royalists with cannon. His deputy, Réal, a former Jacobin, is close to Lucien. He is in charge of the Criminal Investigation Department.

Napoleon listens. He mustn't make a mistake. He speaks of Fouché's duplicity – he is an enigmatic man with his red hair and heavy-lidded eyes. Fouché helped him on 13 Vendémiaire, as a way to re-ingratiate himself with Barras.

He should secure Barras's cooperation – but how can one present oneself as the saviour of the fatherland if one allies oneself with a man who, to the public, is the incarnation of corruption?

No, better to rely on the 'three of a kind': the former priests Sieyès, Fouché and Talleyrand.

'Gohier?' murmurs Napoleon.

'A barrister, fifties, fearful, but acting president of the Directory.' Sighing, Joseph adds that the Gohiers are on the best of terms with Josephine, who is often their guest.

Josephine, again.

SHE IS NOT there when, at six o'clock in the morning on 16 October 1799, Napoleon walks into his house in the rue de la Victoire.

His mother comes towards him, a grave look on her face, followed by his sisters and Lucien. They have been waiting. He does not need to ask; the first things they say are to condemn Josephine, the unfaithful intruder. As if regretfully, they say that she left Paris to go and meet him; Joseph and Louis met Napoleon, but she couldn't find her husband, they laugh mockingly.

He took the Bourbonnais road, he murmurs.

Then he flies into a fury. He will divorce her – pack her bags and put them at the door, he orders. He *will* divorce her.

He would like to rest, but he is too tense and his first visitors are already there. Collot, an army contractor who he has not seen since Italy, appears. He wishes to offer his assistance. As he is talking, the first murmur comes of a crowd that has gathered in rue de la Victoire, singing 'The Marseillaise' and calling Bonaparte's name.

Napoleon hardly listens to Collot. He wanted his return to be discreet. He must still be modest, for a few more days. He will not reveal his guns until he has made sure of all the positions; then he will open a hellish fire. For now restraint and prudence are what's called for.

Collot sees Josephine bags.

'Do you want to leave her?' he asks.

'There is nothing in common between us any more.'

Napoleon curses himself for answering like that, but his resentment is stronger than the reserve he should adopt.

Collot shakes his head and remonstrates. The point now is not to waste time on domestic disputes – 'Your greatness would vanish and in the eyes of France you would be nothing more than one of Molière's husbands.'

Napoleon cannot dispute these words of reason. They open a path in him.

'It is important you do not start as a source of ridicule,' Collot sums up.

Napoleon cannot submit immediately to such a strong argument, which he has already gone over himself, so he flies into a rage to mask his wavering.

'No, my mind is made up,' he says. 'She shall not set foot in my house again. What do I care what people will say!'

He walks out, slamming the door. He knows perfectly well he is lying; he has to take public opinion into account. Yet when he rejoins Collot and the latter insists, saying he is sure that eventually Napoleon will forgive her, he cries, 'If I was not sure of myself, I would tear this heart out and dash it in the fire.'

HE DOES NOT want to think about her any more, but he knows that, whatever he may have said, he has not decided. She is too well placed on the chessboard for him to be able to consider her just an unfaithful wife. But she is that too, and she is still the woman he desires.

Here is Réal, Fouché's deputy, who is asking to see him. Prudence. He is being observed, sounded out. Fouché, says Réal, is ready to support a project that would rescue the Republic from the double threat of Jacobins and royalists. He is the minister of police; he can offer substantial financial assistance. Collot has already offered five hundred thousand francs.

If these men are risking their money, it is because they believe in my chances of success.

There isn't a day to be wasted. Napoleon is received by Gohier, president of the Directory. So, Josephine spends her evenings at this mediocre, stiff, timorous man's house, does she? But he represents the government; he must be outwitted.

'The news that reached us in Egypt was so alarming that I didn't hesitate to leave my army, and set out at once to come and share your perils.' Napoleon says.

'General,' Gohier replies, 'they *were* indeed great, but we have gloriously overcome them. You have arrived in time to help us celebrate the numerous triumphs of your comrades-in-arms.'

So this is what they are going to say! Proclaim the victories of General Moreau, Brune and Masséna, who have prised open the enemy's vice. However, they will not be able to silence, or not immediately, the crowd congregating in rue de la Victoire or those who, on 17 October, will gather in front of the Luxembourg Palace when Napoleon presents himself before the directors.

NAPOLEON has chosen civilian clothes: a tight-fitting greenish frock coat, with a top hat rounding off his strange outfit. He carries, attached by silk cords, a Turkish scimitar.

Cheering breaks out, but he keeps his head bowed, and maintains the same modest attitude before the directors. He lifts his sword.

'Citizen-Directors,' he declares. 'I swear that this will never be drawn except in defence of the Republic and its government.'

He watches them. Will they dare condemn him, reproach him for leaving Egypt, when they hear the crowd which is still shouting his name? They know that a place will have to be found for him in the Republic. He stares at Barras, Gohier and Moulin. He cannot count on them. At the most he can stop these three directors harming him. That leaves Sieyès and Roger Ducos; those two are allies and he must play with them, but everything about Sieyès's face expresses self-importance and mistrust. He wants to retain control of the game.

Lucien has reported what he tells his intimates: 'Bonaparte's sword is too long.'

So he must reassure him – or make himself indispensable, because what other general could Sieyès count on?

He is congratulated. The five directors dare not alienate him.

HE EMERGES from the Luxembourg Palace, parading his good spirits and assurance before the crowd. Today everyone must know that the powers that be have nothing to reproach him with.

He returns to rue de la Victoire. He must tie the threads together, so he receives those who have decided to play this decisive and perilous hand with him.

He listens to Talleyrand. Here is a man who has been forced to resign from his ministerial post and who dreams of winning it back. 'His self-interest vouches for him.' He is accompanied by Roederer, a member of the Institute, and others who speak eagerly and passionately.

Napoleon observes them as they say, 'General, power must be seized.'

But he is the only one who will pay the price of their advice if he goes over the top of his trench too soon. So he chooses to remain in rue de la Victoire, refusing even to receive delegations of officers and soldiers who come to pay their respects and wait out in the street for a long time, trying to catch a glimpse of him.

Seize power?

'Do you think it is possible?' he asks Roederer, who is insistent.

'It is three-quarters done already.'

He merely pushes over to Roederer a copy of *The Messenger*, a newspaper published that morning, 20 October. It is the first sign of a counter-attack by his opponents, perhaps even by Jacobins or Barras. 'Bonaparte,' the article reads, 'left Egypt so hurriedly and secretly only so as to escape a full-scale mutiny by his army.'

Roederer and then Talleyrand protest indignantly. Napoleon observes them in silence. He must act because, if he does not take power, he will be broken – glory fades quickly and someone popular one moment may be disowned the next – but if he acts, he must win. So he must neglect nothing.

HE HAS BEEN right to make it up with Josephine.

She came back in the night and the porter agreed to let her in, despite his instructions. Napoleon heard her and immediately shut himself in his room. She came and knocked on the door. She begged him and he was moved by that beseeching voice. She is at his mercy, as he has so often wished her to be and she never was.

He does not give in. He lets her cry and acknowledge what she has done and ask for his pity. He does not budge, but his feelings are in turmoil, a swirl of desire and self-interest, the pleasure of revenge on the one hand, and personal gain on the other.

She goes away and he thinks she has given up, which fills him with a sense of loss. He feels an even greater longing for her. It is even clearer to him that he needs her. He listens for noises. Someone is coming down the stairs. He recognizes the voices of Eugène and Hortense de Beauharnais who are begging him to pardon their mother.

He is overwhelmed by emotion. He loves Eugène. He shared the perils and pleasures of Egypt with this child. He has seen him become a man and a soldier. He trusts him. Why, at this moment, would he renounce the support of the whole Beauharnais clan? Can he allow himself to be deprived of a part of his family 'army'?

He is not yielding to Josephine but to her children.

He opens the door and Josephine rushes towards him. She starts to caress his face. He smells her perfume again, and feels her body, so slender, cling to him.

He makes love to her all night.

He has become the master of this woman, perhaps because he no longer loves her as he used to, as a blind supplicant.

HE SEES HER smile the next day at the sight of Lucien, who thought his brother's divorce was definite. Napoleon takes Lucien aside. This is not the moment to talk of this, these are my affairs.

Lucien does not insist. Napoleon listens to this lad of twenty-four whose passion is politics and who has managed, with the help of his name, to be a force in the Council of the Five Hundred and to be Sieyès's confidant.

Lucien speaks forcefully. Sieyès, he says, wants a more compact government, made up of three consuls rather than five directors. He expects to organize the transfer of the assemblies from Paris to St Cloud, and induce them to vote for the reform of their institutions.

'Can I assure him that you will agree to be one of the three consuls?' asks Lucien.

'No, good Lord, don't do any such thing!'

It is still too early. We will see later. Sieyès is too identified as a moderate, a reactionary even, a supporter of a return to the monarchy, who perhaps has connections with the Orléans.

'I don't want to wear the colours of any party,' Napoleon repeats.

IT IS A COVERT war he is waging, as rousing as an offensive but all concealed thrusts. He needs Sieyès's support, but without soliciting it or proclaiming it. The directors must be got rid of but, if possible, a coup d'état avoided. He must storm the fortress of the country with the full support of the assemblies, the Five Hundred and the Ancients.

I do not want to be a general who takes power by force.

So he ignores Sieyès at a dinner at Gohier's, and the following day his host reports Sieyès's bitter exclamation, 'Did you see the behaviour of that insolent youngster towards a member of a government that should have had him shot?'

Too late.

He flatters General Moreau: 'I have wanted to make your acquaintance for so long.'

Once again, on 23 October, he goes to the Luxembourg Palace and informs the two directors, without labouring the point, that he is a candidate for the Directory. With expressions of smug regret, Gohier and Moulin tell him that 'the articles of association categorically state a minimum age of forty for membership of the Directory'.

So much the worse for them.

The crowd cheers him as much as ever. The newspapers, which he reads carefully every morning, claim that 'the exclusives won't turn the people against Bonaparte in the slightest'.

On that same day, 23 October, Lucien is elected president of the Council of the Five Hundred. Excellent, a position taken.

But every rose has its thorn – the Bonaparte name has been honoured in the person of Lucien, so people might hope that Napoleon will be relegated to a purely military role.

If you think that's still possible, watch out for when you wake up!

Nothing is certain until one is victorious.

Hasn't Bernadotte just refused to attend a banquet with Napoleon? – 'A man who has breached quarantine may very well have the plague and I have no desire to dine with a plague-carrier,' he said.

Napoleon has only been back in Paris ten days.

XXXVII

NAPOLEON HAS ONLY a few minutes to give to each of his visitors. He takes them by the arm, leads them to one end of the salon. Beyond the rotunda's French windows, the garden is shrouded in mist. A fire is blazing, brightening up the room.

Josephine stands by the fireplace, smiling and chatting as the next visitor waits to see him.

Everyone has to be treated amiably, flattered, asked to come back.

Josephine is wonderful with these officers of all ranks, members of the Institute, deputies and bankers, who are coming to rue de la Victoire because in Paris's upper echelons, which always hum with conjecture and ambition, it is rumoured that General Bonaparte will soon be in government, that he is preparing a coup d'état.

The faubourgs are calm, crushed by poverty and the search for work, and exhausted by six years of hope yielding to disappointment, violence to repression. All the people long for now is enough money to buy food. They dream of peace, so that their young men will not have to fight on the frontiers to make Barras and the other army contractors any richer.

So why not support this General Bonaparte, who is a man of victory and has signed a treaty of peace in the past?

However, it is no longer in the hands of the faubourgs and the street. Questions of power are settled in the salons, barracks and assemblies these days.

Napoleon has understood that everything is decided amongst a few dozen men.

Leaning on the mantelpiece, chatting with Josephine, is someone he recognizes, Staff Officer Thiébaud, who served in Italy, and was one of those who helped him on 13 Vendémiaire.

'You are dining with us,' he says.

JOSEPHINE sits between them.

'You are the only one who has done good things in my absence,' Napoleon says.

He looks at Thiébaud, who seems intimidated and starts to talk of plans for a new Italian campaign.

Is this the moment? Doesn't he understand that the question of power has to be settled in Paris first?

Napoleon loses his temper and interrupts him.

'A nation is only what can be made of it,' he says. 'There is no such thing as bad people for a good government, just as there are no bad troops under good commanders, but what can be expected of people who do not know their country or its needs, who do not understand this age or men, and who only find resistance where they should find succour?'

Napoleon gets to his feet. He cannot stay sitting at table for more than a few minutes. He starts walking around the salon.

'I left peace and I have returned to war,' he exclaims. 'The influence of victory has been replaced by shameful defeats. Italy has been conquered; it has been invaded and France is threatened. I left millions and now penury is rife; these men are bringing France down to the level of their incompetence. They degrade her and she curses them . . .'

He stares Thiébaud out, looking him in the face. Is he reliable?

'What can one expect of generals when there is a government of lawyers?' Napoleon resumes. 'For lieutenants to show devotion, they need a leader able to appreciate, guide and support them . . .'

Thiébaud walks away and Napoleon has to detain him, calling out, 'Go and give Berthier your address!'

HE MUST KEEP seeing the men that count. Have dinner and supper with them. Appear before the Directory again, when he knows the directors are planning to keep him at a distance. 'Let us try, if possible, to make the people forget him,' Sieyès has said.

Sieyès – the only one of the directors who could be an ally – but Sieyès does not want an equal; he only wants a sword that he can use to his advantage and then put back in its sheath once the matter is concluded. Napoleon must also contradict the rumour Barras is spreading. This corrupt beast whose catamites swagger about, who was Josephine's lover, has been saying. 'The Little Corporal has amassed a fortune on his campaign in Italy.'

'That is a slur,' he storms when he is seen by the directors. 'Moreover, were it true that I had concluded such good business in Italy, I would not have made my fortune at the Republic's expense.'

The smooth-tongued Gohier, who timidly pays court to Josephine, answers that 'the valuables packed away in the general-in-chief's coffers no more belong to him than the chicken in the unfortunate's sack whom he has shot. If you had made a fortune in Italy, it could only have been at the Republic's expense!'

'My alleged fortune is a fairy tale that can only be believed by those that invented it!' Napoleon replies.

What do they hope, these lawyers? Don't they see there is only one outcome for me, to win? Be it with some of them, such as Sieyès, on my side, or against them all.

Josephine calms him down. She is clever. She knows all these men. One has to talk to them, win them over – not set them against one.

Napoleon takes a few paces. He agrees whilst revolting against this attitude. He calls Bourrienne to witness.

'Remember one thing,' he says to Bourrienne, 'one must always go and meet one's enemies with a smile on one's face, otherwise they will think one fears them and that makes them bold.'

HE SEES BARRAS and listens impassively as the director tells him in a detached voice, 'The army is your lot. You are going to put yourself at the head of the Army of Italy. The Republic is in such a bad state that only a president can save it. I cannot think of anyone except General Hédouville. What do you think, Bonaparte?'

Bid him farewell and turn on one's heel.

Go and see General Jourdan, who is said to be close to the Jacobins, who, in turn, are said to be preparing a takeover by force on 20 Brumaire. Reassure him without deceiving him: 'I am convinced of your good intentions and those of your friends, but on this occasion I cannot march with you. Rest assured, however, that everything will be done in the interests of the Republic.'

Go and see General Moreau again: give him a sabre studded with gemstones, worth ten thousand francs, from Damascus.

Go and see General Bernadotte, 'the obstacle-man', try to win him over or, at least, prevent him being openly hostile. He will go with whoever wins. So, win.

Now, on 1 November (10 Brumaire), it is no longer the time of reconnaissance and patrols, but of preparations for the attack.

Finally Napoleon decides to have a genuine discussion with Sieyès. The meeting takes place at Lucien's house.

Sieyès has barely sat down before Napoleon starts speaking. He must put pressure on this man, make him understand that he will not be a subordinate but an equal.

'You know my feelings,' says Napoleon. 'The moment to act has come. Have all your measures been passed?'

Don't let Sieyès lose himself in a constitutional labyrinth, interrupt him.

'In that case, occupy yourself exclusively with transferring the assemblies to St Cloud and simultaneously setting up a provisional government. I approve of this government being restricted to three people, and I consent to being one of three provisional consuls with you and your colleague Roger Ducos.'

Sieyès and Lucien's silence conveys their astonishment at this brutal declaration.

'Without that, do not count on me. There is no shortage of generals to carry out the Ancients' decree.'

But which general would dare march against me when they know my goal?

Sometimes, however, he is gripped by anxiety.

One evening, at Talleyrand's, in rue Taitbout, he hears the trot of a troop of cavalry. They halt outside and Talleyrand, limping, rushes to blow out the candles. In the street, a hackney cab waits surrounded by riders.

They might try to arrest me.

Who would protest? Today's allies, the ones who come to rue de la Victoire every day, would join the victors. The people would not move. Who would they rise up for?

Talleyrand relights the candles, laughing. It is only a banker being escorted home.

Yet one must take precautions. Opinion may change. Amongst the cheering, Napoleon hears hostile shouts when he goes to the Temple of Victory, in St Sulpice church, where the Councils of the Five Hundred and the Ancients give a banquet on 6 November in his and General Moreau's honour.

He only eats three eggs and a pear.

At least no one can poison them.

In the church decorated with banners and a great inscription, *United, You Shall Conquer*, it is cold. The band plays stirring airs, but the atmosphere is funereal. Outside it is drizzling. One by one, the dignitaries stand and propose toasts. 'To the armies of the Republic on land and sea,' cries Lucien as president of the Council of the Five Hundred. 'To Peace,' says Gohier. Moreau declaims, 'To all the Republic's faithful allies.'

Napoleon gets to his feet, waits a few moments, and looks round this room where the columns' shadows seem to form a labyrinth. Then he says in a loud voice, 'To the union of all of France!'

He leaves the banquet without delay.

It is more important that he see Sieyès to confirm their agreement, Barras to make him realize he must step down, Fouché to seal their alliance and Bernadotte to verify his neutrality.

ON 17 BRUMAIRE, 8 November, he is at home in rue de la Victoire. He is singing to himself. Everything is ready and he has just reread the tracts, posters and proclamations that will announce the change of government to the people. Then he instructs the generals and officers to convene at his home at six o'clock next morning, 18 Brumaire, 9 November. Troops will take up position on the place de la Concorde since the Council of the Five Hundred sits in the Bourbon Palace and the Council of the Ancients in the Tuileries, and they will only be moved to St Cloud on 19 Brumaire.

He writes to President Gohier inviting him to dine the next evening. That should reassure him. Then Napoleon changes his mind and calls Josephine. Gohier courted her, didn't he? Well, in that case, let her invite that imbecile for tomorrow morning.

She smiles, takes the quill and writes:

To Citizen Gohier, President of the Exclusive Directory of the French Republic

Come, my dear Gohier, and your wife, to breakfast with me tomorrow morning at eight. Be sure you come; I have very interesting matters to discuss.

Adieu, my dear Gohier, knowing that you can always count on my sincere friendship.

La Pagerie-Bonaparte.

It is midnight when Eugène de Beauharnais gives Gohier this invitation for the following day, 18 Brumaire.

XXXVIII

IT IS FIVE O'CLOCK in the morning. Napoleon opens the French window of the salon in the rotunda, and steps out into the garden. The night is cold and bright. On the lawn, he sees gleaming patches of frost in the icy light.

Today, 18 Brumaire, is the first act. He is calm, as always in the moment before a battle, when the troops march off. The dragoons and cavalry of Sébastiani and Murat should already have taken up their positions on the place de la Concorde and at the Tuileries, and the delegates of the Ancients will be starting to arrive at the palace.

Napoleon returns to his room and dresses calmly in the simplest, plainest clothes, which will contrast with the richly coloured outfits of the deputies, directors and even the generals. Before six o'clock – look – here are the first officers presenting themselves at the entrance in the rue de la Victoire. They are booted, with white breeches and bicornes with tricolour plumes. Napoleon takes a turn in the garden, greets them and checks that the guard is in place.

These generals must wait here, with him, until news comes of the decree the Council of the Ancients is going to vote for at the Tuileries, if all goes to plan.

The house is soon full.

He must talk to them so that they each feel personally singled out and involved. Napoleon sits in his small study and signals to Berthier to bring the officers in one by one.

General Lefebvre comes in first. He is a man who must be reassured. Napoleon knows he is worried by this gathering, which may be illegal. So he must win over Lefebvre, who is in command of the 17th division, the troops of the Paris region and the Directory's National Guard. Napoleon embraces him. Does Lefebvre want France to remain in the hands of these lawyers who are looting the Republic? Napoleon puts the Directory in the dock. Then he unhooks his sabre.

'Here, as a token of friendship, is the sabre I wore in Egypt. It is yours, General.'

Lefebvre takes the sabre, his eyes full of tears, and leaves the study proclaiming he is ready 'to throw those bloody lawyers in the Seine'.

First success.

When it comes down to it, men are so easy to steer. Almost all men.

But nothing is won until they have news of the decree, since men do not generally tend to take risks unless they are certain of succeeding.

JOSEPH ENTERS with General Bernadotte.

'How is this? You are not in uniform?' exclaims Napoleon.

Bernadotte explains that he is not on duty and does not want to be part of a rebellion.

'Rebellion? Against a bunch of imbeciles who do nothing but debate from morning to night!' Napoleon replies. 'Perhaps you think you can depend on Moreau or Macdonald or the rest. They will all come over to me. You do not know men. They promise much but perform little.'

He must not make a mistake with Bernadotte, who is jiggling his swordstick and saying, 'You may kill me, but I am not a man who can be detained against his wishes . . .'

He must smile and merely request that Bernadotte not do anything to oppose him.

'As a citizen,' Bernadotte says, 'I give you my word of honour that I will remain quiet – but if the legislature and the Directory order me to act . . .'

Napoleon takes Bernadotte by the arm.

'They will not turn to you,' he says, leading Bernadotte out. 'They fear your ambition more than mine. I am certain that I have no other goal than to save the Republic . . .'

He accompanies Bernadotte to the door.

'I wish to withdraw to Malmaison with a few friends,' he continues.

Bernadotte looks at him incredulously.

One must dare to attempt everything, when the battle is underway.

Napoleon calls Joseph. 'Your brother-in-law, General Bernadotte,' he begins, 'will be dining with you today.'

Josephine can keep an eye on him that way.

NAPOLEON crosses the salon, squeezing through the crowd of officers. He can guess the questions they want to ask. These men are beginning to worry. What if the decree does not come . . .

Josephine appears suddenly. 'Where is Gohier?' Napoleon asks.

The president of the Directory has not come to rue de la Victoire. He declined the invitation and just sent his wife.

Everything can still collapse, and yet Napoleon feels the certainty of success in him, because there is now no other possibility but to see it all through to its conclusion, whatever the consequences.

THERE IS hubbub in the salon. It is eight thirty and two inspector-questors of the Council of the Ancients, accompanied by a State messenger in full regalia, are making their way through the crowd of officers. They are bringing a copy of the decree passed by the Ancients.

Standing in his study, Napoleon glances through the document. It tallies with what was planned with Sieyès. The assemblies are to be transferred to the Commune of St Cloud tomorrow, 19 Brumaire, at noon and 'General Bonaparte is charged with implementing the present decree. He will take all the measures necessary for the safety of the nation's representatives.' He is to appear before the Council of the Ancients to swear an oath.

He rereads it and takes a quill without even glancing at the inspectors. He adds a line granting himself command of the Directory's guard. He already has Lefebvre's support. He has won his first battle. He is calling the tune, not Sieyès.

He enters the salon, holding the document in his hand. He brandishes it, then reads it out. He is, by law, head of the entire army. The officers draw their swords and wave them in the air, cheering.

Who can stop him?

To horse!

The air is bracing at that time of the morning, the sky clear. Napoleon takes the head of the troop and hears the drumming hooves of the cavalcade behind him. The generals and officers follow at a distance of a few metres. Paris is beautiful. A crowd gathers. At the Madeleine, Marmont joins the procession with a group of officers, then Murat's troopers.

Napoleon inhales deeply, his face buffeted by the rising wind.

He leaps off his horse in front of the Tuileries and marches, followed by several generals, to the room where the deputies of the Ancients have been meeting. He sees all eyes fixed on him, that crowd of faces, those high, gold-laced collars. He hesitates.

'Citizen representatives, the Republic was dying,' he begins. 'You knew it and your decree has saved it. Woe betide those who should desire trouble and disorder! I shall stop them, with the help of General Lefebvre, General Berthier and all my comrades-in-arms . . .'

He catches his breath. He does not like these assemblies of 'lawyers'.

'Nothing in history resembles the end of the eighteenth century,' he says. 'Nothing from the end of the eighteenth century resembles the present moment . . . We want a Republic founded on true liberty, civil liberty and the representatives of the nation. We shall have it, I swear on my name and that of my comrades-in-arms.'

'We swear it,' the officers echo.

This is met with applause. A delegate stands and speaks of respect for the constitution, but President Lemercier closes the session. Tomorrow they will reconvene in St Cloud.

He has won the second battle.

He is congratulated, but as long as an engagement is not over, nothing is won. He goes into the garden of the Tuileries. The troops are assembled. They will decide everything. He sees one of Barras's associates, Bottot, grabs him by the arm, pushes him in front of the troops and takes him to task in a loud voice.

'What have you done with the France that I left you in such brilliant order?' he exclaims. 'Theft has become a system. The soldier has been left defenceless. Where are the brave men, the hundred thousand comrades I left covered with laurels? What have they become?'

He pushes Bottot away, takes a step forward.

'This state of affairs cannot last. Within three months it will have led us to despotism. But we want the Republic, we want it resting on the foundations of equality, the morality of civil liberty and political tolerance!

'Soldiers, the army has united with me from its heart, just as I have united with the legislature.

'To listen to certain factions, we should soon all be enemies of the Republic, but we have strengthened it by our labours and courage. There are no greater patriots than the brave men who have been wounded fighting for the Republic!'

Cheering breaks out. Swords and rifles soar into the air.

Napoleon leaps on his horse and inspects the troops.

IT IS ONLY eleven thirty on 18 Brumaire, but Napoleon has the feeling that the first act is over.

There is Gohier, of course, the president of the Directory, who refuses to sign the decree. Acccording to Cambacères, minister of justice, his signature is necessary.

'Jurists always impede the march of events,' Napoleon murmurs.

But Gohier yields and signs, saying that they will see tomorrow at St Cloud whether there is any Directory at all.

Tomorrow . . .

Perhaps it should all have been concluded today, but Napoleon expunges this regret. He does not want a military coup d'état, brutal and arrogant, with its cannonades, salvos and arrests. He wants to be, to use the terms of the posters that are being stuck up around the Tuileries on his orders, and the tracts distributed on the streets, 'a man of sense, an upright man'.

At the start of the afternoon in the Tuileries, Talleyrand enters the office. Napoleon looks questioningly at him. Barras has agreed to stand down, surrendering without a fight. These are the best victories! Why resort to violence when things can be resolved just with threats?

Napoleon calls the officers of his staff and spreads out the map of Paris. Tomorrow, troops must be stationed on the approaches to the Tuileries, on the Champs-Élysées and on the road to St Cloud. He must make a show of force to reassure decent people, and terrorize possible adversaries and prevent them acting.

Fouché comes up, explaining that Paris's barriers must be put in place.

'Good Lord, why all these precautions?' exclaims Napoleon. 'We are marching with the nation and with its force alone. Let no citizen be uneasy.'

Don't they understand that this must be a day like any other in Paris?

'Listen,' he says.

He reads aloud the proclamation to the troops which will be published tomorrow, 19 Brumaire: 'The Republic has been poorly governed for two years . . . Liberty, victory and peace will restore the Republic to the position it occupied in Europe, which only incompetence and treason could have deprived it of . . .'

Is this clear?

'The nation will be whole again.'

He turns towards Sieyès, who is calling for Jacobins to be arrested. He shakes his head in refusal.

He does not say that he has already instructed Saliceti to go and reassure the Jacobins and promise them, in his name, 'a frank and detailed explanation', adding that Sieyès wanted to arrest them and Bonaparte stood up for them. Tomorrow the Jacobins will not be going to St Cloud.

Sieyès bows his head.

Has Sieyès understood that he is not the sole victor on that evening of 18 Brumaire as he hoped to be? That Napoleon has stamped his mark on the whole day?

Tomorrow?

Tomorrow, at St Cloud, it will be true.

'It has not been such an unsatisfactory day,' Napoleon says to Bourrienne in rue de la Victoire. 'We shall see what turns up tomorrow.'

He takes two pistols out of their holsters and goes up to his room with them.

XXXIX

TODAY, 19 BRUMAIRE, Year VIII, 10 November 1799, is the last act.

Napoleon watches the grey sky from the salon. It's drizzling and the fire in the grate is having trouble catching. The room feels damp and cold.

There are fewer people in the house in rue de la Victoire than there were yesterday morning. They talk in whispers. Each of them can be depended on, but he still has to have a word with each in turn, since fears have started to be voiced. How are the two assemblies going to react? Will they let themselves be convinced? They were caught by surprise yesterday. They have had all night to lobby and plan.

Napoleon waves these doubts away, yet he shares them. An interrupted battle is a battle half lost and half won. Nothing is settled. He does not care for this day that is dawning.

Of course, he has made all the military arrangements. Troops will line the route. Murat's men will occupy the esplanade in front of the Château of St Cloud, and thus surround the Directory's guard, who they have to beware of – but no one can say how the day will turn out. Lucien Bonaparte and Sieyès claim that the Ancients and the Five Hundred will vote in favour of the nomination of three consuls and a temporary suspension of the assemblies for a few weeks. But is it definite?

Napoleon regrets not having the situation more in hand. He believes in Fortune, but he does not like improvising, leaving things to chance.

Cambacérès approaches, grave-faced.

'Nothing is decided,' says the minister of justice. 'I am not sure how it will turn out.'

Napoleon shrugs his shoulders. Cambacérès must be reassured.

'In those councils, there are few true men,' he says. 'I watched them all day yesterday, listened to their speeches. Poor stuff, just petty self-interest!'

He walks over to tell General Lannes, who is wounded, not to go to St Cloud. Then, as he kisses Josephine, he murmurs, 'This is not a day for women.'

There may be fighting.

THEY LEAVE by carriage with a detachment of cavalry as escort.

Napoleon remains silent. As they cross the place de la Concorde, he hears Bourrienne murmuring to Lavalette beside him, 'Tomorrow we'll sleep in the Luxembourg or we'll end up here.' With a jerk of his chin, Bourrienne indicates the part of the square where the guillotine used to stand.

The road is choked with carriages, many of which are laden with baggage, as if the people going to St Cloud had already planned their escape. Soldiers' bivouacs are pitched all around the château.

As he is about to cross the esplanade, Napoleon sees members of the Five Hundred, in their white robes with blue belts and red caps, heading in groups towards the pavilion of the Orangery.

He continues on his way and soldiers shout, 'Long live Bonaparte!' but voices are raised amongst a group of deputies of the Five Hundred: 'Ah, the villain, ah, the rogue!' He doesn't turn his head.

This last act of the play must end in victory. If he is defeated he loses everything.

He enters the study adjoining the halls that has been reserved for him It is only furnished with two armchairs, where Sieyès and Roger Ducos, the two future consuls, are already sitting. It is cold and damp and here, too, the fire seems destined to go out at any moment.

Napoleon begins to pace around the room. Having to wait, not being able to act, one's whole destiny being in the hands of others – it is unbearable.

It is only one thirty.

Lavalette announces that Lucien Bonaparte has just opened the session of the Council of the Five Hundred.

SO HE MUST wait, then. Napoleon turns towards Sieyès and Ducos. They are chatting. Can they stand by and let their fates be decided without doing anything? An aide-de-camp enters, Napoleon claps him on the shoulder, and leads him away from the others. The officer murmurs, looking over at Sieyès, that the latter has ordered his coachman to leave his carriage harnessed and hidden in the woods, so that if the affair turns out badly, he can get away. He also tells him that Talleyrand has arrived with the banker Collot and taken up residence in a house near the château.

All of them are cautious, ready to protect their rear. He is playing all the cards in his hand.

Lavalette returns, wearing a preoccupied expression. The Five Hundred, he says, is in uproar. The deputies have been shouting, 'No dictatorship! Down with dictators! Long live the constitution!' The president, Lucien Bonaparte, has had to allow the deputies to swear an oath of loyalty to the Constitution of Year III.

Sieyès smiles. Naturally he is not altogether displeased with the implied accusations made against Napoleon.

'You see what they're doing,' Napoleon calls to him.

Sieyès shrugs. It is true, this oath to respect the whole constitution is rather overdoing it, but . . .

Napoleon turns away and flies into a fury with a major who has not carried out his orders. 'There are no orders here but mine!' he cries. 'Arrest that man and put him in prison!'

He strides up and down. He had felt today would be doubtful. The door opens. What do these deputies want, Generals Jourdan and Augereau, who are said to be Jacobins by persuasion?

Are they coming to prowl around like scavengers, because they think he is going to back down in the face of parliamentary opposition?

They propose a compromise, a joint course of action. They assure him that Bernadotte has men in the faubourgs and is in a position to unleash a sans-culotte movement.

If I don't act, I lose.

Napoleon waves Augereau aside.

'The wine is drawn,' he says. 'It must be drunk. Calm yourself.'

He leaves that room where he feels as if he is suffocating. He will not let himself be hampered by these stratagems, bogged down by these lawyers' speeches.

He enters the Apollo gallery. The Ancients have adjourned

their session and they form a dense mass of red and blue. Napoleon tries to get through them, but he cannot reach the platform.

He must act, that is to say, talk.

'Representatives of the people,' he begins, 'these are by no means ordinary circumstances, you are on the edge of a volcano!'

The deputies are murmuring already. He is ill at ease. He does not like justifying himself.

WHO ARE these men to whom he is saying, 'I swear to you, the fatherland has no more zealous defender than I. I devote myself entirely to carrying out your orders'? What have they done that he should be forced to obtain their consent?

'You forget the constitution!' yells one of them.

He straightens himself.

'The constitution? It suits you to invoke it, does it? Can it still offer any guarantee for the French people? The constitution? Every faction invokes it and yet they each violate it; it is despised by them all.'

He bellowed this. He catches his breath. One of the deputies near him proposes that his speech be printed, but others demand explanations. Let him say more about the danger stirring in La Vendée, the royalists threatening Nantes, St Brieuc and Le Mans.

Hammering out each word, he states, 'I belong to no party, because I am only of the great party of the French people.'

He feels that his words are not striking home. These men in their blue robes, red caps pulled down on their foreheads, white coats and red belts, cannot be convinced.

He turns towards the door.

'You, grenadiers,' he says, 'whose bearskins I see, you, brave soldiers whose bayonets I see . . .'

The deputies get to their feet, muttering angry threats. Yet these are the Ancients, the ones best disposed towards him!

He looks at them. They are hostile. He will never win them over as long as they are in a pack like this. Then suddenly he abandons all restraint, the words pour out of their own accord, brushing aside every thought of strategy or prudence.

'If some orator paid by foreigners were to speak of outlawing me,' he cries, 'let him be crushed this instant by the thunderbolt of war! I shall call on you, brave soldiers, my brave comrades in arms . . .'

The deputies begin shouting.

'Remember,' he cries, 'I am attended by the God of victory and the God of fortune . . .'

He hears Bourrienne murmuring, 'Withdraw, General, you know not what you are saying.'

But what else is there to say to these lawyers who don't want to listen!

'I ask you to take salutary measures which the graveness of the dangers imperiously demands,' he continues. 'You will find my arm always ready to carry out your resolutions.'

HE STRIDES through the Apollo gallery, walking fast, waving away all those like Bourrienne who counsel prudence and advise him not to appear before the assembly of the Five Hundred, where the majority is opposed to him. Don't they understand that it is better to fight badly than not fight at all? He is convinced he will get nothing from these deputies by moderation. Sieyès is silent at his side. On the staircase leading to the Orangery, the writer Arnault, who has just come from Fouché in Paris, speaks to him.

'Fouché answers to you for Paris, General, but you must answer for St Cloud. He thinks it necessary to hurry matters, especially if there is any attempt to entangle you in delays . . . Citizen Talleyrand is also of the opinion that there is no time to lose.'

Nevertheless they try to detain him just as he is about to enter the hall of the Orangery where the Five Hundred is in session. He shakes himself free. This knot must be cut. Escorted by grenadiers, he forces his way through the crowd blocking the corridor, pushes open the door, then walks in alone.

Before him, those men in red caps. Shouts, screams. Faces of hatred.

'Outlaw the dictator! Down with the dictator!' they cry.

A deputy a head taller than the rest rushes forward and strikes Napoleon hard on the shoulder. 'Have you been victorious for this, General?' he asks.

Scattered cries of 'Long live Bonaparte!' are quickly drowned out by the shouting. 'Outlaw, outlaw,' they chant.

For a moment a veil comes down before his eyes. He is suffocating in the scrum. He sees deputies waving daggers. He has scratched his sores and the pustules on his face, and blood trickles down his cheeks. He feels himself being picked up, carried out.

HE IS IN the salon; Sieyès is facing him, calm.

'They want to outlaw me,' he says.

'They are the ones who started it,' replies Sieyès. 'We have to send in the soldiers.'

Napoleon recovers his composure in a matter of seconds. He didn't want a military takeover. He still doesn't. But he must not lose.

Shouting is heard coming from the Orangery.

The doors of the salon fly open. The Five Hundred have voted to outlaw the general.

He must not lose. He draws his sword and shouts out of the window, 'To arms! To arms!'

Then he rushes into the courtyard, followed by his aides-de-camp, and mounts up. Lucien appears, bareheaded. He calls for a horse.

Sieyès shouts, 'They're outlawing us! Well then, General, drive them out of there!'

Lucien, standing in his stirrups, cries, 'A drum roll, a drum roll!'

There is a drum roll. Then silence.

'People of France, the president of the Council of the Five Hundred declares to you that the vast majority of this council is, at this moment, terrorized by representatives armed with stilettos. These odious brigands, undoubtedly in the pay of England, have talked of outlawing the general charged with executing the decree of the Council of Ancients. This small band of madmen have outlawed themselves. These proscribers are no longer representatives of the people, but of the dagger!'

Cheering fills the esplanade and the courtyard.

Napoleon is having trouble staying in the saddle as his horse stamps and shies. He knows that this is the crucial moment of the day, and he is sure he can carry it. He must.

'Soldiers,' he cries. 'I have led you to victory, can I count on you?'

Men raise their muskets and swords and answer, 'Yes!'

This clamour swells and carries Napoleon.

'Agitators are trying to raise the Council of the Five Hundred against me. Well, I will put them to rights! Can I count on you?'

The cry goes up: 'Long live Bonaparte!'

'I tried to talk to them,' resumes Napoleon. 'They answered with daggers . . .'

He has won. It just needs a few more words.

'For long enough the fatherland has been tormented, pillaged, ravaged,' he cries. 'Its defenders have been debased, immolated. These brave men that I have clothed, paid and kept at the cost of our victories, what state do I find them in . . .'

'Long live Bonaparte!'

'Three times I have opened the gates of the Republic and three times they have been closed.'

'Long live Bonaparte!'

'Yes, follow me, I am the god of the hour!'

The cheering resumes. He hears Lucien calling to him, 'Be quiet won't you! Do you think you're talking to the Mamelukes?'

Lucien is right: he mustn't talk any more.

Napoleon leans forward and gives an order to General Leclerc. The grenadiers march off. The drummers beat the charge and head for the Orangery. Deputies of the Council of the Five Hundred can be seen jumping down from the windows, dropping their red caps, shedding their white togas, fleeing into the park. They hear Murat cry, 'Get all this damned rabble out of here!'

It's dark. It is 6 o'clock.

NOW IT IS enough just to wait in the salon. His aide-de-camp Lavalette reports that the Ancients have passed the decree to replace the Directory with an executive commission of three members, but they need the vote of the Five Hundred.

The soldiers go to St Cloud and search the gardens and cafés for the deputies who have fled, to bring them back to the Orangery so that they can vote.

Napoleon strides up and down the salon. The château is silent now. The tramp of soldiers leaving St Cloud can be heard.

Lucien enters the salon towards midnight, radiant.

He reads the decree: 'The legislative body creates an executive consular commission made up of Sieyès, Roger Ducos, former directors, and Bonaparte, General, who will bear the name of Consuls of the Republic.'

Then Napoleon takes his place in the procession that takes the consuls to the chamber where they will each swear an oath of loyalty 'to the Sovereignty of the People, the one, indivisible French Republic, to Equality, Liberty and the Representative System'.

Napoleon says these words last.

At dawn on 11 November 1799, he is consul.

IN THE CARRIAGE taking him back to Paris at five o'clock in the morning, he is quiet. He senses that Bourrienne, sitting next to him in the gloom, is watching him, but Napoleon, eyes closed, doesn't turn his head.

The carriage drives past soldiers lined up along the roadside. They are merry. They're singing,

> *Ah ça ira, ça ira*
> *Les aristocrats à la Lanterne.*

Napoleon knows that whatever he does he is a son of the Revolution, but it is over, like this dawn.

He opens his eyes. The carriage is entering Paris. The streets are empty, silent. The noise of the wheels on the cobbles and the clatter of the hooves of the small escort bounce off the façades with their closed shutters.

For the first time he has a feeling of serene power. After all those months in Egypt, with their uncertainties, their setbacks, after seeing the daggers of hatred glinting at St Cloud, where, at any moment, he could have lost everything, it seems to him that at last he has overcome the final obstacles. Before him stretches the horizon, his life. Everything will now be great. He feels it. He wishes it.

Yes, the Revolution is finished.

He is the one who closes one era and opens another.

At last, at last! The day is breaking and the future is mine!